Take the Cake

a novel by
Sandra Wright

OMNIFIC PUBLISHING
DALLAS

Omnific Publishing
P.O. Box 793871, Dallas, TX 75379
www.omnificpublishing.com

First Omnific eBook edition, August 2010
First Omnific trade paperback edition, August 2010

The characters and events in this book are fictitious.
Any similarity to real persons, living or dead,
is coincidental and not intended by the author.

Library of Congress Cataloguing-in-Publication Data

Wright, Sandra.
    Take the Cake / Sandra Wright – 1st ed.
    ISBN 978-1-936305-32-2
    1. Love—Fiction. 2. Bakery—Fiction. 3. Cupcake—Fiction.
    4. Writer—Fiction. I. Title

10 9 8 7 6 5 4 3 2 1

Cover Design by Amy Brokaw
Interior Book Design by Coreen Montagna

Printed in the United States of America

__Dedication__

For my friends near and far

Chapter 1

Unexpected Kindness

Oh, help, this is going to be visual.

Kate Shannon tripped on a piece of pavement and staggered, one arm flailing for balance as she clutched at her fragile cargo. Equilibrium restored but self-composure now in tatters, she took a deep breath and hefted the carton of eggs more carefully in her arms as she kept walking. She concentrated on taking a few steady breaths, flicking her head as the wind blew her long dark blond hair around her face. Naturally pale skinned, she could feel a tide of heat rushing into her cheeks but kept walking. Fortunately, this was New York so no one gave her a second glance. A few more paces and she was able to pretend it had never happened. Rounding the corner, she looked ahead and felt the familiar lift as she saw the fluttering red canopy heralding the bakery's presence in Greenwich Village. Although it was still early, a small figure stood at the front door, raising a hand in welcome as Kate approached.

"Morning, boss."

"Wren, don't call me boss," Kate reprimanded with a smile.

"Sorry, boss."

"What got you here so early this morning? Did you wet the bed?" Kate fished out her keys and unlocked the door, standing aside to let Wren in first.

"Nope. Just motivated. I can sense victory in the air today," Wren announced with a grin as she followed Kate inside, shrugging out of her jacket and carrying it into the kitchen to hang it up along with her bag. Kate followed.

"Like that, huh?" Kate replied, flicking on the coffee machine as she passed, before carefully setting the egg carton down on the counter in the kitchen, and then stowing her bag in the cupboard. "Bring it on, babe. It's all about you."

"Finally, something we agree on," Wren said as she hefted a wooden framed chalkboard up onto one of the tables and, after a moment's thought, scribbled her quote for the day. She swiveled the board for Kate's inspection, and then carried it outside to hang it on the waiting brass hooks. Wren stood regarding the chalkboard with her hands on her hips before nodding with a "that's that" satisfaction and returning inside.

"What's your poison?" Kate smiled as Wren approached the counter. Wren's bright red pixie cut hair had been spiked up this morning and sported a few plastic daisy hairclips.

"Mocha grande," Wren replied as she disappeared into the back.

"Gotcha." Kate nodded and started to measure the espresso.

"Oh, my God," Wren called from the kitchen. "Where did you get these eggs? They're enormous."

"My neighbor gets them from I don't know where, so I bought some off her last night."

"Are you sure they're from chickens?" Wren appeared, looking doubtful. "Seriously, the birds that laid those must've had tears in their eyes."

"I know. Paul calls them Mothercluckers."

Wren gave a whoop of laughter as she pictured Kate's brother's face. He always had a smart-ass comment to make. She strolled over to accept her coffee from Kate. The kitchen out back was small but held everything she needed: an industrial sized oven, a large stack of cooling racks, and some mixers. Kate stood quiet for a moment, staring off into space.

"Getting in touch with your inner Zen master?"

Kate blinked and came back to the present, shushing Wren as she opened the refrigerator. "Shut up, minx. I'm calculating quantities."

"Really? Because any longer and it looked like you were going to start drooling."

"Hey, you want to be able to lick the beaters or not?"

"Yes'm," Wren replied, trying and failing to look deferential.

"Then scat." Kate shooed her away and got to work with a smile. She measured some butter and sugar into the mixing bowl and set it going before turning to what she called her "magic cupboard" for further inspiration. Pulling the door open, she looked at the stacks of translucent containers as she mulled over Wren's chalkboard quote of the day, wondering how she was going to top it but determined to do so. Opening one of the storage tubs, she pulled out a bottle of food coloring and gazed at it as a vague idea stirred in the back of her mind. Standing at the mixer as she mixed the frosting half an hour later, she smiled to herself. Wren wasn't the only one who could be competitive.

"Boss?"

"Mm-hmm?" Kate didn't look up.

"People are asking what today's one is going to be. What'll I tell them?"

"You got the board?"

"Good to go." Wren held up a small foolscap-sized chalkboard this time.

Kate dictated, and after a brief sigh of dejection, Wren scribbled on the board and carried it out to the front of the store. Kate scooped the frosting into a piping bag and started to swizzle it onto the cakes, flicking a glance at the pièce de résistance she had gotten delivered to the bakery ten minutes prior. A few minutes later, she carried out the first tray and put the items into the glass-fronted display case with all due ceremony. Standing back, she surveyed the fruits of her labor. It was going to be a good day.

Michael sighed and sat at his desk with his chin in his hands as he gazed at the black computer screen. He'd been writing for years now. He knew how it all worked: you got an idea, you started writing, and then you kept at it until it became a book. That process didn't work so well when the ideas weren't forthcoming, and right now he was caught up in what felt like a monumental word drought. He dropped his head forward and rubbed the back of his neck with a sigh, wondering what on earth he was going to do today. The phone sitting beside his laptop rang, jolting him out of his reverie, and he paused before reaching out to answer it with considerable reluctance.

"Forrester," he mumbled, his head in his hands as he held the receiver to his ear.

"I know it's early, but I'm on my way to a meeting and I'm hoping you've got some good news for me."

There had been no greeting, but Michael knew the voice of a stressed editor when he heard it.

"Alistair," he began and heard a heavy sigh at the other end of the line.

"Fuck, when you say my name like that, I know it's never going to be good news."

"So why did you call?"

"I was hoping against hope that you'd have something different to tell me."

"Sorry."

"Have you got anything?" Alistair ventured after a pause and, after a heavy silence on the other end of the line, added, "Well, keep me posted. Is there anything I can do to help?"

Stop calling. "I'll let you know," Michael said aloud.

"Okay, man. Talk to you later."

Michael disconnected the call without saying goodbye. Since his words had left him, some of his social niceties had gone too, particularly where his editor was concerned. He slumped back in his chair, scratching at his morning stubble as he stared at the blank screen. The day hadn't started well. Resolving to quit smoking the night before, he had gone to bed feeling virtuous, but this morning was a different matter entirely. Now he felt tired and out of sorts with the world; there was laundry to be done, a book to be written (or at least an editor to be avoided in the short term), and not a single cigarette in the house for emotional support.

I give up.

Resting his elbows on the desk, he slid forward until his head was resting on his arms and closed his eyes in defeat. It was going to be a long day.

❧

A door slamming somewhere nearby jerked Michael awake, and he groaned as his neck began to ache. He'd fallen asleep sitting at his desk which seemed indicative of his productivity of late. He looked around as he knuckled his eyes, wondering what had woken him up, and then heard his cell phone beep again. It was a text message.

Anything? Anything at all? – A

He looked at his watch. It was nearly ten a.m. and his editor had been in touch with him twice. Alistair must be getting pressure from the top, which meant that he was going to pressure Michael by default. He had to get out of the apartment; otherwise the phone was going to ring again. Getting up, he went back into his bedroom and gathered up his laundry, stuffing it into a large cotton carry bag. He pulled on an old gray pea coat, stuffed his wallet into his back pocket, picked up his keys, and left. Once he was downstairs, he slung the bag over one shoulder and stood on the pavement, looking up and down the street. He'd have to get out of West SoHo; it'd be too easy for Alistair to come looking. Shoving his hands deep into his pockets, he put his head down and began to walk.

Words. He needed to find some words, the more the merrier.

❧

"More?"

"Keep 'em coming, boss. I think we've hit a nerve today."

"Okay." Kate thought quickly. "But we're going to need to order some more supplies in. Remind me to do that later," she said as she shook her head in bemusement. Some days were more surprising than others, and it looked like today was no exception. She slid the next couple of trays into the oven, and then washed her hands and made the most of the momentary lull to head out to the front of the shop. Wren was serving, and Kate moved further down the counter and took a few orders, sliding the coffee orders onto the slot over the espresso machine. Wren was busy frothing milk but scanned the slips and nodded once, indicating that she was on top of things.

Kate gave the store a quick scan, and then picked up a large plastic tub to balance on her hip as she walked out to collect empty cups, saucers, and plates. Some of the customers were regulars and so she stopped to exchange a few words and a smile here and there. Everyone seemed to be happy, and she hauled the tub into the kitchen and began to transfer its contents into the dishwasher. They had lost their kitchen hand to the lure of international travel a few days ago, and Kate was still trying to find a replacement.

"Everything going okay?" she stopped to ask Wren on her way back out to the front of the store.

"Yeah, thanks for clearing the tables," Wren said as she slid out two more coffees to the waiting customers. "Have you thought more about my suggestion?"

"Call her," Kate replied distractedly as she scribbled down another order and slid it across to Wren. "I've advertised but you've seen the applicants."

"I have." Wren pulled a face. "Trust me, I know just the person."

"Good to hear. Just give her a call and get her in as soon as she's able, and we'll take it from there," Kate advised.

Going out into the front of the store again, Kate finished straightening up the tables, topping off the sugar supplies, and getting everything looking neat and tidy to her satisfaction. She ran her gaze over the café, looking for any imperfections, but it seemed that everything was as it should be.

Michael had not been paying any attention to where he was going. He'd dropped off his laundry and just kept on walking, blending in here and there before moving away from the crowds and heading toward Greenwich Village. It felt good to be out of the apartment, although for comfort's sake, he'd avoided going uptown where his publisher was based. He didn't want any reminders of the work he wasn't getting done.

Lifting his chin slightly as he walked, Michael started to pay more attention to his surroundings. He hadn't been into the Village much over the last few months, and he was surprised to see that some of the retail spaces had changed. What had been a shoe repair store now sold comic books, a music store was now an Indian restaurant, and the travel agent had given way to a bookstore. It seemed that the stores were still all independently owned; there were no major franchise names, which meant the area was retaining its individual charm. A fluttering red canopy further down the other side of the street caught his eye. He squinted but couldn't make out the lettering. His curiosity piqued, he crossed the street and walked toward it.

It was a bakery. Michael stopped and peered in at the display in the bay window. A series of bell jars had been set up, some stood on stacks of old hardcover novels, others on folded newspapers. Each jar had been propped on some sort of reading material, no doubt sourced from the bookstore nearby. The cupcakes were little works of sugared art, each one designed to tempt. He hesitated, and then glanced at the chalkboard that was hanging on brass hooks outside. He read the artfully written quote, and a wry smile tugged at his lips.

> Ever feel like your guardian angel
> has just stepped out for a smoke?

Charmed in spite of himself, he stepped inside.

Wren looked up at the movement and gazed at the tall man who stood deliberating in the doorway.

"Holy shit," she whispered to herself.

At that moment, Kate, who had stopped at a table to chat to a couple of customers, threw back her head and laughed. The sound bubbled around the store, catching the eye of the visitor. His eyes flickered toward the source of the laughter, and Wren watched his reaction.

Michael stood in the doorway, fidgeting slightly as he decided whether he wanted to go further inside or not. That was when he heard the laughter; it was such a warm sound that he was in the store before he quite knew what he was doing, looking to see where the sound had come from.

The woman had a slight build and pale smooth skin. Her hair had been pulled back, so he could see a heart shaped face with warm brown eyes that danced with amusement. She stood teasing the two old men sitting at a table, wagging a finger warningly at them in mocking indignation before moving away and out of sight behind the counter.

Michael found that he wanted her to come back and stood there for a moment, waiting.

Wren ran an appreciative gaze up his tall frame, observing him as he stood watching Kate. He was gorgeous and, unlike a lot of striking men she knew, clearly had no idea of his appeal. As he had walked in, the two women sitting at the front table had exchanged quiet murmurs of appreciation, their eyes raking over him while he paid them no attention at all. His hair was a riot of curls that clearly indicated he had rolled out of bed and into the day with barely a thought, and his morning stubble merely served to accentuate a jaw line that begged to be kissed. Not that she would be the one doing the kissing, Wren realized. As soon as Kate had laughed, he'd only had eyes for her. Naturally, Kate had no idea.

Wren more than held her own when it came to dating, but she constantly despaired that Kate would remain single. Men seemed drawn to her and yet somehow she didn't read the signs. Wren told Kate repeatedly when she was being checked out, pointed men out to her, passed on phone numbers, and yet still Kate shied away from relationships.

Kate had finished her conversation and walked back around the counter, giggling at Wren as she walked past.

"Watch out for those two, Wren," Kate said in a voice loud enough to carry to the two old men. "They're getting sassy." With a final playful glance over her shoulder, she continued into the kitchen.

Wren gave the two men in question a wink before turning to the man who stood silently watching.

"Can I help you?" She watched him watch Kate and knew what she was going to do.

Michael gazed at the waitress for a moment, and then looked blankly at the counter. "Uh, coffee?"

"Coming right up," she agreed promptly. "How do you take it?"

"Cream and sugar," he replied and dug out his wallet.

"Sugar's on the table," she replied as she gave him his change. "Go take a seat and your coffee will be right over."

"Thanks."

He paused and looked at the cupcakes on display. The most prominent ones had an orange colored icing that seemed oddly familiar, with a red cherry on top. He leaned forward to peer at the handwritten sign: You Can Do It Cupcake. He raised an eyebrow at the title.

"It's our daily cupcake special. If you're quitting smoking, you get a free nicotine patch."

Michael nodded. Now the frosting made sense. It was a similar hue to the filters on the cigarettes he usually relied on to get through the day. *Quitting today*, he reminded himself.

"I see," he allowed. "Where do you get them from?"

"Uh, I think Kate just went to the drug store and—"

"No," he said, shaking his head, "the cupcakes."

"Oh, they're all made here on the premises by Kate, who you just saw walk into the kitchen."

Michael looked up at that. Now he knew her name.

❧

"Hey, boss, could you spot me for a minute? I've got to …" Wren jigged on the spot by way of illustration.

"Sure. Got any orders?"

"Just one. Tall hunk wants a tall coffee. He's paid," Wren said, grabbing the key for the restroom and ducking out to the back.

Kate went to the coffee machine and went to work. As she waited for the coffee to filter into the cup, she looked for the customer Wren had mentioned. It wasn't hard to see him. He looked miserable, Sir Galahad when Camelot had fallen. She smiled to herself at the analogy. Clearly, she'd been reading too much English literature. She kept watching him as he picked up a packet of sugar and tapped it on the table, lost in thought. The coffee was poured, and she paused for a moment before getting out a plate.

Michael mumbled his thanks as his coffee appeared on the table, then looked up in surprise as a cupcake on a small plate followed. It was the woman he had been watching earlier.

"You look like you needed it," she said, indicating the cupcake with a glance. An individually wrapped nicotine patch had been stuck in the icing on top of the cupcake.

"What gave it away?" His voice felt rusty from lack of use.

"The way you've been playing with that sugar packet was a pretty good clue," she replied, making him realize he was holding it in his fingers as he would a cigarette.

"Thanks," he said, feeling awkward and out of practice. "I didn't expect—"

"That's when random acts mean the most, when they're not looked for." Waving off his thanks, she smiled, and he found himself smiling back. "Enjoy, and maybe we'll see you here again sometime."

"Maybe," he agreed.

She gave a quick smile, and then went back to work, stopping at the stereo to turn up the music slightly.

Michael watched her leave and sipped at his coffee. Regarding the cupcake in front of him for moment, he swiped a finger through the frosting and tasted it. Delicious. Suddenly feeling hungry, he began to eat. He still had no words, but for the first time in a long time, he felt less empty.

Chapter 2

Sins and Salmon

Michael switched off the alarm clock with a slap of his hand and burrowed his head back into his pillow. If he could get back to sleep, he wouldn't have to think about his ongoing failure to write. The ambient noise of the city filtered into the apartment, and he heard a door bang in the apartment upstairs. He squeezed his eyes closed, trying to shut out the day.

Then the phone rang.

With a muffled oath, he threw the pillow aside and sat up, shuffling over his king-sized mattress toward the bedside table where his cell phone was shrilling.

"What?" he snapped as he slid the handset open to take the call.

"Good morning to you too, asshole," replied a droll voice, accompanied by a short bark of laughter.

"Alistair, I see you've decided to give up on charm as a negotiating tool."

He hadn't heard from his editor for a few days, and that had been long enough for him to relax and hope that Alistair had found another project to occupy his time. Now he realized with an inward sigh that the problem wasn't going to go away any time soon.

"Well, it wasn't working, so I figured it was time to move onto well-meaning abuse."

"Noted." Michael waited, but Alistair said nothing. "So was there a purpose to this call?"

"Just to say that it's looking like it's going to be a nice day for writing."

"Maybe if there's something to write about."

"You'll think of something."

"No pressure or anything," Michael replied in a dry tone.

"I'm not about to throw fuel on the fire by saying you're contractually obliged."

"Thanks," Michael said.

"Or that our suppliers are starting to put the heat on," the voice went on.

"Alistair," he warned.

"And your legions of fans are emailing, wanting to know when the next book is due," Alistair continued, ignoring the interruption. "I mean, what sort of editor would I be if I pulled that kind of shit with one of our most successful authors?"

Michael sighed.

"Just because everyone is up in arms because you won't do any interviews—you know how they all eat up that 'reclusive author' bullshit. It just makes them want to talk to you more."

"Thanks, man. All this is really helping," Michael said at last.

"Am I annoying you yet?"

"What, you mean you could tell? And there I was trying to suppress the rage," Michael said.

"Hey, how about we make a deal? Rather than you talking to me on the phone, you could maybe write it down?"

"You're a subtle man, Alistair."

"Wait, I can see something developing here," Alistair continued, warming to his theme. "You could write it down and, fuck me, Forrester, you could probably get whole sentences out of this situation."

"Alistair, I'm warning you," Michael began.

"Or you'll what? Do nothing? Right, like that isn't what you've been doing for the last few months," Alistair replied in a goading voice.

"Fuck you," Michael growled and disconnected the call.

He sat thinking about the conversation and sighed, feeling angry and tired all at once. He was months behind schedule, and Alistair's goading had hit a little too close to home. He flicked the cell phone back onto the bedside table, ignoring it when it slid off and fell onto the floor with a clatter. One of his pillows had fallen off the bed during the night, but he couldn't be bothered getting it. Rolling onto his side, he grabbed the other pillow and tried to get comfortable enough to go back to sleep. He sighed, a loud exhalation in the quiet bedroom, and tried to relax. He realized he was clenching his jaw and yawned, trying to stretch out the tension.

A car horn blared downstairs, followed by a shouted obscenity. His eyes snapped open and he stared at the ceiling. Clearly, it was not going to be his kind of day.

Kate glanced at the clock and returned to her book. It wasn't often that she woke up before her alarm, but rather than try to go back to sleep, she had picked up the book she had been reading the night before. She propped herself up into a more comfortable position against her pillows and turned the page, feeling delightfully self-indulgent.

When the alarm finally shrilled, she closed her book with considerable reluctance and got up. She didn't bother making the bed. It was a Friday; chances were more than good that she would end up having a few drinks after work and get home late. With that in mind, she showered and changed into her customary jeans and shirt, but stopped to stuff her favorite leather boots, a bottle of perfume and her lip gloss into a bag. She grabbed a bottle of water and left the apartment. She'd have something to eat when she got to the shop. A look at her watch revealed that she was running ahead of schedule, so there might be time to sit down and think about the day ahead before the customers started to arrive.

Wren made her way toward the Village, her eyes raking over the closed faces of the other passing pedestrians, wondering where inspiration for her quote of the day was going to strike. Rounding a corner, she nearly tripped over a small dog hunched over, doing its deed. Wren exchanged a sympathetic grimace with the dog walker, who was trying to fish out a plastic bag and control the other six dogs on leads at the same time.

"No good deed goes unpunished," the dog walker muttered in Wren's direction, bending down to clear away the dog's leavings.

Wren stepped aside and kept walking. Her stride faltered for a moment as inspiration struck, and then she grinned and continued on her way.

Kate crossed the street and looked up to see the familiar figure of Wren waiting for her under the red canopy.

"How do you do it?" Kate called out as she drew near. "I'm ahead of schedule and you *still* beat me."

Wren shrugged. "Gotta keep you on your toes somehow, boss."

"Wren, don't call me boss."

"Sorry, boss."

Kate unlocked the door and wedged it open to let in the fresh air, flicking on lights and overhead circulating fans.

Wren walked past her, shrugging off her coat and putting her bag away in the lockable cupboard in the kitchen, then returned to pick up the chalkboard.

"Got your quote of the day?"

"Sure have. Thought it up on the way to work this morning. How about you?"

"I'm feeling good; I just saw the David Beckham billboard on the way in this morning. What's your inspiration today?"

"Dog shit, believe it or not." Wren laughed as she picked up the chalk.

Kate shook her head and flicked on the coffee machine before going into the kitchen to turn on the ovens to preheat.

Wren hung the chalkboard up outside, and then began to check the condiment supplies on each table.

Kate looked up from the coffee machine as Wren started to fill up the water jugs. "Have you had breakfast?"

"Not yet," Wren replied.

"I haven't either. Grab some of the savory muffins from yesterday and zap them in the microwave. They'll be nice with a bit of melted butter and a coffee."

"I'm on it."

Michael looked for his phone and saw it on the floor by the bed. He stooped to pick it up, and then hesitated. Not many people called him these days. He'd been keeping to himself and had little to say, certainly less to write. He picked up the phone and stood weighing it in his hand before tossing it onto the bed and leaving it there.

It had been another late night with nothing to show for it. He had stared blindly at his laptop screen for what felt like hours, and then at the television that had deadened his mind just as much. By the time he had killed a few more hours surfing the internet and decided to turn in, it was already after midnight. He was going to have to get into a better routine. He thought back over the previous evening and snorted to himself. In terms of his social life, he had nowhere to go but up.

Stopping in the kitchen, he swigged back a glass of juice, and then made for the door, deciding to get something to eat while he was out. He just had to get away from the damn computer for a while. He'd find a bookstore; perhaps there was comfort to be found in someone else's words if he couldn't find any of his own. He jogged down the staircase, and then opened the front door and stepped outside, squinting against the daylight. Tugging his baseball cap out of his back jeans pocket, he flicked it out and tugged it into a comfortable position, and then slid his sunglasses on against the sun's glare before he started walking.

The moment Michael stepped into the bookstore downtown, he knew straight away that he had made a mistake; there were books everywhere, all written by people who probably had much better luck at stringing a sentence together these days than he did. He wandered up and down the aisles, picking up and replacing books at random, then scowled as he saw a display stand of his novels. There seemed to be no escape from the damn things. He left the store and kept walking.

☙

"Hey, boss, are they nearly done?"

"Sure. Get the board."

"What do you think this is?"

Kate looked up to see that Wren was already holding it. "Well done. Okay…" She dictated and Wren laughingly wrote it down.

"Beckham's always good for inspiration," she commented.

"Like *that's* what Armani was aiming for," scoffed Kate as she picked up the tray and followed Wren out into the front of the store.

Today's offering was a lush selection of red velvet cupcakes with white chocolate liqueur frosting, white chocolate curls, and a ripe raspberry nestled into the moist folds of sugar. Wren waited as Kate arranged the cupcakes, and then propped the mini chalkboard on a small easel to stand beside them, proclaiming:

I feel a sin coming on.

Wren looked at the cupcakes and then back at Kate. "Nice one," she said.

"I thought so," Kate agreed.

☙

"I don't know where you went in your head this morning, boss, but what the hell did you put in those cupcakes?"

Kate was in the midst of decorating and looked up in concern. "What, no good?"

Wren snorted.

"Yeah, right, like that's gonna happen. They're practically walking out the store. Just tell me those ones there are going to be ready soon."

"Sure, give me a few minutes," Kate replied in an absent voice, popping a raspberry into her mouth. She went back to piping on the frosting on the last cupcake, then put the icing bag down on the counter. Popping another raspberry into her mouth, she chewed as she sprinkled the white chocolate curls over the cupcakes, arranging them just so, as she hummed to herself, feeling very content.

She was putting the latest batch of cupcakes in the display cabinet when she heard Wren greet someone and walk out from behind the counter to hug the newcomer. She looked up to see a slim woman laugh and hug Wren with an ease that spoke of a long friendship. Wren took the woman by the hand and hauled her over to the counter.

"Boss, this is Emily, my friend that I've been telling you about."

"Wren, don't call me boss." Kate laughed, and reached out to shake Emily's hand. "Hi, Emily, you'll have to excuse Wren and me; we have a bit of a routine going."

"It's nice to meet you at last," Emily answered.

Kate assessed her in a glance and liked what she saw. Emily seemed quiet and unassuming, her face was open and honest, her smile reached her eyes, and her mouth looked like it smiled often. Her dark, curly hair framed her face, and she had a warm complexion that was in direct contrast with Wren's.

"Emily is looking for some part-time work at the moment, and I thought she'd be perfect," Wren supplied.

"Have you done retail or hospitality before, Emily?" asked Kate.

"Some, but not a lot," Emily replied. "I'm a quick study, though, and I've got a strong work ethic."

"She's kept up with me in the past," added Wren.

"And that's saying something," said Kate. "Which is good enough for me. Welcome to the team, Emily. When can you start?"

"Uh," Emily looked taken aback. "Well, I guess now is as good a time as any."

"Great," Kate praised. "Wren will show you the ropes, and I'll get some paperwork for you to fill out."

"Okay," Emily replied, and then gave a small laugh. "That was all really easy."

"Hey, it's just synchronicity." Kate shrugged. "I needed more help, Wren knew you, so it's all good. Besides," she added, "any friend of Wren's is a friend of mine, so I think we'll make a great team."

"Not that I want to shoot a job offer in the foot or anything, but are you sure?" Emily ventured. "I mean, I've never had a job interview quite like this before."

"I've never really hired anyone before," Kate replied, then turned to Wren who was about to protest. "You don't count. You told me you were going to work here and it would be fabulous, so I didn't have much say in it." Kate gave Wren an affectionate grin as she glanced at Emily. "She's also vetted everyone else that's worked here too. I trust her judgment, but screw us over and you'll be dealing with her." She nodded toward the smaller woman standing by her side.

Wren opened and closed her mouth, then turned to Emily. "It's true," she admitted. "I just showed up and convinced Kate that she needed me and that's how we've worked ever since."

Kate gave Emily a wry smile. "She calls me boss, but sometimes I really have to wonder who's in charge," she said.

"Tell me about it," agreed Emily.

"So, boss, while I show Emily around, what say you have some lunch?"

"You trying to get rid of me?" teased Kate.

"Hell, no, you're too good a cook, but you ought to eat something besides frosting."

"Okay, I'll make something up."

"How about you eat the bagel I've got ready for you in the refrigerator over at that table," Wren supplied, pointing at a table near the front door.

Kate stared at her. "When the hell did we get married?"

"Please, like you could afford me." Wren snorted.

"Wren, whoever gets you will be one lucky guy, but I just hope he knows what he's taking on," retorted Kate over her shoulder as she went to get her lunch.

Michael kept walking. He paused at a travel agency, looking at the posters and prices, for a moment entertaining the thought of getting out, getting anywhere, getting all the way far, far away. Going someplace where nobody knew what he did, what he used to do, what he was supposed to be doing. He sighed and walked on.

It was early afternoon before he paused at the intersection, waiting for the light to change, and actually took a good look around to get his bearings. He slid his sunglasses down his nose and squinted around at the buildings. Where the hell was he? He knew he was in the Village again, but he must have gotten turned around somehow; his sense of direction felt skewed. Peering ahead, he recognized the red canopy flapping in the breeze, halfway down the next block.

The bakery—he knew where he was now. He walked along the block, and then stood on the other side of the street, staring at the shop front; he wasn't sure what he was doing. He shoved his hands in his pockets and glanced up the street. It was just a bakery, no big deal, so why did he feel like it was? He looked at the chalkboard hanging up out in front of the store, sporting a new quote for the day. At least someone was able to write. He crossed the street for a better look.

The road to hell is closed for repaving.

He grinned and his feet made the decision for him as he stepped inside.

Kate walked out of the kitchen with her bagel on a plate, eyeing it with trepidation. "Wren, do you think you made this one big enough?"

"Relax, boss. I made them for us at home this morning."

"Maybe, but it's the size of a Volkswagen!"

"You work very hard, so you need a good lunch," said Wren with a placid smile. "Now go sit, and I'll bring you a coffee."

Kate nodded and went to find somewhere to sit; she knew better than to argue with Wren.

Michael stood in the doorway of the café, his eyes darting toward the counter. There were two women standing behind the coffee machine, one in the process of teaching the other how it all worked. They were deep in conversation but looked up with ready smiles at his approach. He studied their features but neither was the woman that he had spoken to a few days before, and he was surprised to feel a stab of disappointment.

"Hi there, what can I get for you?" Wren watched him with quiet appreciation. There was something different about him. His eyes were hazel with a generous abundance of eyelashes that women paid a fortune for in mascara to achieve, but despite his striking looks he moved with a kind of shy caution.

"Just a coffee," Michael ventured.

"No problem." She smiled. "You go take a seat and we'll be right with you."

He took his change and nodded his thanks before turning around to look for a table. That's when he saw her, sitting at a small bistro table by herself with what appeared to be a late lunch in front of her. She was leaning back in her chair slightly as she gave an unselfconscious, cat-like stretch before returning to her lunch. She chewed with obvious enjoyment and gave a thumbs-up to the women behind the counter. He hesitated as he looked around the café as he tried to find an unoccupied table.

"You can sit here if you like."

He turned to see the woman, Kate—he remembered her name now—push out a spare chair at her table with her foot. She raised a hand to her face to cover her mouth as she finished chewing and spoke again.

"I won't be here long, and then I'll be getting back to work," she explained, jerking her thumb toward the kitchen.

Michael stood hesitating, shifting his weight has he tried to decide what to do. She was looking at him, waiting for him to say something. He was going to have to find some words.

"I don't want to impose," he began, and she shook her head in denial.

"Sit," she invited again.

He sat down, licked his lips, and tried to think of something to say.

She regarded him over the top of her bagel as she took another bite. He noticed that her eyes crinkled at the edges. Her smile was warm and sincere, and her eyes were framed with expressive eyebrows, one of which was beginning to arch in inquiry.

He was staring. He cleared his throat and gave a start of relief when one of the women silently appeared at his elbow to slide his coffee cup onto the table. He clutched at the saucer, relieved to have something to do with his hands. After keeping to himself for so long, he was feeling the heat of her regard to be somewhat disconcerting.

He wished he could think of something to say.

She glanced down at her plate and appeared to make a decision. Dabbing at her mouth with her napkin, she dusted off her hands, and then stood up and slid the half bagel toward him. He looked at the plate and then up at her in surprise. She smiled and touched his shoulder in passing as she headed back toward the kitchen. He stared after her in astonishment. A moment later she reappeared and set down a plate holding a cupcake. This time when he looked up, she winked and went back to the kitchen.

He hadn't known where he was walking today. Words had hounded him out of his apartment, shooed him out of the bookstore, and herded him along the street until he had ended up here. He considered the bagel for a moment, feeling nourished before he even began, and then took a bite.

Michael paused between mouthfuls to take a sip of his coffee, glancing around the store as he marveled at where he had ended up. He was in a bakery with words outside that made him smile, and a woman inside with warm, crinkly eyes and a soothing presence. He'd found someone who didn't pester him for words. Her laughter sounded from the kitchen in response to a comment from her colleague, and he felt his lips moving into a smile at the sound. He liked it here. He'd have to come back. With any luck he'd think of something to say; perhaps he could find some words for her.

Chapter 3

Knights and Queens

Kate peered at her alarm clock as she switched off the incessant buzzing, and then buried her face back into her pillow with a low groan. The noise woke up the man sleeping beside her, and he squinted at the back of her head for a moment before rolling onto his side and snuggling up beside her, hooking one of his tanned, muscled legs over her hips for good measure.

"Can't we stay in bed?" he mumbled.

"Gotta work," Kate rasped back. She needed water.

"You're the boss. Can't you call in sick?" came the reply, then he ran his hand suggestively over her rump. "I'll make pancakes…"

Kate lay there for a moment considering the suggestion, which certainly had merits. Still, the bakery wasn't going to run itself; Wren was good at everything else she did, but she wasn't "cupcake good," which was something even she was only too happy to admit.

"Sorry, babe, no can do," Kate apologized.

She tried to sit up, and the man grabbed her and pulled her back against his chest, planting a sloppy kiss on the side of her neck and grabbing at her chest. Kate shrieked and slapped at his wandering hands. It was like being in bed with an octopus; his hands were everywhere.

"Thomas! Stop it! What is it with gay men and tits?" Kate finally pushed him off and sat up in bed, her face flushed and hair messy. She looked down at her mussed up camisole and groaned in mock despair. "Look what you've done!"

"What?" Thomas rolled back onto his side and lay with his head propped in his hand, giving her a sleepy-eyed look that had no doubt worked on many conquests.

"You've knocked my tits all outta whack." Kate pushed at them for a moment before giving up and huffing at him in mock exasperation.

Thomas threw back his head and laughed. Kate squinted at him and grinned with affection before crawling off the bed and staggering toward the bathroom. She stopped at the basin to chug back a large glass of water, and then stripped and stepped into the shower, all but groaning with relief as the water hit her skin. She leaned against the tiled wall, trying to wake up, and then yipped with surprise as Thomas yanked back the shower curtain and held out a glass of something fizzing toward her.

"What? It's not like I haven't seen it before. Drink this," he commanded as Kate shrank back and tried to cover herself.

Kate accepted the glass and sniffed at it, eyeing the effervescent contents with caution.

"Relax, Kate. It's a vitamin B tablet. They're a great hangover cure," Thomas said. "Of course," he added as an afterthought, "they work better if you take them beforehand, but it'll help you feel human."

She paused, and then slugged the contents back.

"Good girl." Thomas was waiting to retrieve the glass. "Now you finish up in there, and I'll get us something to eat."

"Thanks, Mom," Kate said as she turned her back to him, and flinched as she received a stinging slap on her wet rump. "What was that for?"

"That was for sassing me," Thomas retorted as he left the bathroom.

Kate shook her head at his bossiness and started to wash her hair. She'd nearly finished when she saw a shadow fall across the shower curtain.

"I see you, Thomas Hall."

"I wasn't trying to hide," he replied. "Are you nearly done?"

"Yep."

"Good. I'm coming in."

"Give me a sec," Kate answered, making sure her hair was completely rinsed.

"5…4…3…2" Thomas counted down, then yanked open the curtain.

Kate rolled her eyes and stepped past him, snatching the towel he was ostentatiously holding up to prevent him from seeing anything.

"Bit late to be playing coy now, isn't it?" Kate asked as she wrapped the towel around herself, and then grabbed a smaller one for her hair. She looked up and saw Thomas's muscular backside as he stepped into the shower.

"I suppose so, but a semblance of modesty is nice now and then."

"You, modest? Please."

"Who said I was talking about *me?*" Thomas said. "I was doing that to protect your sensibilities, although I daresay it's been a while since you've woken up with a man in your bed."

"True," Kate said as she towel dried her hair. "But it's not often I wake up with a screaming queen either."

"You'd better be careful I don't just pour you a saucer of milk for breakfast."

Kate stuck her tongue out at him, aware that she was being childish and enjoying herself anyway, then went into the bedroom to finish getting dry. By the time Thomas had finished his ablutions, Kate had dressed herself into her button down jeans and her Average Joe's T-shirt. She was lacing up her red Chucks when Thomas reappeared, somehow managing to look immaculate despite the fact he was wearing his clothes from the night before: black jeans and a tailored, white, button down shirt that accentuated his olive skin and flashing, dark brown eyes. His short, dark hair had been freshly washed and styled, and the hint of stubble only made him look all the more picture perfect. He looked her up and down and shook his head.

"Oh, Kate," he sighed. "Converse again?"

"What?" Kate looked down at them. "I love them."

"Yeah, but c'mon, can't you wear something a bit more stylish?"

Kate gave him an exasperated look. "Tom, I bake all day so there's no way in hell you're going to get me wearing Jimmy Choo heels."

"I know. I just live in hope is all," Thomas said.

"Dream on," Kate replied. "Actually while you're at it, dream up a Prince Charming for me."

"Oh, please, like he'd go for you when I'm in the room." Thomas snorted.

"Modest much?"

"Not really." Thomas smirked back.

By the time Kate had brushed her teeth and added a quick layer of makeup in a bid to put a bit more color in her face, Thomas had prepared scrambled eggs and was waiting for the toast to pop up.

"Now you look better," he praised as Kate appeared in the small living room.

"Thanks, babe," Kate replied, accepting a plate and glass of juice and indicating the couch with a jerk of her head.

They put their plates down on the coffee table and began to eat. Kate checked her watch and saw that she was still running on time. Thomas looked around his surroundings as he chewed, and sipped at his juice before speaking.

"You know, Kate, this place is looking really homey."

"Coming from you, I'll take that as a compliment," Kate replied as she forked herself some more eggs.

"*Homey*, not homo," Thomas said, nudging her with his shoulder.

"I know," said Kate, nudging him back.

"No, really, the place is looking good. You've got a nice vibe going on here. It's very … eclectic."

Kate looked around the apartment, trying to see it through Thomas's eyes. The walls were covered with pictures that had either been painted by friends or picked up at flea markets over the years, all vying for wall space with framed postcards and little items of interest that had attracted her attention. The room also boasted a series of bookshelves in different heights and different colors, each one home to a diverse range of books, CDs, glass vases filled with seashells, and still more books. Only one shelf alcove was kept bare but for a graceful pair of Buddha-hand figurines.

"Do you mean eclectic in a good way or a bad way?"

"Oh, definitely good," Thomas reassured her.

"It's not as stylish as your place," Kate admitted as she finished her eggs and reached for her juice.

"True, but it'd be a nice place to bring a date home." He gave her an arch look. "If you were to actually go on one."

"I'm a busy woman," Kate hedged. "I don't have time to date."

"Mm-hmm, but you made time to go to the wine bar with Wren last night."

"That's different. That was drinks after work," Kate protested. She hated it when Thomas started grilling her about her love life or lack thereof.

"Right, and I saw a few guys checking you out, which you had no clue about because you weren't even trying to case the joint."

Kate sipped her juice but said nothing.

"You know, Kate, you're a fine lookin' woman and you need to put yourself out there more. What's the worst that could happen?"

"Thank you, Exhibit A," Kate replied dryly, then she rushed on to continue as Thomas's face fell. "Oh, sweetie, no, that's not what I meant. Crap." She slumped back into her chair.

"No, it's okay. I get where you're coming from," Thomas said quietly. "I was still working out what the hell I was, so how were you to know?"

"Well, we know now." Kate sighed.

"Guess I made you gun shy for a while there, huh," Thomas said with a sad smile.

Kate reached over to take his hand, giving it a light squeeze for emphasis.

"Thomas, you can't take *all* the credit for my dating disasters. Besides," she continued, "no matter what your orientation, I think deep down we were always destined to be better friends than lovers. You know I'd much rather have you in my life than not. We're good."

"Good to know," Thomas replied, his expression lightening somewhat. "Still, we're going to have to find you a man."

"Okay." Kate threw her hands up. "Whatever. Knock yourself out. Just do me a favor." She eyed him.

"Anything," he replied instantly.

"Make sure your gaydar is working. I think we both know mine's a little off."

Thomas laughed and Kate checked her watch.

"Okay, Princess, let's hit the road. I've got to get to work."

"I know it's good for me; I just wish I knew why I'm going to drink it." Wren regarded the tumbler full of pink juice, and sniffed at it warily. Her conquest from the night before sighed and rested his hip against the counter. His muscular build and natural vitality had been attractive the night before, not to mention his dazzling smile and shoulder length, fair hair. There was still plenty of him to appreciate, but without any coffee to assist the process, Wren wasn't so sure.

"Because it's full of nutrients from celery, wheatgrass, carrot, ginger, and fresh beet," he replied, counting off the ingredients on his fingers as he spoke. "Just drink it and your hangover will thank you."

Wren drank it down, then gagged and rushed to fill the tumbler with water to follow.

"It tasted like *dirt!*" she accused over her shoulder.

"That's your imagination," he replied as Wren shook her head as if to get rid of the taste. "So," he continued, "what are you doing tonight?"

Wren looked at his kitchen, where she could see he had bowls piled high with fresh produce. She was hung over and longing to eat everything that she knew was bad for her. She also desperately wanted a coffee, but the best he had been able to offer was a cup of dandelion tea. She gazed at the man with regret. Such a shame—he'd been fantastic in the sack.

"I think," she ventured, "I'm going to eat everything deep fried that I can get my hands on."

He pulled a face. "You really ought to go vegan," he began in an earnest tone.

"No, I really ought to go to work," Wren interrupted, grabbing her bag and heading for the door.

He caught her just before she could leave and planted a long kiss on her. Wren sighed and leaned into him, and then broke away to open the door with a small smile.

"You'll call?" he asked.

"Mmmm," she replied, and made her escape while he tried to work out if that had meant yes or no.

What a waste, she thought to herself.

❧

Kate yawned as she and Thomas came to a stop at the light, and Thomas ran his hand briskly up and down her back.

"Wakey, wakey," he said, grinning down at her.

"I'm getting there," she assured him. "Once I get a coffee, I'll be fine."

The light changed and they crossed the street.

"So, what time did we get home last night?"

"All I know is that it was after midnight," Thomas said, draping his arm around her shoulders and hurrying her along.

"What, after midnight and you didn't turn into a pumpkin? What a shame you didn't find Prince Charming after all," Kate teased.

Thomas gave her a droll look. "Honey, if we'd been in *that* fairy tale, I'd have happily changed as long as I could go home with Peter Pumpkin Eater."

His brazen comment shocked a whoop of laughter out of Kate, and she stumbled on, wiping tears of mirth from her eyes as Thomas grinned and kept marching her toward work.

"C'mon, you, let's get you to work. You know it'll do you good," Thomas urged.

They rounded the corner to see Wren standing under the canopy, waiting as always.

"Every single morning," Kate muttered to herself. Thomas looked at her with an inquiring gaze. "She beats me every morning," Kate explained.

Thomas shrugged. "It just means she's keen."

"Hey, boss," Wren greeted her.

"Don't call me boss," Kate replied, and unlocked the door. "You remember Thomas?"

"The man with almost as much style as me? Sure," Wren sassed as Thomas slapped her on the rump by way of greeting.

"Hey, girl," Thomas said once they were inside. "So what's the verdict on last night's offering? Was he Mr. Right or Mr. Right Now?"

Wren pulled a face. "Mr. Right Now turned out to be a vegan, which is why I've got this," she said, holding up a partially eaten bacon sandwich, "for breakfast."

"A modern tragedy!" commiserated Thomas.

"Tell me about it," groused Wren. "I need a coffee," she said to Kate. "Huge."

"Got it," Kate replied.

Wren jammed what was left of her sandwich into her mouth and lugged the chalkboard outside, chewing as she wrote. She stood back to regard her handiwork with a nod of satisfaction, and then went back inside.

Kate had just finished making the coffees for the three of them, and Wren accepted her grande coffee with all the reverence it deserved. She held it in both hands for a moment, just inhaling the freshly brewed aroma, and then took a sip, her eyes all but rolling back into her head with pleasure.

"Wow," Thomas said as he watched the spectacle. "She really takes her coffee seriously."

"If you were as tiny as she is, with a hangover that big, you'd appreciate a coffee too," replied Kate as she cleaned down the machine, looking up with a grin as Emily arrived. "Hey, girl," she greeted. "Need a morning brew?"

"Love one," Emily said. "But shouldn't I be making it?" She stashed her bag in the kitchen and reappeared, wiping her hands on her jeans. "Hi," she greeted Thomas with a shy smile.

"Greetings," he replied as he sipped his coffee.

"Thomas and I go way back," Kate explained.

"Back to when she thought blue eye shadow and pink lipstick was a fabulous look," Thomas elaborated, making Emily laugh as Kate winced. "Oh, Kate, don't be embarrassed. I was right there beside you in my stone washed jeans and matching jacket." Thomas shuddered.

"And on that note, I'm going to start baking," Kate said, sidling away.

"Okay, missy, I'll see you again sometime, thanks for the bed last night," Thomas said, draining his coffee and grabbing Kate for a cuddle before leaving, slapping Wren on the rump for good measure.

When Wren got back to the counter, Emily was laboriously pouring herself a coffee. Becoming a barista was high on Emily's list of priorities, and she was applying herself to the task diligently.

"So, uh, is Thomas Kate's..." Her voice trailed off uncertainly.

"Oh, hell, no, he plays for the other team." Wren laughed. "But the two of them have known each other since college. They even dated for a while."

"Really?" Emily was agog.

"Well, Thomas hadn't come out at that stage, but when he did, he and Kate stayed good friends."

"Oh." Emily thought for a moment. "Makes my life look like white bread by comparison."

"That's not always a bad thing as long as you keep an open mind," Wren reasoned as Emily nodded in agreement. "Anyway, Kate and I went to a wine bar last night for Friday night drinks, and Thomas ended up meeting us there and we just kept on going, which is why he ended up crashing at her place for the night."

"Must be nice to have friends like that," Emily commented and looked at Wren. "Kate's pretty cool, huh."

"Yep."

"So why's she single?"

"Beats me." Wren shrugged. "Guess she just hasn't met the right guy yet."

Michael leaned back in his chair and stretched his arms up over his head, groaning as he heard his stiff body stretch and pop. Relaxing once more, he looked at his laptop screen. It made a nice change to see a document on the screen instead of a blank page, because today, for the first time, he had typed something. Granted it was only a few sentences, but it was a start and certainly more than he'd been able to come up with over the last couple of months. He sat in his chair, thinking of warm, dancing eyes.

Perhaps he'd sit and think a little more and go for a walk later. He looked back at the screen. It still taunted him, but somehow not as much as it usually did. He'd made a mark on the page now. Something was starting. He just wished he knew what.

Michael looked at his watch; it was nearly midday. He puffed out his breath and gazed around his apartment. After his early publishing success, his parents had encouraged him to invest in real estate. He had been somewhat surprised, therefore, to find himself graduating from college and ending up in West SoHo, living in style. The apartment was spacious with polished floorboards and large windows flanking the wall, looking down onto the street. High ceilings and tasteful lighting added to the sense of airiness, but although his mother had helped to choose the furniture and rugs, the apartment often felt cold to him.

He rationalized that by telling himself it was because he lived alone and his work kept him to a relatively solitary existence. Nowadays, he felt that it was because the room took a lot of words to fill, and these days words seemed hard to come by.

Getting up from his desk, he paced the length of the room, hands in pockets as he stared off into space. His gaze drifted toward the row of bookshelves—so many words by so many other people. Of course, there was a shelf that held a collection of his own works, but they weren't helping him now. He needed to find some more words of his own and sitting inside the apartment didn't seem to be helping.

Michael checked the time again. He should eat. His gaze flickered toward the kitchen, where he knew there was a fully stocked refrigerator. For a moment he wavered, rubbing his hands over his stubble as he thought. Setting his jaw, he grabbed his keys and sunglasses and stalked toward the door. He'd go for a walk, do some research, see if he could find any inspiration. Maybe he'd get something to eat while he was out. After all, he knew just the place, but he'd go for a walk first. Maybe if he told himself that enough times, he'd believe it, instead of knowing that going to the bakery had been the first thing on his mind this morning.

❧

"Daydreaming? Or are you still trying to wake up?"

Kate glanced up to see Wren watching her from the doorway.

"A little of both," she admitted, as she glanced down at the cupcakes and put a cherry on the last one.

"God, they look good." Wren sighed.

"I made them with you in mind." Kate nodded.

Wren's tired look brightened. "Really?"

"Yep, in honor of Mr. Vegan, I've made you an antidote."

"What is it?" Wren took a step into the kitchen, gazing at the rack of cakes.

"Peanut butter cupcakes, with chocolate and peanut butter cream cheese frosting," Kate supplied. "And a cherry on top."

"Elvis would be proud," Wren commented. "What are you going to call them?"

Kate told her. Wren jotted it down on the chalkboard. Another day at the bakery had begun.

❧

Michael browsed through some music, scowled his way through a bookstore, and kept walking. Any stops he'd made in various stores just seemed to prolong the inevitable, so after an hour, he'd sighed and turned the corner, picking up the pace somewhat. He was unaware that the closer he got to the bakery, the more he walked with a sense of purpose. He paused across the street to take a good look at the bakery that seemed to have some sort of hold over him. The red canopy bore the bakery's name, and he was surprised to realize that he hadn't even noticed it before.

Take the Cake.

He crossed the street and stopped at the window display. A different collection of cupcakes was in the bell jars today, surrounded by apples and vitamin tablets. He puzzled over this, trying to work out the connection, and then remembered the chalkboard at the entrance. He glanced over at it and felt his mouth curve into a smile before he stepped inside.

Buy organic for health,
but eat cupcakes for taste.

The floor was tiled, and the walls were covered in old wooden panels to match the long, antique counter. A pair of dilapidated wooden bookshelves contained a variety of magazines and newspapers along with a collection of children's books and board games—some new, some old. The tables and chairs were an eclectic mixture of French bistro style and farmhouse, some of which had been hand painted with vines, flowers, and dragonflies, all of which were reflected in the collection of framed mirrors vying for wall space. It was a riot of color and warmth.

❧

"Wow, God must really love her work sometimes," Emily said softly.

"Her work?" Wren asked.

"Only a woman would work to make something *that* fine," Emily replied. Wren looked up to see what had caught her attention.

He was back and this was the third time in as many weeks now. Coincidence? Wren watched as his eyes raked the room, skimming over the two women behind the counter. Wren frowned a little, watching his expression. Was that disappointment? She thought quickly.

"Emily, could you spot me here for a sec?"

"Sure, but I'm not sure I'm up to speed on the coffee machine," Emily said easily.

"Not a problem, if you get an order, Kate can take care of it," Wren said. She stepped away from the counter. "I just have to make a phone call."

He was walking toward the counter now, so Wren turned and walked with what she hoped was a casual stride toward the back of the store. Kate looked up when she entered the kitchen.

"Everything okay?"

"Sure. Just got to get some air. Emily might need a hand with a coffee, though," Wren replied, not breaking stride.

Kate watched her go then popped her head out of the kitchen in time to see Emily write down an order. She wiped her hands on her apron and stepped out into the store.

"Need a hand?" she asked Emily in a quiet voice.

Emily nodded gratefully. "My milk froth is getting better, but I'm not confident enough to inflict it on the public yet."

"No problem." Kate grinned, grabbing a cup and setting the espresso, then jiggling the milk jug under the steam spigot with practiced ease. "You'll pick it up soon enough. Where's this one going?"

"Sir Galahad at table four," Emily said, and then blushed at Kate's raised eyebrow. Wren had pointed him out to her the first time he had appeared in the store.

"Check it out." Wren had given her a nudge to get her attention and directed her gaze to where the man had been sitting. "Seeing guys like that is one of the perks of the job."

Kate gazed over at the table where he sat waiting, frowning over a copy of the *New York Times*. She had to admit that Emily had a point. He sat with a careless grace that hinted at strength.

"Oh, I see he's back again," Kate commented.

"He was here on my first day," Emily replied promptly. "What? I wouldn't forget a guy like *that*."

"I would've thought Wren would have enjoyed looking after him after her vegan experience," Kate said, scanning the order and selecting one of their fresh turkey bagel sandwiches and sliding it onto a plate.

"She saw him then said she had to make a phone call. I guess that's why she went out back?"

Kate thought for a moment. She was sure she hadn't seen Wren holding her phone. Just then, Wren appeared in the doorway.

"Hey, Emily, could you give me a hand carrying the next batch of cupcakes out?"

Emily shot Kate an inquiring look.

"Go ahead. I'll take these out," Kate said. She picked up the cup and plate and walked over to the table. "Hey," she greeted him as she drew near.

He looked up and offered a small nod and smile as he shifted his newspaper aside to allow Kate some room to put down the plates.

"Thank you," he said in a quiet voice.

"You're very welcome," she replied, and then gestured toward the newspaper. "Anything good in it today?"

He glanced at it and shot her a wry grimace. "Not much."

"Well, you can't read doom and gloom while you eat. Mind if I suggest something else?"

He looked puzzled. "Sure," he replied.

Kate stepped over to the bookcase, and after a quick scan, pulled out a book and placed it in front of him. He picked it up and looked at the title.

"*The Berenstain Bears?*"

"Sure, it's not classic literature to some, but I think you'll find it's a perfect lunch accompaniment." She smiled, and then looked a little embarrassed. "Sorry, I know you've been in here before, but I can't remember your name," she explained.

"Michael," he replied.

"Kate," she answered with a wink. "Enjoy your reading. If you need anything, that's Wren over there, and Emily's new but she's here to help too," she said as she returned to the counter, ostensibly wiping down the surface, but keeping a surreptitious eye on him.

"Hey, boss," Wren greeted her in a bright voice. Kate turned to see Wren and Emily carrying two plates of the daily cupcake out to be displayed. "You look like you need a break."

"Do I?" Kate replied, unconsciously reaching a hand up to her hair. "Do I look that bad?"

"Nah, you look good, but why don't you take a load off and I'll bring you a coffee?"

"All right," Kate said slowly. She went into the kitchen to get a couple of items out of her bag, and by the time she reappeared, Wren was already placing a fresh coffee on a table out front, next to Kate's customer.

Kate shot Wren a suspicious glance, but Wren was radiating innocence. Naturally, that meant she was up to something. With an inward sigh, Kate sat down and arranged her things. She sipped her coffee, and then set her cup down to select a fresh piece of paper, picked up her pen, and began to write. As she worked, she watched him from the corner of her eye as he picked up the book and flicked it open to read. After the first few pages, he picked up his bagel and began to eat, still reading. Kate watched him, smiling to herself as she caught the occasional "huh" of amusement.

By the time Michael finished the book and his lunch, his eyes were peaceful.

"So how was it?"

He looked up to see Kate sitting at the table beside him, an empty coffee cup and some sheets of notepaper in front of her.

"I haven't even thought about that book for years," he commented. "But it's still fun."

"That's why I keep it in the store. I get a kick out of watching people of all ages pick it up. I'd love to be able to write something like that—something that makes people smile."

"What about your chalkboard out front? And your cupcake names seem to give people a laugh," Michael pointed out.

"Guess I hadn't thought of it like that," she replied with a slow smile.

He'd heard her laugh and now he'd made her smile. He watched her mouth curl up, trying to remember every detail. "What's that you're working on?" Michael pointed a finger toward the colored notepaper Kate had been working on moments before.

"This? Oh, it's a letter to one of my friends."

"You don't email?" Michael was surprised.

"Sure, but sometimes I like to give people the pleasure of finding something nice in their mail instead of statements and bills."

"Huh," Michael said, leaning forward in his chair as she spoke, intrigued.

"I like to think that there's a certain romance in writing a letter to someone," she continued, a faint pink tingeing her cheeks now. "Because it sends the message that you've set aside time to put pen to paper to someone. You're not forwarding a joke or dashing out an email. You're actually sitting down and devoting some time to that person, and it's something tangible."

She picked up the small sheet of paper and flapped it to illustrate her point, and then put it down with a slight laugh. "Mind you, this isn't exactly *War and Peace*. It's just a note to say I was thinking of them and a really bad joke that's going to make them groan, but it's still something."

"I admire you for that," Michael said in a quiet voice.

She looked at him in surprise. "What on earth for?"

Michael shrugged. "I don't have much luck writing anything lately. I don't think I could manage something complicated like a letter."

"Want a tip about that?" she whispered. She leaned forward, looking conspiratorial and Michael instinctively leaned toward her.

"Sure," he whispered back.

"Say what you have to say and then stop. Don't labor at it so much."

Michael stared at her for a moment, and then began to laugh. If only she knew. He was still chuckling when she looked up to a summons from the counter.

"Gotta go. Sounds like the Pocket Rocket needs me. It was nice meeting you, Michael."

"You too," he replied with a smile. He knew her name. He knew the bakery name. She'd given him more words today. He watched as she gathered up her paper then left the table, running a hand over his shoulder in passing. Michael lifted his hand to grasp her fingers, but she was gone. He watched as she disappeared into the kitchen, and looked up a few minutes later as she re-emerged. She was stuffing the notepaper into a stamped envelope, and she left the store.

Michael sat watching her as she walked over to a mailbox on the other side of the street. She stood gazing at the envelope for a moment, kissed it, and popped it into the slot. She patted the mailbox for good measure and returned to the store, grinning at Michael in passing as she walked through the store and back into the kitchen.

"Is there anything else you'd like?" a voice said beside him.

"Yes," he replied in an absent tone, and then jerked back to awareness as someone giggled. "Sorry, what?"

He looked up to see a small woman with close-cropped hair and a knowing grin, regarding him as she picked up his empty coffee cup from the table. Wren, he remembered.

"I said is there anything else you'd like?"

"Uh . . ." Out of reflex, he looked at his watch. "Not just now. I should probably be going."

"Kate had to take a phone call, but she wanted me to give you this with our compliments," Wren explained, extending a cupcake on a plate toward him. "It's our daily special."

Michael glanced at it then back at her. "What's this one called?"

"*Vegan rehab*." She grinned, and then added, "Private joke."

"Right," he said, accepting the cake and standing up. "Please tell Kate," he felt a stab of pleasure at being able to use her name, "that I said thanks."

"Will do," Wren replied, stepping away and eyeing him appreciatively. "And I'm sure we'll see you here again some time," she added in an assured tone. "And just so you know, she's single."

Michael's forehead wrinkled as he tried to work out if he'd heard her right. Wren leaned forward.

"She's single, you know, available," she repeated. "Just thought you'd like to know is all." She winked.

Michael stood in quiet amazement as he watched her collect some cups off nearby tables and take them out to the back, humming to herself as she worked. He waited for a moment longer, but Kate didn't reappear, so he quietly left the store. Half a block later, he began to eat the cupcake. It was good.

As he walked, his thoughts wandered back over his afternoon, and he shook his head. He had established a comfortable routine for himself, but that routine had faltered when his inspiration had seemingly run dry. By some chance, he had found his way into the bakery. Not once, but three times now. Today he had spent the afternoon reading a children's book and talking to a woman who made him feel rested and exhilarated all at once. It was a curious sensation, and he liked it.

Chapter 4

Cake and Sunshine

Kate opened her eyes seconds before the alarm began to sound, and then reached out to switch it off. She lay there for a moment, gazing at the framed photograph that sat beside the clock, and reached out to gently trace the image's face with a forefinger. No dawdling this morning. She showered and dressed quickly and in silence. The only noises in the apartment were the ambient sounds drifting in from the street and the occasional sounds of water running, the blast of the hairdryer, the clatter of jewelry being selected and discarded, and then the jangle of keys and hurried footsteps.

The slam of the door resonated in the silence.

Mouthing the lyrics to the song blaring through her iPod headphones, Wren glanced at her watch and picked up the pace. She had skipped breakfast but would be able to fix something to eat once she got to work. Dodging her way through traffic, she crossed the street and broke into a light jog. Rounding the corner, she breathed a sigh of relief; she was still running ahead of Kate so her record remained unbroken. She'd made a note of the date yesterday and knew that today was going to be set apart from the norm. She looked further ahead down the block and saw Kate approaching.

"Morning, boss," she called a moment later.

"Wren, don't call me boss," Kate replied with a smile that tried but didn't quite reach her eyes.

"Sorry, boss." Wren waited for Kate to unlock the door, then walked inside and dumped her bag on the counter. First things first: she grabbed a piece of chalk and got the chalkboard ready for the day. By the time she'd hung it up outside, Kate had two coffees ready and was getting out the supplies for the first batch of cupcakes. Conversation was at a minimum, but Wren had known to expect it. She switched on the stereo, selected a disc, and before long, Dido's soothing voice permeated the store.

A quick peek around the corner revealed Kate concentrating on the industrial-sized cake mixer, breaking eggs with total focus on the task at hand. Wren stood there for a moment, then turned and went back to filling up the stainless steel jugs with filtered water. She added slices of lemon and fresh mint and set the jugs out on the small self-service table near the end of the counter. She looked up as Emily arrived and greeted her with a smile.

"Hey, babe," she said as Emily drew near. "Coffee?"

"Please," Emily said gratefully. "I overslept so had to hightail it over here."

"That reminds me." Wren snapped her fingers. "I didn't get to have breakfast so I'll see if there's any—" She broke off as Kate appeared with a small plate.

"Warm, savory cheese and herb scones with plenty of butter," Kate said with a small smile. "That should keep you guys going for a while," she added before disappearing back into the kitchen.

Emily nodded her thanks and watched Kate disappear before turning to Wren with an inquiring look when Kate offered little more than a smile in return.

"Is she okay?" she whispered.

"She'll be fine," Wren said in a confident tone. "Today is just going to be a bit hard on our girl, so we'll have to be gentle."

"Oh?"

Wren could tell that Emily wanted to ask more but wasn't going to impose. She felt a rush of appreciation for Emily's quiet nature and goodwill. She had done the right thing bringing her on board, especially on a day like today.

The two women got busy with the morning routine and enjoyed their breakfast while they worked. After stacking their plates in the dishwasher, Wren paused to peer into the kitchen and stopped short.

"Whoa, you got busy."

Kate had delivered the first batch of cupcakes to Wren and had personally taken care of the window display, before retreating to the kitchen again. She had worked methodically all morning, and now there were over five dozen cupcakes iced and decorated, waiting to be put on display. Wren regarded her for a long moment. Kate couldn't return her gaze.

"You gotta bail for a while?" she asked. Kate nodded and bit her lip. Wren stepped forward and wrapped her arms around her. "All right, then, take care of you," Wren said in a soft voice before releasing her and stepped back out into the shop area. Kate stood blinking against the rush of moisture, and then gathered up her bag. She left the store without a word, leaving Wren and Emily standing behind the counter in silence watching her go. Kate stood outside and looked at the chalkboard then back at Wren, offering a small but genuine smile before she left.

❧

Michael shambled toward the television, yawning and stretching, pausing to grab the waistband of his pajama bottoms that slipped perilously low on his hips as he picked up the remote. He turned toward the sofa, aiming the remote over his shoulder and thumbing a button at random. The flat screen TV came to life as he threw himself onto the sofa with a muffled thump, and he turned a basilisk gaze toward the screen.

After an hour of mind-numbing morning television, Michael gave up on the diversion and powered up his laptop, glancing at the calendar widget that appeared on the screen. The weeks were starting to blur into one another, and he still had very little to show for it. He'd had enough of staring at screens. It was time to get outside and interact with people, and he knew just the person. Scrolling through his contact list, he gave a quiet grunt of satisfaction when he found the name. Decision made, he dialed the number and grinned when the familiar voice answered.

"Watson," he began, and laughed at the war whoop of recognition. Plans were made and a few minutes later he hung up feeling satisfied. Other than the bakery, he hadn't had contact with many people at all over the last few weeks, so getting out and seeing an old friend would be good for him. He got up from his seat and stretched again before strolling back into the bedroom to get changed. It felt nice to have a sense of purpose about the day.

Michael was near Washington Square Park, standing at the light, waiting to cross when movement on the other side of the street caught his eye. It was Kate. She stood alone in the crowd, her gaze turned inward, but that wasn't what held his attention. For the first time that he could recall, she wasn't smiling, and he didn't think he had ever seen her look so lost. Her gaze drifted and for a moment she seemed to look straight at him. They stared at each other across the traffic for a moment, and then Michael lifted his hand and gave her a tentative wave. She gave no sign of recognition as her gaze moved on. Michael paused then lowered his hand. Something was wrong.

The light changed and people surged forward. Michael stuffed his hands in his pockets and crossed the street, keeping a watchful eye on Kate. She walked straight past him, seemingly lost in her own thoughts. She passed close enough for him to catch a waft of her scent, which was warm with a hint of vanilla musk, making him think of cake and sunshine. He reached the curb, and then turned around to catch another glimpse, his shoulder colliding with another pedestrian. He apologized, and then turned again to see where Kate was headed. He caught a glimpse of her hair, and then a bus turned the corner, obscuring his vision. By the time the traffic had cleared, she was gone.

Kate entered Washington Square Park and followed the path toward the dog run. Once there, she leaned against the fence with her face propped in her hands and watched dogs of all shapes and sizes gamboling and playing with each other. From time to time, dogs would wander over to where she stood at the fence for an inquiring sniff, and she would extend her hand, fingers curled into her palm for their inspection before rubbing them behind their ears. Eventually she followed the fence line down toward the gate and let herself in, exchanging smiles with some of the dog owners exercising their pets. Kate wandered around, squatting as some of the smaller dogs trotted over for a hello pat, which she happily obliged.

Kate laughed as a golden retriever snuffled at her ear then swiped his long wet tongue from her hair to her jaw. She gave the dog a quick hug, looking up as a shadow fell across her. She looked up to see an older woman regarding her with interest.

"You got a dog here?"

Kate looked up, squinting against the sunlight and trying to fend off the enthusiastic affections of the retriever. "No, I don't. I just come here when I'm having an off kind of day," she explained.

"Ah." Comprehension dawned on the woman's face. "And there's no better cure than some unconditional canine love."

"You got it." Kate smiled back, and then grabbed the retriever affectionately and gave it a hug. The dog turned and before she could react, had swiped his long wet tongue against her face, making her flinch and laugh. Kate left the park half an hour later, her expression considerably lighter.

Michael stopped at a newsstand for a quick purchase, and then continued on his way to the bakery. He arrived in good time and made a point to stop to check out the chalkboard swinging from its brass hooks.

Live life one cupcake at a time.

He smiled and moved over to look at the window display. The bell jars held cupcakes that were sweet in their simplicity: vanilla frosting with rainbow sprinkles. One of the bell jars held a small framed photo. Michael leaned forward for a closer look. It was a younger looking Kate and a man that was obviously her father. They were leaning against a truck, the man's arm hugging Kate to his chest as they both grinned at the camera. Beside the frame sat a solitary cupcake and a small hand-written sign. *Jack's Favorite*. Now he knew why she had looked so sad. He went inside and sat at a table to wait.

"Psssst, Wren!" Emily hissed.

Wren bobbed up from the display cabinet that she had been restocking. "What?"

Emily jerked her head toward the front of the store. "Sir Galahad's back."

Wren followed Emily's gaze and saw him sitting at a table near the front door. The morning sun shone through the front windows, highlighting his auburn curls. He half-sat half-sprawled in his chair, flicking through a copy of the *New York Times* with careless grace. He was, Wren had to admit, glorious.

"Let's hope Kate gets back soon," Wren whispered to Emily as the two women regarded him with what they hoped were covert glances, along with every other woman in the store. Wren shook her head in admiration; he truly had no inkling that he was the center of attention. She found that very attractive, as her extensive dating history had revealed that attractive men often tended to rely on their looks and fall quite short in other departments.

"Michael Forrester, you reclusive son of a bitch," a voice drawled from the doorway.

Michael looked up, pushing his newspaper aside as he stood up with a broad smile to greet his friend. David had changed little over the years they had known each other, although his body had filled out into a muscular grace that showed his ongoing pursuit of fitness. He had come from work today and so was dressed in more business-like attire than Michael was used to seeing him in. His white blond hair was its customary scruff, however, and a tattoo could be seeing peeking out over his shirt collar.

"Watson, 'bout time you showed up," he replied as the two men enfolded each other in an enthusiastic back-thumping embrace.

"Oh, no." Emily pulled a disappointed face. "The good ones are always gay."

"Uh-uh," Wren replied, shaking her head. "He's straight."

"Are you sure?" Emily was skeptical.

"Sure, I'm sure. He watches Kate like a fat man watches fried food." Wren smirked.

The two men sat down, grinning at each other.

"Dude, I can't believe you called," David said, shaking his head. "How long as it been?"

"Too long if you're asking my mom," Michael replied.

"I know, I know. My folks keep asking after you, as well." David grunted. He cocked his head toward the counter. "I'm on the clock today, man, so how about we order something?"

"Sounds like a plan," Michael agreed.

David sat up straighter in his chair and looked around the store, then regarded Michael with a quizzical expression. "So how did you find this place? This isn't your usual hangout from what I recall."

"Dave, I haven't had a regular hangout for a while," he said with a grimace. "Unless you count my desk chair."

David looked sympathetic. "Yeah, I heard about that but wasn't going to say anything."

Michael raised an eyebrow at that. "My mom?" he asked and sighed at David's nod. "Figures."

"Well, they're worried too," David said in a mild tone.

"Yeah, I know." Michael ran his hand through his hair, frustrated. "It's just … well, you know how it is with deadlines."

"Tell me about it," David deadpanned. "I love that whooshing noise they make as they go by."

"Right," Michael scoffed. "Like you can miss deadlines working at a paper."

"True." David inclined his head in acknowledgment. "But the pressure is still the same, except I get it *every day*."

"True," agreed Michael.

"Although," David continued, "I think it's safe to say that you reap better dividends."

Michael shrugged but didn't reply.

"But enough of that. I need *food*," David said. "I got to work early without breakfast this morning, so I could eat the crotch out of a low-flying duck right about now."

Michael laughed as they walked toward the counter. "With a mouth like that, it's a wonder you're able to charm the ladies."

"Oh, I don't know," replied Wren from behind the counter as she gave David an assessing glance. "He's doing okay so far."

David gave the woman a quick grin then turned his attention to the display cabinet.

Wren was stunned. The guy was cute, she knew she was packing heat in her formfitting shirt, and when it came to the opposite sex, she had an exceptional batting average, yet he had apparently dismissed her with a glance. She took his order, and he accepted his change with an absent-minded thanks, and then walked back to his table. She was still watching his retreating back when she realized that the other man—Sir Galahad—had been speaking to her.

"Sorry, what was that?" She blinked and then took his order, shaking her head as if to clear it.

She passed the order slips to Emily and stood there for a moment, watching the two men resume their seats and start chatting.

He'd ignored her, and she didn't like that. She didn't like that one bit.

"So," David was saying, "what's the draw with this place? I wouldn't have thought it was your usual thing."

"I dunno," Michael mused. "It has a kind of appeal."

That was when Kate appeared in the doorway. David looked at Michael, waiting for him to continue. When the other man said nothing, David twisted slightly in his chair to follow his friend's gaze and grinned in understanding.

❧

Kate felt better. The walk, fresh air, and canine company had been refreshing. She might not be able to find love of the two-legged variety, but it was good to know that she could access unconditional adoration at short notice. She stopped at the window to smile at Jack's photo, and then continued inside, smiling at Michael in passing.

Wren watched as Galahad's gaze tracked Kate as she walked through the store. She sighed and shook her head. It was obvious that Kate had absolutely no idea of his interest, and he was being equally reticent. This was going to take a while.

"So, have you been coming here for long?" David asked, watching Michael with quiet amusement.

"Oh, awhile," Michael replied in an absent tone.

"So I see," David commented.

Wren appeared with their orders, artfully brushing her breast against David's shoulder as she leaned forward with their plates. David nodded his thanks and paid her little attention after that.

"Mmmph," Michael replied as he bit into his bagel, then chewed and swallowed. "It was a surprise discovery, but it has its appeal."

David turned his head to watch the retreating back of the waitress.

"That it does," he said.

Michael followed his gaze. "You're shitting me. You've barely been here five minutes and you've already zeroed in on a target?"

David gave him an innocent glance. "What? Is there something wrong with that?"

Michael glanced back at Wren, who was wiping down the counter with short, angry strokes.

"Nothing at all, but I don't think you've caught her attention."

David gave him a slow smile. "Oh, I think I can handle that," he drawled and gave him a slow wink.

Michael grinned. No work was going get done today, but for the first time in a long time, he felt much better about it. He'd had enough self-flagellation; it was time to live a little, starting one day at a time.

Kate reappeared from the kitchen and draped an arm around Wren's shoulders to give her a loose hug.

"How you feeling, boss?" Wren inquired.

"Better," Kate replied, giving her a quick squeeze, and then nodded toward the cabinet where Emily was cleaning. "How we doing today, Emily?"

"They're selling like crazy." Emily straightened and gave Kate a smile.

"Do you think we need more?"

Emily gave the cupcake display an assessing gaze. "No, at the rate we've been going, I think we'll be okay for a while now."

"Good," Kate replied. "I wasn't ready to shackle myself to the oven again just yet."

"How about I make you some lunch soon?" Wren asked.

Kate looked at Wren affectionately. "What would I do without you?"

"Curl up in a fetal position and sob quietly because you couldn't imagine ever finding someone as fabulous to work with as me?" Wren bantered.

"Probably. I know I'd never find anyone as modest as you," Kate replied.

"Well, there's always Thomas," Wren sassed back.

"Oh, please, that man could make a sequin look shy."

Wren blinked at her. "Are you saying that I can't?"

Kate looked at Emily. "Help," she peeped.

Emily snuffled with laughter. "Uh-uh, you're on your own."

The three women began to laugh.

Michael glanced up to see the source of the laughter and smiled. She was looking better now, and he was glad for it. The men bantered their way through lunch, and then David checked his watch and began to excuse himself.

"I've gotta get back, Michael, but listen, how about we do this again? Don't be such a stranger next time."

"Sure," Michael replied, pleased that he had been able to rekindle a friendship that he had let cool to embers. "How's next week for you?"

"I'll check, but off the top of my head, it sounds good," David said, swigging back his coffee.

The two men stood up and shook hands and gave each other another hug for good measure. David turned to leave, and then turned back as if on an afterthought, "And listen, if you want to come back here, that's fine with me."

"I thought it might be." Michael grinned.

David winked again and left. Michael watched him go and settled back into his seat with a sigh. He didn't want to go just yet. If he was going to be honest with himself, he wanted to see her. He wanted to see Kate. One of the other women appeared with a bagel on a plate and set it down on the table beside him, giving him a shy smile and disappearing behind the counter again. He looked at the plate in puzzlement.

❧

"Kate, why am I looking at you right now?" Wren said in an arch tone.

"Because I'm the best boss you've ever had and you can't help but gaze at me with adoration from time to time?"

"Well, there is that," Wren conceded. "But I'm wondering why you're still here behind the counter, when there's a perfectly good bagel on a plate for you, sitting on a table over *there*." She pointed it out for emphasis.

"Okay, I'm going."

"You're going to eat that and relax, and I don't want to see you back here until you've had a coffee as well."

"Yes'm," Kate replied, snapping off a mock salute and walking toward the table.

Wren and Emily watched her go.

"That's not very subtle," offered Emily after a moment's pause.

"Subtlety wastes time," Wren replied. "And it'd be lost on those two anyway."

Kate sank into her chair and looked at the bagel: smoked salmon again, her all-time favorite. It never failed to amaze her how well Wren looked after her. She bit into it and chewed slowly, enjoying the flavors of the salmon, cream cheese, and capers. She was on her second mouthful when she glanced to her right and saw a familiar pair of hazel eyes. She chewed and swallowed before she spoke.

"Hello again," she said.

"Hello." He gave her a gentle smile, making her blink. He seemed restrained for some reason, watching her as if trying to gauge her reaction.

"How's your day?" she asked, taking another bite.

"It's not bad." He shrugged. "I just caught up with a friend I haven't seen for a long time." He considered it for a moment. "It was good."

"Then I'm happy for you."

"Just like that? You're happy for me?" His eyebrows went up.

"Why not?"

"I—" he began, then stopped. "Thank you."

"You're very welcome."

He watched her in silence, wishing he could think of something to say. He'd had words for David, but David he had known since childhood. This woman was different, and he didn't know what to say that would please her, and he found suddenly that he wanted to please her very much.

She worked her way through her lunch, exchanging greetings with other customers as they entered, enjoying brief conversations here and there. He admired the easy way she seemed to relate to everyone. After a while, she glanced at him again and he shifted in his seat, leaning forward a little.

"So, uh…I don't want to pry," he began awkwardly, cursing his clumsy words. It was a miracle he'd managed to get published. She nodded for him to continue, and he felt a rush of relief. "The cupcake in the window…" He gestured toward the display, and then watched as her open expression became one of polite reserve for a moment.

"It's for my father," she said in a soft voice, looking down into her cup.

"Listen, just tell me to shut up if I'm…" he babbled. He never babbled. What was it with this woman?

"No, it's okay." She reached out a hand to lay it over his as it rested on the table. Her hand felt warm and dry and, he realized, entirely comfortable. "It's a vanilla butter cupcake, Jack—my dad," she nodded toward the photo, "used to love them. He always used to tease me about opening a cupcake shop one day, because I used to make so many."

This time it was Michael who nodded for her to continue.

"I lost him when I was nineteen," she said quietly.

"I'm sorry—" Michael began automatically.

Kate waved him off. "It's not your fault." She smiled.

"So…" He paused. "What happened?"

"Car accident," she said. "I was driving, and we got blindsided by a van. My head got hit pretty hard, and Jack didn't make it."

Michael gazed at her, then without thinking, placed his hand over hers, cupping her hand between his, rubbing his thumb in reassuring circles in an unconscious pattern.

She bit her lip. "So the next thing I know, I'm waking up in the hospital, and my big brother is telling me that Jack was gone, and this…" She lifted her free hand to sweep her hair away from her forehead, revealing a long white scar that ran along her hairline down to her left temple.

Michael winced. The two of them sat in a companionable silence before Kate gave a small start.

"I'm sorry," she apologized in a rush. "I didn't mean to bring you down with that tale of woe—"

"Don't be sorry. I appreciate you telling me," Michael replied. "It's okay. Really."

Kate looked flustered. "I really am sorry, you know. I don't usually go around telling people stuff like that."

"Then I'm flattered that you did," Michael admitted, realizing that it was the truth. The words were coming to him more easily now. "I don't often get to see you for a chat; you seem pretty busy."

Kate laughed at that. "I know, which is why Wren has suddenly started a campaign for me to start taking a lunch break."

"I'll have to time my visits more carefully then," Michael replied, feeling emboldened by the feel of the hand that she seemed content to leave resting between his.

"Well, I'll try to make time to talk to you more in the future too," she teased. "And then the girls will think that you're a special customer."

"So are you," Michael replied, the words suddenly appearing on his tongue unbidden.

"I'm what?"

"Special," he said, then, greatly daring, reached out to gently tuck a strand of hair behind her ear.

Wren watched them from her spot behind the coffee machine, holding her breath as Galahad reached out to touch Kate's hair. Kate hadn't withdrawn, and he was still holding her hand. It wasn't much, but it was a start.

Then there was the matter of Emily.

And there was also the matter of Galahad's friend. *He* was going to be another challenge entirely, but that was okay. In fact, it was better than okay; she liked a challenge.

Wren's small smile widened into a satisfied grin. This was going to be fun.

Chapter 5

Second Mouse Satisfaction

Michael and Kate were still talking quietly at the table when a shadow fell across the doorway of the shop. Kate looked up and did a double take, slipping away from the table—and Michael's hands—with a cry of delight.

"Brother Bear!"

Michael sat watching as Kate launched herself at a man who took two laughing strides toward her before gathering her up into a hug that swept her feet off the floor. Kate cupped his face in her small hands to cover his cheeks with kisses. Her small frame in his arms was apparently no effort.

Michael had seen enough. He gathered his papers and waited for them to pass before he made his way out of the store.

Wren watched him go, shaking her head. "Silly man," she said to herself.

Once outside, Michael walked on, devouring the pavement with long strides, his hands jammed in his jeans pockets, his chin all but tucked into his chest, deep in thought. What had seemed a perfect moment and been broken by the stranger's loud arrival. More importantly, Michael's cautious happiness had evaporated as Kate had torn herself away from his gentle grasp. The way she had thrown herself at the stranger spoke of a long and easy intimacy. Of course she was taken; no one that attractive in New York could be single.

And yet...

Michael stopped short, making the person walking behind him almost trip and have to step around him. Lost in his own thoughts, he was oblivious to the filthy look he received. Kate had called the stranger Brother Bear...and she'd mentioned having an older brother when she had told him about the accident.

His writer's memory clicked into gear, and the clues began to fall into place: the framed picture in the store window, Kate's melancholy state, their quiet conversation, and then the arrival of the person she'd called Brother Bear who had brown eyes just like Kate's. Just like hers because they were *related*. Michael clenched his hands into fists and sighed; he'd been a fool. He could have said something, asked her something, anything. If only he could think of something to say, but it was too late to go back now. He walked on, thinking about the touch of her hair, the warmth of her skin, and the feel of her hand in his. He'd visit the bakery again soon, to set things to rights.

❧

"It's so good to see you!"

Kate had stopped kissing her brother's cheeks and had instead wrapped her arms around his neck, hugging him and wiggling to be set down.

"Easy there, Babycake," he said in a laughing voice as he let Kate down, then looked across to the counter to see Wren grinning at him, and his face lit up with glee. "Pocket Rocket!"

"Oh, no," Wren muttered, her grin faltering as she began backing away from the counter. Paul rounded it, moving toward her with surprising grace despite his immense size as she looked around for a convenient means of escape. She feinted to her left, but he stepped to the right, neatly blocking her access to the kitchen, shaking his head as he began to laugh in anticipation. Wren sighed and straightened up from her crouching stance. "Oh, go on then, you big lug." She opened her arms in surrender.

He whooped and picked her up, giving her a hug that sent the breath out of her in a whoosh before dipping her back onto her feet. Wren staggered back a pace then laughed as she pushed at his chest to get him to move. "Jesus, Paul, and I thought you were the size of a house the *last* time you were in."

Emily, who had appeared in the kitchen doorway to investigate the ruckus, shrank back when Paul rounded on her.

"And who do we have here?"

"Easy, Bear. Play gentle," warned Wren. "This is Emily."

Paul grinned at Emily, who offered him a shy smile in return as he reached out and shook her hand.

"Great to meet you, Emily. I'm Kate's brother, Paul."

"You're related?" Emily's confusion was plain to see as she looked from Kate to Paul and then back again. Paul towered over Kate, and his scruffy jeans and tight-fitting T-shirt only served to emphasize his tanned and very muscular arms.

"Tell me about it." Kate smirked. "Mom used to say that after birthing *him*," she said, jerking a thumb toward Paul, "she was pretty gun-shy for a while, so I'm lucky to be standing here."

"Yeah, right," scoffed Paul. "As if Mom and Dad could keep their hands off each other."

"Eww, parental sex lives, too much information." Wren winced, making Kate laugh.

"Well, they're not here to deny it," Paul said. "Speaking of which…" He moved toward Kate again and draped his arm around her shoulders, pulling her in to kiss her temple. "I saw the window display. Jack would've loved it."

Emily, who had been filled in on the significance of the day by Wren, gave a nod of understanding. "How come you guys refer to your dad by his first name?"

Kate nodded at Paul, who began to explain. "After Mom died, Dad wanted to take us on a holiday to get away, so we came to New York. One day we were in the Natural History Museum and lost sight of Jack. So the two of us were walking along, hand in hand, calling out 'Dad… *Dad…*' and we could see him in the distance, but he wasn't responding, then—"

Kate cut in, "Then Bear here called out 'Jack,' and Jack's head snapped around and he came straight back to where we were."

Wren smiled. She'd heard this story before, but she loved the way Kate's and Paul's faces glowed whenever they recounted it.

Paul continued, "And when he caught up to us, we said, 'Didn't you hear us calling?' And he said, 'Sure, but there are heaps of dads here. You could have been calling to any one of them.' So from then on, he was Jack."

Emily laughed. "That's so cute!"

Kate smiled. "That's so Jack."

"And you've honored him well, sis," Paul said with a grin.

"But how come you're not in the photo?" Emily asked.

Paul smiled. "Who do you think was holding the camera? I'm still there."

"You're always there," Kate replied with a gentle smile.

"Yep, you might not see me, but I'll always be with you, Kat."

☙

Michael peered around in the gloom, smiling when David raised his hand to give a languid wave. He worked his way through the Friday afternoon crowd and saw that David had somehow managed to get a bar table and already had a beer and a shot waiting for Michael's arrival.

"Forrester," David greeted him with a lazy nod.

"Watson," Michael replied, picking up the shot and raising an eyebrow at David.

"Down the hatch," David said.

Michael threw the shot back, then wiped his mouth with the back of his hand and quickly took a sip of beer. "I'm glad you called," he said as he set his glass down.

Michael watched his friend cast a happy gaze around the patrons of the bar, a good proportion of which were women, then thought about his own productivity for the day. He'd gone home from the bakery and, after much thought over a few hours, had written a sentence. Not much to show for the day. Certainly nothing to a journalist with deadlines like David, but given Michael's productivity of late, it was notable. David had called him earlier that evening and invited him out for a drink, and Michael had accepted. It seemed a better option than staring at his computer all evening.

David gave a happy shrug. "Deadlines are met, so my weekend has started. Let's play, Forrester."

"You're on," Michael muttered as he picked up his beer again. He was taking another sip when he felt his phone vibrate in his pocket. He fumbled for it and answered, one hand pressed over his other ear so that he could hear better. "Hello?"

"Hey, son, sounds like you're having fun somewhere."

"Dad." Michael couldn't stop the happy grin on his face. "How are you?"

"Doing good at this end, but we miss you. Your mother wanted me to call. What are you up to this weekend?"

That was, Michael knew, code for "*We both miss you. Come home.*"

"I'm having a drink with David tonight. … Yeah, the Watson kid." He grinned as David raised his glass in acknowledgment. "So maybe Sunday?"

"That sounds great. Listen, I won't keep you on the phone, then, but please come over on Sunday. I know your mother will jump at the chance to feed you."

"You won't hear me arguing," Michael replied. "See you on Sunday, Dad. Love you."

"Will do. Love you too, son. I think your mother's cooking already."

❧

"You mean I don't get a home cooked meal?" Paul said, his eyes pleading. "C'mon, Kat, I'm starved."

Paul had spent the afternoon hanging out at the bakery, making the girls laugh and performing some quality control checks on the cupcake supply. As it turned out, his visit had been well timed in more ways than one. Kate had signed for a delivery of ingredients and had immediately pressed Paul into service with the heavy lifting. He had helped Kate clean up the store after closing and now wanted to do something for dinner. Kate's first instinct had been to suggest take-out, much to Paul's disappointment.

"Oh, come on, then," she said, sighing and picking up her bag. "But I've got to stop for a few things on the way home."

"No problem," Paul replied with a grin.

"And you're paying."

"Fair call," he agreed.

They stopped at a grocery store on the way home, and Kate picked up a few things, after sending Paul to a liquor store further down the block to get a bottle of wine to enjoy with their meal.

Once home, Kate kicked off her shoes and changed shirts, then busied herself making dinner while Paul uncorked a bottle of white and kept up a steady stream of conversation. She directed Paul to "make the table look pretty," and after some searching, he had produced a tablecloth and some candles. Soon they were sitting down to a meal of creamy, chicken and asparagus pasta with crusty garlic bread.

Paul raised his wine glass. "To Jack and Gwen," he said.

Kate chinked her glass against his. "Amen."

"Amen," he replied, and then got down to the business of the meal.

A while later, Paul used the last of the garlic bread to clean up the sauce in his bowl, having already gone back for seconds. He leaned back in his chair and gave a sigh that was replete with satisfaction.

"God, that was good."

Kate watched him with quiet amusement, tucking a foot up on her chair and twirling a strand of hair around one finger, her elbow resting on her knee.

"Don't you cook much at home?"

"Standard bachelor fare," he replied, finishing his mouthful and stacking the plates.

"Meaning what, exactly?"

"Meaning they know me by name at Subway. I cook, but nothing like this." He waved his wine glass at the table. He patted his still-flat belly and gave her a hopeful look. "I don't suppose..." He raised an eyebrow.

Kate laughed. "They're in a box near the sink." She smiled as Paul picked up their dinner plates and went to investigate, enjoying their sibling shorthand. He returned with a cupcake and bit into it, making a happy humming noise to himself as he ate.

"So," Paul said finally, licking some frosting off his fingers, "it's time for the annual question, you ready?"

"As I'll ever be," she said in a resigned tone. "Bring it on."

Paul folded his arms on the table and leaned forward. "How's the love life?"

"How can I put this?" Kate pretended to think for a moment. "Let's just say that if my love life was a person, it'd be lying in a hospital bed somewhere in a vegetative state with a nurse saying, 'Switch it off.'"

Paul laughed and shook his head.

"And now it's my turn," Kate went on. "How about you?"

"Well, let's just say I don't lack for companionship." He waggled his eyebrows suggestively, making her groan. "But," his expression sobered, "it'd be nice to have something more permanent."

The two of them sat in a contemplative silence for a while.

"You know," Paul ventured, "if Mom was still alive, she'd be match-making up a storm for the two of us."

"No doubt about it," Kate agreed. "And Dad would be polishing his shotgun, wanting to know the intentions of any guy that turned up on the doorstep."

Paul grinned.

"So is there anyone on the horizon for you?" Paul asked out of curiosity.

"Not that I'm aware of, but Tom and Wren are usually better at spotting that kind of thing. How about you?"

"Well, I'm looking, so I guess it'll happen when it's meant to." Paul stared into his wine glass, and then took another sip. "We'll get there, Kat."

"Yeah, but it'd be nice to know where *there* is. I've got friends. I've got a great little business that's starting to turn a profit." She sipped her wine and shrugged. "Maybe there are some of us that just aren't destined to have it all."

"Maybe not," Paul replied. "But that doesn't mean you just have to roll over and accept it. Mr. Right isn't just going to knock on your door, Kat. You've gotta get out there."

"I know," Kate replied with a sad little smile. "Just do me a favor?"

"Anything," Paul agreed instantly.

"If I don't end up married and chasing the happily ever after, just promise me you won't let me turn into the crazy old cat lady."

"Done. As long as you make sure I don't end up the sad old bachelor drunk at the bar."

"Brother Bear," Kate said, "you've got yourself a deal."

Paul pushed his chair back from the table and opened his arms. Kate got up and walked around to curl up on his lap, tucking her head under his chin.

"I've missed you," she mumbled into his shirt.

"I've missed you too, sis," Paul replied in a quiet voice. "Let's do this more often, okay?"

"You're just saying that to get more cake," Kate retorted, swallowing down the sudden lump in her throat.

"Saw right through me that time, didn't you?" Paul chuckled.

Kate closed her eyes, listening to the rumble of his laughter in his chest. "Do you miss them?" Kate ventured in a quiet voice.

"Every day." Paul's voice was just as soft.

They sat together, Paul rocking his little sister gently in his arms, closing his eyes and resting his cheek on her head.

❧

David slung an arm around Michael's shoulders and leaned over to shout in his ear.

"Another round?"

"Yeah." Michael flicked some money toward David, who managed to swipe the bills on his second attempt before ambling off to the bar. Michael watched his progress. His gaze drifted, and then stopped when he realized someone was watching him. She shook her blond hair off her shoulders and nibbled at the straw in her drink; the suggestion in her eyes was unmistakable. Michael stared back as he finished his drink.

David returned from the bar with their drinks, setting them down on the table, and followed Michael's gaze. "Nice," he commented. "Listen, man, if you wanna go play, I can find my way home."

"Nah, I'm good," Michael replied, accepting the next drink. "She's not my type."

David glanced across at the woman, and then gave Michael an incredulous look. "Dude, she's been watching you like she's already on her back, and I'm tellin' you right now, that's a serious case of 'fuck me' eyes she's giving you."

"I know," Michael muttered. "But she's not—" He stopped with a shrug.

David watched him, his eyes growing wide. "Oh ho, so you've got someone else in your sights," he guessed, grinning when he saw the look on Michael's face. "I'll take that as a yes. Who is she?"

"No one you know," Michael replied, chugging back his beer in a bid to avoid the conversation.

"Because you haven't made a move yet?" David asked. Michael shot him a quick look. "I'm right again, aren't I? Damn, I'm good."

"Yeah, you're something." Michael gave him a wry grin.

"So what's she like?" David's eyes were alive with curiosity.

"Smart, funny, great laugh, beautiful…" Michael began, pausing as David waved him off.

"Okay, I get the idea. And she's single?"

"That's what I've been told," Michael replied, thinking of Wren.

"Well, if she's that good, you're going to have to move fast. But you know, before you think about the *what if* there's always the *now*."

"What?" Michael's gaze swung from the blonde back to David.

"You heard me." David shrugged. "Why deny yourself a *right now* because you've got a *what if? Carpe diem* and all that shit."

"I don't know," Michael said, feeling doubtful.

"When in doubt, my friend," David said, "have another drink. I'll get us another round."

David went back to the bar, and Michael looked at the woman again. Maybe David had a point. He'd locked himself away for so long. Maybe it was time to live a little.

❧

The next morning, Michael surfaced into awareness with considerable reluctance. That'd been some dream. Even the sheets smelled different, and his mouth felt like someone had poured the Sahara Desert into it. That was when he felt the warmth of another body beside him. His eyes flew open, and the first thing he saw was a mass of blond hair on the pillow beside him.

Where the hell was he?

The woman was nothing like Kate. She had blond hair and blue eyes that had blinked slowly before she offered him a lazy smile as he climbed out of bed to get dressed.

"I've gotta go," Michael began, hoping he wasn't sounding too apologetic as he pulled on his jeans.

"Sure, thanks for the sex." She smiled again as she eyed his half-dressed form with appreciation. Michael felt a rush of relief that she was content to let the situation be what it was: purely temporary.

He was pulling on his shirt when she spoke again. "Honey, just so you know, I wasn't her."

"What?" He looked at her in confusion.

"It was fun and all," she said, waving a desultory hand, "but I know when a guy's thinking about someone else." She considered him for a moment. "You could come back to bed and I'll make sure your attention stays on me this time."

"Thanks, but ..." Michael paused, and she laughed at his obvious discomfort.

"Sweet boy, thanks for the fun and have a nice life." She rolled over and snuggled into her pillow, effectively dismissing him. He paused, but she said nothing more so he left, closing the door quietly behind him.

It was still dark when he got outside, and he sighed when a glance at his watch showed the early hour. He'd shower and go to bed when he got home, and hope that tomorrow would be better. There was no doubt that this evening's "interlude" had provided a measure of release, but he still felt unsatisfied. Perhaps things would look better in the morning.

☙

The next day, Wren made her way to work, stopping in at a newsstand to buy a copy of her weekly indulgence, *Us Weekly*. She leafed through the pages as she walked, dividing her attention between the oncoming pedestrians and the printed page before her. She stopped at a set of lights, snorting with derision as she read about yet *another* sex-tape scandal.

Two hours later, a man stopped outside the bakery and laughed as he read the quote.

> The purpose of life is love,
> and the purpose of digital cameras
> is to make hot movies of that love.

He went inside and strolled up to the counter. "Nice quote. Who came up with that?"

Kate looked up with a ready smile. The customer was tall and blond with wide, blue, friendly eyes.

"That'd be the work of our resident genius, Wren," she replied, inclining her head toward Wren, who was working at the coffee machine and who took a moment to bob a quick curtsey before resuming her task.

"Nice." He grinned, although his gaze hadn't moved from Kate. Wren bit her lip to hold back a grin. "And you are …?" His voice tailed off and he grinned at Kate hopefully.

Kate managed not to yelp as Wren gave her a swift kick in the shins. "I'm Kate. I own the store," she said with a nod.

"*And* she's the resident cupcake genius," Wren added.

"Really?" His eyebrows went up as he nodded in appreciation. "Well, Kate, it's nice to meet you. I'm Tim."

"Hi." Kate smiled. "So what can we get you?"

"Hmm." He made a show of inspecting the case. "Well, I guess that all depends," he said, looking up at her again.

"Depends on what?"

"On you telling me which cupcake comes with your number," he replied with a winning smile.

Kate opened her mouth, but Wren beat her to the punch. "They all do," she chimed.

"Great!" Tim rubbed his hands together. "Well, I'll leave the choice up to you, Kate."

"Take a seat, Tim," Kate managed. "And Wren will be out with the coffee."

"Thanks." He flashed another smile before moving off toward a table.

"What the hell are you doing?" Kate hissed at Wren.

"Trying to help you out," Wren replied in an undertone, scooping out a cupcake and putting it on a plate, before picking it up and grabbing the coffee. "Because sometimes life's just too short to dawdle over shit like this." With that, she sailed out into the store.

By the time Wren returned to the counter, Kate was serving someone else. Emily returned with some more cups and paused to exchange a glance with Wren.

"Wow," Emily whispered. "She's looking pissed. What did you do?"

Wren gave Emily a sly grin. "Relax, Toots. The love doctor is in town."

Emily looked out to where Tim was enjoying his snack, all the while keeping a very appreciative gaze on Kate.

"Him?" she said in a voice that radiated disbelief.

"Yup, but only for now."

Emily looked at Wren in askance. "Are you sure?"

"Positive. Trust me."

Tim left an hour later, and Kate glared at Wren who cleaned up his table. As Wren got back to the coffee machine, Kate sauntered over. "Nice try, Wren, but he didn't get my number," she taunted.

"That's okay. I traded numbers with him on your behalf," Wren said in a flippant tone, walking into the kitchen and leaving Kate blinking in surprise in her wake.

"Hey, boss," Wren began later when there was a lull. "I couldn't help but notice that you were having a very cozy little chat with Galahad yesterday before Paul came in," Wren said in an arch tone. "It looked like the two of you were getting along."

"Who?" Kate looked puzzled.

Wren rolled her eyes, snapping the suspenders she was wearing over her polka dot T-shirt in irritation. "Will you just *try* to work with me for maybe a minute?"

"Well, give me a clue," Kate replied.

"Curly hair, tall, jaw line that just begs to be kissed, hazel eyes, kinda shy, the two of you were holding hands," Wren recited, ticking the items off on her fingers.

Kate stared at her for a moment before comprehension dawned. "Shy? You mean Michael?"

"*Yes*," Wren said with relief. "Thank God, we've got a name. Emily and I have been watching him for a few weeks now, but you're the only one he really wants to talk to."

"Really?" Kate looked surprised and flattered as she kept cleaning the counter.

"Uh-huh," Wren replied, watching the slight flush creeping up Kate's neck. *Come on, little fishy.* "The two of you seem to have struck up a nice little friendship."

"Mmmph," Kate grunted and kept working.

"And then there was Tim today. What did you think of him?"

"Well, he seems like a nice guy," Kate allowed.

Wren stared. "Nice? Is that all you've got to say?"

"Yup." Kate kept cleaning. Her back was to Wren, so the other woman didn't see her lips tightening.

"Well, I would have thought you could say something better than just *nice*."

Kate turned around, resting one hand on her hip and brushing her hair off her face with the other. "Hell, Wren, what else do you want me to say?" Kate was getting angry now, and this was a rare thing.

"I . . ." Wren was shocked into silence, also a rare thing.

Kate sighed and leaned against the counter looking weary. "Wren, you know today has been really hard for me, the shop has been busy, and if you don't mind, I'd rather not end it with a lecture about my love life or—" she held up a warning finger as Wren made as if to speak, "—the lack thereof. Get it?"

Wren closed her mouth with a snap. "Got it," she managed.

"Good."

Kate regarded her for a moment, then turned and slung the dishcloth over one shoulder as she started to unload the dishwasher. "Do me a favor," she said as she collected some stainless steel mixing bowls. "Go out, have a few drinks, have a great time, and get laid."

"That's an official directive, to get laid?" Wren said.

"Someone around here has to." Kate shrugged, stacking the bowls with muted clangs.

The kitchen was quiet for a moment, save for the sounds of dishes and cutlery as Kate unloaded and stacked things away.

"Boss," Wren ventured after a pause. "You know I only nag you because—"

"You care," Kate interrupted and gave her a tired smile. "I know."

"So, we're cool?" Wren said this in a timid voice, and Kate looked at her in surprise.

"Oh, honey." She crossed to her and gave her a hug. "You know we are. I guess I'm just a bit fragile from yesterday is all."

"I know, and I shouldn't have pushed," Wren admitted in a small voice.

Kate gave her another squeeze, and then stepped back, her hands on Wren's shoulders. "Look, I'll make a deal with you," Kate said in a careful tone. "If I go out on a date with someone, will it get you off my back?"

"Sure," Wren said.

"Really?" Kate raised an eyebrow.

"Well," Wren hedged, "maybe a bit."

"That's good enough for me," Kate agreed. "Now get outta here."

After another hug, Wren left a few minutes later. Kate kept working, trying to ignore the scrap of paper that Wren had stuck to the refrigerator door. A number with the name "Tim" scrawled above it in big letters.

She finished cleaning and slowly walked toward the refrigerator and removed the scrap of paper. Maybe Paul had a point. They both ought to do something with their lives. She sighed and, after a long moment, reached for the phone. She closed her eyes, deep in thought, then in a decisive movement, punched in the numbers and waited for the call to go through.

"Hi. Is this Tim?" She listened to the happy affirmative. "Um, it's Kate, from the bakery . . . I got your number this afternoon . . ."

❧

Michael scrubbed at his stubble with one hand as he gazed at his computer screen before leaning back in his chair for a stretch. The combination of a late night, waking up in a strange bed, and the resulting hangover had made for a very unproductive day. Hours later, he found he had accomplished nothing other than a very awkward conversation at three a.m. and three written sentences at best. He sighed and looked at the screen again. Still the same sentence as before: *A laugh that lights up the room, and a smile that can't help but create another.* The hour was late, but he could still hear plenty of activity outside. People were enjoying evening strolls, and traffic was still moving. Everyone seemed to be having a good time, so why wasn't he? He scratched his chin again, idly wondering what Kate did when she wasn't at work.

❧

Kate wasn't used to calling guys to arrange a date, but the pleasure in Tim's voice when she had taken him up on his earlier offer made her feel better. They had arranged a place to meet and he had been waiting for her with a ready smile. It had been a long day at work and so one glass of wine had lead to more before Kate had thrown caution to the wind and ordered a Cosmopolitan.

"Looks like you enjoy a Cosmo," Tim commented as she downed two in quick succession.

Kate nodded. It wasn't often she drank, but when she did she generally made a night of it. "If I could get these things in a sippy cup, I'd be a happy girl," she said carelessly, reaching for the glass as Tim laughed.

Hours later they had made their way home to Kate's apartment. It had been closer for one thing, and Kate had giggled and leaned against Tim all the way up the stairs. Once inside, she had closed the door and turned to see Tim reaching from her. Kate leaned into his embrace, trying not to mind when he swirled his tongue into her ear and sucked on her earlobe. Perhaps it was something that had worked for him in the past, but not this time. Damn it. She'd been lonely for too long. She needed this. She kept reciting that in her head as she closed her eyes and gave herself up to him, all the while knowing that she was cheating them both. She stared into the darkness of the bedroom then closed her eyes tightly as his lips claimed hers.

The next morning Kate rolled toward the alarm clock as it sounded and encountered a warm body instead of her spare pillow. She opened her eyes to see Tim sound asleep although the alarm clock was shrilling beside his head. Clutching the sheet to her chest, she leaned across him and slapped at the alarm until it stopped, lying back onto the bed and regarding Tim with weariness. There was nothing for it. She had to get ready, and he had to go.

"Hey." She nudged his shoulder once, and then again. He grunted and tried to roll over, but she pulled at his shoulder. "Hey, Tim, we've got to get going."

"In a minute," he mumbled, attempting to burrow back into the pillow.

"No, *now*," she repeated. "C'mon."

He showed no sign of movement. Kate regarded him for a moment, and then came to a decision. She had a routine and he was going to have to like it or lump it, preferably the latter. She grabbed at the sheet and quilt and yanked them off the bed.

That woke him up.

"What the fu—" he began when he saw Kate shimmying into a T-shirt that she had dropped on the floor last night. "What are you doing? C'mere." He patted the mattress in an inviting manner.

Kate looked at him over her shoulder and stood up.

"Sorry, Tim, no time. I've got to get to work."

"So call in sick." He put his hands behind his head and rolled over onto his back, quite unabashed at his nudity. Kate regarded him with, she realized, only mild regret, then shook her head.

"It's my business; I've got to be there," she said in what she hoped was a patient tone.

A small "I want" line appeared between Tim's eyebrows. "But I thought—" he began.

"What you want and what I need are two different things," Kate said in what she hoped was a gentle tone. "And I've got a business to run, so I'm going to get ready, okay?" She patted his foot, and then got up and rounded the bed as she headed toward the bathroom. "There's plenty of food in the kitchen," she called over her shoulder. "So help yourself to some breakfast, and then we need to move."

She quickly stripped off the T-shirt and got into the shower, praying he wouldn't try to join her. She showered quickly, shivering under the hot spray. The sex last night had been good, like scratching a persistent itch, but waking up with the morning reality felt very different. She wanted him out of her sanctuary, and soon. Hearing movement, she froze and cocked her head. She heard the refrigerator door open and the sounds of foraging. She relaxed a fraction and began to wash her hair. Good. He was going to eat, and then as soon as she was ready, they could leave.

She reappeared a short while later in jeans and one of Paul's shirts. It was enormous on her, but she had knotted it at the waist to try to cinch it in some-what. She teamed it with a pair of her oldest jeans—given her extensive collection, that was saying a lot—and her faithful red Chucks. Her hair was still wet and her face was devoid of makeup when she entered the kitchen carrying her bag.

Tim saw her and smiled, although she could see that his heart wasn't quite in it. Getting rebuffed now after the night before had left him on uncertain ground.

"Wow, you get ready quick," he commented.

Kate shrugged. "I've got a lot of baking ahead," she replied.

Tim waved a half-eaten apple toward the door. "So, time to hit the road?"

Kate nodded, hoping her relief didn't show on her face. "Yup, sorry."

They left the apartment and made their way down the stairs side by side.

"So," Tim ventured after a brief pause, "how about we catch up for lunch?"

"I can't," Kate replied with a regretful smile. "Business owner, remember?"

"Oh, yeah." He looked disappointed. "That's right." He thought for a moment, "Well, how about breakfast on Saturday?"

"Working again. It's a six-day-a-week operation, so I don't have much of a life," she replied, shrugging her bag's strap into a more comfortable position on her shoulder, hoping he would get the message. What the hell had she been thinking? This awkwardness wasn't her style at all.

"Right." Tim looked at his feet and then back at her. Kate felt guilty. Was she being too harsh? Tim was a nice-looking guy, classic all-American good looks, and they'd had a fun evening together. Lots of women would go for a guy like him, so why wasn't she? "So maybe I'll call you sometime…" His voice trailed off and they both looked at each other, feeling uncomfortable.

"Tim," Kate sighed, looking down at her feet for a moment, trying to find the words. "I just don't know if this is a good time for me. Running my own business takes a lot of—"

"Time," Tim interrupted with a sigh. "I know." He gave her a half-smile. "Still, if you want to catch up again sometime, you've got my number."

On impulse, Kate stood on tiptoe and gave him a gentle kiss. "Goodbye, Tim," she said, and this time she meant it. They both knew she wouldn't call. They said their goodbyes and went their separate ways. Kate watched Tim head off in the opposite direction, and then went on her way, wondering why she felt so relieved and lonely all at once.

Wren walked to work, her eyes darting back and forth over the faces in the crowd as she sought her daily inspiration. She had three more blocks to think of something, and so far the Chalkboard gods hadn't given her a damn thing. She arrived at the corner of Broadway and East Houston, and unhooked her iPod ear buds. Her playlist wasn't inspiring her this morning either, so maybe she'd eavesdrop for a change. She still had nothing as she stood waiting for Kate to arrive.

"Morning, boss."

"Wren, don't call me boss," Kate replied with a smile as she stepped up to unlock the doors.

Wren relaxed. All was forgiven. "Sorry, boss." She stepped into the store and did a double take as she took a good look at Kate. "What the hell happened? Did you oversleep or…" She broke off, her eyes widening. "Or *didn't you get much sleep at all?*"

Kate opened the door and ushered Wren inside, giving her a wry smile. "I woke up on time, but no, I didn't get much sleep. Thanks so much for asking."

Wren was agog. "What did you do?" *She looks like she…*

"I took my own advice from yesterday and called that guy."

"I knew it!" Wren gave a little skip. "So how was it?"

"It was," Kate paused, "okay." She pulled a face. "Pretty lame description, huh?"

Wren turned to face her. "Really? He looked like a nice guy."

"Oh and he is. Nothing wrong with him at all." Kate dropped her bag and flicked on the coffee machine, pulling out a couple of cups. "Before you can ask, yes, we had sex, and it was good sex, but it just felt like we were…like I was…I don't know, going through the motions or something."

While the machine was warming up, the two women put their bags away and kept chattering as they went about their morning routine.

"Tell Dr. Wren everything," Wren said, getting the milk out of the fridge and handing it to Kate, who took it with a nod of thanks.

"Well, you know, I guess I just would've liked a deeper connection."

Wren gave Kate a significant look. "Surely the only way he could get deeper would be with surgery."

Kate coughed to hide her laugh. "Well, yeah, but all I'm saying is that if it's just going to be sex for the sake of it, then I can take care of things for myself in that department."

"True," Wren acknowledged, "but you have to admit that having someone else there with you makes for a great way to pass the time."

"There is that," Kate agreed.

"Did he spend the night?" Wren went on.

"Yeah," Kate sighed and poured the frothy milk into the cups. "Which is why I look like *this*." She gestured to her outfit.

"Ah." Wren's face brightened in understanding. "You grunged yourself down so that he wouldn't get any saucy ideas about seeing you again."

"Yup. Think it's too obvious?"

Wren gave her a pitying look. "Honey, he's a *guy*. There's no such thing as too obvious. He'll be fine."

They sipped their coffee in silence for a moment, giving the freshly ground brew all the loving attention it deserved.

"Tell you what," Wren continued. "Why don't you go fix yourself up and I'll get things started."

"You're a champ," Kate said gratefully.

"Don't applaud; throw money," Wren teased, and slapped Kate's rump to shoo her away. "Now you go get yourself looking nice. I've got a bakery to open, and Emily will be here soon."

"Yes'm."

Kate went out into the kitchen and then opened one of the cupboards, pulling out one of the spare T-shirts she kept in there for emergencies. She looked at the front and grinned; it seemed appropriate. She wriggled into it, and then looked in her bag and cursed when she realized she didn't have her brush.

"Wren!"

"Whassup?" Wren popped her head into the kitchen. "Hey, nice shirt."

"Thanks. You got a brush?"

"Do I look like I have a brush?" Wren pointed at her scruffy short hair.

"What am I going to do? I can't get around with hair like this."

"Gimme a sec. Emily's just got here, so she might be able to help."

Kate heard the women exchange greetings, and then Emily came into kitchen with a smile, already digging in her bag. "Oh, I see what she means. Don't worry, Kate. We'll make you gorgeous."

"Thanks." Kate smiled with gratitude.

Wren cocked her head and considered Kate for a moment. "You know, with a hot little shirt like that, can I do your hair? I've got an idea."

"Knock yourself out." Kate shrugged and Wren set to work.

A few minutes later, Kate was surveying her reflection in a mirror. "Braids? You've put me in braids?"

"You don't like?" Wren looked worried.

Kate laughed. "No, they're cute. I just haven't had braids since grade school, and even then it was only when Gwen could hold me down long enough." She gave Wren a quick hug. "Thanks for getting me presentable, babe."

"Any time." Wren smiled and went back out front.

Reaching for her compact, Kate gave herself a quick dusting of makeup, some mascara, and lip-gloss. Closing the small mirror with a snap, she dropped it back into her bag, and then turned toward the kitchen counter. It was time to start the day.

Wren was making another round of morning coffees for the team when Emily wandered over to stand beside her.

"I wish I could look like you." She sighed.

"Huh? What do you mean?" Wren glanced at her before turning her attention back to the coffees.

"You know," Emily waved a hand at her, "stunning, instead of stunned."

Wren looked down at her outfit. Her favorite black jeans, a blue Paul Frank T-shirt, and tiger print ballet flats. It was simple and funky, and entirely Wren.

"Well…" Wren grinned. "It helps when you're short enough to shop in the kids' section. Keeps the costs down a bit." She cocked her head and regarded Emily thoughtfully. "But I think we can have some fun with your wardrobe."

Emily went pink with pleasure. "Really?"

"Yup, particularly if—and I'm only guessing here—it's going to help you snare someone's interest."

Emily's pink cheeks turned crimson.

"Thought so," Wren added with satisfaction. "Two for two. I'm *good*."

"So," Emily said in a bid to change the focus of the conversation, "if that's me fixed, what about Kate?"

"What about her?"

"You know," Emily peeked into the kitchen to make sure Kate was busy. "That hot guy that looks like he's got a thing for Kate hasn't been in for a while."

"I know." Wren frowned for a moment. "But I think he'll be in soon. There's a pattern of sorts and my gut tells me that he'll be back."

"I hope you're right," Emily said, sipping her coffee.

"Well, if I'm not I'll just have to make the time to fix things until they are."

Kate appeared to accept her coffee, and then looked up at the oversized clock hanging over the kitchen door. It was yet another flea market find, with an enormous face that reminded Kate of the ones she saw at Central Station. She enjoyed her weekend customers as everyone seemed to be in a more relaxed state of mind. She checked her calendar for Saturday and looked up to see Wren collecting empty cups off some of the tables.

"Wren, it's nearly eleven o'clock, time to get ready," she called before heading into the kitchen.

"I'm on it," Wren replied, heading out into the café front with some fabric folded over one arm, and then she saw Michael standing outside reading the chalkboard. She put the fabric down and returned to the counter, biding her time.

☙

Michael had walked through the Village, making his way toward the bakery. He had no idea what he was going to say. He hadn't visited the bakery for a few days, and since his night of drunken debauchery, he'd steered clear while he tried to get his thoughts in order. However circular his thoughts had been, they always returned to one thing: Kate.

Michael looked down the street toward the red canopy of Take the Cake, not realizing that he was already smiling. The store seemed to be a bit busier than usual today, and he could see people coming and going as he made his way toward it. He hoped he'd be able to find a table. As was his tradition, he stopped and checked out the chalkboard before entering.

The early bird gets the worm,
but the second mouse gets the cheese.

As soon as he entered, his gaze automatically went to the counter, looking for Kate. He wasn't disappointed. She was serving some customers, exchanging a few words and a laugh with each of them. She was wearing a black, tight-fitting tee with the unmistakable Rolling Stones logo of red pouting lips with a tongue hanging out which moved suggestively as Kate twisted and turned.

Emily saw Michael pause in the doorway and nudged Wren, who looked up from her coffee making.

"It's him," Emily said with quiet excitement.

"Excellent. Second cast has left the stage and now it's time for the main attraction," Wren replied.

"Huh?"

"Don't worry," Wren said, looking serene.

Michael dropped his newspaper and keys onto a spare table and made his way to the counter to order. Kate was with other customers, so he turned to the small woman near the coffee machine, who grinned at him.

"Your usual?" Wren asked as she got a cup out.

"You know it?" Michael was surprised.

"I remember our 'Specials' as we like to call them," Wren replied blithely. "Anything for lunch as well?"

Michael laughed despite himself. "How about I leave it up to you?" he replied, getting out his wallet.

"Oh, good." Wren gave him a happy smile. "I like it when people come to their senses."

"Is that what they do around you?"

"Generally," Wren replied, flicking a glance toward the kitchen. "Some faster than others."

Michael had no idea what she was talking about but handed over some bills and accepted his change as Wren shooed him back to his table. Later he looked up from his coffee at the sounds of furniture being moved to see a very business-like Wren set to work. Kate had come to his table to collect his plate and Michael made the most of the opportunity.

"Hi, Kate." He smiled, marveling that conversation with her was becoming easier with each visit.

"Hey, Michael." Kate gave him a warm smile. "It's nice to see you again."

"Likewise. So what's going on over there?" he asked, pointing toward Wren's endeavors.

"We're hosting a little girl's birthday party. They're having a High Tea," she explained. At Michael's look of inquiry, she went on. "We don't normally take bookings, but we thought we'd give it a shot and see how things go." She looked over at the activity around the tables, and then grinned back at Michael. "If you think you can handle the estrogen levels, stick around and see for yourself."

Meanwhile, Wren had moved two tables together and produced a vintage white tablecloth. She draped it over the top and then arranged the chairs to fit. Emily appeared with a laden tray from which they decanted a series of mismatched floral teacups and saucers, sugar bowls, and milk jugs. A vase of flowers was added, and Wren scattered rose petals across the table. As a final touch, Emily tied some pastel helium-filled balloons to the back of each chair, each with a lavish amount of ribbon.

Half an hour later, the birthday girl arrived, accompanied by four of her friends and her mother. The girls were all carefully dressed in "going out" clothes, and they oohed and ahhed over the pretty display before carefully taking their seats around the table. The balloons formed a cordon around the table that bobbed gently as the girls chattered and giggled.

Michael watched, charmed as Kate greeted the mother and birthday girl with a broad smile, before signaling Wren and Emily to deliver the main event. The girls broke into squeals of delight as their High Tea was delivered, and Kate settled them down before describing the fare that was being set out before them.

His lunch forgotten, Michael leaned forward, chin in hand as he watched the tea party unfold. The girls were quite taken with the fine display and under the watchful eye of the attending mother began to eat. Kate reappeared and carefully poured each girl cup of milky chai tea. Michael was surprised to see that the noise was kept to a minimum as the girls carefully passed plates, toasted each other with their teacups, and seemed to delight in what appeared to be a fine dining experience for the young group. The birthday girl opened her presents, and soon Kate reappeared with individually boxed cupcakes for each of the young guests to take home with them. The check was discretely presented and settled, and each girl left with her chair balloon carefully tied to her wrist, calling out thanks and goodbyes. Kate stood in the doorway of the shop, waving them off, and then turned to walk back into the store with a pleased smile on her face.

She stopped at the table to assist Emily, who was gathering up the cups and plates. The two of them shared a quiet conversation about the afternoon as they cleared away the leavings of the party. Wren finished serving a customer and went to the table to gather up the tablecloth, being careful to collect the loose rose petals along the way. By this stage, Michael had returned to his lunch and newspaper, and looked up in surprise as a cupcake appeared beside his coffee. He glanced up to see Kate sliding the plate onto the table, a pleased smile on her face.

"This is becoming a habit." She smiled. "But we had some spares from the birthday party and I thought you'd like one."

"Thanks." Michael couldn't help but smile back; Kate's smile was infectious as she turned and went back to the counter. He watched as she dispensed some extra cupcakes to customers free of charge, noticing how everyone was smiling after Kate had spoken with them. He wished he had her easy way with people.

She looked busy, which was a pity; he'd hoped they'd be able to talk a bit more. He decided that he wanted to stay awhile longer and went up to the counter again, where Wren looked up with a bright smile.

"More coffee?" she asked.

"Please," he replied as he turned his head to see what the cupcake of the day was, grinning as he saw the name, and automatically looked at Kate's T-shirt before reading the sign again.

I can't get no satisfaction: *Bitter dark chocolate and cherry with creamy frosting.*

He looked back at Wren, who winked.

"Private joke," was all she offered. "Want one?"

"Sure, why not? I haven't been getting much lately either."

"What, cupcakes?" Wren deliberately misunderstood.

"No." Michael raised an eyebrow at the sign. "The satisfaction."

"Oh," Wren replied. Her mind was working furiously. *He's got to be single.* "And what do you do when you're satisfied?"

Michael shrugged. "I write."

"Really? Been writing much lately?"

He gave a short laugh. "Hell, no, can't get no satisfaction, remember?"

"Ahh." Wren nodded. "And is your ..." she gave a delicate pause as she poured some milk into his coffee, "*girlfriend* able to help at all?"

"Uh, no," Michael replied. "I'm single." His gaze flickered to Kate again, and he looked back to see Wren watching him with a small smile.

"Single," Wren repeated. "Right."

"For now anyway," Michael replied.

Their eyes met again in perfect understanding.

"Well, I hope you get what you want soon then," Wren replied, handing him his cup with a grin. "If there's anything we here at Take the Cake can do to help, let us know."

"I'll bear that in mind," Michael replied gravely, his eye flickering in a subtle wink to Wren before he turned and made his way back to his table.

Wren watched him go, then regarded Kate. She wouldn't give her a push today, she decided. It would be interesting to see what happened of its own accord, but she'd step in if she had to.

Chapter 6

The Fox and the Key

Kate dunked her chocolate croissant into her café au lait before shoving the sopping chunk of pastry into her mouth with a hum of pleasure. Thomas watched her over his magazine, and then silently passed over a napkin for her to dab her chin.

"Thanks," she mumbled as she cleaned herself up, and then leaned forward slightly for him to inspect. "Better?"

Thomas eyed her briefly, and then nodded before reaching over to dust some croissant crumbs off the top of Kate's T-shirt.

"You know, you really are a tit man at heart, even though you're gay," she commented as he fussed over her shirt.

"Hey," he objected. "I just like checking up on the girls and making sure they're okay."

"And how are they?" Kate peered down at her chest, which was now crumb and wrinkle free.

"Very nice." He heaved a reminiscent sigh. "It's just too bad they're not a set of pecs."

"Can't have it all," Kate replied as she finished her croissant, licking her fingers clean before chugging the rest of her coffee. "That was fantastic; I'm going to get another one," she announced, grabbing her bag and standing up from the small table. "You want?"

"Just a coffee for me, babe," Thomas replied with a smile, his attention momentarily diverted by a handsome man strolling past. Kate smiled at Thomas's blatant regard as she walked away from the table and into the café to order.

It was Sunday morning, and Kate was reveling in the thought of the lazy day stretching out ahead of her. She allowed herself one Sunday each month off work and had phoned Thomas to meet for brunch, followed by an inspection of the Hell's Kitchen Flea Market. Thomas wasn't interested in the market but joined Kate occasionally to see "what else was available" as he liked to call it. They weren't the only ones with that idea. The local cafés all seemed to be doing a brisk trade with people sitting at the tables and chairs set up outside, soaking up the sunshine.

"I don't know how you can manage to eat so much," Thomas commented as Kate sat back down.

"Guess I must just burn it off at work," Kate replied as she stuffed her wallet back into her bag. "Which is probably a good thing. Got anything good to report?" Kate gestured at the newspaper he held in a slack grip.

"Well, there are a few showing promise," Thomas answered as he watched another passerby.

"I meant in the paper," Kate deadpanned.

"In that case, no, unless you want to pick up a little holiday property at Martha's Vineyard." Thomas flicked the lifestyle section back onto the table as he reached for a glossy magazine. "Got it," he sighed and turned the page to look at another model advertising expensive wares. "Got it, had it, had *him*." He smiled and turned the page.

"Hang on, go back. Which one?" Kate leaned over. Thomas held up the magazine to show a picture of a bronzed male model. "Oh yeah, I remember him. Weren't you quite keen on him for a while?"

"I was until he opened his mouth," Thomas said in an absent-minded voice as he kept flicking through the magazine. "Lovely to look at," he continued, "but whenever he spoke, all I could hear was the ocean."

Kate snorted. "I suppose at the start you weren't really after him for his conversation."

"You know it," Thomas agreed on a sigh.

"So who have you been seeing lately?" Kate ventured after a pause.

"Well, I've got one that's showing some promise," Thomas allowed. "But the others have just been for a bit of fun."

Kate smiled to herself as she took another bite.

"And what was *that* little smile for?" Thomas asked.

"Well, I had one of those last week," Kate replied, trying not to blush.

"What? No, you don't mean…?" Thomas leaned forward, his face showing delighted shock. "Miss Shannon, are you telling me you got *laid*?"

"You want to repeat that? I'm not sure they heard you in Florida!" Kate hissed, her cheeks flaming now as people at nearby tables shot her amused glances.

"Sorry." Thomas apologized, but his eyes were alight with curiosity. "Tell me everything."

"His name was Tim. Wren got his number for me when he came into the store," Kate began, stopping when Thomas flapped his hands impatiently.

"No, no, no. I want to know the good bits," Thomas replied. "How was the sex?"

"Such a pity," Kate said, shaking her head at Thomas in wonder. "You would've made a lovely girl."

"Spill," Thomas demanded. "Did he stay the night?"

"He did, but—" she said, holding up a hand to forestall more excited questions, "—but that was it. We won't be seeing each other again."

"What, no good?" Thomas's face fell.

"He was fine, but there was no connection."

"Honey, then he wasn't doing it *right*," Thomas said, slapping the table for emphasis.

"Oh, God." Kate dissolved into giggles. "Not like *that*," she said at last. "I meant there was no … emotional connection."

"Ah." Thomas nodded in understanding. "So you want the loveage."

"What?"

"I read it in an article somewhere," Thomas explained. "Women have sex with the men they've fallen in love with, and men fall in love with the women they have sex with." He leaned back in his chair. "So men and women approach the same situation from completely different viewpoints."

"Uh," Kate said, still confused.

Thomas sighed and went on.

"Your guy last week was probably out for some great sex, and although that satisfied a part of you," he said, leering and making Kate laugh again, "you want the loveage as well."

"And that's … what did you call it? Loveage?" Now Kate was looking even more mystified.

"Yup. You want the hot sex, companionship, love—all those goodies, and you're not the Lone Ranger. We all want it, even me."

"Huh," Kate said after a long moment. "Well, I guess you're right."

"And so is Wren," Thomas went on. "For all that she's a love 'em and leave 'em, she's after someone that will see her for what she is."

"And what's that, exactly?" Kate said, intrigued now.

"She's a genuinely warm little person, who is just gagging for someone to look after," Thomas said. "Why else do you think she clucks around you so much?"

Kate looked confused.

"Are you saying that she's..."

"Oh, hell, no, she's a meat and potatoes girl, just like you, but she still wants someone to look after her so she can look after him. Deep at heart she's a nester."

"Right." Kate considered this, and then looked at Thomas. "So what does that make you?"

"Fabulous," Thomas drawled, making Kate laugh again.

Michael finished his breakfast and pushed his plate away before sipping at his coffee and giving a sigh of satisfaction.

"Good?" his father asked with a smile.

"Yup," Michael sighed. "Thanks for calling. This was a good idea."

He had seen his parents a few days ago, but when they called to invite him to join them out for breakfast, he had accepted with alacrity. Hugs and kisses were exchanged when he arrived at their table and the conversation had flowed easily. Michael had a close and easy relationship with his parents, who were both academics. As he ate, Michael noticed how, even after years of marriage, his parents found all manner of excuses to touch each other. Charles finished eating first and relaxed with an arm around the back of Susan's chair, his hand rubbing her upper arm in lazy circles.

"Oh, honey, you know we love seeing you," his mother said, reaching over to rub his wrist.

Michael felt a pang of guilt. She was right, of course. The more difficult work had become for him, the more he had shut everyone out. His editor, Alistair, had given him a week's breathing space but had started to call him for some carefully worded conversations.

"So, Michael," his father began. Michael braced himself because he knew what was coming. "How's it all going? With work, I mean."

"Well," Michael scratched his stubble, "it has its moments." He thought about the last few weeks, about Kate, and smiled.

"Looks like it," his mother observed. "What's her name?"

"What?" Michael was startled out of his thoughts by his mother's amused question. "What makes you think it's anyone?"

She shook her head. "Michael, I've been married to your father for thirty-five years and I've watched you in and out of relationships, so I know a goofy grin when I see it."

Michael shifted on his seat, all too aware that his father was watching him with a considerable amount of amusement.

"Uh," he temporized.

"Might as well give it up, son. You know she'll get it out of you anyway," his father advised.

Michael shot him an affectionate glare. "Thanks for your support, Dad," he muttered.

"Just calling it how I see it." His father shrugged. "Plus, of course, while she's grilling you, it means I get off the hook for a while."

"Well," Michael began again, "work hasn't been happening much at all lately, but I'm sure you knew that was still the case."

Susan's face creased with concern. "Oh, Michael, writer's block?"

Michael gave a mirthless grin. "It's beyond a block now, Mom. It feels like the Great Wall of China."

"Anything we can do to help?" Susan leaned forward to put her hand on Michael's.

He smiled. No matter how old he got he'd always be their boy.

"No, it's okay," he said, even though it wasn't.

"Well, you know we're here for you, son," Charles chimed in. "At least let your mother feed you once in a while."

Charles's eyes crinkled as he smiled, and for the first time Michael noticed that his father's auburn hair was slowly shifting toward a paler shade, white and gray hairs interspersed with the red. His mother's chestnut hair still fell in thick waves around her shoulders, but it too was beginning to pale at her temples. He thought of Kate again and her conversation about losing her parents, and he looked at Charles and Susan through new eyes.

"Thanks, it'd be nice to see more of you," Michael replied and meant it.

"So, what's going on with your work? How are you dealing with it?" Susan gave Michael a shrewd gaze. "I seem to recall your way of coping with stress was to hide away from the world. Would I be right?"

"Yes," Michael admitted with a groan. His parents knew him all too well.

"And has it worked?" she continued.

"No," Michael admitted again, shifting in his seat as his father grinned.

"And what have we learned from this?"

"You going all teacher on me?" Michael replied, trying to divert the conversation. Susan pursed her lips but her eyes were twinkling at him, so Michael sighed and began to talk. "All right, so it hasn't been working. I've started going out for walks, just taking things in and ..." His voice trailed off.

"And what?" Susan asked in a gentle voice.

"And I don't know." Michael shrugged. "I think I've found something ..." His words trailed off again.

"Or someone?" guessed Charles.

"Maybe." Michael considered the situation. "Or maybe not. I don't know."

"Well, I guess there's only one way to find out," Susan prompted. "And is she nice?"

Michael grinned as he thought of Kate's laughter, and her easy way with people. "Yeah, she's one of a kind."

☙

"Another one? What do you want to look at more of those for?" Thomas asked as Kate tugged him across to another stall offering original artwork and prints. Kate had begged and cajoled Thomas into keeping her company at the flea market, but after watching Kate carefully work her way through a stack of secondhand books, his patience was wearing thin.

"I just like them," Kate replied. "So I'm going to have a look. You don't have to come."

"Well ..." Thomas paused and Kate turned to look at him.

"What?"

Thomas scuffed the ground with his shoe, his hands in his pockets. "See here's the thing, Kate," he began. "I've got a date this afternoon."

"You have?" Kate's eyes widened. "And you're wasting time at a flea market with me when you should be getting ready?"

"Something like that," Thomas agreed, then went on in a hasty tone. "Not that time with you is wasted."

"Oh, I got what you meant." Kate waved away his concern. "You go get ready. You know I can spend a whole day here and you've got a much better offer."

"Thanks, Kate," Thomas said, wrapping his arms around her for a quick hug. Kate closed her eyes and felt the warmth emanating from his body to hers. Thomas stepped back, but kept his hands on her shoulders, looking into her eyes. "You sure you're okay?"

"Sure." Kate scrunched her nose at him. "And make sure you tell me all about it later. I want to hear who the lucky guy is."

"I will." Thomas gave her a quick, soft kiss. "Later, Kate."

"See ya, Tom," she replied, swatting his rump as he turned to stroll off.

"Don't touch what you can't afford," Thomas sassed.

"I don't have that much small change on me anyway," Kate teased back, pleased that their old camaraderie was intact. She watched him walk away and didn't fail to notice the admiring glances that followed his passage. He looked like a Calvin Klein model in his scruffy jeans and fashionably tattered T-shirt. She turned away with a smile and walked over to the art stall that had caught her attention.

The sun was shining, and she had a whole day ahead of her to spend on whatever she wished. She felt blessed. She gave the artist operating the stall a quick smile, and then began to flick through some of the prints, stopping and admiring from time to time but not tempted to buy. She checked her watch and kept strolling, stopping at another artist's stall, deciding to give herself a present. She began to look at the limited edition prints, realizing that the pictures were good. Kate flicked through a few more; they were *very* good.

She picked one up and held it at arm's length. She loved it. It was a small print, a stylized fox sitting amongst some flowers. The fox's red coat was made up of small symbols that reminded her of Louis Vuitton: very stylish. Her mind was made up and she could already picture it hanging in the store.

❧

Michael realized that he was walking with no particular destination in mind. He glanced around him, looking at all the shops and traffic, and decided to go somewhere different for a change. He'd heard his mother talking about the Hell's Kitchen Flea Market. It wasn't his usual thing, but of course, the longer he stayed out, the longer he'd be away from the computer. He hesitated a moment longer, and then crossed the street.

He made his way through the market, feeling out of place as he walked past an array of stalls offering vintage and contemporary women's fashion, pausing to admire some hand bound leather journals before realizing they were point-less. Perhaps that would change in time, but he wasn't about to tempt fate buy purchasing some more blank pages that would no doubt come back to haunt him. Michael sighed as he paused and looked at the crowds of people. Getting off the beaten track was one way of making new discoveries, but it might help if he knew what he was looking for in the first place. That was when he saw her.

He moved toward her through the crowd, watching as Kate laughed and joked with a woman at a stall. They exchanged bills and Kate took careful pos-session of some flat packages. She'd just bought something. Michael stopped and gazed at her for a moment. He was used to seeing her with her hair up and off her face when she was working. It was a curious sensation, seeing her outside of her usual environment. Kate was wearing her hair down, and he admired the way it fell over her bare shoulders. She laughed and joked with her usual ease, and she turned away with a smile and a wave, strolling through the crowd with a careless grace. Her good mood was evident by the half-smile that played on her lips.

Michael stood, watching her navigate the crowds. A toddler clutching a stuffed toy wandered out into her path and she half-tripped and caught the child by his shoulders. The child clutched at her legs as they staggered around in a laughing waltz before Kate got her balance again. She grinned and exchanged a couple of words with the child's parents before continuing on her way. Michael began to follow her progress, trying to think of something to say. He wanted something witty, something that would warm her eyes. He liked her smile and he wanted to see it again.

Kate strolled through the market, feeling pleased with herself. All she had to do was find some picture frames and her new purchases could be displayed in the shop. She stopped to buy a warm pretzel and was chewing with great enjoyment when she turned and bumped straight into someone's chest.

"Mmph!" she half-choked and swallowed as she apologized on impulse. "I'm sorry, I wasn't looking where I was going." She felt warm hands clasp her upper arms as she stumbled a half pace backwards, and looked up to see a man looking just as startled as she was.

Michael had been following at a hesitant pace, longing to be able to say something to her, clenching his hands in frustration. Why was this so hard? He'd stopped to consider the situation. He didn't feel intimidated by her; quite the contrary. He'd felt more comfortable with her than he had with anyone else for years. He'd drawn closer until he could reach out and touch her and still the words stuck in his throat. The situation had resolved itself before he could realize what was happening. He had just taken a step closer just as she abruptly wheeled about and collided with him. He automatically reached out to balance her as their impetus knocked her back a step. Her wide, brown eyes looked up at him as he steadied her. He could feel her hair brushing against his hands where he held her upper arms, and her skin felt warm from the sun. He smiled at her, realizing that he hadn't heard a word she'd said.

"Are you okay, Kate?" he asked, the words bubbling up and out.

"I'm fine." Her forehead creased in puzzlement. "You look familiar. Have we met?"

He dropped his hands from her arms as if scalded. She had no idea who he was. He rubbed the back of his neck with one hand, feeling awkward.

"Uh, yeah. I'm Michael," he replied.

She gave him a polite stare.

"We've talked at your store a few times. You shared your lunch with me," he clarified, trying to fill in the blanks. *Please, please remember me.*

To his vast relief, her expression cleared as her mouth formed an "O" of recognition.

"Michael, right. Please forgive me. I meet so many people during the week. Of course, I remember you now," she apologized as her cheeks turned pink. "This is so embarrassing, but when I see people out of context, I have a hard time placing them."

"It must be nice to know that many people," Michael observed, feeling his momentary tension begin to ease.

"I didn't mean to make you feel awkward," she said, reaching out to grasp his forearm, and he looked at her in surprise. "Jack—my dad—used to rub his neck like that when he was a bit uncomfortable too."

"I was actually coming over to say hello," Michael explained. "In a city this big, it's not often that I bump into someone I know. I just didn't realize you liked to do it literally."

"I like to be thorough." Kate grinned. "Are you out shopping today?"

"Not really. I just had brunch with my folks and thought I'd go exploring afterward."

"It's a lovely day for it," Kate offered. "Have you found anything interesting?"

"You know," Michael said, "I think I have."

They fell in step with each other and began to stroll through the market. Occasionally a gust of wind would blow Kate's hair onto Michael's shoulder, carrying a cloud of her scent. It made him think of cupcakes and sunshine and was a smell he would forever associate with her. They kept talking, and Michael found that she managed to surprise a few laughs out of him along the way. He was even more delighted when he made her laugh in return. It was as if she had tapped into a hidden well of conversation he didn't know he had and the words kept flowing. They reached the edge of the market and stopped to look back at where they'd been.

"So," Kate said, looking up at him, "I guess we've seen everything here today."

She may have, but Michael had found himself watching *her* reaction to everything instead.

"You want to get a coffee or something?" He paused for her reaction, and then decided to tease her. "I know this great place if cupcakes are your thing."

"I don't think I could eat anything else. I seem to have been grazing all morning," she said, rubbing an apparently flat tummy.

He tried to hide his disappointment.

"Still," she went on, "coffee never goes astray. Do you know of any good cafés around here?"

"I'm sure we can find something," Michael replied. "Want to keep exploring?"

"Sure." She smiled, and to his surprise slipped her arm through his in a show of familiarity as they began to follow the path out of the park.

Michael looked at the blue sky, and then glanced at Kate's hair as she chattered away at his side. The sun was revealing auburn tints to her hair that he hadn't noticed before, and her yellow and white sundress flowed around her as they walked. Everything about Kate seemed warm: her hair, laughing eyes and smile, even her smell. He smiled as he realized that for the first time in a long time, he felt content. He didn't care how long she stayed with him today, only that she stayed awhile longer.

❧

Later that afternoon, Kate opened the door to her apartment and walked inside, hanging up her keys on the hook beside the door and putting her sunglasses on the deep, wooden mirror frame, adding her earrings to the modest collection in the Chinese teacup.

She walked with a lazy pace into the living room, tossing her bag onto the couch but holding onto the prints she'd purchased from the market. She unwrapped them, letting the paper fall to the floor as she held them out for inspection, one at a time. They were small, no bigger than a sheet of copy paper, but there was a whimsical charm about them. She propped two of them up on her bookshelves and put one beside her bag to take to work in the morning. It had been a delightful day.

After bumping into Michael, they had ended up spending much of the afternoon together. They had started with a coffee, and then it had seemed only natural to browse through some of the nearby shops. A bookstore had been open and she hadn't been able to stop herself from going inside, apologizing to Michael in advance.

"Books are my addiction," she had warned him. "It could get messy."

He had laughed at that.

"No, really. I get this blank stare while I'm in the zone. Wren swears that one day I'll start drooling."

"Which one's Wren?"

"The little one, the Pocket Rocket," Kate had clarified.

He had snapped his fingers. "Now I know exactly who you're talking about."

As soon as they had stepped into the store, she had lost track of time. They had meandered around the store for a while, acquainting themselves with the layout, and then Kate had started browsing in earnest. She'd started to drift toward a display stand at one point, and only barely registered that Michael had stiffened slightly before pulling her attention elsewhere.

They had been in the store for over an hour before making their way back outside, squinting in the daylight. Kate had looked at her watch. The day had gotten away from her, and it was only right then that she'd realized she'd felt more relaxed and satisfied than she had in a long time.

They'd both made their goodbyes with considerable reluctance.

"Maybe I'll see you at the shop again sometime?"

"You can count on it," he'd replied with a grave smile.

"And as a special treat, I promise to recognize you," she had teased.

She smiled to herself, remembering his warmth, thinking about his smile. His eyes were always so serious, like he was trying to absorb everything around him all at once.

There was still more that she had to do today. She went into the bedroom to change into her yoga gear, and then flicked out her yoga mat onto the living room floor. She lit her aromatherapy oil burner and switched on some relaxing music. Soon she was taking deep, even breaths as she flowed from one pose into the next, feeling centered and strong. Her mood was as peaceful and satisfied as it had been when she'd heard Michael laugh.

Michael was still thinking about Kate's smile when he arrived home. He'd taken a risk going into that particular bookstore with Kate, but it had all gone well. He'd managed to keep a lower profile than he'd thought, a fact which he made a mental note *not* to mention to Alistair. Editors didn't like it when their favorite authors started to drop off the radar. They'd had a coffee together and somehow he had kept talking. Kate had entertained him with anecdotes from the store, and he'd told her about his parents. The words had been so easy, had felt so right.

He felt relaxed and at ease with the day. He walked into the expansive living room, but only switched on a few lamps, wanting to keep the lighting low and warm. He paused in the kitchen and poured himself a glass of wine, kicked off his shoes, and sprawled on the couch. Picking up the remote, he switched on the TV, gazing at it for a while before switching it off and opting for some music instead.

Michael sipped at his wine, then got up and wandered around the room. He felt a little restless now that he was alone. The music wasn't quite satisfying him either. He gazed at his surroundings, and then saw his laptop. He stood staring at it for a while, sipping his wine, deep in thought.

Finally he walked toward it and switched it on, taking a seat as he waited for it to power up. His last document appeared on the screen. He sat thinking about his day, and then setting his glass aside, began to type.

Kate switched off the small lamp by the couch and set her book aside with a small yawn. After her yoga, she had hunted through her things, finally uncovering a small frame that was just right for the fox print. She'd combined the two and nodded at the happy result. She had fixed herself a small meal that she'd enjoyed with a glass of wine before settling down on the couch to immerse herself in a book. As always, the printed words had carried her away for the evening, and she had been a little surprised at the hour when she'd finally emerged from the pages.

She felt pleasantly warm from the wine and almost boneless from relaxation as she wandered out of the bathroom, wearing clean underwear and an old T-shirt of Paul's that she had begged him for. She didn't have many of Jack's shirts left and was trying to make them last as long as she could by interspersing them with items filched from her big brother. Crawling into the bed, she checked her alarm and snuggled into her pillow, thinking of Michael as she drifted off to sleep.

It wasn't until he yawned that Michael thought to check the time and was shocked to see that it was after midnight. He looked at the screen: he'd written a few thousand words. He'd done it; somehow he'd broken through the block. Tired as he was, there was no clear way of knowing if what he'd written was useable, but for the time being, he was surprised and pleased. He looked at the time again and realized he needed to get some sleep if he wanted to stop in and see Kate tomorrow. Or maybe that was too soon? He'd see how he felt about it in the morning.

Michael switched off the lamps and went into the bedroom, shucking off his jeans and throwing them over the back of a chair. He began to tug his shirt off over his head, pausing and sniffing at the shoulder. It was still there, incredibly faint, but he could detect it: Kate's scent. He wouldn't wash it just yet, and he smiled at his sentimentality.

He crawled into bed, tugging the sheets over his body as he settled down for the evening. He'd found words for her and she had unlocked words for him. No one else had been able to do that: not his editor, not his friends, and not his parents. Only Kate had been able to draw them out; somehow she had found the key to him, one that he hadn't realized he had lost. Michael's eyes fluttered closed and his breathing evened out. After a long time, his eyelashes flickered, and for the first time in months, Michael dreamed.

Chapter 7

Late Night Surprise

"Morning, boss."

"Wren, don't call me boss."

"Sorry, boss."

Kate unlocked the door and stood aside, whistling under her breath to the music on her iPod as she let Wren in ahead of her. Wren slung her bag into the kitchen closet and reappeared, flicking on the espresso machine and getting the chalkboard. Kate followed her, shucked off her bag and hung it on the hook beside Wren's.

Wren propped the chalkboard up against the counter and stood watching Kate, tossing a piece of chalk from one hand to the other.

"So," Wren ventured, "how was your day off?"

"Fabulous," Kate replied, smiling to herself and tapping her fingers on the counter as she waited for the coffee machine to start up.

"Oh, really?" Wren wandered closer, folding her arms and leaning over the counter toward Kate. "And what did you do?"

For a split second, Kate considered telling Wren about her encounter with Michael and their subsequent afternoon. She had gone to bed thinking about him and had woken up feeling restless. *Those* kinds of dreams hadn't happened to her for a long time. She decided to keep the day to herself. Telling Wren would mean the inevitable dissection, and then Wren would very lovingly try to manipulate the situation to what she considered was everyone's best advantage.

Kate had found herself daydreaming on the way to work, thinking about the color of Michael's eyes and his impressive height compared to her small frame. She remembered the sensation of colliding with his chest and the feeling of warmth that had rushed into her as he all but loomed over her, making sure she was all right.

Kate was later mortified that she hadn't been able to recognize Michael at first glance. Given her usual work hours, it wasn't often that she had the opportunity to see people out of context. She had apologized as fast as she could, but not before she had seen a flash of disappointment on his face. To her relief the conversation after that had flowed easily. At first she had kept up the usual jovial patter that she used in the store, but after a while, Michael's quiet company had somehow managed to soothe and relax her. Gradually, her conversation had slowed, become a little less witty, a little more genuine.

She had always been tactile, but she had surprised herself when she had slipped her arm through his as they had meandered through the city in search of coffee. Even now she smiled at the sensory memory of the way the muscles in his arms had flexed and relaxed at her contact, and then the warmth of his arm seeping into hers. He had even smelled good. She was used to men's aftershave, plenty of products certainly wafted in and out of the store all day, but she hadn't been able to place which brand Michael used. He had smelled warm and musky, with an undertone that she still wasn't able to place. And to think that earlier in the day she had been enjoying the sensation of time to herself. Michael had somehow managed to change that.

Wren waited and watched as Kate stared off into space with a slight smile, and then cleared her throat. Kate blinked and returned her attention to the present, looking at Wren who raised an eyebrow but said nothing.

"I went to the flea market and found a couple of great art pieces," Kate replied. "They're in my bag, so I'll get them out once we've had our heart-starters."

Wren watched Kate closely. Kate was looking very happy, but seemed to be trying to hide it. Given Kate was generally an open book, this was enough to give Wren pause. "Mm-hmm, and what else did you get up to?"

"Well, I wore a *dress*," Kate went on, rolling her eyes as Wren feigned a shocked response of her own.

"You did?" Wren replied, clapping her hands to her cheeks. "Which one?"

"Remember the yellow and white halter-neck one you made for me?"

"Rowr." Wren nodded with approval. "And I bet you looked great. Did you pick up anyone?"

"Uh," Kate stalled for a moment. "Nope, but I had a great day. The sun was shining, I saw some great things, bought myself some presents." She picked up two cups. "Mocha for you?"

"Yeah," Wren replied. "Grande, thanks." Sometimes she forgot that Kate only gave herself one day off a month, and she obviously cherished her free time. Wren gave a mental shrug, perhaps her radar had been off after all.

"How about you?" Kate said as she wiped down the spigot and passed Wren her mocha. "What did you get up to, or should I say, who?"

"You know me too well," Wren replied, toasting Kate with her cup before taking a sip. She gave it some thought, and then wrinkled her nose at Kate. "He was cute enough, but nothing serious."

"Right, but did you have a good time?" Kate called as she ducked into the kitchen to turn on the industrial oven for pre-warming.

"Yeah, we did," Wren conceded. "He was nice but young and forgettable." Wren sipped her mocha again as she turned the piece of chalk over and over in her fingers, then gave Kate a smug smile. "But I'm pretty sure he'll remember *me* for a while."

"That good?"

"Oh, I was *very* good. I think the next woman he's with will offer some thanks up to my tutoring skills."

Wren put down her cup and wrote on the chalkboard. When she was finished she held it up to show Kate who laughed and gave her a thumbs-up. Wren carried the chalkboard outside and hung it carefully on the hooks, grinning to herself as she went back inside.

Emily arrived a few minutes later and stopped to read the chalkboard before entering the store, laughing and shaking her head. "Good weekend?" she asked as she put her things away.

"Very satisfying," Wren replied with a smile. Sewing and creating always made her feel good, sometimes she had to admit, albeit very quietly, that it was even better than sex.

"Where's Kate?" Emily asked, then paused as she heard the mixer start up. "Never mind." She glanced at Wren. "Has she told you what today's cake is?"

Wren shrugged. "Nope, but when she saw the quote for the day she said she had an idea, then just got straight to work. We'll find out soon enough."

"Guess that's why she's the boss," Emily agreed.

"So how was your weekend?" Wren asked as she began to fill the water jugs.

Emily paused as she picked up a tray of bagels that she would be turning into the daily lunch specials. "It was good." She considered, then looked at Wren and blushed.

"Look at you! What's his name?" Wren dropped a slice of lemon into one of the jugs with a plop and turned to give Emily her full attention.

Emily heaved the tray onto the island behind the main counter and opened the refrigerator built in underneath, so her reply was muffled as she took out some ingredients.

"Sorry?" Wren called. "I didn't quite catch that."

"I don't know what his name is; I just think he's cute. He works at a bookstore," Emily confessed. "And he seems really nice." She gave a small shrug. "I bought something and we just got to talking."

"Nice," mused Wren. "It's a good start. Do you know if he's seeing anyone?"

"I don't think so. He asked if I had a boyfriend so maybe he's available too," she said in tones of quiet hope.

"Well then, what are we going to do about that?" Wren paused and pointed her paring knife at Emily for emphasis as she spoke. "I'll tell you what we're going to do. We're going to find out who he is, and then make sure he falls madly in love with you."

Checking the oven, Kate smiled to herself as she listened in on the girls' conversation. Thank God for Emily. The heat would be off her for a while, and she was all the more thankful that she hadn't told Wren about Michael. The Pocket Rocket would have gone into paroxysms of joy at the prospect of having not one, but *two*, friends' love lives to oversee.

"Wow," Emily commented. "You make it sound so easy."

"What can I say? I've got plenty of experience." She looked up at Emily and gave her an urchin grin. "Mind you, it's generally of the short term variety."

Both the women laughed, and then got back to work.

In the kitchen, Kate paused and considered Wren's glib comeback. She didn't judge Wren for what Tom called the "love 'em and leave 'em" approach, but she hadn't failed to see the flash of vulnerability on Wren's face when she had dismissed her Saturday evening encounter. Wren needed more but wasn't ready to admit it yet.

A while later, Kate delivered the daily cupcake special along with an array of the usual butter cake and vanilla frosted ones that had always been Jack's favorite. They were all frosted in different colors with different sprinkles, making the display cabinet look lush and inviting.

"Ohhh, I'd better have one of *those* with lunch today." Emily sighed. "What are they?"

Kate set the tray down and adjusted a few cupcakes so they could be displayed to their best advantage.

"I've made these in honor of our Pocket Rocket," Kate replied, speaking in a voice loud enough to carry to Wren who had been collecting cups from a table at the front of the store.

"Wait! Wait! I'll get the chalk!" Wren hurried forward, setting down her cups with a clatter and picking up the little chalkboard that sat on an easel on top of the counter. "Okay. Ready. Fire away."

"That's what she said," Kate replied, laughing as Wren gave her a look of amused exasperation. "In honor of our dear Wren..." She inclined her head toward Wren who gave a gracious nod of acknowledgment in return. "I give you *Sugar Mama Cupcakes,* a caramel cupcake topped with white creamy frosting and sprinkled with shattered caramel toffee."

"I think I just gained two pounds," replied Emily in a mournful tone although her expression was still covetous.

Wren finished writing and propped up the chalkboard, then nodded approval to Kate.

"Nice one," she said.

"Thanks," answered Kate. "I'm pretty pleased with them myself."

"Not as pleased as I was on Saturday night when he—" Wren began, whooping with laughter as Kate and Emily both gave an affected squeal of dismay and clapped their hands over their ears.

❧

Michael woke up feeling more refreshed than he had in a long time. His dream still clung to him, following him into the bathroom, back into the kitchen, whispering to him as he plugged in his espresso machine and gave a massive yawn. He headed back toward the bathroom, stripping off and standing under the hot shower spray for a long time, gazing sightlessly at the tiles as his dream played in his mind's eye once more.

He had been in a maze of white walls, stumbling along and feeling his way by touch, squinting against the bright light. He hadn't known where he was, but he knew there was something or someone waiting for him at the center. He ran his hands over the seemingly endless white walls, losing his way and coming up against dead ends countless times. Finally, he saw a speck of color on one of the walls and had run toward it. A word: laughter. He knew what he was looking for now.

Michael had kept searching, darting forward whenever he saw a word scribbled against the white. First there had only been the one word, then two, then five. Then he saw a steady stream, unraveling and coiling around the walls of the maze, guiding him on.

He ran on, trailing his hand along the wall's surface, his fingers brushing over the words that dipped and swirled, guiding him ever onwards. After what had felt like an eternity of searching, he rounded a corner and stopped short. The corridor of the maze had opened into a small room, three white walls, and the fourth... the fourth was the shop front of Kate's store. He stood gaping at it, looking down to see the words had slithered off the walls and were pooling around his feet, swirling with an invisible current, eddying toward the store. He took an uncertain step forward.

The door opened, and Kate stepped out. She was wearing the sundress she had worn at the market. Her hair was still down, and her smile was a beacon of warmth against the white surroundings. The words surged and crested against Kate's feet, making her look down and laugh as they swirled into the store. She had held the door open and extended a hand toward him in invitation.

It didn't take a genius to interpret that dream; it seemed even his subconscious realized that Kate restored his words. He wrapped a towel around his waist and stood brushing his teeth, deep in thought at the bathroom basin. His head jerked when he heard the phone ring, and he spat and rinsed before padding into the room to snatch up the handset.

"Hello," he offered in a soft growl.

"Michael," said a voice in a very careful tone.

"Alistair," he acknowledged. "How are you?"

"I'm ..." Alistair hesitated. "I'm well. Did you have a good weekend?"

"Thank you, I did," Michael replied, and then paused. He wasn't a talkative man by nature at the best of times, but for some reason of late, Alistair brought out the worst in him.

"Dare I ask?"

"Yes, Alistair," Michael said in a quiet voice. "I've been working."

There was a slight pause, and Michael pictured Alistair leaning forward in his chair, eyes bright with curiosity.

"And?"

Michael shrugged even though he knew Alistair couldn't see the gesture. "It might be something," he allowed, "but then again, it might be nothing at all."

"It doesn't matter," Alistair rushed in. "The fact that you're writing again is all that's important."

"I'm not going to meet deadline," Michael cautioned. His contract was for a number of publications within a certain timeframe, and this time he was falling well past the mark.

"That's not for you to worry about," Alistair said in a reassuring tone. "Leave that to me. I won't let anyone bother you."

"Thanks," Michael replied, surprised to discover that he appreciated this source of unexpected support.

"Anytime, Michael. Look, I know that I'm a pain in the ass, but that's what they pay me for," Alistair went on. "I'm here to help. Just try to remember that next time you want to kill me."

"I'll try," Michael replied in a dry tone. "But I'm not promising anything."

Alistair laughed. "I'll take what I can get." He paused. "So," he began delicately, "are you able to tell me anything about it?"

"Uh," Michael stalled. To be honest, he wasn't entirely sure what he'd written. It had been a stream-of-consciousness ramble that had run on for a few thousand words, and he hadn't had the opportunity to re-read it yet. "You know, I'm not entirely sure what it's going to be at this stage. I'm still getting a sense of it myself."

"Okay," replied Alistair, the disappointment evident in his voice. "We can talk about it later."

"Thanks, Alistair. I appreciate it."

"Any time. I'll give you a call in a week or so. How does that sound?"

"Fine," Michael grunted.

"Try to control your enthusiasm. I'm doing my job, remember?"

"Yes, dear," Michael sighed, startling a laugh out of Alistair. "Can I go now?"

"I think I'll let you. Talk to you later."

"Okay."

Michael hung up, staring at the handset for a moment before tossing it onto the bed. He turned to leave the room, and then glanced back. Hitching his towel into a firmer position around his waist, he tugged at the quilt and sheets, making the bed and rearranging the pillows for the first time in longer than he cared to admit. He picked up the phone again and paused before dialing.

"Hey, Watson," he began. "You free for a run sometime?"

Plans were made, and he snapped the phone shut, this time with a distinct sense of satisfaction. Yesterday at the market with Kate had been fun, and it made him want to get out into the world again.

❧

Michael had made his way over to Washington Square Park and was doing some warm-up stretches when he looked up at the sound of his name being called. He waved, and David waved back, jogging toward him.

"Hey, thanks for the call. The way things are going at work it's good to be out of the office."

"No problem. You sure you've got time?"

"Yeah, I'm just waiting for a few people to call back with some quotes, and the deadline for those isn't until tomorrow. All good," David replied. "You ready?"

"As I'll ever be." Michael straightened up. "But it's been a while, so be gentle."

The two of them set off at a steady pace, talking as they jogged.

"You been up to much?" asked David.

"Well…" Michael paused to think of what to say. "I guess you could say I've gotten some work done."

"Cool," David replied.

They kept jogging, and when David remained silent, Michael shot him a quizzical glance.

"That's all you've got to say?"

David shrugged. "I figure you'll tell me more when you're ready. I question people for a living, so I know when people are ready to talk and when they're not."

Michael thought about this for a few more paces. "Thanks. I wish there were more people like you out there."

"Have you told your folks you're writing again?"

"I haven't had a chance to. It only started last night."

They rounded a curve on the path and veered to the side as some cyclists wound their way past. They were nearing the dog park and Michael grinned as he saw the dogs and owners playing. Maybe he'd get a dog one day.

"Well, you'll tell them when you're ready," David suggested.

"Again with the thanks."

They jogged on through dappled shade and open sunny stretches of pathways. Michael's lungs were starting to burn, and he felt sweat pooling on his back and chest. It had been a long time since he'd done this. A sideways glanced showed that David barely looked winded. Michael realized he was going to have to jog more often. How had he managed to lose his fitness so fast?

"So," he gasped after a while, "how's your work?"

"Aw, hell." David grimaced. "I guess it is what it is. All the papers in this town are having a hard time, so I'm thinking about quitting."

Michael shot him a surprised look. He hadn't realized David was so unhappy at work. "What's going on?"

David shrugged. "It all seems to be going to shit. The paper's in trouble with a few lay-offs here and there, so it's not looking good."

"Is your job in trouble?" Michael asked.

"I'll be fine, but it's not as much fun as it used to be. Still, I've got a few options."

"Such as?" Michael asked.

"All in good time." David shot him an amused glance. "I'll tell you when I'm ready."

"Point taken," Michael conceded with a grin, and they jogged on.

"Hey," David ventured after a while, "do you ever think it's funny how we both ended up making a living in publishing?"

"Yeah." Michael smiled. "Sometimes."

"Me as the History major, you studying Economics, what the hell happened?"

"We discovered booze and rock-n-roll, my friend."

"True," conceded David. "And damned if we didn't have a good time."

"Amen to that, brother."

They looked at each other and laughed.

Jogging in silence for a while gave Michael the time to mull over David's comments. Their lives had started out on different career paths and yet they had ended up on a kind of parallel. Having known each other from an early age thanks to their parents, everyone had been delighted when the two boys had been accepted at the same college. What the parents had been a little *less* enchanted by was David's decision to start playing guitar in a local band while Michael had starting writing review articles for local music magazines. Their parents had, after a few "summit meetings" as Charles had called them, been concerned that the boys find a life path that would ensure a steady income, although they had been careful to encourage and support them all the way through college, lest they rebel and drop out.

In the meantime, Michael and David had somehow stumbled across their futures by accident. David had a natural way with people that encouraged conversation, usually much to their surprise as they found themselves revealing far more than they wanted to. Michael, on the other hand, was a natural observer. He was quieter by nature and tended to stand back and take everything in, chiming in on later conversations with a knowledge and complexity of understanding that left people wondering at the depth of his insight.

Although Michael was the natural writer of the two, David was the one that had delved into the media world first. He had completed his degree and had been offered a job with a small newspaper. He had become well connected through the band circuit, and his network of contacts had become legion. David's people skills seemed perfectly suited to journalism, and so his career began.

It had been Michael's mother, Susan, who had inadvertently changed Michael's career direction. She had been helping him unpack his books from college and had found some files that he had filled with random pieces of writing. After asking what they were, Michael had suggested in an off-hand manner that if she needed the files for work she could ditch the contents. Susan hadn't done that, a fact she was thankful for even now. She had taken the files into her study and, later that night, had begun to read. Charles had sleepily come in to see if she was coming to bed at a very late hour, and she had wordlessly handed him one of the files she had finished and kept reading the next.

They read through the night, and a few days later, Susan casually asked Michael if he had any more writing. Michael had nodded and mumbled through a mouthful of cereal that he had an extensive collection on his MacBook. He'd referred to the files as "just some assorted ramblings, nothing much." Susan and Charles had, with Michael's amused permission, shown his work to some people in the publishing industry and things had never been the same after that.

By the time Michael and David had completed the park circuit, Michael thought he was going to die, much to David's amusement.

"Just go on," he wheezed. "Leave me, save yourself."

"Aw, c'mon, it's not that bad." David laughed.

"Just promise me you'll put up a plaque where I fall, saying something touching about my courage and dauntlessness." Michael bent over double, bracing his hands on his knees, trying not to throw up. He hadn't had enough water to drink.

"You're the better writer out of the two of us. I think I'll leave it up to you."

"Damn." Michael straightened up with a groan and squinted at David. "And I'm in no shape to dictate. Guess I'll have to pull through."

The two men walked toward the edge of the park and back out into the streets.

"That's my boy." David clapped him on the back. "I'm proud of you."

"Bite me," Michael replied.

"Speaking of which," David said, a distinct gleam in his eye, "what was the name of that place we met at for lunch a while back?"

"Take the Cake. It's in the Village. Why?"

"It was good. I might go there again sometime," David replied.

"Really," Michael responded, watching David's expression.

"Yeah, really." David said. "I need lunch. How to you feel about a Tube Steak?"

Michael grimaced. "You want street meat after a jog like that?"

"Hey." David cuffed him on the shoulder. "It might have been a workout for you, but I'm well ahead of the game. I need mustard and onion too, and I can smell a vendor here somewhere. C'mon."

After waving David off, Michael walked home slowly, already feeling his muscles protesting after his exertions. David had returned to work somehow still managing to look fresh, which firmed Michael's resolve to go jogging more often. As he strode through the crowds, deep in thought, he completely missed the admiring glances from the women in the street … and from a few men. He moved with an unconscious grace and assurance that, centuries before, could have commanded armies, but all he knew was that he felt rank and desperately wanted another shower.

"A hot dog." Kate stared at Wren, who had given a guilty start from her corner in the kitchen. "I slave over a hot oven to create culinary delights, Emily wears her fingers to the *bone* creating gourmet bagels and you come in here with a *hot dog?*"

"Don't be mad," Wren pleaded. "I just felt like one!"

"Oh, Wren." Kate shook her head. "I just don't know what I'm going to do with you." She gave the hot dog an arch look. "You know that's not even real meat, right?"

"Don't spoil the illusion!" Wren yelped, taking another bite and trying to talk with her mouth full. "I know it's plastic, I know it could withstand a nuclear war, but I *wanted* one."

"Fine," Kate sighed. "I'll make sure we've got Tampax in the ladies' room next week."

"Huh?" Wren looked mystified, and Kate smiled at her.

"You always crave stuff like that when you're due, same as I usually want sweet or savory."

"It's cheese for me," commented Emily as she carried a tray of cups inside and stacked them into the dishwasher. "And you know it's only a matter of time before we're in sync."

"Men have it so easy." Wren contemplated her hot dog for a moment, and then resolutely bit into it again. "They never have to put up with this shit."

"Babycake!"

Kate looked up with a delighted smile of recognition. Paul was coming into the store, and he stopped short and stood aside to let a female customer leave who brushed against him, offering a smile of thanks for his chivalry as she passed. Paul stood stock still and watched her leave, his eyes following her progress with an appreciative gleam. When he turned back to Kate, he looked pole-axed. He wandered toward the counter and stopped in front of it, looking at Kate.

"Wow," he said. "That's all I've got to say, wow."

"I take it you saw something you like?"

"Something like that," Paul replied. Kate had a cupcake on a plate and was making some more coffee.

Wren appeared, wiping crumbs off her hands with a dishcloth, and beamed at Paul.

"Hey, Paul," she called as she glanced at Kate. "You gonna take a break, boss?"

"You know, I think I will."

"Ah, the privilege of power," Wren replied with a wink. She loved working with Kate and was delighted to see just how relaxed Kate was today. Maybe she had needed the Sunday off even more than she thought. She made a mental note to have a talk to Emily to see if they could somehow reduce Kate's workload a little.

Kate selected a "Jack" cupcake and followed Paul to a table, where he was already opening the file he'd been carrying and was making some room for their cups and plates.

"So, what's the verdict?" Kate asked as she sat down.

Paul licked some frosting from the corner of his mouth, and then glanced at Kate.

"Kat, do you have an idea as to how the business is going?"

"A little." She shrugged. "Seems to be going okay. Why?" She looked worried. "What's wrong? Am I wrong? Am I struggling more than I thought?"

Paul gave her a look that was rich with affection. "Calm down. You're doing better than okay. Seems you've found yourself a good little niche here in the Village after all. How was your weekend?"

"Uh…" Kate was flummoxed at the change in topic. "It was good. Great, even. I didn't realize how tired I was until I had the chance to relax."

Paul regarded his sister. He loved her with all his heart, which was considerable, and always would. After Jack's and Gwen's passing, the two of them had grown even closer. Partners had come and gone and had always been welcomed into the fold, but their bond had grown stronger over the years. Kate was, he had to admit, a striking woman—sister notwithstanding—having a quiet kind of beauty that drew people to her. He took enormous pride in her success but had watched with concern as faint purple smudges of fatigue had appeared beneath her eyes as the years went by. He had cautioned and advised, and now he was in a position to remedy the situation.

"Would you like to have more?"

"Oh, God," Kate groaned. "Now you're just talking dirty."

"I'm serious, Kat. You can all give yourselves a two-day weekend, just like the rest of us. How 'bout it?"

Kate gaped at him. "Are you sure?"

"Definitely. Your turnover has been steadily increasing and you're sitting in a good place. You've got some good cash reserves now, good staff. I think you need to start to pace things before you burn yourself out and it goes south."

Kate sipped her coffee, her mind racing. She set her cup down and looked at Paul. "You're really serious."

"Yup."

"How long have you been thinking about this?"

"About twelve months," he admitted, then held up a hand as she opened her mouth to protest. "I wanted to make sure it was a long term trend, not just a spike in your sales."

Kate shook her head. "How is it that you ended up with a degree in Business and yet you work as an Urban Ranger at Central Park?"

Paul shrugged. "Guess I found something to do that I enjoy more. How did that Literature degree of yours work out?"

"Point taken," she replied.

"That's what she said," Paul shot back, making her laugh. "I guess we found our passions led us elsewhere, but look at it this way, I'm in a position to help my favorite sister, my youngest sister, my oldest sister ..." He paused and raised an eyebrow.

"Your only sister," Kate completed the old joke and waved for Paul to continue.

He nodded and went on. "... with her business decisions, and make sure that she's okay, *and* I get to stop in and see the hotties that her business attracts. And although you've got a Literature degree you don't think you use, I've got an extensive collection of notes and letters from you at home and I know your friends often keep them too, so I think we're doing okay." He toasted her with his cup and took a swig.

"You've kept all my notes?"

"Yep."

"Even the one that I wrote on the back of a dry cleaning docket?"

"Even that one. It's one of my favorites because it tells me that you were having a busy day but you still had a moment to think about your brother, grab any piece of paper that came to hand and write something to him."

Kate thought about Paul's business suggestion and her forehead wrinkled with concern. "You're really sure about this?" she asked as she waved a hand at the printouts Paul had spread across the table to illustrate his point.

"Totally."

Without breaking her gaze, Kate lifted her chin slightly. "Hey, Wren, you got a sec?"

"Hang on," came the reply. Wren finished serving, Emily took over and Wren appeared at the table.

"Sit down," Kate invited her.

"What's all this about?"

"Well, Paul here has just made a suggestion and I thought I'd see what you think."

"Oh?"

"How would you feel if I were to close the store Sundays and Mondays, and we all have a two day weekend?"

Wren stared at her. "I think I could tongue kiss you right now."

"I think that means she thinks it's good," observed Paul. "Although if you girls want to try the practical demonstration, I've got no objections, Wren, so long as your intentions toward my sister are honorable."

☙

That night Kate let herself into the apartment and slipped into her usual routine. Jewelry was dispensed into teacups, keys were hung up, and her bag was slung over a chair. She wandered about the apartment, her face blank with thought. Dinner was cooked and eaten, followed by a glass of red wine. The television was switched on and stared at for a long time. After a few hours, Kate sat up with a huff of exasperation. It was no use trying to relax, because her head wouldn't stop buzzing with activity. Paul's revelation this afternoon had floored her, although she had to admit that she was thrilled.

Maybe she'd go see a movie. It was better than lying on the sofa like a corpse.

A quick change later, she was skipping down the steps. She walked a couple of blocks before finding a cab. She had no idea what was showing, but she knew the Quad Cinema between Fifth and Sixth Avenue had late shows. It'd probably be an independent or foreign film, but that suited her just fine.

☙

Michael woke with a start, cursing when he saw the time. After getting home, he'd had a long, hot shower and re-read his writing effort from the night before. After a quick lunch, he'd sprawled on the sofa, staring drowsily at the television, not even realizing he was falling asleep. Now it was late at night. He sat up with a sigh and scrubbed at his hair with his hands.

Rather than loll about in the apartment, he decided to catch a movie at the Quad, knowing that they always had something worth seeing. He left the apartment and was just settling himself into a seat at the cinema when he saw movement in the aisle, his eyes widening as he saw who it was.

"Kate?" he whispered.

Her head snapped up in surprise. "Michael?" she whispered back. "What are you doing here?"

"Same as you, I'd imagine," he replied, inclining his head toward the still darkened screen.

"Oh, right." She gave a sheepish laugh. "Sorry. I wasn't expecting to see anyone I knew here at this hour." She paused and looked at him. "So are you stalking me or something?"

"Well, given I got here first, I'd have to say it's a case of you stalking me."

"True," she conceded, then glanced around at the array of empty seats. "Uh, so it seems a bit silly to know you're here and sit somewhere else. Do you mind if I ...?" She indicated the seat beside him.

"I'd be delighted," he replied with a smile.

Kate had barely sat down when the lights began to dim.

"So," murmured Michael after a pause, "what's your stash?"

She looked at him, her eyes luminous in the dark. "Huh?"

He held up his bucket of popcorn by way of explanation.

"Oh, right. Let's see, I've got Junior Mints, Goobers, and I'm pretty sure I've got some Reese's Cups in here somewhere too." She dug around in her bag and produced a packet with a triumphant smile. "And a small vat of Coke."

"I'm impressed; you take your snacking seriously." He paused. "Do you allow incursions?"

"Absolutely, but I'll be expecting popcorn in return."

"Deal."

Arrangements made, they smiled and settled back to watch the movie. Unfortunately for Michael, although it seemed that Kate was thoroughly enjoying herself, he wasn't able to keep track of the movie at all. Her scent swirled around him, as did the memory of his dream. He could feel the heat of her body soaking into his, and he reveled in it.

Chapter 8
Limited French and Possibilities

The closing credits began to roll, and the other movie patrons started to gather themselves and file out of the theater. Michael and Kate remained relaxed in their seats, talking in quiet voices and laughing occasionally as they discussed the movie.

"That was…" Michael said as he tried to find the right word and gave up with a laugh. "I don't know what the hell that was."

"I didn't know this one was screening until I got here, but some of his other movies are quite a trip. Did you like it?"

"You know, I think I did," Michael replied slowly. "I had no idea what to expect."

When he had decided to catch a late night movie, Michael had no other expectations beyond keeping himself occupied for a couple of hours. He had arrived at the cinema and purchased a ticket for whatever was screening at the next show, grabbed a snack, and wandered inside to take a seat. At first when he had seen Kate walking up the aisle in the dim lighting, he thought he was seeing things, but when he had realized that serendipity had again brought her to him, he had felt a rush of pleasure.

Michael had followed the movie with a diminished level of attention as his mind kept wandering to the woman who sat beside him. He wondered if she realized she leaned into his shoulder during the more dramatic scenes, or shifted in her seat when the characters' tortuously slow entanglement began to gain speed. He had enjoyed the movie, but enjoyed Kate's reactions to it all the more. She allowed herself to be truly immersed in the storyline. The way her breathing quickened, the slight involuntary movements she made told him that, for her, a movie was a complete sensory experience.

"Who's the director?" Michael turned a little in his seat so that he could see Kate's face more clearly.

"Uh, Jean-Pierre something. I'll have to check the poster on the way out," Kate admitted. "His movies are like a kind of fairytale for grownups. You really ought to see some of his other films. I'd be curious to see what you think."

"What are they?" Michael asked. Even if he'd known, he would have asked. He just wanted to keep her talking, to keep her with him.

"*The City of Lost Children* and *Amélie* are two of my favorites," Kate replied, then had to stifle a yawn behind her hand. "Sorry."

"Don't be." Michael looked at his watch. "It's nearly midnight." He got to his feet and extended a hand to help her up, which she accepted with a smile. It seemed only natural that he kept her hand in his as they walked down the aisle toward the exit, past the tired usher who was holding a garbage bag as he collected discarded drink cups and popcorn buckets. They emerged into the evening and stopped on the sidewalk, smiling at each other. Michael released her hand with considerable reluctance.

"Have you got a busy week planned?" Michael asked, still wanting to prolong their time.

"As always," Kate answered with a smile. "It never stops, but I guess I've only got myself to blame for that one."

"You don't look too sorry about it," he observed.

"It's starting to pay off. My brother has been going over the books for me, and I'll be able to give myself more of a weekend soon." She yawned again, apologizing with a laugh.

"You're going to need a break," Michael said, "but for now we'd better get you home. Which way are you headed?"

"I'm in West Village."

Michael's eyebrows went up at that. "Really? I'm in West SoHo." He'd wondered where she lived, and now he'd discovered they were closer than he thought, which perhaps explained why they had ended up at the same cinema. "You want to share a cab?"

Kate looked up and down the street, which was quiet. "Sure," she agreed. "Why not?"

Michael crooked his arm, which she accepted with a smile, and they began to walk. They'd barely gone a block before Michael flagged down a cab and helped Kate inside. The cab took off with a lurch, sending Kate, who had been settling into her seat, crashing into Michael.

"Oops, sorry." She laughed.

Michael looked at her and smiled, feeling brave. "I'm not."

They gazed at each other and Kate smiled. "Neither am I," she admitted, glad that the dim interior of the cab hid her blush.

"I know this wasn't a date, but would you mind if I …" He raised an eyebrow at her in silent query as he dipped his head toward hers.

"Not at all," Kate whispered, lifting her face toward his.

Their lips met in a soft kiss, parted, and went back for more.

"Well, for an evening that wasn't a date, I had a great time," Kate said with a smile.

"So did I," Michael replied. "Maybe we should arrange to bump into each other again soon." It wasn't a question.

"That sounds like a great idea," she agreed, then looked up in surprise as the cab slowed to a halt, and she realized that they had arrived at her address. "But for now, I guess this is goodnight."

"Allow me." Michael had gotten out of the cab and opened her door. He instructed the cabbie to wait and escorted her to the front door of the building. Michael quirked an eyebrow at her and offered a grin. "One for the road?"

Their mutual eagerness had them bumping noses and exchanging a husky laugh again before their laughter subsided into the sweetness of each other's mouths.

"Well, Kate, I guess I'll be seeing you soon," Michael said, still holding her hand and tracing gentle circles on it with his thumb. "Maybe we can arrange a date sometime."

"I'd like that," she said softly as dimples appeared on her cheeks, making him smile.

"Good night," he said and turned to walk back to the cab.

"Sweet dreams," she called, and for a moment he hesitated, his gaze flashing back to her, before he shot her a broad smile and climbed back into the cab.

❧

"It's about time," Wren commented with a raised eyebrow the next morning.

"What?" Kate was surprised at Wren's remark as she appeared with the tray of cupcakes.

"You've been daydreaming all morning, and for the first time ever you're—" Wren looked at her watch, "—ten minutes behind schedule."

Kate laughed, setting down the tray and leaning forward into the cabinet to arrange the cakes, hoping that the action would hide her flushing cheeks. She hadn't gotten much sleep and had felt out of breath all morning. It seemed that her mind wanted to replay the kiss with Michael at every opportunity.

"Not for long," Kate replied. "Get the chalk."

"What do you think this is?" Wren held up a stub. Kate hadn't even noticed her pick it up. She really had to work to get her focus back today. She'd never been this distracted after a kiss before. She thought for a moment, and then dictated, knowing full well that Wren was going to be curious, but she was too happy to care.

Wren raised an eyebrow and wrote down the words with a smile, and then propped up the chalkboard, watching as Kate headed back into the kitchen. Something was definitely going on. She knew that if she asked too many questions Kate would clam up, but she was content to wait and see.

Michael liked what he saw, as he leaned back in his chair, cracking his knuckles and shaking out his hands as he gazed at the screen. He'd woken up with words tumbling out of his head, his fingers itching to type them out and up onto the page. With barely a conscious thought, he'd stumbled out of bed and over to his desk, sat down, and began to type. He had no idea what he was writing about, which for him was a departure from his normal style. His previous novels had been mapped out in meticulous detail, character biographies and intertwining relationships carefully noted and explored. This time there was none of that; he simply sat and typed. By the time the stream of words had slowed to a trickle, he was aware of a mild ache between his shoulders.

Michael looked at his watch and snorted with surprise at the hour. He had been working for longer than he thought. He sat for a moment, considering his options, and then with a sigh got up and changed into his jogging gear. He'd taken to going for early morning runs, although glancing back at his laptop, he couldn't find it in his heart to begrudge the altered morning schedule today. He stopped long enough to fill up his water bottle and grab his keys, and then he was gone.

Jogging around Washington Square Park, Michael stopped for a few breathers and drink breaks. After his initial jog with David, he had woken up stiff and sore, which had been a bitter lesson to learn. Without David to spur him on this time, he set himself an easier pace and noticed that he didn't seem to be struggling as much as he thought he would. His decision to quit smoking had definitely done him some favors. By the time Michael had finished the circuit, he was well and truly ready for a shower, and he jogged home slowly. Once home, he stood in the kitchen, flicking through the mail he had collected in the foyer downstairs. There was nothing of note, and he headed toward the bathroom for a shower. He wanted lunch, and he wanted to see Kate. There was no reason why he couldn't do both.

The city noises hummed around Michael as he made his way toward the Village. He'd taken his time with a shower and a careful shave, picking out clean jeans and a button down shirt. The jog had left him feeling hungry and energized, and he found himself paying more attention to his surroundings as he walked, enjoying his newfound sense of purpose. David had called, wanting to meet for lunch, and unsurprisingly they had both agreed the bakery would be the perfect spot. He felt his phone vibrate in his pocket and answered without checking the number.

"Forrester," he said, weaving through a group of students that were mingling outside a music store. "Alistair, hey."

"Hey, yourself," Alistair replied, taken aback at Michael's voice. "How's things?"

"Good," Michael said. "I'm just taking a break for some lunch, and then I'll be back working this afternoon."

"You're still writing?" Alistair worked to keep the surprise out of his voice but wasn't entirely successful. After months of dealing with a dour-sounding Michael, this new incarnation had caught him off-guard.

"Don't worry," Michael replied in a dry tone. "I'm as surprised as you are."

"It sounds like it's going well."

"Whatever it is," agreed Michael. "I still don't know what to tell you about it, but give me a few days and I'll send an outline."

Alistair found himself in a quandary. He was eager to get his hands on whatever it was Michael might be working on, but didn't want to push for fear of dampening this sudden onset of creativity.

Michael snorted. "It's probably better I send you something soon before I change my mind."

"Well, whenever you're ready," Alistair agreed quickly to seal the offer. "Get it to me when you can." He paused. "And Michael?"

Michael hunched his shoulders a little as he walked, trying to listen to Alistair's voice over the sounds of traffic. "What?"

"You sound good. Better than you have in a long time." Alistair chose his words with care. "Whatever you've come across that's helping you out, hang onto it."

"Oh, I plan to," Michael replied. He looked up at the intersection and saw that he was only a block away now. "Gotta go. We'll talk again soon."

"All right then," said Alistair. He hung up and shook his head in wonder.

He'd been worrying about Michael over the last few months, watching as the deadline had come and gone with nothing to show for it. Now it seemed that there had been a change in fortune, and he couldn't help but wonder what the cause of it was.

Worrying is like a rocking chair:
it gives you something to do
but doesn't get you anywhere.

Michael smiled at the chalkboard, and then stepped inside. Worrying seemed to be something he'd been doing less of lately. His gaze went straight to the counter inside, and he saw Kate serving some customers, and then turned to where he heard his name being called. David gave him a casual wave from the table he'd commandeered and was folding up his newspaper as Michael approached.

"I see you've brought your work with you," Michael said, nodding at the paper.

"You'd think so." David snorted. "But I'm not so sure anymore."

Michael started to pull out a chair from the table to take a seat, and then glanced over at the counter again. Kate was nearly finished with her customers; maybe he'd go say hello first. He glanced at David. "You want a coffee?"

"It's why I'm here," David answered, then got up and tossed the newspaper onto the table. "Let's eat."

Wren was emerging from the kitchen as Emily appeared in the doorway with a conspiratorial grin.

"He's back," she said.

Wren gave her a blank stare. "Who is?"

"Galahad, and he's brought his friend again," Emily said, jerking her head back toward the store.

Peering over her shoulder, Wren saw Michael flanked by a man with fair hair. "Oh great," she muttered to herself. "It's Mr. Wonderful."

"You know him?" Emily looked at her in surprise.

"I don't need to," Wren said in a dismissive tone. "I know his type." She paused and gave David a more considered once-over. He was looking good: not too preppy, not too casual. He clearly had a sense of his own style and knew how to work it to his best advantage. She gave her shirt a quick tug to smooth out any creases and raked her fingers through her hair to freshen up the style. Today she was wearing her favorite navy blue Capri pants and a fitted, orange T-shirt that bore the slogan "100% organic." She was looking good today, too, and that made her feel even better. Two could play at that game. Strolling out into the storefront, Wren gave Michael a broad smile of welcome.

"Hey, stranger," she greeted him. "Great to see you again."

David raised an eyebrow at this and glanced at Michael. How often had he been coming here? He watched Michael glance across at another woman who was serving some other customers, saw her give him a blushing smile and got his answer. He glanced down to conceal his smile. He didn't know what was going on between the two, but his friend looked happy, and for David, that was enough.

The two men ordered and argued good-naturedly over who was paying. David was about to return to the table when he noticed Michael lingering at the counter. He glanced over to see Michael scrutinizing the cupcake special, and then looking at the woman he had exchanged a smile with earlier. He'd have questions for his friend when they got back to their table.

David leaned forward to read the chalkboard propped up on the counter. *Sweet Possibilities, Black Forest Cherry Delight.* He looked at the cupcake name, and then at the quietly chatting couple. Interesting. He glanced over at the espresso machine to see that their coffees were ready, and he reached out to take the cups as they were slid across the counter toward him. With a careless smile of thanks, he took them back to the table.

Wren felt indignant. She'd offered Mr. Wonderful a smile, gazing up at him through her eyelashes in a manner that she knew worked well, and yet … nothing. His gaze had flickered across her and he had offered her a smile, a polite smile at best, and then he was gone. What the hell was wrong with her? Better yet, what the hell was wrong with him? Snatching up the dishcloth, she wiped the frothed milk off the steam spigot with quick, angry movements.

As David ordered lunch and headed back to the table where he'd left his newspaper, Michael lingered by the counter with Kate. She'd finished with her customers, waved them off, and then turned to him with a brilliant smile.

"*Bonjour*, Kate," he greeted her, smiling as the words came easily. "*Comment allez-vous?*"

"*Très bien, merci*," she replied, and then winked. "But that's all the French I've got."

"Same," Michael confessed. "Lucky for us there were subtitles last night."

Kate laughed and leaned toward him. "Remind me to teach you my foreign language game sometime," she suggested, enjoying the way Michael's face lit with curiosity. "I think you'll like it."

"You're on," Michael answered. Standing in front of her, he knew he was already looking forward to seeing her again.

"Have you ordered?"

"Uh." Michael was distracted by her smile, and looked over at Wren who nodded, holding up two laden plates in silent answer. "Yes, we have."

"Oh." Kate seemed a little disappointed at the prospect of their conversation running short. "Well, I'll send over dessert for you later."

"Only if you join me," Michael countered, surprised at his easy daring with this woman.

"Then you've got a deal," Kate replied.

"But we still don't have a date," Michael said, wondering where his words were coming from. In the past it had been nothing for him to labor for days over a page of dialogue, and yet here he was, tripping over himself to keep talking to a woman whose smile kept him warm.

"No, we don't," Kate agreed, "but how about you ask me later? I'll make it easy for you and let you know in advance that my answer is going to be yes." She reached up and tucked a strand of hair behind her ears and stood regarding him with one hand on her hip, her face lit with a smile of easy challenge.

"That's good to know," Michael replied, turning from the counter with considerable reluctance as he heard David call his name. "Very good in fact."

"I'm glad you think so," Kate replied, glancing over at Wren who stood watching them both at the coffee machine, and she gave an inward sigh. No doubt this conversation was going to be dissected beneath Wren's loving scrutiny later.

Michael took the plates from Wren with a smile of thanks and strolled toward the table, already feeling satisfied and replete. Setting the plates down on the table, Michael sat and then looked up to see David looking amused. "What?"

"Nothing." David sipped his coffee.

"Doesn't look like nothing," Michael commented as he bit into his bagel and chewed slowly.

"Let's just say I'm beginning to see the appeal of this place," David replied, flickering a glance back at the counter to where Wren was serving someone, and then indulging himself in a more leisurely study of her once he had assured himself that she was unaware of his scrutiny.

Michael followed David's gaze, and then regarded his friend.

"You too?"

"Maybe," David conceded. "But it's early days yet."

"Okay," Michael said, taking another bite. "So what's going on at work, anything you can tell me about?"

David sighed and ran a frustrated hand through his hair, making his blond hair stand up in uneven spikes. He looked, Michael realized, tired and uncertain, which was unusual for him.

"How much time you got, Forrester?"

"All the time you need."

Kate smiled as her latest customers left and put the bills in the till, bumping the drawer shut with her hip. She stood and surveyed the store with satisfaction. Business had been at a steady pace for the morning. All of the tables were occupied and people were laughing and talking over their meals. Others had finished and were now giving the cupcake cabinet speculative looks that she knew would lead to buying. Everyone looked happy and content, and Kate gave a sigh of satisfaction, knowing that in some small way she had contributed toward it.

She glanced over to where Michael was sitting and watched him as he talked to his friend. He was leaning forward on his elbows, his shoulders hunched as he listened to his friend speak. He had a languid feline grace and he listened with an intensity that suggested a long friendship.

His friend was still talking, occasionally waving his hand as he made a point, and Michael barely said a word. He nodded in encouragement now and then, and it seemed he only spoke when he wanted to clarify something. For the most part he sat and listened, soaking up all the words that were offered to him.

"Sounds like a good offer," Michael commented at last, when David's conversation petered out.

"Yeah," David sighed.

"And you know your parents would be thrilled," he added.

David gave him a tired smile.

"Well, I can't say that I've set my life course by what they wanted, but I'll admit that factor would be a bonus," he confessed, then slid his elbows forward on the table and propped his head in his hands. "Fuck," he cursed in a quiet voice. "I'm tired, Michael."

"Hey." Michael leaned forward and rested his hand on David's shoulder. "Can you take some time off?"

"Probably." David's voice was muffled.

"Then do it," Michael suggested. "Come crash at my place if you want. Just get away from the office and have a think about what you want. Life's too short for this shit. You've got to do what makes you happy."

"Oh, really? That's your theory?" David looked up at Michael with a cynical expression. "Because I don't think you've been following that advice for the last few months."

Michael shifted in his seat. David's words had stung, but it had never been said that the truth would be easy. "True," he agreed, "but I think we both know my head was too far up my own ass to see straight."

David looked at him with a straight face for a moment before his mouth quirked into a grin.

"And anyway," Michael continued, "things are different now."

"And how," David replied. "I wouldn't say you're a happy camper yet, but you're at least interacting with the world again. What happened?"

Michael looked over to where Kate stood chatting to the other two women behind the counter. "I guess I got lucky," he said.

❧

"Wren, it's your lucky day."

"Mmm-hmm?" Wren pulled herself away from her *Vogue* magazine to give Kate an owlish blink. Things had gotten quiet enough for Wren to make herself a quick coffee and flick through her glossy magazine indulgence.

"I should have known better than to disturb you when you're at your devotions," Kate said, "but I wanted you to know that I've been thinking about what you suggested last week."

"You'll have to remind me; we've had a few talks since then," Wren replied, marking her place and flicking the magazine closed.

"The one about us getting a bit more style," Kate began.

Wren became more interested. "Keep talking," she said.

"I don't know what I want, but I'm thinking that you probably have it all mapped out," Kate went on.

"Uh-huh," Wren said.

"So, I can either pitch a few ideas at you, then you can do what you want and let me think it was my idea," Kate continued, "or I can just let you do what you want and love what you come up with."

The two women regarded each other.

"So what's your preference?" Wren asked after a pause.

"Well, either way I think the outcome will be the same, so how about you just do your thing."

A slow smile began to appear on Wren's face. "Do you know how long I've been waiting for this moment?"

"Probably about as long as you've worked here," Kate supplied.

"You'd be right," Wren agreed. "So how far can I go?"

"I'm thinking whatever you come up with has to be machine washable, or able to withstand the occasional splatter in the kitchen," Kate supplied, "but other than that it's all up to you."

"Accessories?" Wren cocked her head.

"Within reason," Kate allowed, "you know I can't do frou-frou." She gestured to herself as an example.

Wren took in Kate's usual work attire: jeans, Chucks, and a T-shirt. "You mean can't or won't?" she asked. Kate had pulled her hair up into a ponytail, and today she had moonstones swinging from her ears. Wren had to admit that Kate had style, and she was blessed with a lovely figure, but surely there had to be a way of showing it off a little more.

Kate sighed and gave Wren a long stare. Wren held up her hands in surrender.

"Okay," she conceded, "minimal accessories. But when you say free rein, do I have your word on that?" Wren looked at Emily who had been stacking some clean glasses on a nearby shelf. "Hey, Emily, you're a witness to this, right?"

"Sure," Emily said. "But what am I agreeing to?"

"I'm giving Wren artistic free license to give us a new look here in the store," Kate answered.

Emily's face dropped. "But what's wrong with the place? I think it looks fantastic." She waved a hand to encompass the store.

"Oh, no," Kate broke in. "The look of the store is my domain. I'm talking about us." She pointed from herself to Wren then to Emily, and gave Emily a shy smile. "You really think the place looks that good?"

"Absolutely." Emily nodded. "It's unique. I love how you've just jumbled everything in together. Have you noticed how some of our regulars don't even bother bringing a book with them anymore? They either help themselves to a book off the shelf, or they just sit and look at all the stuff you've got hanging up."

"Good." Kate was pleased. "That's just what I've been hoping they'd do."

"It's working," confirmed Wren. "Mind you, some of our regulars come in to look at other points of interest." She gave Kate an arch look. "Not that I'm naming names or anything, *Kate*."

Kate shook her head in mock exasperation, and flicked a quick look at Michael's table. He was looking over at the counter toward her, and she gave a brief smile before glancing at Wren to see her wearing a smug I-told-you-so expression. Without saying a word, Wren picked up her magazine and flicked it open, giving Kate a wide-eyed innocent look and began to leaf through the pages as she strolled toward the kitchen.

"You know," Emily ventured, "for a smart woman, she can be a bit dense sometimes."

"Wren?" Kate looked at Emily in puzzlement. "Really?"

"For sure. She can't see what's right in front of her." Emily shrugged. "It's a case of who watches the watcher."

"But who—" Kate began, stopping when Emily raised an eyebrow and tilted her head in David's direction. She watched as David kept talking to Michael, his eyes tracking Wren as she walked the length of the counter and disappeared into the back. "I see," she said after a thoughtful pause. "Well, this is going to be interesting. I don't think she even likes him."

"I know, but sometimes what we think we want and what we actually need are two different things," Emily speculated.

❦

"So what is it you want to do?" Michael ventured.

"I wish I knew," David admitted. "But I've got a bit of time up my sleeve to work things out. Speaking of which…" He looked at his watch. "I've got to head back to work." He got up from the table and walked around to stand beside Michael's chair. "Thanks for letting me vent."

"Any time," Michael replied, and he meant it. "You take care. Call if you want some company, okay?"

"Will do," David answered. With a final smile, he left the store.

Michael watched as David walked out, and then finished his coffee. It seemed that just as his luck was changing so was David's, although time would tell just how successful each of them would be this time around. He looked up as he felt a gentle hand on his shoulder and saw Kate smiling at him.

"Are you staying awhile longer?"

"Sure," Michael replied and was rewarded with a smile.

"Oh, good, I'll get some lunch then. It'd be nice to have some company." She made to return to the counter, and then turned back. "Another coffee?"

"If you're having one."

"Coming up."

Kate walked back to the counter, sticking her tongue out at Wren who was beaming at her. "Not a word," she warned her as she grabbed herself a bagel out of the display cabinet.

"I didn't say anything," Wren protested.

"You didn't have to; your thoughts were screaming at me," Kate answered with a smile. "But in the meantime you can make a couple of coffees for us." Picking up another plate, Kate added two cupcakes.

"Sure, boss."

"Don't call me boss," Kate shot back automatically as she carried her two plates past a grinning Emily. "And that goes for you too, Emily."

"Okay, boss."

Kate stopped short at that and turned to face a giggling Emily. "Did I just hear that?" She looked back at Wren, who was making a show of being very busy with her coffee prep. "Have you gone viral now?"

"Looks like it, boss," Wren said in a cheerfully unrepentant tone.

"No respect," Kate muttered in an amused tone as she carried on toward the table where Michael sat waiting. She set the plates down and settled herself on a chair, glancing at Michael and noting with an inward groan that her face was feeling warm.

"Are you okay?" Michael said, reaching out to brush a finger against her cheek. "You look a little flushed."

"I'm fine," Kate said, ducking her head as her cheeks flared warmer still at his touch. "But do you ever get the feeling you're being watched?"

"Feeling I'm … oh." Michael glanced back to the counter in time to see Emily duck behind the coffee machine.

Wren swept toward them, bearing two cups and a serene expression, setting the cups down and giving Kate a beatific smile. "You've been working hard, boss. Give yourself a break. Take as long as you like. Emily and I can hold the fort."

"Thanks, Wren, that's … really subtle of you."

"Just trying to help is all."

"Thanks, Wren, and you can go away now," Kate replied, rubbing her forehead with one hand and looking mortified. She watched as Wren went back to the counter and fell into a whispered conversation with Emily, and then gave Michael a pained look. "Sorry about that," she offered.

"She means well," Michael suggested as he stirred some sugar into his coffee.

"Try being on the receiving end sometime," Kate muttered as she picked up her bagel. "So how's your day?" she asked as she took a bite.

"Getting better all the time," Michael commented. They fell into an easy conversation, and Michael again found himself wondering what it was about Kate that seemed to make talking so easy. He and David had the ease of a long friendship between them, and more often than not David sought him out as a sounding board. Listening and observing was something that came naturally to Michael, although with Kate he often found himself in situations where he wanted to talk. He wanted to tell her things about himself and to get her talking in return. He felt greedy for her words, knowing that they would stimulate more of his own.

"So you're jogging now?" Kate looked impressed. "That's something I've never tried."

"It was hard at first." Michael winced, remembering the pain of his first run with David. "But it's getting a little easier. It's just good to get out and get some fresh air."

"So what made you decide to sniff the great outdoors?" Kate teased as she took another mouthful.

"You," Michael admitted, then felt surprised at the unexpected honesty before he could filter his answer.

Kate's chewing slowed as she regarded him with surprise, then swallowed. "Me?"

"Why not?"

"I'm …" She shrugged, looking bewildered. "Well, I guess it's a bit unusual to be credited with something like that." Kate had finished her lunch by now and sat twisting her teaspoon, the clinking noises it made against the saucer breaking the sudden silence.

"Have I freaked you out?" Michael ventured after a pause.

"No, it's just I …" She paused and blushed. "Thank you."

❧

Wren and Emily were still watching them from behind the counter.

"I think he's just paid her a massive compliment," Wren observed in an undertone.

"Really?" Emily looked over at their table. "How can you tell?"

"Because Kate is looking very pink, uncomfortable, and pleased all at once," Wren said in a thoughtful tone. "I don't think I've ever seen her look like that before."

"I would've thought she'd be used to guys saying nice things," Emily replied as she opened the fridge for a quick inventory. "She's easy on the eyes, so she must get guys hitting on her now and then."

Wren snorted. "Please, it happens all the time but she's absolutely clueless." Wren put her hands on her hips and regarded the pair who still sat talking in quiet tones. "Well," she amended, "usually anyway. Galahad seems to have gotten through her defenses, so I'm hopeful."

"Oh." Emily's expression cleared. "She's been badly burned then?"

"No," Wren said after some consideration. "But her track record isn't good. Her first serious boyfriend was Thomas, and look how that turned out. I don't know about you, but if I slept with a guy for a few years and then he switched teams, I'd be a bit gun-shy too."

"She would've gone out with other guys since then, though, surely?"

"Sure." Wren wiped down the coffee machine and flicked the dishcloth over one shoulder as she kept tidying up the counter. "But she uses the store as a great barricade. Which is why I've given things a couple of very subtle nudges in the right direction." She straightened a couple of trays with a deft touch and nodded when everything was aligned to her satisfaction.

Emily closed the refrigerator door and gave Wren an exasperated look. "Subtle? Wren, I wouldn't call your comments to Kate earlier very subtle."

Wren turned and gave her a look of wounded pride. "I didn't say the nudges were to her." She glanced over at Kate and Michael, who were still talking, and felt a surge of glee as she watched Michael reach out and take Kate's hand. "I nudged *him.*"

Emily stepped forward and peeked around the coffee machine to see the latest development before giving Wren an impressed look. "You're good, I'll give you that."

"Thanks," Wren said, looking pleased. "Hell, I had to step in and do something. It was obvious they were attracted to each other, but they're both so damn shy it would've taken ages."

"You couldn't let things take their course naturally?" Emily teased.

"If there's one thing you should know about me by now," Wren replied, "it's that I don't do suspense."

❧

"So I know you've been waiting for me to ask," Michael began, smiling as Kate sat up a little straighter in her chair. "Kate, would you like to go on a date with me this Saturday?"

"Oh, this is all so sudden." Kate smiled. "I don't quite know what to say."

"You did tell me earlier that you were going to say yes," Michael pointed out.

"That's right, so I did," she replied. "Well, then, thank you very much for asking. I'd love to."

"I have to say that knowing the answer in advance makes it a lot easier."

"Glad I could help," she said. "So what are we going to do?"

"I hadn't actually thought that far ahead," he admitted, making her laugh. "I thought maybe dinner somewhere?"

"That sounds great," Kate said, and she meant it. It had been a long time since she had felt this comfortable with someone. She enjoyed talking to him, and with a surprise she realized that she was already looking forward to seeing him again, although he was already sitting right in front of her.

"Good." Michael smiled. "I'll book us in somewhere. In the meantime, don't be surprised if we bump into each other again."

"You know, you could always just keep coming here. It's nice to see you any time," she said, then stopped in surprise. Had she just said that? How was it that he managed to wheedle such an admission out of her?

"Done." He smiled and bit into his cupcake. As always, it was perfect. The cherry flavor burst on his tongue, surrounded by bitter chocolate and sugar sweetness. "God, this is good."

Kate glanced at her watch as she nibbled at her own cake. The afternoon was well on its way, and she had been keeping a casual eye on the number of customers coming through. Wren and Emily seemed to be staying on top of things okay, and a quick look at the cabinet showed that they had enough cupcakes to see them through the afternoon.

"I'm sorry." Michael's voice broke into her train of thought. "Am I keeping you from work?"

Kate blinked as she detached herself from her mental running tally. "Not at all. I was just checking to make sure we had enough stock for the afternoon. It looks like the girls are doing fine," she reassured him. "But what about you? Do you have to be back at work somewhere?"

"Nope, I'm a free agent most of the time."

"Really? What is it that you do?" As soon as she asked, she regretted it. Michael's expression became more composed, and he paused to lick his fingertips before he answered.

"I'm a writer," he admitted.

"Wow," Kate enthused. "Published?"

"Sometimes," Michael replied. Modest by nature, he still had a hard time accepting praise for his work. It seemed strange that something that had come to him by accident should bring accolades and a very comfortable income. It was even harder to accept compliments when he had generated so little in recent times.

"Ah." She gave him a sympathetic look. "Going through hard times?"

"Something like that, but things are looking up."

"Well, that's good news then," Kate answered, then bit into her cupcake. She was chewing contentedly when she noticed Michael was looking amused. "What?" she mumbled around a mouthful.

"You've got a little …" he began, and then reached forward. Kate paused and sat still as he gently cupped her chin and rubbed his thumb across her top lip. He held up his thumb long enough for her to see the smear of frosting, before he licked it off. She sat still, watching his tongue flicker over the pad of his thumb, and realized she wanted him to kiss her again. Saturday suddenly felt too far away.

Michael tasted the sweetness on his tongue before the sugar dissolved, and he stared at Kate's pink lips. Her tongue darted out to moisten them, and it was all he could do not to haul her over the table and into his arms. Saturday was too far away.

"You know…" he began, then stopped and coughed as his words struggled against a throat that was suddenly tight. "We've got a few days until Saturday. How about I walk you home tonight?"

"Okay," Kate ventured, licking her lips again. "I think I'd like that," then added, "very much."

They gave each other a shy smile of recognition. This time they were both aware that something was starting.

Chapter 9

Sweetness and Spice

It was with some relief that Kate saw the last customer for the afternoon leave the store. The day had finished on a quiet note, and she was pleased to see that Wren and Emily were well ahead of schedule. The two of them worked together like a well-oiled machine, finishing tasks and trading gossip and friendly insults like the old friends they were. Kate went outside and was just reaching up to take the chalkboard down from its hooks when someone grabbed her in a bear-hug from behind. She yipped with surprise, and then relaxed when she heard and felt the deep rumble of laughter. She was set down and she turned to see Paul beaming at her.

"Bear, you're lucky I didn't try and elbow you in the nuts." She gave his shoulder a laughing swat.

"Good to see you too, sis." He laughed, grabbing her in a headlock and ruffling her hair, a move he knew she hated. Kate protested and managed to squirm away from him, reaching up to smooth her hair in what she knew would be a futile gesture. Paul never did things by halves. He took down the chalkboard and carried it inside for her, setting it down by the counter at Wren's direction. "So how's the day been?"

"We did okay," Kate answered. "I started a count earlier and the takings were looking good."

"Want me to finish?" he asked, and Kate gave him a surprised nod. "Thanks, that'll give me time to do a quick inventory of the kitchen for tomorrow."

"No problem," Paul answered as he headed toward the till. He popped the drawer open and started to tally, scribbling down figures on the scrap of paper Kate had started earlier. "Doing good, Kat," he commented with a grin when she reappeared later. "Those weekends must be so close now you can almost taste 'em."

"They do sound pretty good," she admitted. "I'm thinking if we close Sunday and Monday it'll be a good start."

"A to the men," Wren chimed in, making Emily laugh.

"When do you think you'll start?" Paul asked, putting the takings into a nondescript bag and zipping it closed.

"Probably two weeks," Kate replied. "Wren, we'll need to make up some kind of sign to give people the heads up."

"Already on it," Wren replied. "I figured we'd put notices up in the windows and a smaller version on the tables, so I'll bring them in soon."

"Let me know when your first weekend is going to be, and I'll come install those magazine racks for you," Paul offered.

Kate brightened at that. "You've got them good to go?" She walked over and gave him a hug. "How do they look?"

Paul hugged her back. "The copper polished up beautifully. The place is going to look great. Which reminds me …" He released Kate and fished in one of the pockets on his cargo pants. "I found these for you the other day." He pulled out some octagonal pieces of cardboard and handed them over.

Kate accepted them, looking puzzled, and then started to laugh. "Where did you get these? I love them!"

Paul looked pleased. Wren and Emily came forward to have a look, and Kate handed them over.

"Old Speckled Hen," Emily read aloud, and she began to laugh. Wren reached out for one as Emily finished reading. They were English beer coasters, and each one featured the same gentleman fox wearing a red hunting jacket, with a different slogan on each.

"This one's my favorite," Wren said, holding one up that showed the fox looking very pleased under the slogan: *Nothing slips down easier than a hen with no bones.* "What are you going to do with them?"

"Oh, they're going to have to be framed. What a foxy whiskered gentleman he is," exclaimed Kate, a broad smile of delight on her face. "They can be hung up next to my fox. It'll be a great little display." She nodded toward the fox print on the wall and gave Paul a grin. "Thanks for these."

"You're welcome," said Paul, smiling with delight at the pleasure they had brought to his sister. He'd found them in a bar when he'd been having a drink with some friends, and had known immediately that they would appeal to her quirky sense of humor. Paul leaned against the counter as the others kept working awhile longer before Wren and Emily announced that they were leaving for the day.

"See you tomorrow, boss," they chorused from the door, giggling as Kate rounded on them.

"Get outta here," she called. "Don't let the door hit your ass on the way out!" She turned back with a chuckle to see Paul giving her a quizzical look. "It's an ongoing joke," she explained.

"Ah," he said. He hefted the bag of takings. "You want me to drop this off in the night safe?"

"Would you mind?" Kate said with relief. "That'd save me a trip."

"No problem, it's on my way home."

"I owe you," she said with a grateful smile.

❦

Kate had waved Paul off and was pulling out a chair at one of the tables to wait for Michael when she heard a knock on the front window. She looked up to see Michael peering through the glass, his face breaking into a smile as she stood up from the table and walked over to let him in. He stepped into the store, smiling down at her and then around the empty store with an expression of faint wonder on his face.

"It's so quiet," he commented.

"The people make a big difference," Kate agreed, "but a bit of peace and quiet never goes astray."

Michael looked at her peaceful expression. "You really love it, don't you?"

She gave him a surprised look. "Shouldn't I?"

"Of course," he said. "But it's not just a business venture for you, it's a passion." He looked around the store. "I mean, just look at the place. It's amazing."

"You're the second person to say that," Kate replied. "Emily was saying the same thing earlier. She thinks this place is part home, part bakery, and part gallery."

"And she's right," Michael said. "And it's very *you*."

Kate gave an embarrassed laugh. "And what's that?"

He took a step closer, reaching out to take her hand. "It's warm…" His thumb made a slow circle on her hand. "…welcoming…" He dipped his head. "…and sweet." He brushed his lips across hers, and Kate's eyes closed as she leaned in for more. The kiss was very soft and over before Kate was ready for it to be.

Michael pulled away, still holding her hand and gestured toward the door. "Shall we?"

"Yes," she said, smiling and reaching back to the table to pick up her bag.

He waited while she locked the door, and then took her hand and set a leisurely pace as they walked.

"So how was the rest of your afternoon?" he asked after a short pause.

"Long," said Kate, looking up as he chuckled.

The streets were still busy as commuters made their way home from the working day, and Michael charted a careful course through the crowd, shielding Kate from being jostled. By the time they got to the next corner, Michael had taken to walking with Kate's hand held up against his chest, and she was close to his side. Their conversation ebbed and flowed, and they seemed equally content to fall into an easy quiet now and then. The light changed, and the crowd surged forward.

"Are you in a hurry to get home?" Michael asked as they reached the curb on the other side.

Kate thought for a moment. "I guess not. Why?"

Michael's eyes crinkled at her. "How do you feel about a pre-date date?"

Kate's mouth twisted into an amused smile. "You need a warm-up?"

"Well, given you told me in advance you were going to say yes, I figure a practice date can't hurt."

Kate ducked her head and giggled, then looked back up at him, feeling carefree. "This is crazy, but sure, why not?"

"Great. Come on." Michael kept walking, leading them up West 4th Street. Kate looked ahead down the block, and then up at Michael. "Washington Square Park?" she guessed.

"Well done," Michael replied. "I figured we've got time for a bit of a walk there before I see you safely home."

"I love that park," Kate enthused. "The dog runs there are wonderful."

"You have a dog?" Michael looked at her in surprise.

"No," Kate said with a rueful smile. "But I go there when I need some unconditional canine love. It's a wonderful tonic."

"I'll have to remember that," Michael mused.

Soon they entered the park and were happy to stroll along the pathways until they found a park bench that wasn't occupied.

"Shall we?" Michael gestured toward the bench, and Kate nodded. They took a seat, and Kate adjusted her bag to a more comfortable position against her hip as she sat.

"So what did you get up to this afternoon?" Kate asked after a brief pause.

Michael shrugged. "A bit of writing," he said.

"Anything good?"

"It's a bit too early to tell, but I'm enjoying it all the same." He paused. "It's been a while since I've been able to get anything down. Not long ago just writing a grocery list would have been a literary achievement."

"Ah, you had a block?" Kate asked in a sympathetic tone.

"Massive," Michael sighed.

"Sounds awful."

"It was, but it's getting better now."

"Then I'm glad for you," she said.

Michael looked down at her with a brief smile, and then they both went back to gazing at the park vista. After an infinitesimal pause, he carefully lifted his arm up and around Kate's shoulders, resting his hand on her upper arm. "This okay?"

"Better than," she agreed, and Michael stilled as Kate settled her head against his shoulder.

"So keep talking," Kate encouraged. "What happened? How did you get writer's block in the first place?"

Michael grimaced. "I guess one day I woke up and realized I didn't like what I was writing." He sighed and looked down, crossing his legs at the ankles. "Then I began to hate it, and then..." He looked at Kate and shrugged. "One morning I woke up and discovered I had absolutely nothing to say. The words were just... gone."

They both sat there in silence for a while.

"It was like that for me, losing Jack," Kate ventured in a quiet voice. "One minute he and I were talking, just driving into town, nothing special, and then..." Her voice wavered for a moment before she continued, "and then..."

"Do you remember anything?" Michael asked, intrigued that someone so small and vital could carry the weight of so much pain.

Kate shook her head against his shoulder. "No. Paul told me later that they'd had to cut the car open to get me out," she went on in a faraway voice. "We got hit on Jack's side, and the car was pushed into a telephone pole. By the time help got to us, they knew that Jack was gone, but I was still alive."

Michael rested his cheek on the top of her head, rubbing his hand on her arm, cupping her other hand as he pulled her closer.

Kate closed her eyes, still talking. "The next thing I knew, I was waking up in the hospital, and just like that, everything I knew would never be the same again."

"I'm so sorry," Michael murmured.

"You know what I keep thinking about, though?"

"What?"

"Jack's last words. I was teasing him about a song on the radio. He used to torment Paul and me as kids by getting song lyrics wrong on purpose, so the last thing I remember is Jack singing along to the Beatles." She paused and began to sing in a soft voice, *"Lucy knows this guy with lions..."*

Despite the somber conversation, Michael's shoulders twitched in amusement at the thought of "Lucy in the Sky with Diamonds" getting butchered in the name of dad humor.

Kate lifted her head to look at him. "I know, right? Not the most profound last words for a lifetime, huh?"

"No," he agreed. "But you have to admit that it gives his life joy." Michael gazed down at Kate's open face and continued, "There are worse ways to go out of this life, and I think going out singing is pretty good."

Kate blinked at him. "You know, I'd never thought of it like that." She looked at him for a long moment, and then rested her head against his shoulder again. "Thanks," she said at last. "That really helps."

"You're welcome," he replied.

The two of them sat quietly, watching the procession of pedestrians and dog walkers that ebbed and flowed through the park. The sun was beginning to set, and they found themselves watching the colors of the park shift from the warm hues of the day to the cooler tones of dusk. The conversation between them moved from one topic to the next, and after a while the two of them drifted into a contented silence.

"Sometimes," Kate ventured after a long moment, "there's a lot to be said for a companionable silence."

A rumble of amusement came from Michael's chest. "Isn't that a contradiction?"

He felt Kate's shoulders shake with silent laughter. "I was hoping you wouldn't pick up on that."

Michael found himself glancing from the park vista to Kate's head resting near his chest. *A companionable silence:* he'd never really taken note of the phrase before and yet here he was with a woman that gave him silence and words in equal and satisfying measure. Michael began to relax enough that he almost jolted when Kate's voice roused him from his reverie.

"Michael," she said in a quiet voice, "how long have you been writing?"

"Ever since I could, I suppose." Michael frowned for a moment as he tried to remember. "Mom said I was always quiet, so growing up the only child of academics, it's no surprise that books were always a good companion."

"True," Kate agreed. "You're never alone if you've got a book."

"Yeah," he sighed. "After college, Mom went through some papers of mine, one thing led to another, and about eighteen months after that, I was published. People wanted more, so I kept writing. The rest of my life had to be scheduled in around publication dates." He gave a small chuff of laughter. "And then suddenly I found that I'd been writing for twelve years that had flown by, but had no idea what to do with my own time."

"Ah." Kate nodded. "You got busy burning up the decade when you should've seized the day."

Michael gave her a startled look. "You were the same?"

"A little, although not the same extent as you. I was always looking to the future, always trying to plan my next step. I studied literature at college and was thinking about teaching. When I lost Jack, though, it made me realize that it's about making each day important, because you never know when they're going to stop."

"Is that why you and Wren do the special cupcakes and chalkboard quotes every day?"

She nodded, and some hair fell across her face. Michael watched as she hooked the strands with her fingers and tucked them back behind her ears, the movement setting the moonstones at her ears dancing.

"It might only be a small thing, but it's my way of celebrating each day."

"I think it's beautiful," Michael replied.

The day was drawing to a close by the time Michael and Kate began to make their way out of the park. They both walked at an easy pace, holding hands and talking with an easy intimacy. What had begun as a friendship was fast becoming something more, a fact the two of them were aware of. Neither of them felt compelled to rush into anything, and their mutual exploration of each other's personalities added to the pleasure of anticipation.

"Here you are, safe and sound," Michael commented as they drew to a halt in front of Kate's apartment.

"Thanks." Kate smiled. "I enjoyed our walk; it was a great way to finish the day."

"Maybe we could do it again sometime?" Michael asked, raising an eyebrow with a slight smile, enjoying the flush of color that the fresh air had brought to her cheeks.

"I'd like that," Kate replied. Now she was confused. It hadn't been a date, but they had just spent a couple of hours together, walking, talking, and taking in the sights that the park and the city had to offer. Should she invite him upstairs? Would he say yes? What if he said no? She bit her lip in confusion, looking up when Michael began to speak.

"So, I guess this is the part where I leave you to enjoy your evening," Michael said, twining their fingers together and giving her a gentle tug to bring her a step closer toward him.

"Something like that," she agreed.

"It seems a shame, though, to let you go without wishing you a good night," he said softly.

"Well, when you put it that way," she said, pretending to give the suggestion careful consideration, "it seems only fair that we end on a good note."

Michael dipped his head toward hers, and Kate noticed just before her eyes fluttered closed that they were both smiling. The kiss was soft and sweet. Their lips met and broke apart, returning again and again. Kate felt the tip of Michael's tongue brush gently against her lips, and she parted them slightly to allow him access. He tasted her carefully before breaking away and resting his forehead against hers for a moment.

"Good night, Kate," he said, reaching up to brush her hair off her face.

"And to you," she replied, her eyes drowsy. With great effort, she moved to walk up the stairs, pausing at the top to look back and wave.

Once inside, she got changed and began fixing dinner, her mind replaying the conversation with Michael in the park as she began humming. "Lucy knows this guy with lions…," she sang in a quiet voice with a sad smile on her face. "Oh, Jack," she sighed. She wished he could have seen the success her bakery had become. She wished he was still around to see the "heart family" of friends she had surrounded herself with. Jack had always impressed upon Kate and Paul the importance of family, particularly as they had so few relatives to call their own.

"Most people don't have a choice who they get in their family, but you guys do," Jack had told them with a twinkle. "Friends are the family that you choose for yourself."

Taking his advice, Kate had set about acquiring a heart family of her own, which included people like Wren and Thomas, and now Michael. She wondered what Jack would have thought of him. Michael was a friend, or at least he had begun as such. Now she could feel herself standing on the precipice of something more.

There was a lot yet to learn about Michael, but she had a feeling Jack would have approved of their mutually careful approach. She remembered some advice Jack had given her, and her smile dipped for a moment. The cream began to bubble as the salmon danced across the surface of the pan, and she picked up the wooden spoon to stir it, hoping for some distraction, but the memory, once unlocked, unraveled and began to play as she sipped at her glass of wine.

"Kat," Jack had begun, rubbing the back of his neck with one hand, a sure sign he was nervous. Kate had looked at him, waiting for him to speak. "You know that since your mother passed, we've never really had any deep conversations."

"We said what's been needed to be said, Jack," Kate had said in a gentle voice. It was true enough. While Jack had never been big on conversation, since Gwen's passing, the three remaining members of the family—Jack, Paul, and Kate—had always made sure to voice "I love you" whenever they could. Jack might have been of the "if you don't have anything to say, keep your trap shut" school, but when he spoke, his words stuck in the heart.

"Well, just give an old guy a chance here." Jack had smiled. "I don't know what I'll do at retirement, hell, I might not even make it that far," he had joked, pausing when Kate's face went white. "Life can be long or short, but it's the quality of the hours in between, you know that, right?"

"Right," Kate had agreed, wondering where the conversation was going.

"I just …" He paused, then started again. "I just wanted to pass on one bit of advice. It's what my dad told me, and the old man was right, so I figure it might do my kids some good as well." He reached out and took Kate's hand, holding it between his own, rubbing the back of her hand with his thumb. His hands were warm and calloused and smelled slightly of a curious combination of gun oil and fish. "When you do meet the right man and you want to make a life together, make sure you're friends in the bargain."

Kate had raised an eyebrow at that.

"No," Jack had patted her hand for emphasis. "Hear me out. All that romantic stuff, and the … uh …" His ears had turned pink at this. "… the other side of things." He squinted at her to make sure she was following what he was too embarrassed to voice to his baby girl, and, at Kate's amused nod, had continued with a slight sigh of relief. "You know," he had said in a gruff tone, "that stuff don't always last. Passion can wax and wane, but a good intimate friendship will just keep getting better with age."

"Is that what you and Mom had?" Kate had asked, leaning forward slightly.

Jack had given a wry grin, his gaze turning inward to the past. "Oh yeah. Hell, once I met that woman, I knew my life was never going to be the same." He winked. "Gwen and I loved each other hard for over twenty years. Mind you, we fought just as hard too."

He had reached up and stroked his mustache with a reminiscent smile on his face until he remembered Kate was sitting quietly with him at the table. He had cleared his throat. "Just promise me you'll remember that, Kat. Any good relationship has friendship at the core."

"Sure thing, Dad," Kate had replied, a little puzzled at Jack's quiet insistence. "Have you had this talk with Paul?"

"Yup." Jack had sat back at that, reaching for his beer and taking a swig. "My old man told me I'd know when the time was right to pass the advice on. Seemed to me that today was the day."

Jack had given her a small smile and had sipped at his beer again, clearly uncomfortable with the somber conversation. Kate smiled, and then reached over to give him a kiss and a hug.

"Love you, Dad," she had whispered in his ear.

"Love you too, Kat. Always. You remember that."

He was dead a week later.

Kate sighed as she remembered his words, wiping her eyes against the sudden moisture and telling herself that it was from the cracked pepper she was adding to the dish. She didn't like feeling maudlin and knew that even Jack would be shaking his head at her if he could see her now. And anyway, there was plenty in her life to smile about these days. More so now that she had met Michael.

She smiled as she thought of his gentle smile and the way his auburn hair had ruffled in the breeze as they'd walked. The wind had blown the scent of his aftershave around her in delightful clouds, and the combination of that, with the touch of his hand, brush of his lips, and the comfort of his arm around her shoulder, had left her with a sense memory that made her feel warm.

The words were bubbling in Michael's mind as he unlocked his front door and strode into the apartment, kicking the door closed behind him. Throwing his keys onto the table, he reached for the phone. He had his favorite Chinese take-out on speed dial, so it was the work of a moment to place his order, and then he strode into the living room toward his desk to boot up his laptop.

He felt energized and eager to write. Again, he had no clear structure in mind, but he knew once he gave the words access to the page they'd settle and grow and flourish beneath his fingertips. The take-out was delivered, and he forked into it while he kept his attention on the screen. The chili peppers hit his taste buds, making him draw a sharp breath, and he scooped some steamed rice into his mouth to try and cool the burn. He chewed and swallowed with caution, wiping his eyes as they began to water. He hadn't eaten spicy food for a while, and now his taste buds were going into overdrive, protesting at the sudden abuse. Getting adventurous now and then seemed to come with a price. As his mouth began to cool, he stirred some rice into the other container, hoping to reduce the chili pepper effect for the next mouthful. Just because the first taste of adventure was a shock, it didn't mean that he wasn't keen to go back for more.

He sat cross-legged on his sofa, picking at his take-out containers. His laptop was on the coffee table and he squinted at the screen, reading what he had written during the week. He still had no clear sense of what he was hoping to achieve, but found that the mere act of writing again was more soothing than he had ever given it credit for. Perhaps if he gave his words some more structure ...

Twisting on the sofa, he peered across at his desk to the stack of blank index cards that hadn't been touched in weeks. For years now they'd been an integral component of his writing, and yet this time he'd started work without even giving them a moment's thought. Dropping the fork back into one of the containers, he set it down on the coffee table and uncoiled himself to walk over and pick them up, along with a pen.

He made his way back to the laptop in a thoughtful mood, turning the cards over and over in his hands. Sitting down again, he stared into space, the pen poised over the top card on the pack. Words flitted through his head, possibilities, characters, plot devices, and yet none of them held any appeal. He sighed and flicked the pen toward the table, not caring as it skittered across the surface and over the edge, landing silently on the rug. The cards followed, spraying in a graceful arc across the wood grain of the table.

Michael leaned forward and snagged a container toward him, and then retrieved his fork and began to eat. He chewed slowly, staring at the cards on the table. Indexing and mapping out his characters and story lines had always been his style. Meticulous planning and attention to detail was his trademark, and yet this time it seemed his well honed habits were going to languish in a corner somewhere. His writing this time around seemed to be far more organic, evolving and developing into something unexpected. He wasn't used to dealing with the unexpected, but he had a feeling he was going to like it.

He scooped some more take-out into his mouth and chewed with relish. He'd gotten used to the burn now, and it was good.

⟡

"Morning, boss." Wren yawned.

"Wren, don't call me boss," Kate answered as she slid the key into the lock. She shot Wren a sidelong look as she opened the door and stood aside to let her enter. "You okay?"

"Sorry, boss." Wren gave a jaw-popping yawn again. "Just get me caffeinated and I'll be fine."

Kate watched as Wren disappeared into the kitchen to hang up her coat and bag, and then reappeared to lug the chalkboard outside. Kate shed her coat and bag as well, and then switched on the coffee machine.

"Forgot the chalk," she explained as she plucked it out of the glass beside the register and went back outside to write her quote of the day.

"Did you get any sleep last night?" Kate asked in concern when Wren stumbled back through the store, almost sleepwalking.

"Sure." Wren yawned again as she dropped the chalk back into the glass with a plink. "I was up late working on some gear for the store and watching a bit of TV."

"What was on?" Kate asked.

"A documentary about Woodstock," Wren answered as she collected the glass jugs from a shelf behind the counter and filled them up with water from the tap. "Free love in the sixties might have sounded like fun, but it came with a price."

"Oh, really?" Kate started to froth some milk, and after a considered gaze at Wren, got out a grande sized cup for her. Wren really looked like she needed all the caffeine she could get.

Wren slumped against the counter as she waited for Kate to finish the coffees. They both looked up at a whoop of laughter from outside, and smiled as Emily giggled her way past the chalkboard and into the store.

"Okay, Wren," she said as she reached the counter. "I have to ask. How on earth did you think that one up?"

Wren grinned. "I was just telling Kate that I watched a show about Woodstock last night."

"Ah." Emily nodded. "That explains it then."

"Right. Now I have to see for myself," Kate said, setting down the milk jug and, against Wren's protests, walked outside. She had to smile when she read Wren's artful scrawl.

When you give freely of yourself,
your reward might be a serious case of crabs.

Kate laughed and shook her head, wagging an admonishing finger at Wren. "And this is why we're not uptown," she said.

"And it's why you love me," Wren replied, poking her tongue out. "Now finish making my coffee, woman!"

"Yes'm," Kate drawled as she made her way back to the machine. She smiled to herself as she poured the foamy milk into their cups, and the three of them took a quick break to enjoy their morning ritual.

"So what's the special going to be today?" Emily asked.

"I've been thinking of a few variations," Kate replied, "but Wren's little effort out there has just bumped one to the front of the queue."

Wren tried to look modest. "Just doing my bit to help," she answered, and then straightened up as a thought hit her. "Fuck, I must be more tired than I thought. I forgot to show you the pretties."

Kate and Emily exchanged a baffled look.

"The what?" Kate said.

"Stay there," Wren instructed, and went into the kitchen to fetch three flat packages that had been wrapped with black tissue paper which she set down on one of the tables.

"Wren," Kate began, "what have you been up to?"

"Nothing that you didn't given me permission to do," Wren replied with a wide-eyed look.

"But we only had that conversation *yesterday*," Kate objected. "You can't have done them already."

Wren stopped unpacking and stood with an exasperated hand on one hip. "I could if I started them back when we first started talking about it weeks ago."

Kate regarded Wren with an amused expression. "That sure of yourself, huh?"

"Something like that." Wren shrugged. "Now check these out and prepare to fall in love." She looked on as Emily began to pick with careful fingers at the package Wren had handed her. "Emily," she sighed. "It's *tissue* paper; you're meant to rip the shit out of it."

"Oh," Emily replied, "well, in that case . . ." She ripped the parcel apart with both hands, and Kate followed suit.

There was a long silence, broken only when Wren huffed out the breath she had been holding. "Will one of you *say* something?"

"Wren," Kate began, and then stopped and swallowed. "I don't know what to say, they're . . ."

"Beautiful," Emily supplied.

Kate gave a mute nod, her throat suddenly tight. The colors of the fabric blazed against the black tissue paper. She reached in and pulled the garment out with reverent hands, holding it up to inspect it closer.

It was an apron, the likes of which she had never seen before. It was made of sturdy black cotton, but that was where the practicality ended. Wren had sewn a patchwork of Chinese brocades, ribbons, and braids in a multi-hued pattern that sang to the eyes. Kate glanced over to see Emily regarding hers with an expression of awe, and knew that her face must mirror the other woman's expression.

"They might look delicate," Wren broke in, "but they're machine washable, like you wanted. And look." She stepped toward Kate and pulled out a smaller package. "Yours is a bit different." Opening the bundle, she revealed a sheet of soft, clear plastic that affixed over the apron panel by way of a series of clear snaps. "There you go, so anything will wipe off." She gave Kate and anxious look. "Have I done good?"

Kate looped the apron over her head and tied it around her waist, then swept Wren into a tight hug. "You've done good, kiddo," she said in a muffled voice. "I love them."

"I need to get in on that action too," Emily chimed in, insinuating herself for a group hug.

When they broke apart, Kate and Wren both sniffed a little, and then laughed at their foolishness.

"You really like them?" Wren asked again.

Kate gave her a sigh of amused exasperation. "Wren, if we don't start wearing them, I'll have them framed and hung up instead because they're works of art."

Emily nodded in happy agreement, and Wren beamed.

"Now I've gotta get baking." Kate looked at her watch.

"Speaking of which," Wren said, "what was it about the chalkboard quote that gave you the cupcake idea?"

"You'll find out."

Ꙩ

"You know I'm capable of being a patient man, but you're going to have to tell me sooner rather than later."

"I know, Alistair," Michael replied. "But I don't really know what it is myself, so how the hell can I describe it to you?"

"Interesting point," Alistair conceded.

Michael leaned forward and rested his elbows on his desk as he listened to Alistair. The phone calls from his editor were fewer these days, but all the same, he knew that the publishers were going to want something soon.

He'd woken refreshed after another night of solid sleep. It hadn't escaped his notice that his words had returned and taken the place of his insomnia. The nights he slept the best were inevitably the days that he'd seen Kate. He'd gone for his morning jog through the park, past the bench where they had sat together. Today he'd taken a different route, stopping in at the large dog run. He'd stood, leaning against the fence, watching the dogs run and play together. Some of the more inquisitive ones had trotted up to the fence and sniffed at his hand, allowing a quick pat. Kate had been right; the unconditional acceptance and enjoyment of the day seemed to rub off. He had jogged home, feeling more awake than he had in a long time.

"Look," Michael suggested after a while, "why don't I send you the first few chapters of what I've done, and you can see if you can make any sense of it."

There was a startled pause.

"Did you say chapters? As in *plural?*" Alistair asked.

"Yes." Michael couldn't help but smile at the careful way Alistair posed the question.

"What, uh…" Alistair cleared his throat. "How many words are we talking about here?"

Michael flicked a glance toward his laptop. "Last time I checked, about thirty thousand, give or take."

"Right," Alistair replied, sounding a little hoarse this time. "Okay, Michael, if you're comfortable letting me have a look then I'd love to see it."

"Okay, give me a minute and I'll send it through," Michael replied, tapping the space bar on the laptop to activate it from sleep mode, and wedged the phone between his ear and chin as he began to type.

"You're sending it now?"

"No time like the present."

"Michael," Alistair said, "I have no idea what changed in your life recently, but keep it up."

A vision of Kate flashed into Michael's mind. "I plan to."

David had set out with a plan, and yet despite his well thought-out intentions for the day, he found himself pacing the sidewalk across the street from the bakery. He jammed his hands into his pockets and scuffed his shoes on the pavement while he thought. He'd made his career decision, and now it was time for the other one that he had been considering. He looked over at the bakery, squinting as he saw movement again. He thought he caught a glimpse of her red hair as she bent over at a table to collect a cup, and then she moved toward the back of the store.

David sighed and looked down at his feet, scuffing again. Finally he looked up and set his jaw.

"Fuck it," he muttered and set off across the street. He'd had enough indecision in the last month to last him a lifetime. He knew what he wanted now.

As he reached the door to the bakery, his gaze flickered across to the chalkboard, and he grinned at the phrase before stepping inside. He took a moment to orient himself and looked at the counter to see where she was.

"Hey, isn't that the guy that's been in here with Galahad?" Emily asked with a nudge as she passed.

Wren looked up from her task, snorting when she saw who had come in. "Yeah, it's Mr. Wonderful," she answered in a dismissive tone, bending over the cups to pour in the milk and then tracing a quick pattern in the milk froth.

Emily watched as David approached the counter, his gaze rarely shifting from Wren who seemed to be going to great lengths to avoid acknowledging his presence. "I dunno, Wren. Seems to me you might want to think about cutting him a little slack."

"Whatever." Wren straightened and picked up the saucers. "But for now I'm busy."

David reached the counter just as Wren slid away and carried her order out toward her waiting customers, a bright efficient smile on her face. He watched her go, and then turned to Emily who gave him a sympathetic smile.

"Give her time," Emily suggested, startling David.

"You knew?"

Emily looked over at Wren who had paused at the table for some conversation with some customers. It seemed that as long as David stood at the counter, she wasn't in any hurry to come back. Emily pursed her lips and watched her. It wasn't like Wren to run away from something. Or someone. She fixed David with a measuring gaze.

"You be gentle," she cautioned him.

"I always am, but how did you know?" he said, confused.

"You're not the only one paying attention around here," Emily replied. "Now, what can I get you?"

David hadn't thought any further than seeing Wren again, and now he floundered. He looked around, and then gave Emily a hopeful look. "What do you recommend?"

"Well, there's always the cupcake of the day," Emily suggested.

"Which is?" he asked.

Emily inclined her head toward the small chalkboard that sat on a brass easel. David followed her gaze and read the name, then gave a short laugh.

Woodstock Afterburn: *Spicy Chocolate Temptations.*

"You've talked me into it," he said with a grin as he remembered the quote outside. "But hold the crabs."

"Done." Emily winked. "Now you go take a seat and we'll be right over."

David made his way to an empty table, feeling confused. What the hell was it with this store? First Michael had fallen under its spell, and now he was back here again, watching the small red-headed woman with the bird-like eyes and quick smile.

"Hey, Wren," Emily called.

"Yeah, babe?" Wren said in an absent tone. She was slicing lemons to add to the water jugs. She'd made it a point to keep herself occupied with small tasks that kept her behind the counter.

"We're getting low on cups. You mind checking out front?"

"Kinda busy here, Emily," Wren replied.

"Really? Looks like you're hiding to me," Emily said. Wren shot her a disgruntled look, then silently picked up a large plastic tub and hitched it onto her hip, stalking out to the front of the store to clear tables. "Atta girl," Emily said with a slight smile.

Wren worked her way through the tables, leaving David's until last for a faster getaway back to the sanctuary of the counter. She reached for his cup and saucer and added them to the tub without making eye contact.

David watched her, and then cleared his throat. "So," David said, "I take it you and the boss get along?"

"She's the best," Wren answered, picking up his plate and adding it to the plastic tub she balanced on her hip.

"So I see. You've put it out there, so it's obvious she's good to work for."

"Huh?"

David pointed to Wren's apron, then over to where Kate was serving behind the counter. "She's earth, the other one—" he indicated Emily who was walking back from delivering a coffee, "—is water, so she must be easy-going as well." Then he turned back to Wren. "Which makes yours wind." He gave her a pleased smile. "Am I right?"

Wren stared at him, dumbfounded.

"What?" he said under the weight of her scrutiny.

"You're the only one that's picked up on that," she said, choosing her words with care. "It's … unexpected."

"What's the big surprise?" David waved a hand at her apron again. "The patterns are obvious if you look." He glanced again at Wren's apron. The brocades shimmered as she shifted her weight from one foot to the other. The patterns coiled and swirled in tones of blue, silver, and gray. Silver ribbons fluttered slightly in the breeze that wafted into the store from outside.

"Maybe I just didn't think you seemed the type to notice," she admitted at last.

David leaned back in his chair with lazy grace and regarded her with amusement. "I think you'll find I always pay attention."

"Really." Wren was intrigued, despite herself.

"Oh, yes." David leaned forward again and in a quick movement plucked at a ribbon that floated off the hem, tugging at it in a way that had her taking an involuntary step toward him. "I often take in the details of beautiful things, particularly when they don't know that they're on display."

Wren regarded him for a moment, wondering why she was indulging him. He wasn't her usual type at all, and his self-assuredness made her feel as if she was charting unfamiliar waters.

❧

Kate wandered out of the kitchen and saw Emily standing quietly, watching the front of the store.

"Whatcha doin'?" she asked, and was surprised to see Emily shush her to silence. She walked over to where Emily was standing and saw Wren and David. David was tugging at a ribbon on Wren's apron as the two talked. Wren hesitated and then put down the plastic tub and pulled out a chair.

"Works every time," Emily said in tones of quiet satisfaction.

"What does?" Kate asked, not taking her eyes off the duo.

Emily gave her a quick look, and then resumed her gaze. "I've worked in a few bars here and there. It's the oldest trick in the book. Take two regulars, mix them together, and let them stew."

"Really?"

"It never fails," replied Emily. "You wait; it won't be long now."

"It might take Wren a while to realize that, though," Kate commented.

"She's a smart girl," Emily said. "She'll get there if Mr. Wonderful is patient."

"Mr. Wonderful? Is that what you call him?"

Emily gave her a droll look. "No, that's Wren's name for him." She glanced back at David. "Thing is, she was being facetious, but it turns out she might be right."

"Emily, you're an interesting woman," Kate said after a moment.

"I know. Modest, too."

It was with some regret that Kate watched Wren carry the chalkboard inside, lean it against the wall and then flip the window sign to CLOSED and pull the door shut. Michael hadn't come in after all. Oh, well. She went back to taking the remaining cupcakes out of the cabinet, putting some aside for Emily to take home as she'd requested.

The three of them made short work of cleaning up. Kate counted up the takings and bagged it up, throwing the bag into the small safe that she'd had built into one of the kitchen's lower cupboards. She'd drop it off at the night safe later in the week, staggering the drop off day as she'd mentioned to Paul.

"So I guess we'll head off." Wren appeared in the kitchen doorway. "See you tomorrow."

"I'll be here." Kate smiled. "Did you have a nice chat with Michael's friend?"

"David," Wren supplied, standing awkwardly in the doorway as she mentioned his name. "Uh … it was … interesting, I guess."

"Interesting can be good," Kate agreed. "He seems like a nice guy."

"Yeah, well, we'll see," Wren said in a carefully dismissive tone.

"Mmm-hmm." Kate smiled.

Wren narrowed her eyes. "What's that supposed to mean?"

"Nothing," Kate said. "You go have a nice night."

"Yeah, you too."

Kate was shrugging on her coat when a barrage of rapping on the front window brought her to the doorway. Wren was standing with her face up to the glass. When she saw Kate, she gave her a happy thumbs-up, and then went on her way. Kate stood there for a moment, baffled, and then went back into the kitchen to collect her bag. When she opened the door to leave, she saw what Wren had looked so happy about.

Michael was leaning against the wall, hands in pockets as he gave her an easy smile. The breeze ruffled his hair, blowing his scent toward her.

"Hey." He smiled.

"Hey, yourself," she answered, not bothering to hide her broad smile of delight. "What are you doing here?"

He shrugged, then straightened up and took a step toward her and waited as she closed up the shop. "I thought I'd walk you home again."

She straightened up and smiled at him as she took a step closer.

Michael reached up to put his finger under her chin to draw her gaze back up to his as he dipped his head toward hers and gave her a soft kiss. They drew apart a fraction, and looked at each other. Kate nodded, and Michael smiled before leaning down to kiss her again. Kate closed her eyes and stepped closer still, until her chest was pressed up against his, feeling a rush of pleasure as Michael wrapped his arms around her to hold her close while their mouths explored each other's.

They broke apart and regarded each other. "I don't know about you," Michael admitted, "but Saturday is just too damn far away for my liking."

"I'll second that," Kate replied. "But if it'd make you feel better, you can keep kissing me."

Michael's mouth twisted into a grin. "You'd let me do that?"

"Just trying to help the situation is all," Kate said with a smile, dropping her eyes to his lips.

"I think I'll take you up on that offer," Michael said, and leaned down to kiss her again. This time he reached up a hand to cup her head against his lips, stroking his thumb against her throat. She gave a small hum of pleasure and ran her hands up his arms to hold him closer still.

They stood underneath the canopy of the store, kissing for a few minutes more before breaking apart with a quiet laugh.

"Come on," Michael said, giving her another quick kiss. "Let's get you home." He looped his arm around her shoulders and pulled her close. He'd ended up working most of the afternoon, and when he realized the time, had rushed out of his apartment to get to the bakery, hoping to catch her before she left for the day. Wren had stopped short when she'd seen him quietly waiting, and he'd held a finger to his lips for quiet. The look on Kate's face when she'd seen him had been worth the haste.

Kate felt a rush of pleasure at Michael's words and settled her bag into a comfortable position on her shoulder. The weight and warmth of Michael's arm around her felt good, and she smiled up at him as they began to walk.

"So, how was your day?" he asked, glancing down at her as she began to speak, looking forward to her words.

Soon they were lost in each other, and then they were lost in the afternoon crowd.

Chapter 10

The Fox and the Bear

"Morning, boss."

"Wren, don't call me boss," Kate chided. She wasn't going to admit it, but the morning banter with Wren always made her smile. When she first realized she was going to need staff, it had taken a while for her to get her head around being an employer. The fact that Wren made a game of it had made the assimilation process much easier for the two of them.

"Sorry, boss," Wren said, waiting for Kate to unlock the door.

"Have you got a quote for the day yet?"

"Getting there," Wren replied. She was considering a few options that had sprung to mind on her way to work. "Have you ever noticed how office workers look?"

"Huh?" Kate looked up at her as she opened the door and ushered her inside. "Can't say that I have. Why?"

"Most of them wear black."

"Well, I guess it's a serviceable color, it goes with everything," Kate said, flicking on the coffee machine and heading through to the kitchen to put her bag away. Wren followed, still talking.

"I know, but c'mon, a bit of color here and there wouldn't kill them. You look next time you're at the traffic lights. They all look like a big flock of crows."

"Murder," Kate replied absently.

"What?" Wren looked puzzled.

"They're called a 'murder of crows.' You know, like a 'pride of lions,'" Kate explained as she got out a couple of cups, then smiled and waved as she got out a third. Emily had just arrived.

"Hey, guys," Emily said as she walked past. Kate and Wren chorused a greeting in return.

"So, on to other things. How's Michael?" Wren said with a speculative glint in her eye.

"Good, he's good," Kate replied as she became very focused on the task at hand, so that she could avoid Wren's gaze.

Michael had stopped by the bakery once more during the week for lunch, but had turned up twice more at closing time to walk Kate home. Although Kate was quite used to walking home alone, the days when Michael hadn't been waiting for her gave her a slight pang, and she was aware of the lack of his presence more than she was ready to admit. He never assumed she didn't have plans and told her in advance when he would be there. Even when he wasn't expected she found herself watching for him all the same.

"Tomorrow night's the night, huh?" Wren continued, smirking as she saw the telltale show of color on Kate's neck.

"Mmm," Kate replied in what she hoped was a casual tone. She poured the coffee into their cups and spooned on some extra milk froth. Emily appeared, and they toasted each other before taking their first sip of the day.

"Oh, that's good." Emily said, sighing in appreciation. "I swear this job is turning me into a cake and coffee addict."

"Right there with ya, babe," Wren replied, then glanced back at Kate. "So what's today's special?"

"Depends. I've got a couple in mind, but what's your quote of the day going to be?"

Wren thought for a moment. "I think we'll go with: *Remember you're unique, just like everybody else.*"

"Oh, I *like* that one," Emily gave a happy endorsement as Wren picked up the chalk and walked around the counter.

"Of course, I could come up with a lovey-dovey quote, but maybe I'll save that for tomorrow," Wren said over her shoulder as she headed toward the door.

"Thanks, no pressure or anything," Kate called after Wren, who blew her an unrepentant raspberry as she carried the chalkboard outside.

Emily and Kate regarded each other over their cups. "Don't you start," Kate warned.

"I wasn't even thinking of it," Emily countered. "Wren is all smug now, but she's next."

"Good," Kate replied. "It'll be fun when it's not me in the spotlight."

Wren returned. "Right, so that's done. What's the cupcake going to be?"

"I'm thinking ... *Nothing Beets You, Baby*, a chocolate beet cupcake with chocolate ganache frosting."

"Nice," Wren commented, scribbling on the smaller chalkboard and setting it on the counter. "Now on to more important things. What are you going to wear tomorrow?"

Kate had taken her apron down from its hook in the kitchen and was tying it up at the back, giving herself a bit of time to think. "I haven't thought it through yet." Wren looked at her, aghast. "What?" Kate said in a defensive tone. She was lying. Kate had been thinking about the date all week, although it was safe to say that her thoughts had been wrapped up in Michael rather than what clothes she would be wearing at the time.

"I don't know what I'm going to do with you," Wren said in apparent despair.

"Maybe you could pick on someone else?" Kate replied as she checked that the plastic cover was snapped onto the apron properly. "Emily hasn't said much about her mystery man lately."

Both women turned to regard Emily, who had looked up from her bagel preparation at the mention of her name and was now giving her best deer-in-the-headlights impression. "Thanks, boss," she muttered as Wren advanced toward her.

"Any time. Now if you'll excuse me, these cupcakes aren't going to bake themselves," Kate replied and made a quick getaway.

"I've gotta say, Wren, people have been raving about the aprons," Emily commented as they stood drying glasses and stacking them in rows on one of the counter tops later that morning.

"Really?" Wren asked with a pleased smile. Kate looked up from doing a quick inventory of the remaining cakes and nodded her agreement as she kept a silent tally running in her head.

"Yup, everyone wants to know where they're from," Emily continued. She put down the dishcloth she'd been holding and ran a gentle hand down the front panel. "They're so gorgeous. I can't believe I've got one."

While Kate left her apron in the store each night, Emily had been taking hers home, lovingly spot-cleaning it when required and poring over the stitches and beading that Wren had worked into the design. She loved finding the tiny details Wren had included, and last night had been delighted to find a tiny silver seashell bead dancing on the hem of the main panel of watermarked blue silk and seed pearls sewn over the white oriental blossoms on another.

"What are people saying?" Wren said, curious to hear what sort of reaction her work had garnered.

"Oh." Emily thought for a moment. "They comment on the fabrics and the patchwork and that they're something really funky for a bakery."

Wren nodded thoughtfully, intrigued that it had been a few days and still no one else had cracked the code but David. She frowned a little, thinking of the way he had gazed at her, and then had seemed to see right *through* her, as if there was nothing she could hide from him, and she had moved toward him, instead of away.

❧

Michael was walking back to the apartment after his jog when his cell phone began to ring. He fished it out of the zip pocket in his running shorts and managed to answer it before it could divert to voice mail.

"Forrester," he said as he continued walking.

"Michael, hi. It's Alistair. Just calling to let you know I read the chapter you sent to me."

The careful tone of Alistair's voice had Michael slowing down his pace. "And?"

"And it's…" There was a considered pause. "It's good."

Michael reached the intersection and waited for the light to change. "You're not saying very much, Alistair."

"Probably because I don't quite know what to say."

Michael snorted. "That's rare." The light changed, and he began to cross. "Just cut the bull and tell me what you really thought."

"Michael, I don't know what the hell you're on … or what the hell you've been doing, but keep it up. I think this is …"

"What?" Michael frowned as a bus took off from the curb, drowning out Alistair's voice. "Sorry, I didn't catch that. Could you repeat it?"

"I said I think this could be your best work yet," Alistair said in a slow, careful tone. He didn't want to jinx the process any more than Michael did, but he'd been asked to critique, and praise had to be given where it was due. He'd received the email from Michael with a heavy heart, not knowing what to expect. Twenty minutes after he had started reading, he'd had his assistant clear his schedule for the day, and he had hunkered down in front of his computer in complete absorption. By the time he'd finished reading, his heart had been thumping with stealthy excitement.

"Well, that's …" Michael began, then cleared his throat. "That's unexpected."

"Just calling it how I see it, Michael," Alistair replied.

"And it's appreciated," Michael admitted with a reluctant smile. *It's good. Alistair said it's good. I'm back.*

"Seriously, I don't know what's been going on, but your whole tone has changed. It's very … optimistic."

"There have been a few changes lately," Michael allowed, "but that's all I'm willing to say."

"It's okay," Alistair said quickly. "You don't have to tell me anything more than you're comfortable with. Just tell me you're going to keep writing."

"I will, Alistair. As long as the words keep coming, I'll keep writing."

"Then that's all I need to hear," Alistair said, and Michael could hear the smile in his voice.

❦

"Whatever you're going to say, I'm not listening," Kate said as she brushed past Wren with another tray of cakes. The morning trade in the store had been brisk enough, but now the afternoon was slowing down as more people left the city to escape for the weekend.

"Come on, you didn't know what I was going to say," Wren protested.

Kate slid the tray home, and then put her hands on her hips. "Was it something about shoes?"

"Maybe," Wren mumbled, swirling a piece of ribbon from her apron around a finger. "I wasn't going to talk *clothes*; I wanted to talk about *accessories*."

"Same difference," Kate replied, and then stopped and gave Wren a hug, "but points for trying."

"It was worth a shot. Better luck next time, huh?" Wren admitted.

"Something like that." Kate laughed, and carried the empty tray into the kitchen.

Emily approached Wren where she stood at the counter and leaned toward her. "You know full well that Kate could show up wearing sackcloth and he'd still think she's gorgeous."

"Yeah, I know. But I was trying to get her to think of her image a bit more." Wren nodded as she watched Kate go.

"Image isn't what he's interested in either, even though Kate's wrapped up in a pretty package. He likes her for what she is, pure and simple," Emily reasoned.

"It must be nice," Wren said in a quiet voice, "to have someone like that." Her gaze flickered toward her feet, and then she looked at Emily, who was startled to see her looking so vulnerable.

"He'll find you, Wren," Emily replied.

Wren shrugged and put on a brave face. "Well, he's taking his time. He doesn't write, doesn't call …"

❦

The afternoon wound its way to a close, and Kate had just switched off the coffee machine as she glanced over at the woman working beside her.

"How're you doing there, Emily? Nearly done?"

Emily looked up as she shut the dishwasher drawer and slung a dishcloth over her shoulder. "Just about, boss," she began, laughing when she saw the look on Kate's face. "I can't help it—blame Wren!"

"I don't know what I'm going to do with you two," Kate said, shaking her head.

"It just kinda trips off the tongue," Emily explained. "But anyway, I'm about finished up here. All the dishes have been washed and stacked, we're fine for supplies tomorrow, and I've updated the order sheet." She turned to wave a hand at the inventory order sheet that Kate kept on the refrigerator door. "So it's all good."

"Excellent, then I think it's drink o'clock. I'll get the glasses; you get the booze." She walked to the kitchen doorway and looked at Wren. "Ready for a drink?"

Wren gave a fervent nod.

"Emily, you want to get out that dip platter I made earlier?" Kate asked as she collected some wine glasses out of the cupboard and carried them out into the store.

"Got it," Emily replied, opening the fridge and getting out a large serving plate, then tucked a bottle of wine under her arm to follow Kate.

Kate waited for Emily to set the platter down on the table before swooping on it for a snack. The wine bottle followed, and Kate picked it up, still chewing as she poured everyone a glass.

There was a rat-a-tat at the window, and Kate looked up, waving enthusiastically for Paul to come in as she finished chewing. Wren opened the door and Paul stepped inside, beaming at everyone, sassing Wren and Emily before swooping his little sister up into a big brother bear hug.

The four of them settled down for a drink and enjoyed the process of winding down the working day. Kate sat and watched her brother as he sent the girls into fits of laughter and was pleased to see that Emily was able to hold her own against everyone's exuberant personalities. An idea stirred at the back of her mind and she encouraged it, mulling it over as she sipped quietly at her wine. She wondered what Paul would make of it, and what he could see for the future.

"Morning, Betty," Wren called as she got to the newsstand the next day on her way to work.

"You're a sight for sore eyes." The vendor looked up and beamed, dropping her reading glasses so that they swung off the imitation gold and pearl chain around her neck. "You want your usual?"

"Yup. How you doin', Bets? Still breakin' hearts?" Wren grinned.

"Now, don't you sass me," the old woman said, sliding the latest copy of *InStyle* and a packet of gum toward Wren, who handed over a few bills in exchange.

Wren waited for her change, and then stopped and looked at Betty. She'd been stopping at this newsstand for her magazine fix on the same day every month, and Betty was always there, rain, hail or shine. "Hey, Betty, can I ask you something?"

"Don't see how I can stop you," Betty replied in a placid tone.

Wren rested her elbows on the magazines and leaned in. "What did you want to be when you grew up? Did you have any dreams about what you wanted out of life?"

Betty regarded Wren for a moment, and then gave a dry chuckle. "Oh, the things you young ones come out with. No wonder you're all screwed up."

"Huh?" Wren stood and watched as Betty rolled up a magazine, and then flinched as the older woman swatted her firmly across the head with it. "Fuck, Betty, what was that for?" Wren yelped as she jumped back a pace. The old woman laughed until she was overcome with a coughing fit. All Wren could do was stand and wait for her to recover.

"Oh, God, that was good, the look on your face," Betty wheezed.

Wren waited, her lips twitching as she tried not to laugh at the woman's mirth, even though it had been entirely at her expense.

"You kids can be real dumb shits. Living the dream, chasing your dreams, *bah*," she said in a dismissive tone. "Honey, you're never going to find a damn thing if you think there's always something better ahead."

"Is that what you did?" Wren asked, leaning in again after making sure Betty had put the magazine away.

"Hell, no," Betty went on with a twinkle. "I was going to be an artist, but I figure it's never too late to pass on a bit of wisdom once you get as far down the track as I have."

"An artist, huh? What happened?"

"I met Earl, we got married, and I got knocked up is what happened," Betty said, reaching over to take some bills from another customer.

"Any regrets?"

Betty shrugged. "Can't miss what you've never had, and Earl and I have certainly had some times." She gave the kind of reminiscent smile that Wren could see hinted at a youth that had seen its share of fun. "You just have to make the best of what you've got and grab opportunities when you can."

"Gotcha."

"And then when you get to my age and the kids have moved out, you go enroll yourself in an art class."

"You have?" Wren replied, charmed. "Are you enjoying it?"

"Let's just say I'm enjoying it more these days than I would've in the fifties." Betty leaned forward. "They got *nude* models at the community college these days," she said in a loud whisper.

"Betty," Wren said, laughing, "you're a dirty old woman."

"Hey, I can dream, and some of those men are *fine*. But like I tell Earl, those boys would be wasted on me. It'd take me all night to do what I used to do all night." She flicked a second packet of gum at Wren. "Now go on, you get, and have a good day. I've got a business to run."

"Yes'm," Wren said, leaning over to kiss the old woman's powdery cheek. "You have a good weekend."

"You have a good one too, Wren, and whatever or whoever you're up to, get some for me while you're at it."

Wren walked away laughing, wondering if she'd be as free with her words at Betty's age. She hoped so.

ℇ

"Morning, boss," Wren called, waiting as always.

"Wren, don't call me boss."

"Sorry, boss." Wren gave her an unrepentant grin, popping her gum and standing back as Kate unlocked the security door and rolled it up. "So, tonight's the night, huh?"

"Yeah, thanks, Wren. It's good that you're not trying to make me nervous or anything," Kate said, standing aside to let Wren in.

"No problem."

"I'll do the coffee. You put some music on," Kate instructed as she got out a couple of cups.

"Gotcha."

"And—" Kate pointed an admonishing finger, "—no Barry White."

Wren pouted, but sifted through the discs, and soon the lilting sounds of Lily Allen filled the store. Emily arrived, and the three of them got ready to start the day.

"Got a quote yet, girl?" Kate asked as she leaned against the kitchen doorway.

"As a matter of fact, I do," Wren replied, tossing the stub of chalk from hand to hand. She picked up the chalkboard and wrote, a slight smile on her face, then turned and showed it to Kate and Emily.

I'm not going to follow my dreams;
I'm just going to find out where they're going
and hook up with them later.

"Very zen." Emily nodded.

Kate gave Wren a quizzical look. "I'll say. What happened to Little Miss Plan?"

Wren gave a happy shrug. "Meh, just a thought. We'll see how long it lasts."

Michael jogged around the park, thinking about Kate and seeing words everywhere: carved into stonework around the park, describing statues, sprayed on fences. Amazing that he hadn't noticed them before now. He was going to be seeing her tonight. He picked up his pace, jogging faster as he tried to speed up the day.

He paused at a water fountain to catch his breath and stood stretching his calves, then checked his watch. It was earlier than he'd thought. He sighed and looked around the park. He had a whole day to kill. Maybe he'd jog a bit more. He managed three quarters of another circuit before slowing to a walk, pleased to see that his fitness was improving.

Stopping to grab a newspaper on his way home, he flicked through to the music section as he walked and grinned when he realized he was reading some of David's work. Not for much longer, though, he realized as he thought back to the night before.

An exuberant David had phoned him, crowing with success and demanding celebratory drinks. Michael had been only too happy to toast the future success of David as he re-entered academia as "Associate Professor Watson." The night had wound its way on as the two men laughed and celebrated David's new career. By the time Michael had gotten home, there was a definite stagger in his step, and he had drifted off to sleep thinking of brown eyes.

Now he shook his head with a grin, tucking the newspaper under his arm as he thought about the previous night. He wanted breakfast, and then maybe he'd do some more writing. It looked like it was going to be a nice day. For a moment he was tempted to spend it outdoors, but more words were whispering. He'd do some work first and then see how things went. He enjoyed a hasty breakfast after he showered and changed, and then sat down in front of his computer. He started typing slowly at first, and as the speeding of his typing increased, the outside world began to recede.

Hours later Michael looked at his watch again and shook his head. Two hours to go. He paced the length of the apartment, picking up the occasional book off a shelf and giving it a cursory glance before discarding it. He felt nervous, which he told himself was ridiculous. He and Kate had been getting to know each other for a while now, so there was no reason why this evening should feel any different; except this wasn't just bumping into her or walking her home after work. This was a date and somehow that made it entirely different. Now that he realized how anxious he was feeling, he was glad he hadn't confided in David. He didn't think he could have handled the teasing.

            ❧

"Are you looking forward to it?" Wren asked as Kate slide a tray of cupcakes into the display cabinet. "Of course, you are," she said as Kate shot her a look of amused exasperation. "Have you thought about what you're going to wear?"

"Well …" Kate slid the cabinet door shut and leaned against it. "I figured I'd start with clothes and take it from there."

Wren sighed. "You really don't care what you wear, do you?"

"Of course I do, but the whole evening isn't going to depend on what I'm wearing." Kate snorted.

"I know that," Wren said, "but it can certainly help. Just tell me you'll be wearing good underwear." This was said with a hopeful expression as Wren slid a coffee toward a startled customer with a broad smile.

Kate gave a startled whoop of laughter. "Wren! I'm not putting out on the first date."

"I wasn't saying you had to," Wren replied, "but feeling totally hot inside and out can do wonders for a girl's confidence."

"Duly noted," Kate said, flipping a quick salute before turning as some more customers approached. It looked like it was going to be a busy day.

At last Kate departed the bakery that afternoon under a chorus of catcalls from Wren and Emily. The pair remained unrepentant even after Kate had fired back a volley of empty threats to fire them both. She glanced at her watch and seeing that she had two hours before meeting Michael, decided to spring for a cab. The cab would cost her a few dollars but she knew there was one thing she wanted to do before all else: Sleep.

Letting herself into the apartment, Kate headed for the bedroom, and after a quick bathroom stop, stripped down to her underwear and crawled onto the bed. She set the alarm on her cell phone and curled up under the coverlet for a quick half hour nap. She had no idea how late the evening would be and wanted to be as fresh as possible. Yawning, she closed her eyes and had just enough time to wonder if she would be able to get any sleep before going under.

            ❧

After her nap, Kate had taken her time getting ready. Light makeup, loose hair, and one of Wren's creations. It was a simple halter-neck dress that fell in a graceful empire line with the hem brushing her ankles. Flat sandals completed the look. The last thing she wanted after a day on her feet was a pair of heels, and in her mind's eye, she could all but see Wren sighing and shaking her head. She looked at the time and realized Michael would be there any minute. A thought struck her: maybe he was as nervous as she was. On impulse, she walked toward the front window and peered down toward the street, smiling when she saw Michael pacing. He was there already. She grabbed her purse and headed for the door.

Michael looked up as he heard the front door open, and then Kate appeared. He gazed at her as she made her way down the front steps toward him.

"Hi," she said in a soft voice.

"Hi," he answered. "You're beautiful." Without thinking, he raised a finger to trail it across her suddenly warm face.

"So are you," Kate replied. She hadn't meant to blurt it out like that, but damn it, he *was*. Emily had been right. God *did* love her work.

He stepped closer and reached out, cupping a hand in the small of her back to draw her close as he dusted a kiss against her lips. She swayed against him for a moment as their mouths met again and again. In the quiet moment of sweetness, Michael did what he had wanted to do for a long time and reached up to cradle the nape of her neck, turning her head slightly to kiss her eyelids and then the side of her throat. When he drew away, Kate's eyes stayed closed for a moment, before they fluttered open to regard him with a soft smile.

He slid his hand down her arm to twine his fingers with hers. "Shall we?"

He took her to a small restaurant called Resto on 29th Street, and they were shown to a quiet table for two. Michael seated Kate with old fashioned courtesy, and then ordered a bottle of wine after checking what she liked. Two glasses were poured, and they settled into their evening.

"So this is…" He paused.

"Good, but kinda weird?" Kate completed, making him laugh.

"Something like that," he admitted. "I might have worded it differently."

"Of course." Kate inclined her head. "You're the writer, after all."

"Now and then," he admitted with a smile, touching his wine glass to hers for a quiet toast.

Kate paused to watch his Adam's apple bob as he swallowed, and curled her hand around the stem of her wine glass to curb the sudden impulse to reach out and trail her finger down the column of his throat. He put his glass down, and she realized she had been caught staring, so she sipped at her wine to cover herself. It was good.

Michael watched the play of light over the wine in Kate's glass and against her hair. He wanted to twine the long, dark blond strands around his fingers and pull her face toward his.

They both looked up as the waiter appeared with the menus, and the quiet mood was broken as they chose their meals, then they were left alone again.

Michael reached out and took Kate's hand. "I don't know about you, but maybe if we keep close, we can get through the jitters."

Kate laughed and gave his hand a squeeze, fluttering her fingers over his wrist, feeling his pulse beneath her fingertips. He was right. The warmth of his hand over hers made her feel better already.

"It's going to make it hard when our meals arrive," she commented.

"True, but there's always footsies," he agreed, grinning in delight as she laughed again.

Like almost every other time, they fell into an easy conversation. Their meals arrived and were enjoyed, then the table was cleared, and still they kept talking. Michael soaked it all up, a wellspring of words and worlds between them to explore. Kate encouraged him to talk about his writing career, and although he wasn't ready to reveal everything just yet, he found that he was willing to share details with her that he had rarely shared with anyone else. He wanted to get to know her better. He wanted her to get to know him.

"It must be amazing, creating whole new worlds and taking people on an adventure of your own making," she commented.

"Sometimes," he admitted. "When it's all working, it's an amazing rush. Other times, not so much."

"Do you get pleasure out of the process?" Kate cocked her head and regarded him, running her fingers in small circles over the back of his hand. It was a soothing gesture that relaxed him even more, and the coil of words inside his chest loosened further.

"I'm not sure," he replied after considering it for a moment. "It used to feel like a ..." He tried to find the words. Kate waited, and the words came to him. "It used to be like a compulsion, and it was as if writing was what sustained me for the better part of a decade." Michael frowned to himself, trying to articulate the situation. "I guess," he ventured after a while, "once the writer's block kicked in, I realized that I didn't have much of a life outside of writing."

"No life?" Kate asked. "Surely you must have had something else besides your writing. What about dating? Relationships?"

Michael looked amused. "I've had a few," he allowed. "Although occasionally they complained that my writing was always the third wheel and they didn't like competing."

"Were you writing about them at the time?"

"No, I wasn't, although I'm not sure if that was the factor working for or against me at the time." He glanced down at Kate who was looking thoughtful. "What about you?"

"Me?" She looked startled.

"Yeah, you," he teased. "Come on, 'fess up."

"Uh…" she floundered for a moment, and then recovered. "There isn't really much to tell. When I first opened the bakery I was in a dating wasteland, which suited me just fine. I was channeling so much of my energy into the store that there really wasn't any room in my life for anything else. Or anyone," she added.

"Surely there must have been someone," he pressed. He couldn't imagine a woman like Kate being single, although now that they had met, he was very grateful that she was.

"Okay, so there *was* someone serious," she said in a guarded tone. Michael was beginning to regret asking the question when he saw the flicker of hurt on her face, but she rallied soon enough and continued, "I'd been in a relationship for a couple of years, and we kind of drifted apart." Her mind wandered off into thought for a moment, and then she gave a short laugh. "And by the time we split, we had become friends more than anything else." She sipped her wine, licking her lips as she set the glass back down on the table. "Probably a good thing really, given what happened," she said, and then looked amused at Michael's obvious curiosity. "But that's for another time. Suffice to say that, yes, I've dated since then, but nothing really serious. I guess the bakery has been my main squeeze for a while now."

"Has that situation been by choice?" Michael asked.

"A little," she agreed. "A bit by necessity and mostly by circumstance." She looked at him with a wry smile. "Think about the logistics. All of my time and energy had to go into the store, so I guess I really didn't have much of a life for a while there. I don't know of many guys that would be patient enough to date someone who'd say, *Thanks for dinner. See you next month.*"

"I know I would have," Michael replied, realizing the truth as soon as he spoke.

"Really?" Kate couldn't stop the shy smile of delight.

"I couldn't wait a week, which is why I've been hanging around the store. Walking you home might not be much, but it's a way of spending time with you, so I'll take what I can get."

"Flatterer." She laughed, giving his hands a playful swat.

"You're welcome," he replied, reaching to snare her hand as she began to withdraw, and lacing his fingers with hers.

"It's not easy in this town," Kate went on. "Finding someone, I mean. For all that we're surrounded by people, everyone seems to lead quite solitary lives. It can be hard making the connection."

"I guess," Michael answered. "I suppose it's not really something I've thought about all that much. Other things have kept me busy."

"There's the rub," Kate replied. "Everyone's in a hurry all the time in this town."

A waiter took their plates away and returned with the dessert menu. Michael cast a quick glance at it, and then left it on the table. The menu was full of mouth-watering words like *chocolate* and *cream*, but he found Kate's words to be all the more tempting.

"Is that why you have a store that encourages people to take their time?"

Kate gave him an amused look. "Have you seen the store when it's busy? There's not much leisure going on there."

"Ah, yet you've got a supply of books and magazines for people to read, the walls are covered with art. I've even watched people stand and talk to you about the cupcake names, and Wren entertains people with her quote of the day. You might have started with the cupcakes, but it has become something much more."

So much more, he added silently, watching Kate as she thought it over, realizing that he wanted to kiss her again.

"You know," she said, "I think I understand your writer's block now."

"I'm glad someone does," Michael replied with feeling.

"How were you feeling just before it all happened, before you stopped working?"

Michael gave the matter some thought, aware that Kate was prompting words about a subject he had rarely spoken about to anyone else.

"I guess," he began slowly, "I was feeling tired." He sipped his wine and shrugged. "Burned-out, I suppose. The fun had gone out of it."

Kate leaned forward, resting an elbow on the table, and he instinctively mirrored her position as their heads bent toward each other. "So you found yourself in a position where the occupation that had sustained you for so long felt like a monumental chore?"

"Yes," he said, surprised that she could understand him so well.

"And then you began to resent it?"

"*Yes*," he said with feeling. "It was draining. At first I stopped writing out of spite, I guess, which in retrospect wasn't the smartest thing to do."

Kate gave him a sympathetic smile. "Like you were cutting off your nose to spite your face?"

Michael chuckled at her turn of phrase. "Something like that," he admitted.

"I guess writing would be like being in a relationship of sorts," Kate mused. "You spend your time with it, and it has its ups and downs."

Michael sipped as his wine, watching Kate as she spoke. Their hands were still entwined on the table top, and he ran his thumb over the palm of her hand. It was a curiously intimate moment, and one he was enjoying.

"When you're in love with a story, you have to take your time to follow it and to fall in love again," Kate said. "You need some time. And maybe you need to be in love with a story because you're going to spend years of your life inside without seeing anybody. Working sixteen-hour days and weekends, you need to be in love with every detail. If you don't have that, then how can you write if you don't love what you do?"

Michael raised Kate's hand to his mouth and placed a gentle kiss on the center of her palm, making her breath hitch in her throat as his breath tickled against her skin. "Is that what the bakery is like for you?"

"Sure," Kate replied, trying to focus on what she was saying, rather than the warmth of his hand and the feel of his lips against her skin. "Getting the business up and running was never going to be easy. I can't tell you the number of times I cried myself to sleep from sheer exhaustion, wondering when things were going to get better."

"But you kept at it," he said in a soft voice, dusting a kiss across her fingers.

"It felt like it was all that I *could* do," Kate replied, mesmerized by the way he kept brushing his lips across her hand. She could feel a tingle of heat beginning in her chest, swirling over her clavicle and up into her face, flooding into her lips and cheeks.

Michael turned her hand in his and kissed the inside of her wrist. "You want to go somewhere else?"

Kate looked at him with luminous eyes. "Yes, please."

Chapter 11

Skylines and Dumplings

After settling the check, Michael guided Kate out into the street, and the two began walking.

"Where to next?" Kate looked up at Michael.

"I thought maybe an after dinner drink somewhere different might be nice," he offered. "A friend of mine told me about a bar down on 32nd and said it was good."

"Sounds good," she replied, tucking her arm though his as they walked. "It's not often I get to do stuff like this."

"Like what?" He glanced down at her in surprise. "You mean dating?"

She smiled and nudged him as they walked. "No, I mean … well, that too, I suppose. But what I meant was getting the chance to go exploring for an evening." She blinked up at him. "It's nice." Michael gave her a pleased smile, and Kate realized again how tall he was. She barely came up to his shoulder, and every time he put his arm around her she felt comforted and protected all at once.

"What's that smile for?" Michael's voice roused her from her thoughts, and she glanced up to see him smiling down at her before shifting his gaze back to the sidewalk.

"I'm just having a really nice time." The air was crisp but not too cool, and there were lots of people out enjoying the evening.

"Glad to hear it. I am too," he said.

A few minutes later, they had reached the building Michael had been heading for. Kate shot him a curious glance as he led them inside and pressed the button for the elevator.

"Can you guess yet?" he said with a grin.

"I'm thinking it's a bar, but I don't know which one," Kate answered.

The elevator doors opened with a soft chime, and Michael led them inside. They were the only ones there, and so he took the opportunity to wrap his arms around her and give her a soft kiss.

"Thanks for this evening," he said in a quiet voice.

"Shouldn't I be the one thanking you?" Kate answered, looking up at him. The cupid's bow of her lips curled into a smile before Michael bent his head to claim them with his own. They were still kissing when the elevator stopped and the doors opened, and Michael broke away with reluctance as they stepped into the foyer.

"The M Bar," Kate said, reading the sign on the door. "I never would've thought of doing this."

"Well, I figured it would be a chance for us both to do something different," Michael said as they went inside. "You spend so much of your time at street level, I thought you'd like the chance to look out over the city."

Kate looked around the bar and then up at Michael with a beam of delight. "This is wonderful."

The bar opened up into a rooftop area, with round tables and chairs set up in random order, and one end of the room was covered with twinkling Christmas lights. The overall decoration was minimal, as the real backdrop to the bar was the New York skyline itself, and the eye was drawn straight to the illuminated Empire State Building.

He ducked his head to hers, brushing his lips against her temple. "Would you like a drink?"

"Please," she replied. "Vodka, lime, and soda."

He nodded as he ran his fingers down her arm to take her hand again and began to lead her through the crowd. Finding a space at the bar, the two of them made small talk while they waited, and then Michael noticed a couple of guys nearby giving Kate's bare back some covetous glances. Oblivious to their blatant interest, Kate kept smiling and talking to Michael, who kept her hand in his.

The barman arrived, and Michael placed their drink order with some relief. He'd be glad to get away from the crush at the bar and from the unwanted attention. The drinks were dispensed, and Michael turned with both glasses and indicated an area of the room with an inclination of his head. Kate glanced back at him as she pointed to a bench seat, and he nodded.

Each wall of the bar had long bench seats with red cushions, and they managed to find a space over at the far wall. Michael set their drinks down on the low table in front of the bench and sat, watching as Kate settled herself beside him. Their easy intimacy remained, and Kate rested comfortably against his side as they toasted each other, and then sipped their drinks and gazed at the brilliantly lit cityscape.

"It's so beautiful," Kate said, sighing and tipping her head back to rest it against the padded wall behind her.

Michael tilted his head to rest it against the top of Kate's, breathing in the sweetness of her scent. No matter where they were, she always seemed to smell of sunshine and cupcakes. "Yes, you are," he murmured in reply, smiling when he got a soft chuckle in response. Kate let herself lean more against Michael's side, and felt a surge of pleasure as he automatically lifted his arm to rest it around her shoulders.

Their conversation drifted on. Michael's thumb drew lazy circles on Kate's upper arm, and Kate rested her hand on Michael's knee, her hand soaking up his body heat. As Kate spoke, Michael gave in to the temptation that had been at him all evening, and twined his fingers in her hair, running his fingers through the silken lengths in a languid caress.

Seeing their glasses were empty, Michael glanced over toward the bar. Kate watched the tendons in his throat as he moved his head, and then acting on impulse, reached up to brush a kiss against his jaw. He turned back and gently cupped her chin in his hand so that he could kiss her, taking his time, exploring her warmth with his. When they broke apart, he was surprised to see Kate give him an urchin grin.

"That might have been a bit forward of me, but I couldn't resist," she admitted.

Michael rubbed his nose against hers, giving her another small kiss. "You don't hear me complaining. Maybe you can blame the alcohol?"

Now it was Kate who reached up to slide her fingers around the nape of his neck, licking her lips as she leaned in for more. "I don't think so," she whispered before their lips met. "I know exactly what I'm doing."

Wren had jammed her iPod headphones into her ears and was mouthing the words to a Lily Allen song when she collided straight into someone's chest.

"Sorry," she muttered as she stepped aside to walk around them and was then startled when a hand shot out to grab her arm. She looked up with a quick retort, but the words died on her lips as her eyes rounded in surprise.

"*You?*" she said, blinking as her shock was greeted with a low rumble of laughter. It was Mr. Wonderful.

"Are you okay?"

Wren nodded and stood there in surprise as he kept talking. He asked her questions: about her day, if she'd made any more aprons, wanting to know if anyone else had cracked the secret code. She found herself answering, and as she talked he listened. They fell in step with each other, strolling along the streets of the Village. It wasn't until she saw the lights of Chinatown that she realized he'd been steering them both here all along.

"It's Friday night." He shrugged in answer to her silent question. "I don't know about you, but I'm not much for cooking, and I want dinner." His hands were in his jeans pockets, but he crooked an elbow toward her invitation. "Join me?" After a pause, she slipped her arm through his, and they kept walking.

Half an hour later, Wren glanced around the crowded restaurant, wondering not for the first time what the hell was going on.

"You okay?"

She glanced back in time to see David pop another piece of dumpling into his mouth. He chewed, watching her with a steady gaze as she toyed with her chopsticks.

"I'm fine." She shrugged. "Just surprised is all."

"What? You don't like the food?" David asked in a mild tone, his eyes not leaving hers.

She shook her head and scooped up some steamed crab, chewing it with pleasure. "The food is great. I just don't know what I'm doing here." Wren grimaced. "Sorry, that came out wrong." She scooped up some more crab, watching David as she ate. He was working his way through his dumplings with every sign of enjoyment, glancing around the restaurant, exchanging small talk with the other couple that was sharing their table.

"I'm flattered," David drawled. "But if it makes you feel any better, everyone has to eat and we just happen to be doing it together."

☙

"I see a gap at the bar," Michael said later. "I'm going in."

"Kiss for luck?"

"Absolutely," Michael murmured, dipping his head to hers again before getting up and moving inside to get some fresh drinks. Kate watched him go, admiring the way he wove his way sinuously through the crowd with little effort. She felt more relaxed and happy than she had in a long time.

After another leisurely drink, they left the bar and walked the streets, feeling warm and relaxed from a combination of the alcohol they'd consumed and the intimacy that was growing by the hour between them. Kate stumbled slightly on an uneven piece of pavement, and Michael wrapped his arm around her waist to steady her, his fingers splaying around her, grazing the underside of her breast. She turned as he righted her, so they were standing face to face.

"You okay?" He smiled as she hiccuped.

"Better than," she affirmed. "And getting better and more betterer all the time."

Michael threw his head back and laughed, and Kate laughed as she watched his Adam's apple bob. She'd never seen him laugh like this before, and it was intoxicating.

"More betterer? That's a word?"

"It's a Jack word." Kate grinned.

"Then that's good enough for me," Michael said, his smiling fading as he looked at her smiling up at him. She had so many different smiles. This one turned up at the right slightly, creating a dimple that was provocative and challenging. He dipped his head and kissed it, before trailing kisses to her lips. Kate gave a low hum as she wrapped her arms up around his neck, shivering slightly as Michael's hands ran over her bare back. They drew apart and smiled at each other, before Michael wrapped his arm around her waist once more as they continued on their way.

"Can I say that I want to see you again soon?" Michael asked as they drew closer to Kate's apartment. Their pace had slowed the closer they got, as neither of them were willing to see the evening end.

"Sure," Kate admitted with a smile. "Perhaps it's just as well that we're as bad as each other."

"Or as good, depending on how you look at it."

"This is true. So I guess this is it." Kate turned to face him. "I had a great time."

"The first of many, I hope," Michael said, running his hands up her forearms and resting them on her shoulders as he drew her into his chest.

"I'd like that," she agreed.

This time their kiss was long and sweet, their lips were gentle as they said a silent goodnight before either of them said the words that would bring the evening to a close. When they parted, Kate turned with a reluctant smile toward the door, and Michael waited until she had her keys out before he began to turn away. He had gone a few paces when he heard Kate's voice.

"Michael?"

He turned to see Kate leaning out of the door, her hair blowing in the soft evening breeze, sending more of her scent toward him.

"Yes?"

"I hear tomorrow's going to be a beautiful day, especially in the afternoon."

He couldn't stop the smile that started to spread his face. "Really?"

"It's the word on the street," Kate said in a solemn voice. "Or at least, from here anyway." She cocked her head and smiled. "Spend it with me?"

"I'd love to."

"Great." She grinned. "I'll see you then."

Michael waved at her and turned to go home, this time a bit lighter at heart.

Chapter 12

Honey to the Bee

Michael wrapped an arm over his chest, pulling against it to stretch the muscles, and then repeated it on his other side, going through his routine warm-up stretches. He'd half-walked, half-jogged his way over to the park, and after his warm-up was completed, he set off along the path. As he jogged, he exchanged nods of acknowledgment with other runners whose faces had become familiar. He felt his body begin to grow warmer, and sweat prickled between his shoulder blades. His head felt hot, and he ran an impatient hand through his hair, pushing it off his face, although after a few paces his hair fell forward into his eyes again. He was going to have to get a haircut soon.

Michael ran on, thinking about his writing, thinking about Kate. He increased his pace, willing himself to push through the burn that was beginning in his thighs and chest. He gulped for air, running faster still, his long stride devouring the path before him. He'd completed half a circuit when, to his surprise, David appeared on one of the smaller arterial paths and joined him. The two of them exchanged a quick grin and a fist bump before settling into a matching pace. Neither of them spoke until the circuit was completed and they slowed to a stop near the park entrance, their usual starting point.

"Good weekend?" Michael asked by way of greeting.

"Yep." David nodded. "Yours?"

"Great," Michael replied, grinning as he thought of the time he and Kate had spent together.

"So, how did the date go? Did you guys end up at the M Bar?"

"We did, and thanks for the suggestion," Michael said. "That's a great place. You go there much?"

"Now and then," David replied as he did some quick cool-downs stretches. "It's my go-to place when I want a low-maintenance evening." He raised an eyebrow at Michael. "So, what sort of an evening did you have?"

Michael shrugged and gave a slight smile. "It was good."

David nodded. High praise indeed. Although he was a writer, Michael was inclined to be a man of few words when something was important to him. David suspected that the bakery was going to have more of an impact on his friend than even he was aware of. There was also, he realized, the matter of Wren.

"You got a busy week ahead?" Michael asked as they both headed out of the park at a brisk walk, still cooling down from their jog.

"Patchy, but yeah." David shrugged. "I gave them two weeks' notice, so I just have to finish a few articles and tie up a few loose ends and I'm outta there."

"How were your folks with the news?" Michael asked, stretching his hamstring muscles as they waited for the light to change. It was still early, but the morning traffic was already getting busy. The two men stood in their running gear chatting, as other people in business clothes gathered at the intersection.

"How do you think they were? They're over the moon. It's what they've always figured I'd end up doing anyway," David said with a rueful smile. "Although, points to my mom, she managed to hold off on any *I-told-you-so* comments."

Michael laughed. The light changed and the crowd surged across the street.

"Want to grab lunch later this week?" David asked as they reached the curb on the other side.

"Sure. Give me a call. Usual place?" Michael replied, thinking of the bar David seemed to favor.

"Uh-uh, I'll see you at the bakery," David replied.

"Oh, really?" That stopped Michael in his tracks and he looked at David. "So, the place is getting to you too, huh?"

"Something like that," David conceded. "But it's still early days yet."

❧

"Morning, boss." Wren popped her gum as Kate approached.

"Wren, don't call me boss." Kate smiled, unlocking the security grill and then the door lock, pushing it open with her hip.

"Sorry, boss." Wren shrugged, giving her gum another pop. "So," she continued, taking off her light coat as she followed Kate through the store toward the kitchen, "how was it?"

Kate flicked on the coffee machine and went to the back to dump her bag. She straightened and made a play of looking at her watch. "I'm impressed. You almost waited a whole second before you asked how—" She broke off as Emily appeared in the doorway, breathless.

"I'm here." Her announcement was unnecessary as she hurried in to hang up her bag. "Have I missed anything?"

"Not yet," Kate said in a resigned tone.

Wren muffled a laugh as she and Emily followed Kate out toward the coffee machine. Kate picked up the stainless steel jug and held out a hand in silent request. Emily had anticipated this and had already grabbed the milk for her. Kate accepted it with a smile and began to get the coffee ready. She shot the two women a look as they both stood leaning against the counter, watching her work, waiting for her to talk.

"You're both driving me nuts and you know it. Would I be right in thinking that you're going to stalk me until I tell you about the date?" Kate ventured at last.

"Is that what we're doing?" Wren looked at Emily with an expression of mild surprise.

"We're just standing here, is all," Emily said.

Kate poured the frothed milk into the cups, sketched a quick line into the foam that created a coffee colored leaf, and handed the girls their morning heart-starter.

"Well," Kate said, "if that's the case, maybe we ought to start—"

Wren held up a finger to stop Kate's words. "Uh, boss, now that you mention it, Emily and I *might* be a bit curious about your date, and maybe it would be nice if you told us about it now," she said. "You know, otherwise it could be hard to get things going."

"Hard to concentrate," Emily agreed.

"Right," Wren agreed with a quick sidelong look at her cohort. "It could be hard to get going until you—"

"Fess up and tell us everything," Emily completed.

Kate sipped her coffee and slumped against the counter. "Oh, God," she said in a long suffering tone. "All right, what do you want to know?"

"Just the important details," Wren said as she sipped her coffee. "Like *everything.*"

"Well . . ." Kate sipped her own coffee and thought, unable to stop the smile of satisfaction that was spreading across her face. "It was wonderful." She took another sip and smiled again.

"What was?" Wren was all but vibrating with impatience. "What did you wear? Did he kiss you? Of course he kissed you," Wren answered her own question as Emily laughed. "Where did you go?"

"Calm down," Kate said, flapping her hand at Wren in a shushing gesture. "I'll talk. It's obvious you're going to be useless until I tell you anyway."

"You got that right," Emily said, watching Wren who had hoisted herself up to sit on the counter, crossing her feet at the ankles and swinging them back and forth as she waited for Kate to keep talking.

"Okay, but I'm going to keep this short because we've got work to do," Kate admonished. "First off, I wore that lilac halter-neck dress you made for me, Wren."

"Great choice, the color on you is stunning." Wren nodded.

"Thanks, glad you approve," Kate replied.

"It leaves her back bare—perfect for a bit of hand-on-skin contact—and it makes her tits look fantastic," Wren said on an aside to Emily.

"I—" Kate stopped, nonplussed. She hadn't even considered that when she chose the dress; she just liked the color. Wren waved her free hand in a wind-up gesture for Kate to continue, so she did. "Uh, yeah. Anyway, he took us to dinner at a little place called Resto on 29th, and then afterward we went for drinks at a rooftop bar on 32nd called M Bar."

"And was there kissage?" Emily asked with a knowing smile.

Kate felt her cheeks warm up as she grinned again. "Yes," she said. "There was *much* kissage."

Wren hopped down and finished her coffee in an unladylike swig before throwing her arms around Kate. "Well done, girl," she declared, and then held Kate away at arm's length. "And did he stay the night?"

"Wren." Kate wriggled away with a laugh. "He did *not*."

"Huh," the smaller woman said in a thoughtful tone.

"Really." Kate shot her a glance as she picked up their empty cups and put them in the dishwasher. "Now, have you got a quote for us today?"

"Hmm, tricky," Wren said, putting a finger to her lips in apparent thought.

"When you're ready," Kate said, glancing at Emily who shrugged. No help there, but she knew that Wren, or rather the chalkboard, was going to have something to say about things.

"I've been thinking about this over the weekend, about *you*, I should point out, and can think of nothing better than: *If life is the flower, then love is the honey.*"

Kate laughed at that and watched as Wren picked up her stub of chalk and collected the chalkboard to carry outside. Emily followed Kate as she wandered into the kitchen and stood, hands on her jeans-clad hips, deep in thought.

"Don't tell me she has you stumped," Emily began, but was waved into silence.

After a minute, Kate looked up with a gleam in her eyes. She'd known Wren was going to make some sort of comment about love or sweetness and had been racking her brain all weekend to think of some sort of baked retaliation to the chalked gauntlet. "I think I've got it." She turned toward the industrial ovens and switched them on.

"Can't wait to see the comeback." Emily grinned, and then went back out into the store to start the day. She watched as Wren came back inside looking very pleased with herself. Emily waited until Wren was occupied with slicing the oranges and lemons for the water jugs before launching a quiet attack of her own. "And how was *your* weekend, Missy?"

"Me?" Wren faltered and the knife skittered off the lemon and onto the chopping board with a dull thud. "It was fine," she answered in a noncommittal tone.

Emily didn't push the issue but could tell Wren was a little off—and she was pretty sure she knew why. For now, she'd keep an eye on Wren, who had now turned back to the chopping board and begun slicing. Emily went back to making up the bagels, shooting Wren a glance from time to time. After a few minutes, Wren went to the stereo and put on some 1970s disco. It wasn't long before the two of them were singing along under their breath, swiveling their hips and shuffling around in time to the music, good mood restored. It was impossible to stay in an unsettled mood when disco was on.

Kate poured flour into the mixer and watched the beaters whir it into a creamy batter with the other ingredients, spinning to pick up the vanilla essence, shaking her groove thing in time to the music as she added the sweet spice to the mix. She smiled as she watched the batter smooth out, humming as she got out the trays, thinking about the weekend.

"Is that them?" Wren arched an eyebrow as Kate later appeared from the kitchen with the first tray.

"Sure is," said Kate, feeling smug. "Get your chalk."

"Okay, boss." Wren touched two fingers to her forehead and flicked them out in an odd little salute that Kate had never seen before. "Fire when ready."

Emily put down the storybooks she had been tidying and strolled over, interested to see what Kate had come up with. Kate put the tray into the display cabinet with a flourish and stepped back, hands on hips as the girls surveyed the special for the day, and then looked at her expectantly.

"Today's is *Bee Still My Heart*," she intoned. Emily choked back a laugh as Kate continued, "Bee hive honey cupcakes with honey buttercream frosting, topped with peanut butter crunch."

"Damn," Wren muttered.

"I believe you mean *touché*," Kate said with a twinkle in her eye.

"Do you think there will ever come a day where you don't have a cupcake to match the quote?"

Kate gave her a laugh and a hug. "We'll just have to wait and see."

Wren glanced up at the door as a shadow of movement blocked the morning light, and then she went back to work as the customer walked inside. It wasn't him.

Emily handed over some change to her customer and bid them a good day, then turned to regard Wren. "Hey, girl, are you okay?"

"I'm fine." Wren jerked her head up in surprise as she frothed milk for another coffee order. "Why's that?"

Emily shrugged. "Every time a customer comes in, your head goes up like a sniffer dog. Are you expecting someone?"

"I don't know," Wren admitted. She was silent as she finished getting the coffee order ready and slid the cups across the counter to her customers with a broad smile.

Emily decided to investigate her suspicions further. "I was in Chinatown on Saturday night and I could've sworn that I—" she broke off as she glanced over and saw Wren standing still. "What?"

"What did you see?" Wren said in a quiet voice.

"Uh, well, I saw you with…" Emily flicked a glance toward the kitchen doorway and then leaned over and spoke in a quieter tone. "I saw you with a guy…and you looked…happy."

"Did I?" Wren gave a hesitant smile.

"You did. Actually at first I wasn't sure if it was you because you looked different."

"How?"

Emily thought back. She'd been out getting dinner with company of her own, and her gaze had flickered into the restaurant for only a moment, but it had been enough for a double take and a knowing smile. "I don't know really. Quiet? No, that can't be right. You were talking, but you just looked more…" She paused and searched for the right word as Wren stood waiting. "*Involved* in the conversation."

"Really?" Wren mused. Perhaps Emily had a point. Her dinner with David had certainly been something different.

"Were you guys on a date?"

"No, maybe, I don't know," Wren stumbled. She huffed and glanced up again. "We just got some dinner." She turned back to her task, and then looked up again. "But nothing happened. He saw me home and that was it."

"I believe you," Emily said quietly.

Wren went back to work, and after a while, the frown of concentration eased into a calmer expression as she lost herself in the mindless chore.

It was true. She wasn't expecting David to come into the store today. They hadn't made any plans. Saturday night certainly hadn't been planned, and yet here she was, watching the door like a lovesick teenager.

"So," Emily went on, "that guy I saw you with . . ."

"What about him?" Wren held up an empty cup in silent query to Emily who nodded. She got out a third for Kate and started to make them another coffee.

"He looked an awful lot like Mr. Wonderful," Emily said, pausing in surprise as she saw a slight flush on Wren's cheeks. "Wren, are you blushing?"

"No, it's just warm in here," Wren said, giving Emily a pointed look.

"Right. My mistake." Emily nodded. "But, c'mon, was it him?"

"It might've been," Wren admitted. "We . . . ah . . . bumped into each other, literally, and ended up getting something to eat."

"Really," Emily said, watching Wren froth the milk with an ease that spoke of years of experience. Wren was a little different today, a little more subdued than usual. Even her clothes were a little quieter than usual. Usually she dressed in an eye-watering array of colors and styles that came across as effortlessly stylish. Today, however, she wore jeans and a vintage T-shirt with a scarf knotted at her throat. Fashionable to be sure, but it wasn't her usual cutting edge style. "And did the two of you get up to anything else?"

"Uh, we got ice cream," Wren said, "and we talked."

Emily accepted her coffee from Wren and carried the third cup into the kitchen for Kate before she returned to the front where Wren stood sipping from her cup.

"Okay, so you *talked*," Emily repeated, picking up the thread of the conversation. "And then what?"

"He saw me home," Wren said again and sipped her coffee while Emily processed what she'd said.

"That was it?"

"Yup."

"Huh," Emily said after a while. "Well, this is interesting."

"Tell me about it," Wren agreed.

Some more customers came in, and Emily turned toward them with a smile. "I'll look after these guys. How about you take a break?"

"Okay, thanks." Wren stepped away from the coffee machine and, instead of grabbing one of her beloved glossy magazines that she kept a small stack of in one of the cupboards, she stood in thought for a moment. She fingered the waistband of her jeans, flicking the small locket that hung there so that it swung back and forth while she thought and then, decision made, she went into the kitchen.

Kate was bent over a tray of cupcakes, piping on thick swirls of honey buttercream frosting. She looked up as Wren appeared and flashed a quick smile before getting back to her task.

"Hey, boss, I've been thinking," Wren began.

"Mm-hmm?" Kate hummed as she kept frosting.

"About earlier when we were talking about your date." Kate nodded but said nothing, so Wren continued, "You know when I asked you if Michael had stayed the night and you said no?" She paused for a moment, flicking the locket again. "I was kinda wondering…" Her voice trailed off as she shifted her weight from one foot to the other.

Kate looked up at this and finished the cupcake she was working on with a flourish, then straightened up and put the frosting bag on the counter. "Spit it out," she said. "What do you want to know?"

"Well," Wren paused for a moment, and then rushed on, "isn't that kinda hypocritical?"

"Huh?"

"You know, after Tim," Wren went on. "I mean, he was a date and you slept with him, so what's different about Michael?"

Kate sighed and glanced down at the floor for a moment, toeing her Chucks against the floor tiles as she thought, and then leaned against the counter and folded her arms over her chest in a protective gesture. "I get what you mean, and yeah, you're right," she said at last, "but there was a difference. Tim was … well …" she floundered. "You know the history with Thomas, right?" At Wren's nod, she went on, "With Tim, I wanted, *needed,* to feel that I still had what it takes to feel attractive to a man."

"But you *are,*" Wren said.

Kate sighed, hugging her arms tighter to her chest. "Thanks, Wren. I guess I just wanted to know I could go out with someone that knew what they wanted, knew what they were without taking me along for their journey of discovery," she finished in a quiet voice.

"Is that what it was like with Thomas?"

"Huh?" Kate looked up with eyes that were still gazing into the past. "A bit, I guess. We loved each other, but I just didn't have the right … uh … accessories." Her mouth pulled into a wry smile. "He tells me now that he'd always had his suspicions, and he just happened to be with me when he made his decision."

"Everyone loves you, Kate. You know that, right?" Unable to help herself, Wren stepped forward and rubbed her hands on Kate's forearm. "You're a strong, sexy woman."

"Thanks, babe, but there are times when I need to get that feedback from the opposite sex, you know?"

"Ah," Wren replied as realization dawned, "you mean the kind of feedback that's—"

"Horizontal," Kate supplied. "Yes."

"Right. So Tim was a booty call for your self-esteem, and Michael's for your heart?"

"Maybe," Kate allowed. "I think so."

Wren gave her a hug. "Good luck then, boss."

"Wren, don't call me boss," Kate replied automatically. She stood there for a moment, and then her arms crept up around Wren's shoulders as she returned the hug.

❧

"Dammit," Wren groused as she stacked the magazines onto the bookshelf again. "Hey, boss," she called. "When did Bear say he was going to put up those magazine racks?"

"Next weekend," Kate answered, slicing a bagel in hand and putting it onto a plate for a waiting customer, which she handed over with a smile.

"What's happening?" Emily returned with some cups and plates that she began to stack into the dishwasher.

"Paul's going to do some chores here next weekend when we have our first two-day weekend. Speaking of which..." Kate looked up at Wren, who held up a handful of flyers.

"They're on every table," Wren confirmed in response to Kate's silent question.

"That's my girl," Kate said with a grateful smile.

"I know," Wren sighed. "I'm just that good."

"The guy that gets you will be a lucky man," Emily said, giving Wren a sly wink, which the smaller woman endeavored to ignore. Wren muttered about tidying the front of the store and made her escape.

"Speaking of lucky men," Emily murmured, nodding her head toward the door when Kate looked at her in confusion. Emily watched as Kate looked over to the store front, and her face lit up at the tall man who entered, an answering smile on his lips.

Kate dropped the dishcloth she'd been holding and walked out from behind the coffee machine, pausing with her hand on the end of the counter, feeling oddly shy as Michael started toward her.

"Hey," Kate said with a smile as Michael approached. "I wasn't sure if I'd be seeing you."

"I wasn't sure either, but my feet just kind of steered me here." Michael grinned.

For a moment the two of them hesitated with just the right amount of awkwardness, and then closed the gap between them. Kate smiled as Michael slid his hand around her waist to pull her toward him as he dipped his head to give her a quick kiss. He was pulling away when Kate caught his wrist with her hand.

"Is that all I get?" she said, feeling bold. She saw Michael's teeth flash as he grinned before lowering his mouth to hers again.

He'd smiled when he had seen the chalkboard quote outside. Kate had told him that the board was Wren's domain, and then had told him about the friendly rivalry the two of them had between the quotes and the cupcakes. He was already curious to see what Kate had come up with in response.

"How's your day going so far?" Kate asked.

"Good, getting better all the time," he replied. "But I shouldn't be keeping you from your work." He felt an irrational surge of pride as her face fell. She wanted him to stay. He wanted to stay too, but he looked at the oversized clock hanging on the wall behind the counter. "It's nearly lunchtime, so I'm guessing you guys will be getting pretty busy."

"Probably," Kate agreed.

"More than likely," Wren quipped as she strolled past with a coffee order. "But if you two want to play sucky face some more, then that's fine too." She laughed at the indignant blush on Kate's face.

Michael reached up to cup the nape of her neck with one hand as he rubbed his thumb across her pink cheeks. "What are you blushing about?" he whispered.

"That she was right," Kate replied, smiling as he gave a low chuckle, and then brushed his lips against hers.

"Listen, I'll leave you to it for a while," Michael said, breaking away at last. "I've got some errands to run, but I'll see you here this afternoon."

"Really?" Kate smiled, delighted that he wanted to spend more time with her.

"I'd like to walk my girl home if that's okay," Michael replied, and then stopped, his eyes widening a little as he realized what he'd said.

They stared at each other for a moment.

"Your girl, huh?" Kate said at last.

"Something like that," Michael agreed. "Assuming that you agree, of course. If it helps your decision any, you've always been my girl in my head."

"Really," Kate commented.

"Yup," Michael said, venturing a slight grin.

"Sounds like you've put a bit of thought into this situation, Michael."

"It does, doesn't it," he agreed.

"Seems a shame to waste all that mental effort. Guess I'd better go along with it and see how we go."

"You're a woman with a discerning mind," Michael said giving her another kiss. "Yet another reason I'm crazy for you."

"Another reason, huh? So how many are you up to?"

Michael scrunched his forehead in apparent concentration. "Last count I think it was up to seven."

"Seven?" Kate gave his arm a light punch. "Only seven?"

Michael laughed, dodging away. "Well, if you work a bit harder, then you could—" He broke off as he saw the display cabinet. He read the cupcake sign and turned to her with a look of mock lust. "I think I'm up to number eight now."

"Yeah, right." Kate reached for the dishcloth she'd left on the counter and started twirling it in preparation to snap it at him. "You can tell your story walkin'."

"I'm going," Michael said, side-stepping Kate to lean in to give her another kiss. "But I'll see you later this afternoon." With that, he waved to the other two women and left the store.

Kate turned back to the counter with a snort of amusement, slinging the dishcloth over one shoulder. She stopped short when she saw Wren and Emily regarding her with twin expressions of interest. "What?"

"Nothing. Did we say anything?" Wren said.

"I didn't say anything," Emily replied, and then got back to work on her bagels.

"Right, just as it should be," Kate retorted, feeling her cheeks warming up again as she walked toward the kitchen.

"Just one little thing, though," Wren commented, popping her head around the door.

Kate looked up from washing her hands. "Go on," she said warily.

"So you're more at ease with him than I've seen you with any other guy," Wren started, pausing as Kate shook the excess water off her hands and reached for a hand towel. Kate didn't refute what she had said, so Wren continued, "So if you guys are like that and you haven't even slept together yet then ..."

"Then what?"

"Then I don't know, really. One minute you guys look like the cutest couple on the planet, the next you're treating him like a friend."

"Huh?" Kate was confused.

"Hey." Wren held her hands up. "I'm just sayin' those are some confusing signals you're putting out there."

"Is that what I'm doing?" Kate began to wrap a strand of hair around her finger, pulling it as she thought.

"Maybe, maybe not," Wren said. "But it's safe to say that Sir Galahad is pretty taken with you. How do you feel about it all?"

"Good," Kate conceded. "Really good." She thought about it some more and elaborated. "Scared, terrified." She gave Wren an uncertain smile. "You know what that's like, right?"

"I could give you a master class on the subject," Wren scoffed, and then gave her a stern look. "The trick is deciding what you're going to do about it."

❧

Michael let himself into his apartment and broke into a light jog toward the kitchen counter as his phone started to ring. He grabbed the phone and tossed his keys onto the counter, rolling his eyes as they skidded across the granite top and fell onto the floor with a metallic clatter.

"Forrester," he said.

"It's Alistair," the voice said. Michael walked around the counter and bent over to pick up his keys, spinning the key ring on his forefinger as Alistair spoke. "Got any news for me today?"

"Hard to say," he hedged. "What is it that you're wanting to know?"

"Have you written more?" Alistair shifted a little on his seat, anxious for the answer.

"Surprisingly, yes," Michael replied, a smile forming as he thought back to the visit he'd just had with Kate—and their conversation.

Alistair felt his shoulders relax as he released a level of tension he hadn't be aware he'd been carrying over the weekend. He had to report on the progress of the authors within his portfolio this morning, and he had paced the corridors of the office, biding his time until it seemed a respectable hour to call the shining star on his list. "Anything more you can send through to me?" he asked, and when Michael paused, hastened in to fill the silence. "When you're ready, of course."

"Of course," Michael repeated, amusement clear in his tone. "Not that you're wanting to rush me or anything."

Alistair gave an internal sigh of relief. Michael was relaxed enough to make a slight joke, so things were still going well. Granted the man wasn't one of his more high maintenance writers, but he had a talent that made the publishing market hungry, and the appetite for Michael Forrester was growing.

"Sorry, but you know how it is," he admitted.

"Yeah, Alistair, I think I do. I've done another few thousand words since the last time we spoke, but can you give me another couple of days? There's a bit I want to finish before you have a look."

"Sure," Alistair agreed. "I'll be looking forward to it."

Michael hung up and set the handset back in its cradle before strolling over to his desk and switching on the laptop. He'd work for a couple of hours, and then go see Kate. As it powered up, he headed toward the bathroom for a shower, making a deal with himself as he began to peel off his sweaty clothes. He'd clean up and then do some work.

Hours later he gave his laptop a light shove as he got up and pushed his chair out from the desk. He'd made enough of a start for today, and it was look-ing good. Getting up, he walked the length of the room, stopping to look out one of the tall windows, watching the people and traffic below. He glanced at his watch. It was already early afternoon, although he'd known that from the sunlight streaming through the windows.

Shoving his hands into his jeans pockets, he stood and stared down at the hardwood floor, lost in thought. His writing was going well, and if he was going to be honest, it was one of the more pleasurable writing experiences he'd had of late. He ran his hand through his hair, and then with a grimace, headed toward the phone to make a long overdue call.

He'd left it until the last minute as usual, but luck was on his side. A short cab ride later, Michael took a seat in the salon and waited, picking up an outdated magazine and discarding it almost straight away when he saw a copy of *The New York Chronicle:* David's newspaper, at least for the time being anyway. He picked it up and rifled through the pages until he found the music and review section. Scanning the pages, he stopped when he saw the familiar by-line and began to read, smiling here and there at David's witty turn of phrase.

He envied his friend's light touch with words, the way his deadlines came and went on a daily basis, the way David could write something and have it go to print that day without spending slavish hours over it all. His name was called, and he looked up and gave a nod, then stood and set the newspaper aside.

ℰ⌇

"Hey, boss," Wren said. "Tall and handsome heading your way."

Kate looked up with a smile, and her mouth dropped in an "oh" of surprise. "Wow," she said at last, "you look different."

Michael's striking auburn hair was nearly all gone. The scruffy curls he had run his hands through impatiently of late had been cut short. It may have been carefully styled when he left the barber, but the combination of wind and his own nervous habit had ruffled it up considerably. It stuck up in spikes and clumps that looked chaotic and endearing all at once.

"Oh, yeah." He gave a self-conscious laugh. "It's been a while since I've had a haircut and I was getting scruffy, so I thought I'd better get myself looking decent."

"Fuck," Wren muttered. "If that was him looking scruffy, how good does he look when he makes an effort?"

"I hear ya, sister," Emily said in a fervent undertone.

"I'm back ahead of schedule, but I've managed to leave my phone at home, so I wanted to drop by and see if I could walk you home tonight."

"I think I'd like that," Kate replied, folding her arms on the counter and leaning over toward him. "In fact, I know I would." She watched him smile, and wondered again how Wren thought she was giving out mixed signals.

"That's good to know. So it's a date then." He grinned.

"Sounds like. I'll see you at closing time." She smiled.

He turned to go, and then hesitated and turned back. His gaze dropped to her lips, and then he looked at her with a shy smile. "One for the road?"

Kate gave him a lazy grin. "C'mere," she invited. Michael walked up to the counter and, bracing his hands on it, lifted himself up so that he could lean over and kiss her. When they parted seconds later, Kate could already feel the warmth beginning low in her belly. Michael gave her a heart-stopping smile and left the store. Kate watched him go, thinking that it was going to be a long afternoon.

Chapter 13

Argon and Shiraz

"*I* think she's seen the light," Wren commented to Emily.

"How so?" Emily was stacking plates on one of the shelves behind the counter. It was approaching closing time, and they were going through the usual late afternoon ritual.

"You saw her at lunchtime with Michael?"

"Yeah, what of it?"

"I called her out on her behavior," Wren replied. "All that flirtation-and-retreat thing she's got going on." She snapped the lid closed on a container and put it back into the refrigerator.

"Which would be different *how*, exactly, from what you do yourself?" Emily said, shooting a look at Wren who looked up in surprise.

"Me? What are you talking about?"

"I see you, Wren. You're the original femme fatale when you think you've got the upper hand, but Mr. Wonderful has put you on the defensive and you've got no idea what the hell you're going to do about it." Emily slid the last plate onto the pile and turned to face the smaller woman, leaning against the counter with one hand on her hip.

Wren stared back at Emily, momentarily speechless, which told Emily that she had hit her mark.

"You sound pretty sure of yourself," Wren managed at last.

"Hey, you're not the only one keeping an eye on what's going on." Emily shrugged. "I just can't help but notice that you're happy to call Kate out on her behavior, but I'm the one that you've confided in about your date."

"It wasn't a date." Wren was quick to object. "And anyway, you're the one that spotted us; Kate didn't."

"Whatever," Emily said. "But you're confiding in different people about different things and stepping in when you think it's needed. When are you going to let people look out for you for a change?"

"Huh?" Wren was confused.

"Honey." Emily moved closer and slung an arm around her friend's shoulders to take the sting out of her words. "You're always pushing us into the spotlight, but staying behind the scenes as much as you can for yourself. When do you think you'll decide to step out and have a go yourself?"

"I don't push everyone," Wren replied, but the denial sounded weak even to her ears.

"Don't think I didn't miss that my bookstore guy just happened to have one of our specials when I saw him last Friday. What was that mystery errand you popped out for that afternoon?"

Wren stayed silent, but a slight upward curl of her lips admitted her guilt.

"You know we love you, but sooner or later you're going to have to take a chance."

"Take a chance on what?" Wren asked.

"On yourself," Emily said, tweaking Wren's nose before turning back to the final tasks of the day.

Wren watched her for a moment, and then slowly went back to work, mulling over Emily's words.

Kate had finished counting the day's takings and bundled bills that she added to the zip-up bag. Bending over, she flicked the combination on the concealed safe and added the bag, before closing the door and turning the lock again. She opened the cupboard and pulled out her bag and then gathered up the paperwork that she would need to work on that evening. It was time to complete her monthly order for ingredients, and she found it quicker to do it online at home rather than fuss about with the paperwork too much in the store. Besides, the task always seemed that much more bearable when it was accompanied by a nice glass of wine.

She headed out into the front of the store to see Wren and Emily were nearly done. The floor had been swept, the tables wiped down, and now they were just finishing stacking the freshly washed cups and plates.

"You guys nearly ready to go?" she asked as she set the order book on the counter.

"You sound pretty eager," Emily teased. "Could it be because you're expecting a certain someone?"

Kate groaned. She was going to have to accept the teasing as one of the perils of dating in front of an attentive audience. "Is it that obvious?"

"We're just happy for you," Emily clarified. "Besides, it's really exciting, isn't it?"

Kate cocked her head. "Is something going on with you as well?"

"There might be," Emily conceded with a modest nod. "Bookstore guy and I are going to a movie later this week."

"You didn't tell me that," Wren accused.

"Didn't I?" Emily gave her a wide-eyed look. "Gosh, I guess it must've slipped my mind."

"Yeah, right," Wren groused and then brightened. "So who asked who on the date?"

"He did," Emily answered. "But try not to congratulate yourself too much."

"Am I missing something?" Kate asked, giving the two of them a curious look.

"Nope, we're going to head off in a few, though, and leave the coast clear for you-know-who," Wren said.

"Uh-huh," Kate replied, giving them a curious look as the two women exchanged a conspiratorial grin and quickly finished their jobs before getting their bags. She waved them off and had just gotten back to her paperwork when she heard the girls exchanging greetings with Michael outside the store. True to his word, he'd arrived to walk her home.

"I won't be long," she said as he approached. "I've just got to finish up a couple of things and then we can go."

"No rush," he said easily.

Her eyes crinkled in a smile before she bent back to her task, working her way quickly through the list, her pen flicking across the check boxes as she scribbled quantities. Michael folded his arms and leaned over the counter, watching her in silence as she worked, noting the line of concentration that appeared between her brows.

Looking up, she hesitated and then reached over with a smile to brush her fingers over the tips of the shortened spikes of hair on his head. "This is going to take some getting used to," she commented.

"You don't like?" Michael asked.

"It's great. I just haven't seen you with short hair before is all," she answered. She turned her attention back to her paperwork. She registered Michael shifting away from the counter, but wanted to get her last task done before she could relax for the night. A moment later, she felt the warmth of him as he stood behind her, resting his chin on her shoulder.

A shiver of delight rippled through her as he spoke, his breath sending warm puffs of air against her cheek.

"Do you think you could get used to it?" he asked, nuzzling against her neck.

"I'll try," she answered. She had intended to sound teasing, but the feel of him against her had the words coming out as a croak.

Michael began to kiss the side of her neck, something he'd wanted to do all day. "How about now?"

"Getting there," Kate replied, closing her eyes and swallowing hard before looking at the paperwork again as she tried to focus.

"How's the paperwork going?" Michael said, peering over her shoulder at the sheet of paper, and then kissing her cheek.

"I'd, uh …" Kate stopped and cleared her throat. "I'd say it's coming on nicely." She felt his smile against her skin.

"You're talking about the paperwork, right?"

"I thought I was." She laughed. "But I could be mistaken."

Michael wrapped his arms around her waist, offering nothing more than support while she finished. Kate blinked at the page, realizing that she had been staring sightlessly at it, and then gave up. She folded up the pages and stuffed them into her bag. As long as Michael was providing that level of distraction, there was no way she was going to be able to think straight.

The two of them had fallen into an easy physical intimacy that was growing by the day. The more time she spent with him, the more she wanted him, and the suggestion of hardness behind her before he shifted his hips away told her that he felt the same.

She gathered up her bag and turned in Michael's arms to face him. "Shall we?"

"I was thinking we could stop in at a wine bar or something on the way home for an after work drink," he suggested.

"That sounds great," Kate agreed. Michael was wearing a plaid button down shirt over a gray T-shirt, and she could see a few chest hairs poking over the neckline. Unable to resist, she kissed base of his throat. Michael kissed the top of her head in response, running his hands up her arms and onto her shoulders so that he could steer her toward the door.

Once outside, he waited for her to lock up, and then took her by the hand as they started to walk. They had barely gone a few paces before he shook her hand free and wrapped his arm around her waist. "You were too far away." He grinned. "I like being able to hold onto you."

Kate laughed as she put her arm around him too, hooking her thumb into one of the belt loops on his jeans as they kept walking. "So where are we off to this time?"

"How does the 8th Street wine cellar sound to you?"

Kate considered it and nodded. "I've been there a few times but not for a while. It's a nice place."

The last time she'd gone there had been for a few drinks with Wren, and she had woken up with Thomas in bed beside her the following morning. The memory of that made her realize she'd not heard from Thomas for a while now, and she smiled, thinking that his date had obviously gone well for him to have dropped off the radar recently.

"I figured we could always end up having dinner there as well," Michael suggested, and then watched as Kate tugged at her coat as she thought.

"Okay," she said, "but I probably shouldn't have too late a night because I've got some paperwork to process at home."

Michael slowed their pace as he glanced at her. "I'm sorry. I didn't think to ask if you had something else on. I'm making assumptions here."

"No, it's fine, really," Kate reassured him. "It's something that doesn't take too long." Kate paused and gave it some thought. "Actually, I can probably hold off on it for a day or two."

"If you're sure," Michael said in a cautious tone. He hadn't stopped to think about any commitments she might have had. The luxury of determining his own working hours and his eagerness to see her had clouded his judgment.

"Sure, I'm sure. We had a busy day, so a glass of wine will be a great way to decompress," she said, and then added, "Of course, the company doesn't hurt either."

"You've read my mind," Michael answered as he hugged her closer.

"Speaking of reading, how's the writing going?" Kate looked up at him expectantly.

"Not bad," Michael admitted. "Better than I expected, as a matter of fact."

"Is that your own humble opinion?" Kate teased.

"Actually, it's my editor who's the one getting excited this time around." Michael thought for a moment and then went on. "I never know what to make of my writing until someone else has had a look at it."

"It's a very introspective thing to do," Kate agreed. "Don't you get lonely sometimes?"

They crossed the street and kept walking, Michael steering them out of the way of oncoming pedestrians now and then, keeping Kate firmly tucked against his side. Her thumb was still hooked on his belt loop, and he felt her hand tap against his hip as she made a point when she spoke.

"A little," he admitted. "But it became a habit. I got used to my own company so it became a way of life." He gave a dry laugh. "Then, of course, the writer's block kicked in, and Alistair got a lot of mileage out of calling me his reclusive author."

"Alistair?"

"My editor," Michael explained. "I'd withdrawn a lot over the last few months. I stopped doing a lot of things because I was just so caught up in what wasn't happening."

Michael glanced down at the ground for a moment as they walked, and then shoved his free hand in his pocket, hunching his shoulders forward a little as he clutched Kate tighter. Kate was quiet; judging by his self-protective behavior and body language she could tell that the conversation had hit a nerve.

"That can't have been much fun," she ventured after a few more paces, surprised when Michael gave a dry chuckle.

"No, it wasn't much fun at all." He huffed out a sigh at the thought of how his life had been a few short weeks ago. "I stopped going out, stopped seeing my friends, just holed myself up at home and got bitter." Michael pulled a face. He wasn't proud of his self-indulgent behavior at all. "Alistair had taken to phoning me practically every day to ask how things were going."

"Surely he must've known that would just make things worse."

"He did, but he admitted the other day that he was also hoping it would make me so pissed I'd write something—anything—as long as I started work again."

"Well, he's either very brave or incredibly stupid."

Michael gave her a droll look. "What makes you say that?"

"I don't think I'd like to see you in a bad mood: the whole tortured artist routine." Kate gave a dramatic shudder.

"I'm not that bad," he protested in a mild tone, and then gave it some more thought. "Actually, I'm not sure. Other than getting pissed at Alistair, I don't think much has ever made me that angry."

"You're too even-tempered?"

"Nope, I just wasn't getting out and seeing many people," Michael replied.

"So what changed?" Kate watched him as he spoke, the way his eyebrows drew together in a slight frown when he was choosing his words carefully, how his eyes crinkled with humor.

"Well, here's the thing," Michael replied, "I had to escape Alistair one day, so I went out for a walk and didn't pay any attention to where I was going. Then I looked up and realized that I'd ended up at a café."

"Really? There are a few of those around," Kate said, playing along.

"Yeah, there are," Michael agreed, "but there's something different about this one. They make great cupcakes, plus the chick that runs it is totally hot." He gave a mock growl and tried to nip at her throat, grabbing her as she laughed and tried to dodge away.

"So then what happened?" Kate said when they had stopped tussling and resumed their walk.

"I guess there was something so disarming about the bakery that it gave me an overdue wake-up call. I suddenly realized I had to get my head out of my ass and get back to work."

"Really?" Kate gave him a pleased smile. "Who would've thought a cupcake could do that?"

"That and the chalkboard," Michael added. "I wasn't sure if I wanted to go in or not, but the quote outside gave me a laugh and," he paused as he waved his arm, "here we are." He came to a dead stop, which made Kate stumble forward a pace.

"You meant that literally." Kate laughed as she straightened up and looked at the doorway. "I love the feel of this place," she commented as Michael took her by the hand and led her down the stairs. "It's like a basement for grown-ups."

Michael grinned at her over his shoulder. "I like the way you see things. You've got a great filter on life."

They paused at the bar to get a table. Michael put his hand on the small of her back to guide her through the bar toward a small table in a corner, and then held out her chair for her to sit down. Kate set down her bag and shrugged out of her denim jacket. She was wearing a simple leaf-green T-shirt with a v-neck that gathered between her breasts. She wore no jewelry save for a simple pair of hammered silver disks that swung at her ears.

"May I?" Michael asked, leaning forward and gesturing toward the earrings.

"Sure." Kate leaned forward obligingly, and Michael captured one between his fingers to look at the intricate pattern of irises that had been engraved onto the disks. He released it and ran his fingers down the side of her neck, smiling as she shivered. "Was that just an excuse for you to cop a feel?"

"A bit," he admitted. "Did it work?"

"Like a charm," she replied.

"Thanks, I'll have to remember that," he replied, watching as she gave him a quick wink and then scanned the menu that sat on the table. After a moment, she reached up behind her to loosen her hair from its customary ponytail and shook it loose. Michael watched as the dark blond strands flowed around and over her shoulders, and the way her arms and breasts moved as she quickly ran her fingers through her hair to smooth it. He looked up and saw that she was watching him with a slight smile.

"So, was that an excuse for you to make me watch you?"

"Maybe," she conceded. "Did it work?"

"Like a charm," he replied. He shifted his weight and scooted his chair closer to hers and then reached out to drape his arm around her shoulders. "Now, how about that drink?"

☙

Kate took another sip of her wine and leaned back in her chair, smiling as Michael ran his hand up and down her arm absently as they spoke. Without realizing it, the two of them seemed to be in physical contact all the time in one form or another: lightly touching the other's arm to make a point, leaning against each other, and frequently stopping to exchange a gentle kiss.

"So tell me, Michael," Kate ventured at last, "what is it that you're writing?"

Michael had been about to take a sip of his wine, and now he stilled. He held his glass suspended for a moment, and then took a deliberate sip before carefully sitting the glass back down on its coaster.

"I don't normally make a habit of talking about it while it's still a work in progress."

"I can understand that," Kate said in what she hoped was an encouraging tone. "But can you give me a hint?"

"It's about …" Michael licked his lips, he could taste the Shiraz he had just sipped, "… relationships, interconnectivity, the gulf stream …" He paused and sipped his wine again. "And argon."

"Argon?" Kate cocked her head toward him. "It sounds like something from Jason and the Argonauts."

Michael laughed. He always felt uncomfortable and exposed when he talked about his writing before the finished product had been released, but Kate had a way of coaxing words out of him. He gave her shoulders a squeeze, and she shifted closer to rest her warm hand on his thigh as he continued to speak.

"If I were being practical, I could tell you it's a substance used in fluorescent lighting."

"And if you were being a writer?" Kate prompted.

"Then I could tell you that every breath we take into our bodies contains maybe one percent of an element called argon. It doesn't react with anything, and our bodies can't break it down, so we breathe it in, and then breathe it back out."

"And then what happens?" Kate shifted a little in her seat, sipping at her wine, watching Michael's face. He was frowning a little, thinking before he spoke in low, measured tones. Kate leaned forward, keen not to miss a word.

"To the argon?" Michael shrugged. "Nothing. It keeps circulating around the world, everyone breathing it in and out, over and over."

"It just keeps going forever?"

"Mm-hmm," Michael said, setting down his glass. "Each breath we take contains, I don't know, maybe millions of argon atoms." He reached up and gently traced the tip of his finger along Kate's lower lip. "We could be breathing the same atoms that were inhaled by Leonardo da Vinci while he painted the Mona Lisa, or by Christ and his Disciples at the Last Supper, or even the dinosaurs." He brushed his lips against hers in a soft kiss.

"And it's all interconnected," Kate replied, gazing at Michael.

"Mm-hmm." He nuzzled at her temple as he kept speaking. "The debates of philosophers, the battle cries of Waterloo, sighs of ancient lovers, and now…" He brushed a kiss against her cheek. "…the two of us."

Kate sat there for a moment, absorbing his words, and then her eyes fluttered closed as he kissed her again. Her hand floated up to rest against his cheek to keep Michael's lips against hers as they gently explored each other's mouths.

Michael broke away and rested his cheek against hers for a moment, his eyes closed as he breathed in her scent, the familiar bouquet of cake and sunshine. He imagined the argon swirling from his body into hers, wondering if the element had somehow led him to her. He wondered if it had led him to the wellspring of words that his life had suddenly become.

&

Wren put her magazine down and reached for her glass, glancing over at the door of the Club Room, and then did a double take.

"I don't believe it," she muttered to herself, sipping her wine and watching as David made his way toward the bar. "Out of all the bars in this town, he walks into mine."

She hadn't been in the mood to go straight home after work and so, after a quick detour, had found a bar that looked good and gotten herself comfortable at a table with her glossy magazine and a glass of wine. Wren leaned back in her seat, enjoying the opportunity to watch him as he ordered his drink and exchanged a few words and a laugh with the barman. He looked a bit tired today but still moved with the easy self-assurance that she always noticed about him. Wren watched as he accepted his drink, stuffed his change into his hip pocket and turned to survey the room with his back against the bar.

David's face went blank with surprise as he saw Wren sitting at a small table against the wall, and she raised her glass to him in a silent toast across the room. Smiling, he picked up his glass and made his way toward her.

"May I?" he asked, indicating the empty chair, pulling it out and taking a seat when she nodded. "So, you've had that kinda day too, huh?" He nodded at her glass.

"It wasn't so bad." Wren shrugged, sipping at her wine. "I just couldn't decide what I wanted to do tonight, so I figured I'd come have a drink first." She set her glass down and waved a hand toward the drink David was still holding. "You too?"

"Something like that," he agreed. "Busy day at work, and I wasn't quite ready to go home and be a couch potato."

The two of them looked at each other and then both sighed at the same time, which made them laugh.

"I guess if neither of us feels like doing much, we might as well do it together," David ventured and caught the eye of a waiter to wave him over. "Join me for dinner?"

"Sure," Wren said, surprised at her easy acceptance. Once again, her evening had taken an unexpected turn, and it involved David. "They've got a decent tapas menu unless you want to go through to the dining room."

David got a copy of the menu and scanned it briefly, then looked up at her with an inquiring smile. He had left the office with no clear plans for the evening other than having a drink on his way home, but now things were looking up.

"That sounds good, let's make ourselves comfortable."

❧

"So how's your wine?" Michael asked, watching Kate as she sipped at her glass. They'd had a couple of drinks now and had ordered some small dishes to snack on.

"Nice. Want a taste?" She held out her glass.

"Don't mind if I do." Michael leaned over and kissed her again. Kate's mouth opened like a flower beneath his as she leaned into him. He had rested his hand on her thigh and now slid it up over her waist to pull her against him. When he broke off the kiss, Kate drew in a shaking breath and licked her lips. "Penny for your thoughts?" he prompted.

Kate looked at Michael, feeling the familiar warmth begin as it spiraled down low into her abdomen, and then lower still where it began to stoke the embers. Michael's touch on her arm added fuel to the fire.

"I'm thinking that maybe I don't want you to go home tonight," Kate said, before sliding her hand around the nape of his neck and pulling his face back to hers. This time when they broke apart, Kate was smiling. "How is it that we always end up necking like a pair of teenagers?"

"I have no idea," Michael murmured as he kissed just under her earlobe. "But you won't hear me complaining." He hooked a finger in the neckline of her T-shirt and tugged at it so that he could drop a kiss on her collarbone. Looking up, he saw a warm flush begin at Kate's throat and sweep up into her face.

"Just so you know," Kate declared as she trailed a finger across Michael's stubble, "I don't make a habit of this."

"Nor do I," Michael said, watching Kate's face as she smiled at his answer. Her eyes were heavy as she gazed at him, and he could see the effects her arousal was having on her. Her lips were full and pink, matching the high color in her cheeks, and her breathing was shallow. He could smell the sweetness of the wine on her breath, knowing it was interlaced with the eternal argon that was swirling into his own body as he inhaled.

They were distracted from each other when their food arrived: a platter of olives, dips, and crusty bread to be torn apart and eaten with their fingers.

Kate chewed slowly, enjoying the saltiness of the olives, then tore off a piece of bread to dip in some olive oil. It had been a busy day, and she ate with relish. A warm dribble of olive oil ran down her thumb, and as she licked it off she looked across at Michael. He had been about to sip his wine, but instead he sat watching her, his eyes dark as he watched her tongue flicker over her skin.

⸎

It wasn't long before Kate invited him back to her place, an offer he accepted with alacrity.

"Make yourself at home," Kate called over her shoulder as she dropped her bag by the door and headed for the kitchen.

Michael paused in the living room, gazing at the profusion of color and warmth in the room. It reminded him of the bakery. Artwork, prints, and post-cards jostled for space, making the walls glow with color. He smiled as he saw the bookshelves and made his way toward them, curious to see what sort of reader Kate was. Running his fingers over the book spines, he saw that she seemed to be as eclectic in her reading tastes as she was with everything else. Tudor history, science fiction, autobiographies, the whole range was there. His eyes flickered quickly over the shelves, and he noted that he didn't see any of his books there. He wasn't sure if he felt relieved or disappointed, and he turned when he heard Kate's footsteps approach.

"I should've known that you'd home in on the books." Kate smiled as she walked toward him, a bottle of wine in one hand and two glasses in the other.

"Force of habit." Michael smiled. "You've certainly got a good collection going here."

"But none of yours," Kate added. "I'll have to change that. I think I'd like to see what you've come up with in the past." She cocked her head as she looked at him. "Come to think of it, I haven't looked up any of your books yet."

"No rush," Michael replied, taking the glasses from her and dropping a kiss on the tip of her nose. "You'll probably find something on Google."

"Hell, I can probably find myself on Google." Kate laughed.

While Michael poured the wine, Kate kicked off her shoes and socks, sinking down onto the sofa beside him and stretched out her legs, crossing them at the ankles. She leaned forward and fumbled for the iPod dock remote, and soon one of her "chill" playlists was filtering through the apartment. Michael passed her a glass of wine, and she accepted it with a smile of thanks, chinking her glass against his before taking a sip.

Michael rested his arm around Kate's shoulder, and she snuggled in against him, rubbing one of her feet up her calf as she gave a mild stretch of contentment.

"What's that?" Michael gestured with his hand that held his glass of wine toward Kate's feet.

"What's what?" Kate didn't understand what he was looking at and moved her feet to look at the coffee table.

"Not the table. You." Michael laughed, putting his class of wine down so that he could grasp Kate's calf, pulling her leg across his lap. Curious, he traced his forefinger across the flowing script that ran around her inner ankle.

"There's one on the other ankle too, see?" Kate lifted her other leg slightly to show him.

Enchanted, Michael maneuvered Kate so that she sat perpendicular to him, her thighs across his lap so that he could look at both ankles. It took him a moment to realize that the words he was reading weren't in English.

"Latin?" he guessed and got a nod of acknowledgment. He mouthed the words to himself and then turned to her, curious to find out more. "I can't even guess. You'll have to tell me."

Kate leaned forward. "This one," she said, tracing her finger across her left ankle, "says 'Receive Joy,' and the other says 'Give Joy.'" She leaned her shoulder against the couch, her breasts pressing against Michael's arm as he rubbed his hand up and down her thigh, his other hand gently cupping an ankle.

"There's a story behind them," he said in a quiet voice, gently tracing a finger over the inked pattern, staring at the contrast of the ink against her pale skin, the way the letters flowed in a fluid wave as she flexed her foot.

"It's something I read about when I was in college," Kate began. "The Egyptians believed that when you reached the afterlife, your heart was weighed by the god Horus and you were asked two questions: did you find joy in your life, and did you bring joy to the lives of others." She glanced down at the tattoos and gave a small smile. "I figured that was as good a template for a happy life as any."

Michael nodded, his gaze not moving from Kate's face as she spoke. "And the Latin?"

"I was a Literature major, so Latin made a kind of sense." She smiled and wrinkled her nose at Michael. "And anyway, it's like having a special secret, and I can choose who I let in on it."

Michael reached over to pull her up and onto his lap and wrapped his arms around her waist as she dipped her head to kiss him. His arms tightened around her as she hesitantly touched the tip of her tongue to his lips, and he opened his mouth to draw her in. Within moments the kiss became urgent, more heated. Kate began squirming and then to Michael's shock she wriggled out of his arms and off his lap completely.

"I'm sorry," he said, lifting a hand out of reflex to run it through hair he realized was no longer there. "Have I done something wrong?"

"Quite the opposite," Kate murmured and rose up on her knees so that she could throw a leg over his hips to straddle him where he sat on the sofa. She draped her arms around his shoulders, her fingers curling against the nape of his neck, and Michael closed his eyes as she lowered her mouth toward his. Michael's hands floated up from her hips to clutch convulsively at the hem of her T-shirt, and he bunched the soft fabric in his hands before breaking off the kiss to gaze at her. Kate leaned her weight back, creating a delightful friction that had him biting his lip as she looked at him.

"What is it?" she whispered.

Michael dropped his head to rest his forehead against her throat, breathing in her familiar scent.

"I want …" He stopped and licked his lips, trying to gather his thoughts. "I want to touch you, so very much." He looked into her eyes. "Can I have you?"

"Only if I can have you." Kate smiled.

It was, Michael reflected later, the smile outside the bar that had sealed his fate. The way she had bitten her lip in an instant of vulnerability before she had given herself over to the evening ahead. Trailing kisses across Kate's collarbone, he gently pushed her T-shirt up, watching with hooded eyes as she reached down to assist, taking it off and dropping it onto the floor before reaching to remove his. He had leaned forward as she had tugged at his collar, the sight of her disappearing for a moment as the shirt was pulled over his head. And then they were touching and tasting, their hands restless as they explored the topography of each other's bodies.

Kate began to move her hips against his, making him groan into her mouth, and she shivered as he ran his fingertips and down her back, cupping her backside to pull her harder against him.

He reached up to trace the swell of her breast with a finger, following the edge of the lace cups, sliding the strap off her shoulder until she reached behind to unfasten the clasp, clutching his head to her chest.

"Kate," he muttered between kisses, "I need … Can we …" He was stuttering, trying to find the words.

"Yes," she answered, knowing that he was trying to say. She climbed off his lap and pulled him to his feet and took him to her bed.

David finished his drink, set the glass down with a flourish, and gestured at the almost empty glass Wren was nursing. "Can I get you another?"

Wren glanced at her drink and finished off the mouthful that was left. "Sure, why not?"

David excused himself from the table, returning a while later with two more glasses of red wine. He raised his glass to hers in a brief toast as he sat down, and then leaned back in his chair and crossed his legs. The evening had taken an unexpected, but by no means unwelcome, turn.

He looked up as he heard Wren give a quiet snort of amusement, and then followed her gaze to see a couple in a nearby booth indulging in an overt display of affection. David raised an eyebrow at Wren and looked at the couple again, glancing away quickly as the woman's hand disappeared beneath the table. He couldn't see what she had done, but winced in sympathy as the man gave a sudden jerk. Enthusiasm was one thing, but style went a long way as well as far as he was concerned.

"Do you think it's love?" he asked in a dry tone.

"Please," Wren scoffed. "She's practically eating that guy. I'm almost tempted to send her some cutlery so she can make a better job of it."

"Oh, I don't know," David mused as he looked at the enthusiastic couple. "There certainly seems to be a level of fondness there."

"For the next couple of hours at least," Wren agreed. "I don't think that's Hallmark love you're looking at there."

David took a sip of wine and glanced at Wren again. "You don't sound like a believer."

Wren considered this for a moment. "Did you know that the word 'love' has more definitions than any other word in the dictionary? Just one little word, four letters, but it's one of the most difficult things in the world to define. It's like they invented a word for the condition and have been struggling to define it ever since," Wren mused, holding her glass of wine up to admire the way the light shone through the red hue. She was pretty sure she had some silk at home that color.

"Condition? You make it sound like a sickness," David replied in an amused tone.

"Well, it is." Wren paused. "It's viral. One person falls in love, and then it gets transmitted. You can't eat, you can't sleep, and the only thing that can cure you is someone else that's suffering from it as well."

There was a thoughtful silence between the two.

"All that fuss over just four letters," Wren mused.

"True, but it's just four out of twenty-six," David pointed out.

"Interesting," Wren said in a thoughtful tone as she leaned her elbows on the table and propped her chin in her hands. "I hadn't thought of it like that."

"Sure. You're freaking out over four letters, but just think about the Roman alphabet: twenty-six letters supporting our entire culture." David picked up his folded newspaper and gave it an idle glance. "Twenty-six fragile little squiggles that underpin everything we do."

"Who said I was freaking out?" Wren said, frowning a little.

"Hey." David shrugged. "You can get your freak on all you want. At least you're prepared to talk about the subject without getting starry-eyed and grabbing the nearest bridal magazine."

Wren made the mistake of snorting with laughter just as she was about to sip her drink and was sent into a spasm of coughing as the alcohol hit her windpipe. Within seconds she was bent over in her chair coughing and sobbing for air as she tried to clear her throat. By the time she had gotten herself under control, David was helpless with laughter himself. Wren accepted a napkin and a glass of water from a passing waitress with a watery smile, and mopped at her streaming eyes, still giving the occasional cough as she settled back down.

"The last time that happened I was in grade school."

"Oh, God, I'm so sorry," David wheezed. "Are you okay?"

"I think I'll live," Wren replied. "I can't believe that just happened, though." She picked up her glass of water and took several small careful sips. "I suppose I should be used to expecting the unexpected whenever you're around."

A sound woke Michael up, and he blinked into the darkness of the room for a moment, unsure of where he was. The sound came again, and he realized that it had come from Kate, her head tucked against his shoulder. He hadn't understood what she had said, and so he lay there in silence wondering if she was going to repeat herself.

She shifted her head a little, a small frown appearing on her forehead, and he gently reached over to brush a strand of hair off her face. Kate gave a soft sigh and repositioned herself against him in her sleep, her hand creeping up to rest on his chest. It was a small gesture, but to Michael it felt like a significant moment.

He knew he was falling in love with her.

Chapter 14

Afterglow and Google

Kate blinked and opened her eyes to discover Michael dropping a trail of kisses along the valley of her breasts, working his way up toward her throat. Michael's hazel eyes crinkled as he gave her a sleepy smile. "Good morning," he rumbled, before leaning in to nuzzle the side of her neck, nibbling and sucking on her delicate skin. Kate closed her eyes again, putting her arms around him to hold him closer, reveling in the feel of his body on top of hers and turning her head for his kiss.

"Kate," Michael said as he raised himself onto his elbows.

"I know." Kate arched up to kiss his throat. "I want you, too." She twisted in his arms to reach for the bedside table. There were the sounds of a foil packet tearing, breathless fumbling and laughter, and then silence as his mouth was on hers again. He put his hands on her hips to hold her steady as he slid into her, and they held their breath for a long moment delighting in the heat and pressure where their bodies met.

Michael began to move, rocking further inside her as Kate made a soft growling noise and sank her teeth into his neck. Kate hooked her ankles around his hips, wrapping him up in joy as she felt an itch begin to tingle underneath her skin.

Kate's world shrank to nothing but the feel of Michael's body on and in hers. She screwed her eyes shut as she urged him deeper, shivering as she tried to get closer still. The itch was getting stronger now and was maddeningly just out of reach. Michael slid a hand under her shoulder, pulling her toward him.

"Let go," he urged. "I've got you."

Kate could feel the pressure of release growing stronger as it moved through her to follow the path that Michael's hand was taking, down between the two of them.

"Oh." She tried to move away, the feeling was too much, but Michael held onto her and sank his teeth into her shoulder. The shock of it sent the pressure inside her flaring up and out, making her skin want to scream as her muscles contracted around Michael, and he followed her into pleasure with a hoarse groan. Afterward, Michael held onto her so tightly that it almost hurt, but she clung to him anyway.

"I want to spend the day in bed with you," Michael said at last, brushing a kiss against her temple, pushing the sweaty hair off her forehead.

"Sounds good," Kate replied, "but…" She turned to look at the bedside clock and gave him a regretful smile.

"I know," he sighed. For the first time he found himself wishing that he had an office job, somewhere to go that would fill up his day instead of sitting at home and thinking about Kate as the hours ticked on.

Wren popped another piece of gum into her mouth and checked her watch, breaking into a light jog when she saw the time.

David had seen her home again after dinner and, after nothing more than a brief kiss on the cheek, had turned and left. Wren had stood at the top of the stairs, jingling her keys from palm to palm, wondering why he hadn't kissed her properly, and why she wanted him to. The man was infuriatingly hard to categorize, which made it even harder for her to read the game play, if he was even playing a game in the first place. She could not, for the life of her, work out what it was that David wanted, and much to her surprise, she realized she wanted to know very much.

She reached the bakery and noted with satisfaction that she was exactly on time.

Fifteen minutes later, she was still waiting when Emily arrived.

"What's going on?" Emily said as she drew near.

"Not sure." Wren frowned. "But it's not like the boss to be late. I think I'll give her a call." She dug in her bag for her cell phone and had started to dial when Emily tapped her on the arm and pointed. Wren turned to see Kate hurrying down the street toward them, throwing her hands up in the air as she saw them looking at her.

"I know, I'm late," Kate said as she reached the door and began to unlock it. "Sorry, guys."

"No problem, boss," Wren said as she and Emily followed her inside, "so long as you're okay."

"Oh, I'm good," Kate said in a breezy tone, flicking on the coffee machine and dropping her bag in the kitchen. She returned to the front of the store and powered up the stereo system, selecting a Kylie Minogue album to get the day started.

Wren raised her eyebrows as the synthesized pop music began to pulse through the store, and she exchanged a surprised look with Emily. "Someone's in a good mood this morning," she commented.

"Well, she did see Michael again last night," Emily replied as she tied on her apron, brushing it down to smooth out a slight crease. "We'll find out soon enough anyway. Let's get the day started."

Wren followed Emily out into the store and waited as Kate finished making their morning coffees, accepting hers with a smile of thanks.

"So, boss," Wren ventured, "you're looking pretty happy this morning."

"Thanks, Wren," Kate replied. "I'm feeling pretty damn good this morning, so it's nice to see it shows."

Wren took a step closer. "Oh, it shows, all right," she said, flicking Kate's hair aside to examine the pink rash that marked the side of her neck. "So how's Michael this morning?"

Kate clapped a hand to her neck in a bid to cover up the stubble rash and gave Wren a horrified look. "Is it that obvious?"

"Not if you wear your hair down," Wren reassured her.

"I can't do that when I'm baking," Kate remonstrated, ducking down to peer at her distorted reflection in the chrome side of the coffee machine. "Damn," she swore softly.

"Maybe you can just put your hair up while you're in the kitchen and take it down when you're out here," Emily suggested.

"Maybe some concealer," Kate muttered.

"Wait a minute, hang on here." Wren waved a hand. "What's with the big cover up?" She shrugged at Kate. "You got laid. Are you ashamed of it?"

Kate thought back over the morning and couldn't stop the slow smile that spread across her face. "Hell, no."

"Well, then, just put your hair up and be done with it." Wren nodded. "Chances are most of the people that notice the rash will be jealous anyway."

"Good point," Emily noted. "I know I am," she added on a sigh.

Kate hesitated, and then reached for the hair elastic she wore around her wrist, and pulled her hair up into a ponytail. She ran her fingertips over the spot on her neck where Wren had pointed out the stubble rash and could feel the warmth of the irritated skin.

"Don't worry about it," Wren advised. "You'll be so busy soon, you'll forget it's even there. Anyway," she went on, sipping her coffee, "we've got more important business to attend to."

"Right. What's today's quote, Wren?" Emily asked, stirring sugar into her coffee and taking an appreciative sip. "And by the way, I love your shirt."

Wren glanced down at her chest and then looked back at Emily with a grin. "Isn't it great? It's a 1970s men's tuxedo shirt. I had to make a few modifications, but I think it looks pretty damn good."

Kate agreed as they fell to admiring Wren's handiwork. She'd teamed the shirt with jeans and a pair of two-tone brogues, creating a very eclectic look, but one that was entirely Wren. Kate glanced at her own attire with a mild pang. Michael had delayed her considerably this morning, not that she was going to complain. She had managed to wriggle into her jeans and a deep violet shirt before having to make a dash for the door. Michael had insisted on escorting her to work, and they had spent a long time standing at the corner kissing each other goodbye for the day before she literally had to run.

"You know, Wren, one of these days I might just unleash you on my wardrobe," Kate ventured, laughing at the look of amazed delight on Wren's face. "What? Come on, it's not that big a deal."

"Not that big a deal," Wren said to Emily. "You know how long I've been waiting for this? *Years*." She turned back to face Kate and pointed a stern finger. "I won't be forgetting that offer."

"Yes, ma'am," Kate said, laughing. "But before you start giving me an overhaul, how about you give us a quote for the day?"

Wren put her cup down and reached for the chalk, squinting at Kate before breaking into a smug grin and walking over to pick up the chalkboard. She propped it on a table and wrote quickly, then showed it to the girls. Kate rolled her eyes and Emily applauded at the words:

Love is friendship on fire.

"All right, all right, let's get to work," Kate said, waving the girls on as she headed back into the kitchen. She was going to have to think hard to come up with something to match that one.

Emily was making up the bagels for the day and Wren was checking the condiment supplies on the tables when Kate appeared with the first tray of cupcakes.

"Okay, guys, here they are," Kate announced as she slid the tray into the display case.

"All right, boss, what have you come up with today?" Wren wandered up to the counter with her tub of sugar packets and napkins, setting it down as she waited for Kate to reveal the daily special.

Kate flicked her ponytail and gave Wren a smug smile. "I think I'll call these ones *Lemon Afterglow*, lemon meringue cupcakes."

Emily laughed as Wren and Kate exchanged a nod, equally acknowledging each other in the ongoing competition.

Wren gave the golden meringue tips a considering gaze and then arched an eyebrow at Kate. "Afterglow, huh?"

Kate felt her cheeks redden.

"Definitely afterglow," Wren said with satisfaction. "Nice one, boss," she added as she carried the tub out into the kitchen.

"That's a really great shirt she's got on," Emily commented as she watched Wren go.

"She's very talented," Kate replied, reaching over to snag a slice of cold turkey meat for a quick snack.

"So why is she waiting tables?" Emily asked, swatting Kate's hand with the spatula as Kate swiped another slice.

"Beats me. I love her to bits, but those talents of hers are wasted here, I know that much."

"Hmmm." Emily slathered a bagel with cranberry jam and kept working. "I guess as long as she's happy. Life's too short to have an average day at work."

❧

David walked out of the elevator and headed past the reception area toward his cubicle, calling out greetings as he went. It was his last week on the job at the newspaper, and it was a good feeling.

He stopped in at the kitchen long enough to grab himself a coffee, and then settled down at his desk. He was drumming his fingers on the hard wood, waiting for his computer network log-in to finish, when someone leaned over his shoulder to deposit a cupcake in front of him. Twisting in his chair, he looked up to see Karen, one of the Food and Wine editors, grinning at him.

"What's this for?"

"A bakery sent some over this morning chasing a review, but I don't need the carbs so I'm sharing the wealth. Send me an email later letting me know what you think of it."

"Sounds like a fair trade," David replied with a grin.

"You're welcome. You'll be helping me with the article, so just make sure you get back to me this afternoon."

"Will do." David touched two fingers to his forehead and flicked them out in a quick salute, turning back to his computer as Karen headed over to the next desk, cupcake box in hand.

He sipped his coffee and peeled off the cupcake wrapper, taking a healthy bite. He chewed as he scanned his emails for the morning. The cupcake seemed nice enough, but he knew where Karen could get better. He set the cupcake down beside his coffee and started to type. Every so often he took another bite, and each time he did, he thought about Wren. They'd run into each other twice now, and each time they did, he realized that he wanted to see her more. The next time he saw her, he was going to get her number and, as he realized he didn't know it, her last name.

☙

"Hey, Kate," Emily ventured. "What did you say Michael's surname was?"

"Forrester. Why?" Kate answered, looking up from the mixer to see Emily mouthing the name, deep in thought.

"Huh? Oh, Brad and I were talking the other night, and I couldn't remember what you said his surname was. Brad had a few guesses, but I'm not sure if we're talking about the same guy." Emily cocked her head. "Have you looked him up?"

"No, but I haven't had the chance to yet. He told me I'd probably find something if I looked on Google, though," Kate replied. She switched off the mixer and considered her options. "How's stock looking out front?"

Emily stuck her head back into the shop front and had a quick look at the display cabinets. "We'll hold for an hour or so yet."

Kate leaned against the counter, playing with her ponytail while she thought. Decision made, she collected her laptop from her bag and powered it up.

"You're going to look him up now?" Emily said, surprised.

"It's as good a time as any," Kate answered, plugging in the power cord after she'd glanced at the battery status. It only took a couple of minutes for the laptop to be ready, and she clicked on the Google page and typed in her search.

"You guys are quiet. What's going on?" Wren popped her head into the kitchen.

"Kate's looking up Michael on the net," Emily answered, glancing up at Wren briefly and then looking back at the screen.

"Oh, I'll be in on that. Lemme see," Wren said, stepping up to the counter to gaze at the screen.

Kate tapped her fingers on the counter as she waited for the page to load. When it was complete, her eyes widened. The three women stood silent, staring at the search results, which numbered in the tens of thousands: reviews, publishers, distributors, articles, book club groups, fan societies, online book sellers, and media interviews.

"Huh," Wren ventured, reaching over to scroll through some of the search results. "Well, he's an author, all right." She looked at Kate who was still staring at the screen. "And you didn't know he was *this* Michael Forrester?"

"Can't say that I did," Kate replied.

"C'mon," Wren scoffed, "a book hound like you didn't connect the dots? Didn't the name even ring a bell?"

"It did," Kate replied. "Of course it did, but I thought he was someone much older, not…" Kate waved a hand as she searched for the right word.

"A total hottie?" Emily supplied.

"Yeah," Kate admitted with a sheepish grin.

"Didn't he mention anything about this?" Emily asked.

"Not really, but then again, I guess I never really asked," Kate replied. "I asked him what he did, he said he was a writer and that he'd been published, and we left things at that."

"He didn't offer any other information? Not even a clue?" Wren asked, raising an eyebrow. She reached forward and opened a link to Amazon, scrolling through the bibliography of Michael's work that was available. "Holy shit, I think I've read a couple of these."

Emily leaned closer to read over Wren's shoulder, and then reached out to point at the screen. "I've read that one. It was really good." She looked at Kate. "Have you read any?"

"I don't think I have," Kate admitted. "I mean, I've been aware of them but just haven't gotten around to any of them yet."

"What are the odds." Wren sighed. "You've even got a degree in Literature. Guess this means we can't call you a groupie."

"Guess so," Kate admitted with an uncomfortable laugh.

Emily touched her shoulder. "Are you okay?"

"Sure." Kate was still distracted by the screen. Why hadn't he said anything? She suddenly felt as if the information Michael had given her would fit on the head of a pin. It made her feel unsettled.

"You don't look okay," Emily commented. "What's got you freaked out, that he's famous, or that he didn't tell you?"

"I'm not sure," Kate admitted. "Either way I feel pretty weird." Kate stood chewing her thumbnail as she stared at the screen and then shook her head. "Anyway, we've got customers now so we'd better get back to work." She snapped the laptop shut and shoved it back into her bag, moving to the mixer and getting back to work. Wren and Emily exchanged a quick glance before heading out into the shop front to take orders.

When there was a lull in orders, Emily turned to Wren. "Do you think she's going to be okay?"

"Can't tell," Wren muttered, cleaning the milk froth off the steam spigot. "I don't think so. Let's hope the boy turns up soon because I think he's going to have some explaining to do."

Michael pulled on a clean pair of jeans and then went back into the bathroom to grab a towel. He gave his hair a brisk rub, and then hung up the towel again before heading out to the kitchen. Barefoot and shirtless, he stood in front of the refrigerator as he considered his options before grabbing the milk. He uncapped it and gave it a cautious sniff before getting out a box of cereal and a bowl. Padding into the living room with his breakfast, he switched on the TV and settled back on the sofa. He glanced at his watch and sighed; there were hours to kill until he could see Kate again.

Staring at the morning news shows, he finished his cereal and set the bowl aside, yawning and scratching his bare chest. He kicked his legs up onto the sofa and pulled the cushions into a more comfortable position. He didn't feel like doing any writing just yet; he'd watch some TV for a while instead. Five minutes later he got up from the sofa with a growl and switched on his laptop, the words bubbling in his mind. He knew they would pester him until he got them out of his head and onto the screen. He pulled out the chair from his desk and sat down, stared out of the window for a moment, and then took a deep breath and began to write.

Kate slid another tray of cupcakes into the display cabinet, and then headed back into the kitchen. She paused to wash her hands and push her hair off her face before getting out her laptop. The laptop had been put into sleep mode, so she tapped the space bar to wake it up. The search results page was still on the screen, and she clicked on the Amazon page to read Michael's biography. It was a short synopsis, but it gave her a snapshot of his career. Published in his early twenties, Michael had since gone on to be nominated for the National Book Award three times. Kate looked at the books available and swallowed hard. In the last ten years, Michael had written and published nine books, all of which had received positive critical acclaim. She shook her head. She couldn't believe it was the same Michael she knew, and more still, that she hadn't read any of his books.

Scrubbing her face with her hands, Kate sighed. Why hadn't he told her? Had she even asked? She knew they'd discussed his writing, but he seemed to shy away from talking about himself too much. Perhaps he was just a reticent person by nature. Or perhaps there was more to it than that. There was one way to find out.

Her cell phone chimed. A new text message had arrived. Picking up the phone from where it had been resting on the counter, she looked at the screen.

I miss you. Can I see you tonight? xM

Kate looked from the laptop to her phone and gave a wry smile. The timing was impeccable. She hit reply and composed a message.

I miss you too. See you at closing? xK

She hit send and snapped the phone shut, moving back out to the store to get a coffee. Business had been going at a steady pace today, so she could take a break for a while. Wiping her palms on her jeans, she reached for the milk jug, only to have her hand slapped away by Wren.

"Uh-uh, let me. You go take a seat and occupy yourself with lustful thoughts for a while, boss," Wren admonished, flapping her hands to shoo Kate out from behind the counter.

"If you call me boss, does that mean I can call you *Bossy?*"

"I've been called worse." Wren shrugged as she set to work making a coffee.

Emily appeared at Kate's table with a turkey bagel sandwich and one of Wren's glossy fashion magazines. "She means well." Emily winked.

"I know. Can you imagine what things would be like if she used her powers for evil?" Kate replied as she started to flip through the magazine. "I don't know why I look through these things. I'll never wear anything like *that*," Kate commented, pointing at an extravagant couture creation for emphasis.

"Tell me about it," Emily replied, gesturing toward her cargo pants and T-shirt. "I think this—" she patted her apron, "—is the closest to couture I'll ever get."

Wren arrived with the coffee which she set down with all due ceremony. Kate groaned at the artful "K & M" that had been written in the coffee foam.

"I should turn this into a working lunch," Kate commented as she made a move to get up.

"Stop right there. What are you going to do?" Wren said in a commanding tone.

"Uh, well, I need to order some more supplies. The checklist has been done. I just need to submit it online."

"And how long does that take?"

"Five minutes, maybe ten, tops," Kate said in a meek voice.

Wren considered this and then nodded once. "I'll go get your laptop. You're not to go behind the counter until you've finished your lunch."

"Yes, ma'am," Kate replied. Emily smothered a laugh and went back to work.

Wren delivered the laptop and the handful of papers Kate had left on the counter, and Kate set to work. True to her word, the order was submitted minutes later, and Wren approached the table again ready to whisk the computer away. She paused when she saw Kate staring at the Amazon page again.

"You really didn't know," Wren said in a quiet tone, watching as Kate shook her head.

"I had no idea," Kate replied. "He never even so much as hinted."

Wren took a seat at the table, and Kate wordlessly turned the laptop so that Wren could see the screen.

"Well, it figures," Wren said after a while, and then went on as Kate looked at her in puzzlement. "You were never going to end up with some bonehead. The man's obviously talented; you've got a literature degree." She shrugged. "It's a perfect match."

"Maybe." Kate was looking pensive again.

Wren leaned against Kate, nudging her with her shoulder. "So, come on, how was last night?" She watched as a flush of color rose up Kate's neck and filled her cheeks. "That good, huh?"

"Oh, it was more than good," Kate said in a strangled tone.

"So what's the problem?" Wren questioned.

"I don't know," Kate replied. "Maybe there isn't one. It's just ..." She waved a hand in a vague gesture. "I just don't like secrets."

"They're okay if they're *good* secrets," Wren said after a thoughtful pause.

"True, but you know, the last guy I was with that kept a big secret was Tom," Kate said. "And we all know how that turned out."

"Ouch." Wren winced. "Okay, point taken." She reached over and patted Kate's hand. "Just give the guy a chance, can you do that?"

"I'll try," Kate said.

"C'mon, everyone else seems to be singing his praises, so there's nothing wrong with seeing what all the fuss is about."

David paused outside the bakery and read the blackboard with bemusement. Entering the store, he made his way over to the counter. Just as he'd hoped, Wren was working, although for the moment she had her back to the store.

"It looks like you're singing a different tune," he called out.

Wren jumped and turned around at the sound of his voice. "Hey," she greeted him, rubbing her suddenly damp hands on her backside. "What are you doing here?"

"It's good to see you, too," David said with an amused smile.

"Sorry." Wren grimaced. "That came out wrong. It's nice to see you, too," she ventured. "I just wasn't expecting to see you today."

"As opposed to the other times we've bumped into each other?"

"I guess," she acknowledged, shifting her weight from one foot to the other.

David rested his elbows on the counter and leaned toward her. "So, have you changed your mind about love?"

"Huh?" Wren stared at him.

David nodded over his shoulder toward the entrance. "Your quote of the day. It sounds pretty optimistic for someone that was calling love a virus last night."

"The…" Wren's mind went blank as she tried to remember what she'd written, and then her memory caught up with her. "Oh! Right, no, that one was for Kate."

"Ah." David nodded. "She's the boss, right?"

"Right, that's her over there." Wren pointed to where Kate sat hunched over a magazine.

"Gotcha," David replied and after a quick glance at Kate, stepped forward to inspect the cupcake of the day. His eyebrows went up when he saw the cupcake name. "Nice," he approved. "So I take it things are going well?"

"They could be," Wren said after a careful pause. She liked David, but she wasn't about to discuss Kate's love life with Michael's friend.

David looked up from inspecting the display cabinet at Wren's cautious reply. "For what it's worth, Michael's pretty happy these days," he said.

"Mm-hmm," Wren said, tight-lipped on the subject.

David spread his hands in a placatory gesture. "Hey, I'm not here fishing for details. I actually came to talk to you about getting some cakes."

"Okay." Wren nodded.

"And your name and number," David added.

The two of them exchanged a long look.

"Smooth," Wren said at last.

"I thought so," David replied, swallowing his grin as Wren went to get a piece of paper and a pen.

❧

Michael looked at the word count and gave a huff of surprise. Over the last few weeks he'd churned out over a hundred thousand words. That would keep Alistair quiet for a while. He tapped a few more keys, finished off the paragraph he'd been writing, and then closed the document.

He rested his chin in his hands and stared out the window, wondering what Kate was doing. He glanced at his wrist and then realized he didn't have his watch on, or a shirt for that matter. He looked at the top right corner of his MacBook to check the time and gave a start of surprise. It was already mid-afternoon; he'd been writing for over six hours. No wonder he'd managed to produce so much. No wonder he was hungry, he realized, rubbing his bare stomach.

Getting up, he headed toward his bedroom to grab a shirt. He didn't feel like being cooped up for the rest of the day. He'd get outside for a walk and grab something to eat before he saw Kate. He still had a few hours to kill, but for the time being, the words in his head had gone quiet. He'd make the most of it and get some fresh air. He opened his closet and glanced at his button up shirts, but reached for a soft old T-shirt instead and grabbed his sneakers.

Kate watched as the girls finished their chores for the afternoon. Emily was humming to herself, and Wren seemed distracted. Kate held off on asking what was going on, however, as she had enough distractions of her own for the time being. The girls finished up and departed, and they exchanged a chorus of goodbyes before Kate was left alone in the shop. She wandered back into the kitchen and picked up her bag, looking at her laptop again and deciding to leave it in the store for another night. She looked up at a quick tattoo of knocking on the front window and saw Michael. She couldn't help but smile at the grin that split his face. The door was barely open when Michael had her in his arms.

"Missed you," he said, before giving her a kiss that started the itch beneath her skin all over again as he ran his hands up her arms to cup her face. Kate's lips parted as she leaned into his kiss, and he licked the tip of his tongue into her mouth.

The discoveries she had made earlier in the day could wait, because all she wanted to think about was right now. She fisted a hand in the fabric of his T-shirt as she tried to pull him closer and then closer still, putting a hand on his bicep to get better traction.

Michael was the first to break the kiss, resting his forehead against hers. Kate ran her hand up the nape of his neck, but there was no longer any hair for her to twine her fingers in, so she settled for running her nails over his scalp in a lazy caress. "I'll give you forever to stop that," Michael muttered as he pulled Kate's T-shirt up and ran his hands over her bare back, pulling her hips soft against his.

The itch was getting more insistent now, and Kate closed her eyes as she felt his hardness against her, shivering as his warm hand rested on the small of her back. Somehow she mustered enough willpower to open her eyes and take a small step back.

"We should get out of here," she said, taking a step further as Michael took her hands and followed her.

"Where to?" Michael asked, his eyes not leaving her as she led them out of the store.

"How about a drink and then we take it from there," she suggested. She was going to have to tell him about her discovery sooner or later, and a glass of liquid courage might help.

"Deal," Michael replied, releasing her hand so that she could lock up the store. When she straightened up, he draped his arm around her shoulders and they began to walk. "So how was your day?"

"Busy, but not quick enough," Kate admitted as she leaned into Michael's side. "This is much better."

Michael tightened his arm around her and smiled. "You want to go back to the basement again, or shall we try somewhere else?"

"Basement is good," she agreed, putting her arm around his waist as they walked.

It didn't take them long to make their way to the bar, and soon they were settling at a table for two with a bottle of wine being set down before them. The wine was poured, and they made themselves comfortable, moving their chairs closer together.

"So," Michael said again, toasting Kate's glass before taking a sip, "how was your day?"

Kate gave him an amused glance, thinking about the daily routine of running a store which didn't seem to vary that much from one day to the next. "You really wanna know?"

"I really wanna know," Michael said, repeating Kate's words. "You're talking to a guy that has been staring at a blank computer screen these past few months. Tell me news of the outside world," he said, giving the words an extra relish that made Kate smile.

"Well, let me think." Kate sipped her wine, giving herself time to think, then set her glass down and reached over to steeple her fingers against Michael's. "Customers came in and bought stuff," she began.

"Always a good sign," Michael encouraged.

"Wren sassed me," Kate continued, "but that's nothing new."

"Routine can be good," Michael said, slipping his fingers through hers, rubbing his thumb over her hand.

"Mm-hmm," Kate replied, shooting him a cautious look. "And I, ah, looked you up on the internet."

There was a telling pause.

"Uh-huh," Michael said at last. "So, the secret's out then."

"Kinda," Kate agreed. "What with Wren and Emily seeing it too."

"Right," Michael said, releasing her hand to pick up his wine glass, which he gulped at this time. "So, what did you think?"

Kate chose her words with care. "I think I'm impressed," she began, "and surprised."

Michael swirled the wine in his glass peering into the liquid depths, and then looked at Kate.

"I mean," she went on, "I know you'd told me you were published, I just didn't expect to discover you had fan sites or talk about movie options."

Michael grimaced. "Kate, you know that stuff isn't real, right?"

Kate blinked at him. "How can you say that?"

Michael reached up to run his hand through his hair in an entirely unconscious gesture and had to settle for rubbing the back of his neck. "Well, of course, it's real, but you know…" He trailed off, not knowing what to say.

"I don't know." Kate twisted in her seat a little, resting a hand on his thigh, the warmth of his body helping to reassure her. "But maybe you can tell me about it."

Michael sighed and gazed at Kate for a long moment. She said nothing in return, but sat waiting for him to speak.

"My writing…" He stopped and cleared his throat, looking up as a waiter approached the table with menus. "Can you give us a minute?" The waiter nodded and withdrew. "My writing," he began again, "is something that just … happened. It wasn't something I sought out. When my folks got interested, I kind of went along for the ride. Then I got published and it seemed that everyone was getting excited about something I'd only ever done as a hobby or a way to kill the time."

"That's how my cupcakes started." Kate smiled. "And look where it got us, huh?"

"So you do understand," Michael said, feeling a rush of relief.

"I'm not sure I'd go that far," Kate cautioned, "but it seems we both fell upon our current paths."

"For sure," Michael agreed. "For me, it was like everyone started taking my musings far more seriously than I ever had. The next thing I knew, I was meeting with editors, going to book signings, giving interviews." He sighed again and gazed at Kate. "I felt like a fraud. It was like it was all some kind of fantasy, but I was the only one getting the joke. I still feel like that sometimes."

Kate sipped at her wine while she considered what Michael had told her. He sat quiet now, his heart in his mouth as he waited for her reaction.

"So, you know this makes you kinda weird, right?" Kate said at last, wrinkling her nose at him.

"What?"

"What are you, some kind of reclusive author with a cupcake fetish?"

"Something like that," he admitted. "I guess it's something you don't hear Stephen King talking about."

"Definitely not," Kate said in a solemn voice, and then gave a dramatic sigh. "Trust me to always attract the weirdos." Now that they had laid their cards on the table, she was feeling like she had gotten a weight off her chest. It had been easier than she had expected.

Michael leaned forward to nuzzle the side of her neck, making her squirm against him. "I suppose that's what you get for being so attractive."

Sensing the drop in tension, the waiter approached the table. "Are you ready to order?"

Michael looked up with a smile as he reached for the menu while Kate topped off their glasses. "Thanks."

❧

Wren let herself into her apartment and headed straight over to her bed, throwing herself onto it with a sigh of relief. She rolled over onto her back and stared at the ceiling, and then glanced over at her laptop, sitting at the small table in front of the window. She considered her options for a moment before she got up and walked toward the desk.

She switched on the laptop and went to get herself a glass of juice while it powered up. Taking a seat at the desk, she clicked to open her email and sat drumming her fingers while she waited for her messages to download. Minutes later, she was surprised to see an email from an address she didn't recognize.

How about we bump into each again soon? In the meantime, I thought you might be interested in this. David.

She clicked on the attachment and read the contents. She had to give credit where it was due, the man was good: it was an article about an upcoming exhibit at the Fashion Institute of Technology. She read the article and shook her head in quiet amusement while she chugged her juice, her eyes never leaving the screen. An exhibition about fashion and politics: he'd remembered her conversation about Chanel.

He was definitely good, and she was definitely in trouble.

❧

"So how's your writing going?" Kate said as she scooped up some more risotto. "Your words still giving you trouble?"

"Quite the opposite," Michael said, reaching for another slice of bread. "They won't give me much of a break." He paused and chewed with obvious enjoyment before he continued. "When I got back from your place this morning, I went for a run and thought I'd catch up on some sleep." He paused to leer at Kate who coughed into her glass of wine. "But then I got busy brain."

"Busy brain?" Kate looked up from her meal, licking her lips.

Michael shrugged as he kept eating. "The characters kept talking to me, so all I could do was keep writing. I even managed to lose track of time, so I haven't eaten much today." He looked up to see Kate regarding him with a quizzical expression. "What?"

"Your characters talk to you?"

"Uh." Now he felt foolish. "Well, yeah, sometimes." Kate waved her fork for him to continue, so he went on. "I guess, when the story is flowing well, it all unravels in my head visually." He stumbled for a moment, realizing that he was talking about his writing process with Kate more than he ever had with anyone else. "When I'm truly involved with it, it's more like I'm transcribing what's going on, rather than creating it myself."

Kate gazed at him and took another mouthful of risotto while she considered what he'd said. Michael glanced at her and then occupied himself with his meal, feeling foolish at what he'd revealed.

"Well, I guess that means you're a strange man, Michael Forrester," she said at last, and then leaned over to give him a quick kiss. "But I like you anyway."

"That's good to know," Michael said with some relief.

"Oh, I don't know," Kate replied. "I have my moments where Wren is sure I'm not going to appear on the cover of Sanity Fair anytime soon, so perhaps like attracts like."

They finished their meal, the conversation bantering back and forth as they teased information out of each other, each taking a quiet delight as successive details were revealed. Michael discovered Kate had a love of classic literature, which explained why she hadn't read any of his books to date, and Kate discovered Michael had started reading books from his childhood, having been re-introduced to the Berenstain Bears courtesy of the bakery.

The evening wound on, and Kate ended up pink-cheeked and giggling perhaps more than the conversation merited, leaning against Michael more and more. After a while Michael slid his hand under the curve of her knee and hitched her leg over his thigh, pulling her closer to him. Kate leaned in toward him.

"Mr. Forrester, it appears that you have an ulterior motive this evening."

"It would appear so," he agreed. "What do you propose we do about it?" He smiled into her eyes.

"One or two things spring to mind," Kate replied after what she hoped was a thoughtful, rather than a tipsy, pause.

Michael ran his hand along her thigh. "Such as?" he said in a quiet tone. "I'm going to need a demonstration to be able to follow your point, you understand."

"You writer types, always so literal," Kate answered with a shake of her head. She leaned forward and brushed a soft kiss against his mouth, then gently ran the tip of her tongue along his lower lip before he parted them and let her in.

The waiter reappeared and removed the plates with as little noise as possible, carrying them back toward the kitchen with a small smile.

Michael watched the waiter walk away, noting the smirk on the man's face as he approached another server. "They're talking about us," he said.

"Wasn't that the woman who waited on us the other night?" Kate asked after glancing to where Michael was looking. "I guess we are getting a little hot and heavy for public viewing." Michael ran his hand up Kate's side in a bid to pull her closer still. "We're either going to have to behave or leave," Michael whispered. "They look like they're contemplating bringing out a mattress for our use right here on the restaurant floor."

"You want to take this somewhere else?" Kate said in a breathless tone.

"Hell, yeah," Michael replied.

Chapter 15

Serenity and Sleepovers

"Morning, boss."

"Wren, don't call me boss."

"Sorry, boss." Wren popped her gum with satisfaction as she followed Kate into the store.

"Another day, another dollar," Wren sang as she hung her bag up on the hook and closed the cupboard, waving a greeting to Emily who had just arrived.

"Is that today's quote?" Emily asked as she dropped her bag to shrug out of her coat and carefully tie on her apron.

"Uh-uh, I can do much better than that," Wren said as she walked out to the coffee machine where Kate had already started to make their morning coffees. Wren stood a few paces away, hands on hips as she assessed Kate's wardrobe choice for the day. Kate looked up to see Wren watching her.

"Do I meet with your approval?" she asked, pouring some milk into a stainless steel jug and starting to froth it.

"It's a start," Wren commented with a business-like nod. After repeated begging, Kate had given Wren a few pairs of her jeans to be jazzed up, and today she was feeling particularly pleased with her creative vision. Kate's jeans featured a strip of carefully frayed gold ribbon that had been stitched to the leg seams. After Wren waved an imperious hand, Kate obediently gave a slow turn, revealing the gold dragonfly that Wren had silkscreened onto the back upper thigh of one of the legs.

Kate poured the steamed milk into the first coffee, set it on the counter, then reached back to tie her apron. Wren made her twirl again so that she could make sure the dragonfly would still be visible. Emily picked up the coffee cup and took an appreciative sip before cooing over Kate's refreshed wardrobe.

"Wren, do you think you could do the same for me?" she said with a hopeful smile.

"Nope, sorry," Wren said, then continued just as Emily's smile faltered. "I'll do something different for you. No duplications or knock-offs for my girls."

"Really?" Emily's face lit up with excitement.

"Absolutely," Wren replied, reaching for her stub of chalk. "I'm happy to do it for you, Emily. We'll set up a time for me to raid your closet, and then Brad won't know what's hit him. Speaking of which…" She turned to Kate. "What does Michael think of the new style?"

"I don't think he's noticed," Kate commented, pouring the next shot of espresso into the second mug, and nodding her thanks as Emily handed her the milk.

"You're kidding, right?" Wren asked in disbelief.

"C'mon, I'm usually in a T-shirt and something," Kate answered, frothing the milk as she talked.

"Yeah, Wren, it's not like he's David," Emily teased, nudging Wren as she passed.

"Well," Wren spluttered, "yeah, but—"

"I can't see Michael taking me to a fashion exhibition," Kate said, flicking a wink at Emily as she poured the milk over the fresh coffee, and then spooned on the milk froth. "How about you, Emily?"

"Nope, Brad looks like he has a migraine coming on when I want to go see a chick flick," Emily supplied, "although he goes along with it anyway."

"And yet here's Wren dating a guy she admits drives her nuts, but he takes her to see stuff she's interested in all the time," Kate said, raising an eyebrow at Wren.

"Dating?" Wren protested. "Wait a minute, have I ever said we were dating?"

Kate gave Emily an amused look as she handed Wren her mug. "I wouldn't say you've come out and admitted it, but I'd have to say that all signs point to yes."

Wren took her coffee and leaned against the counter.

"C'mon, Wren," Emily chided. "What would *you* call it?"

Wren shrugged. "I don't know. *He* seems to think that we're dating, but I'm not so sure."

"Okay." Kate set down her cup and put a companionable arm around Wren's shoulders. "Let's examine the facts, shall we? How often do you guys see each other?"

Wren mumbled something into her cup as she sipped at her coffee.

Kate cocked her head and raised an eyebrow at Emily, who had started to get the ingredients ready for the sandwiches and bagels to be made for the day. "Sorry, I didn't quite catch that."

Wren sighed. "Once or twice a week."

"Hmm." Kate sipped at her coffee and nodded thoughtfully. "And how about on the weekends?"

"Sometimes," Wren allowed again.

"How often over the last month have you seen him on a Saturday night?" Emily piped up from her place at the counter. She paused at her task as she and Kate waited for Wren to answer.

"I guess," Wren said, the words coming slowly, "we've caught up three Saturdays in the last month."

"Ah," Kate said, raising an eyebrow to Emily, who nodded.

"What?" Wren looked up, and then looked from Kate to Emily and back again. "*What?*"

"Wren, try not to take this too hard, but it sounds like you've got yourself a boyfriend," Kate said.

Wren gaped at her for a moment before picking up the chalkboard with a flourish and reached for the chalk. "If you'll excuse me, *some* of us have work to do."

Kate and Emily watched her go.

"Subtle," Kate commented and then turned to Emily. "So how are things going with you and Bookstore Brad?"

Emily gave a quiet smile of satisfaction. "All good, boss. How about you and writer boy?"

"Great," Kate replied. "He's cooking me dinner tonight, and I'm having my first sleepover."

Emily's eyebrows went up at that. "Finally," she said, slathering some avocado onto a bagel. "I was starting to wonder if you were ever going to spend a night at his place."

"Hey," Kate objected, "I've been to his place before."

"Uh-huh," Emily answered, "but this will be the first time you've stayed the night." She paused and waggled her spatula for emphasis. "This means things are getting serious."

"Right." Kate was amused now, glancing over at Wren who was making her way back inside, tossing her stub of chalk from hand to hand. "Okay, girl, so what is it today?"

Wren reached the counter and leaned over with a broad smile. "Today's is: *Seek serenity, and if you can't find it, seek cupcakes.*" She dropped the piece of chalk into its glass with a plink and dusted her hands with satisfaction as she gave Kate a superior look. "Top *that*, boss."

"Damn." Kate turned and walked slowly into the kitchen. "That's a good one, I'll give you that." She stood in front of the oven, hands on hips, thinking hard, and then pulled out one of her recipe notebooks. Thinking back to Wren's daily quote, a random word association began to flicker through her mind, and then she began to smile as she shut the notebook with a decisive snap. She knew what she was going to make.

❧

"You're cooking?" David asked, shooting Michael a quizzical look.

"Yup," Michael answered.

The two of them had met up for a morning jog and were making their way around the park for a second time. Michael's fitness had been increasing by the day, and he was at last starting to push David's endurance, albeit only slightly so far.

"So what are you going to make?"

"I haven't quite worked that bit out yet," Michael admitted, making David give a huff of laughter. "I'll figure that out when I back home."

"Just so we're clear," David said, "are you actually able to cook?"

"C'mon," Michael protested, "you've eaten my cooking before."

"If you can call it that, dude, but that was years ago. Have you progressed much past bachelor fare?"

"Oh, yeah," he grunted, although he had to admit that David had a point. For a while there, he had subsisted on a small repertoire of tried and true recipes before his mother had taken him in hand and proceeded to give him a thorough kitchen education. The subsequent years of self-sufficiency and an assortment of girlfriends to impress had led to a level of culinary finesse that would have made David very surprised indeed.

"There's a ringing endorsement," David commented, "but you know there's no shame in ordering Chinese."

"Give me a break," Michael protested, cuffing David on the shoulder as they jogged toward the park gates, laughing.

"How's it going with you and Wren?" Michael asked, groaning as he leaned forward over his hips into a cool-down stretch, reaching his hands toward the ground.

"Going good," David allowed, his lips curving into a slight grin.

Michael straightened up from his stretch and looked at David. "It must be good for you to be grinning like that," he commented.

"Huh?" David looked surprised.

Michael waved a hand to indicate David's face. "My mom said I had a goofy grin like that when I was starting to get to know Kate, so it looks like you're not too far behind."

"Right." David gave an amused snort as they went through the rest of their stretches, and then looked uncertainly at Michael a few minutes later. "Is it that obvious?"

"Yup," Michael replied, "but if you want to be absolutely certain, I can take you over to see the folks so that my mom can—"

"No," David cut in hurriedly. "That's fine. God, she'd be straight on the phone to *my* mom."

The two men began to walk out of the park, still talking.

"I don't think she'd be that bad," Michael said in a mild tone.

"Oh, no? She told my folks about you and Kate weeks ago," David replied with a grin.

Michael gave him a surprised look. "Really? But I only just told them her name last week."

"Apparently she was just excited that her boy had met a girl." David patted Michael on the shoulder. "So imagine how happy she'll be when she finds out you're not only still happily dating, but you're cooking your girl a romantic meal."

Michael gave him a hard look. "You wouldn't."

"Why not?" David waggled his eyebrows, enjoying himself immensely.

"Because then I'd tell yout mom about you and Wren," Michael retorted.

They walked on while David considered his options.

"Okay," he conceded with a slight sigh. "You win."

"I thought you'd see it my way," Michael said in a placid voice.

They stopped at the intersection and then crossed when the light changed. The two men were hot and sweaty from their run, and their faces were red with exertion. They still drew a number of appreciative looks from women as they passed by, but neither of them paid the female attention any heed as they kept talking about the women in their lives.

"So this is what it's come to, huh?" David mused. "We're two strong, independent, thirty-something men, but we're still afraid of our moms."

"Guess that means they've done their job right after all," Michael said with a laugh.

"Still hard at work, I see." Wren popped her head around the kitchen doorway, her eyes sparkling. She could almost taste victory this morning. She was sure her serenity quote would have Kate stumped.

"Nearly there," Kate said, flicking her hand at Wren in a shooing gesture. "I'll be out with the first batch in a couple of minutes."

"Did you think of a cupcake to match the quote?" Wren leaned around the door frame a bit more, trying to peer at the box Kate was opening.

"I guess you'll have to wait and see," Kate replied. "Go on back out there. You'll see what I'm up to soon enough."

"How about a hint?" Wren wheedled.

"Nope," Kate said, smiling as she picked up the frosting bag and aimed it at the last cupcake. She'd dip into the box's contents once Wren was out of the way.

"If I do my puppy eyes?"

"Uh-uh, scat," Kate said. "Go on," she said in a warning tone when Wren hesitated. "Don't make me come over there."

"Going now," Wren squeaked and headed back out into the store.

Emily looked up with a laugh as she saw Wren re-appear. "No luck?"

"None," Wren admitted. "But I still think I've got her on the ropes this time." She swiped a slice of tomato off the chopping board and popped it into her mouth before Emily could protest.

"You've said that before," Emily replied, making up another chicken sandwich, "but she gets you every time." She slid the finished sandwich onto a plate and added a small garnish before putting it into the display counter.

Wren watched her work, admiring her deftness of touch. "What did we ever do without you? My sandwiches were never *that* good."

"They always taste better when someone else makes them," Emily replied with a shrug. "I prefer the ones you make." She looked up as a thought occurred to her. "Does Kate ever eat cupcakes?"

"Uh." Wren thought. "Actually now that you mention it, probably not as many as you'd think. She seems to have one every other day, and I know she has a soft spot for frosting."

"Oh, who doesn't?" Emily grinned, and then glanced over Wren's shoulder. "Heads up, moment of truth at four o'clock."

"What?" Wren spun around to see Kate appear with the first tray of cupcakes.

"Here you go," Kate announced as she slid the tray into the display cabinet and then straightened with a flourish as she faced Wren. "You ready?"

"As I'll ever be," Wren replied, having darted around the counter to pick up her chalk.

"*Peace Out*, vanilla cupcake with chocolate frosting topped with *Reese's Pieces*. Get it? Serenity…peace…pieces." Kate gave Wren an expectant look.

Wren scribbled furiously on the mini chalkboard and held it out in front of her for critical inspection with a sigh.

"Well, I'll be damned." She sighed. "You've done it again, boss."

"Only just," Kate said, giving Wren a quick hug. "You really had me on the run this time."

"I still didn't win, though," Wren said, managing a wry grin. Damn. She really thought she had her this morning too. She was just going to have to try harder.

"One day." Kate chucked her under the chin and then headed back to the kitchen. "You'll get me one day."

"Mmph," Wren said, crossing her arms and giving Kate a mock pout. "Well, you know I'll be waiting."

"You know you love it," Kate called over her shoulder.

Michael frowned with indecision at the laptop screen, unsure if he loved or hated what he had written that morning. There were a lot of words on the screen, but their tone had become less assured as he had begun to tire. He re-read the pages and shook his head. It felt like a half-hearted attempt at best. Experience had taught him to remove but not delete, so he cut and pasted the bulk of the day's efforts into a separate document. Perhaps it could be recycled into something more pleasing later. He got up from his seat and stretched, then checked the time. He still hadn't decided what he was going to cook for Kate, and he stood at his desk, staring out the window, and let his mind wander. After a while, he shook himself out of his daze and picked up his wallet and keys, hesitating as he looked at the laptop again. No more words came, so he turned and left with a clear conscience.

Walking through SoHo, Michael glanced at his surroundings and the people around him as he made his way toward his usual grocery store. Strolling past a small gift shop, he pulled up short and then backtracked to the display window, peering in at a small reclining Buddha figurine. It reminded him of Kate and made him smile. Words began to whisper at the back of his mind. He walked on, and the words followed.

A few stops later, Michael had purchased everything he needed, and the words had accumulated to become a dull roar. Shifting the bags handles to a more comfortable grip, he walked on, stopping in at a liquor store to pick up a bottle of wine that he added to his load. Pausing on the sidewalk, he considered his purchases and the trip home, and hailed a cab. Shoving the bags of groceries across the backseat, he got in, and after giving his address, rummaged around for one of the receipts before realizing he didn't have a pen. The words kept coming, but he'd be home soon.

❧

"Is it time to go home yet?" Wren gave the clock a mournful look. "Surely it's home time somewhere."

"Not yet," Emily replied as she finished stacking the morning's baking pans, "but we're getting there."

"Not soon enough," Wren groused. "I'm ready to start my weekend."

"Big plans?"

"No," Wren admitted. "But I'm looking forward to sleeping in and not having anywhere I have to be. How about you, are you going to be seeing Brad?"

"Yup." Emily grinned. "We're going to catch a movie tonight and then find what Brad calls a 'cheap and cheerful' for dinner."

"Sounds good. And after that?" Wren raised an eyebrow meaningfully.

"Ah, well…" Emily hedged. "We'll see how the evening goes. How about you and David? Any sleepovers yet?" She was stacking plates for a moment before she realized there had been no reply. "Wren?" She turned. Wren was wiping down the coffee machine with a look of fierce concentration. "Wren?"

"I'm not saying," Wren replied at last.

"Why not?" Emily was curious now. It wasn't like Wren to keep quiet on the subject, and she was surprised when Wren turned and gave her a hesitant look.

"Because I'm not entirely sure what's going on, but whatever it is, I don't want to jinx it," she said at last. "David's… different."

"And it's making you different too," Emily added.

"Different good or different bad?" Wren asked after an anxious pause.

"There was nothing wrong with you to begin with, and it's nothing bad. You're just… different. Whatever he's doing, babe, he's doing it right."

Wren considered this. "If you thought it was something bad, you'd tell me, right?"

"If you promise never to shoot the messenger," Emily clarified. "I've seen too many friendships go down in flames because friends have said what they thought."

"Pinky swear," Wren replied, offering a hand. The girls shook on the deal with solemn faces and then began to laugh.

"Seriously, though," Emily said as they caught their breath, "David's got you in a good place, so I really hope things work out."

"We'll see." Wren nodded.

"Speaking of good places, Kate and Michael seem to be happy," Emily ventured as they both got back to work.

"For sure," Wren agreed. "She handled the whole 'famous author' thing a lot better than I thought she would."

Emily looked up from wiping down the counter. "What, you thought she'd freak out?"

"Not as such." Wren shrugged. "But she's a person that likes to keep things honest. You know Paul, and you've heard stories about her parents, so you know she's from a family of straight shooters."

"Straight, yeah, so Thomas must've rocked her world a bit," Emily mused.

"It did," Wren agreed. "She told me that she and Thomas had a *lot* of talks about that once she got over the shock. She also saw a therapist for a while too."

"Really?" Emily looked amazed. Kate seemed to be one of the most grounded people she knew.

"I know she comes across as Little Miss Confident, but think about it. She loses her father in a car accident while she's driving, then her first *serious* boyfriend reveals that he's gay. She still has a lot of self-esteem issues at times, but she's working on it."

"Wow." Emily went back to wiping the counter down, slower this time as she processed what Wren had said. "I guess that'd be pretty hard."

"For sure. She lost the man that was the cornerstone of her life in the blink of an eye, and then a year later the guy that she'd totally bared herself to in every sense of the word totally rejects her. It's a lot for a young woman to take."

"She's told you all this?"

"Not in so many words." Wren rinsed out the steel milk jug and began to wipe it dry. "She's said a few things here and there, and Paul has made the odd comment. Thomas was the one that has told me the most, so I've pieced it all together over time."

"Thomas?" Emily looked up in disbelief. "He told you?"

"Granted we were both drunk at the time." Wren shrugged. "But yeah. He told me all about it. He loves Kate dearly, just not in *that* way, which is why he's still around. Even though he's hurt her, he's still very protective."

"Isn't that a double standard?" Emily rinsed out her washcloth and hung it over the sink to dry.

"Might be to some, could be his way of atoning. Either way, he's not going anywhere until Kate tells him to."

"I wonder what he'll make of Michael," Emily mused.

"I think as long as Kate's happy, he'll be okay, but if he hurts her, I wouldn't want a bitch queen like Thomas against me. But speaking of which…" She nodded toward the door, and Emily turned to see Michael walking toward the counter, pushing his sunglasses up onto his head.

"Hey, Wren, Emily." Michael nodded at each of them in turn with a smile. "How's your day been?"

"Busy as usual, but we're winding down for the day now," Emily replied, running an appreciative eye over his jeans and T-shirt. *Brad. Remember Brad.* She gave a quiet sigh; just because she was on a diet didn't mean she couldn't appreciate the buffet. Emily watched, amused, as Wren turned the full force of her charm on Michael and it had no effect.

"Michael, you're looking *good*. Are you here for your girl?" Wren rested her elbows on the counter and leaned forward to give him a leisurely inspection. Her grin broadened as he gave a slight cough to cover his embarrassment.

Emily delighted in the slight tinge of pink that colored Michael's cheeks at the mention of Kate.

"I am," he replied with a smile. "Is she here?"

"She's out running an errand," Wren answered, "but she's due back any minute. You want a coffee while you wait?"

"If it's no trouble," Michael began, reaching for his wallet.

"Sorry, Michael, your money's no good here," Wren said, rebuffing his offer with a smile. "Take a seat and we'll bring it over."

Michael flashed a smile of thanks and strolled toward a table against the wall. Emily smiled too as she realized he had chosen a spot where he could keep an eye on the door while he flicked through a copy of an old *National Geographic* that he had snagged off the bookshelf. Emily cast her gaze around the store, and seeing nothing urgent that needed doing, strolled over and leaned against the counter next to the cash register to chat with Wren while she made Michael's coffee.

"They make a cute pair," Emily commented.

"Sure do, and his style is loosening up too," Wren replied as she waited for the espresso to filter through into the cup.

"Well, yeah, I guess he's looking pretty relaxed," Emily said in a doubtful tone, wondering what she was missing as she looked over at Michael again. He was leaning back in his chair with his legs stretched out and crossed at the ankles as he flicked through the magazine, smiling here and there.

"No, I meant his style," Wren clarified as she reached for a saucer. "Remember how he always used to wear button-down shirts and leather shoes? Look at him now."

Emily hadn't paid much attention to what Michael usually wore, but she had to admit on closer inspection that Wren had a point. Michael was wearing an old pair of jeans and a T-shirt that featured the iconic image of Che Guevara. A pair of gray Converse completed the outfit. Emily smiled when she noticed them, wondering if he knew that they were also Kate's usual footwear of choice.

"How about," Wren began, spooning the milk froth into the cup and placing it on the saucer, "you take this over to Michael, and then we can start cashing out and closing for the day. It's getting on, and I think Kate's going to want to close on time when she gets back. We might as well get a head start on things for her."

"Sounds good. You want to put some more music on?" Emily asked as she picked up the cup and saucer.

"On it," Wren said as she headed over to the stereo and started to flick through the CD case that sat on top of it.

Emily rounded the counter and collected the coffee to take over to Michael. Now that she had a better look at him, which in itself was never a hardship, she saw that Wren had been right. Both the jeans and the T-shirt looked old and soft, and he hadn't shaved for a couple of days, making him look all the more relaxed. He looked like a man taking his ease rather than the distracted and polite man they had initially called Sir Galahad. Kate had told them about his writer's block a few weeks ago, and that he was now writing again.

Emily had told Brad about Michael's identity, and on their next date, he had given her a copy of Michael's last book. It had taken her a week to read it, as she had found herself in the unusual situation of constantly putting it down and walking away from it the closer she got to the finish because she hadn't wanted the story to end. There was no doubt that Michael was a very talented wordsmith. When she had discovered just how famous Michael was in the literary world, she had felt shy around him when he had appeared in the bakery days later. It felt strangely intimidating to know someone who was so obviously talented and highly regarded. It made her feel quite ordinary by comparison. Wren had soon helped her put things into perspective, pointing out that Michael had to make a living just like anyone else. Emily had watched him on subsequent visits and was reassured by his natural reticence and obvious deep affection for Kate.

Wren, on the otherhand, hadn't read any of Michael's books in years, as she gave all of her devotion to *Vogue* and *Harper's Bazaar*. Her apparent lack of interest about Michael's literary achievements meant that she treated him in her usual disarming, harmless, flirting way that he responded to with an endearing mixture of warmth and embarrassment. His lack of ego had him fumbling for words whenever Wren called him out on his striking good looks, which amused and amazed her.

"She should be back soon," Emily said in a gentle tone, setting the cup down and turning the saucer so that the cup handle was pointing the right way for Michael to pick it up. "She's just running a couple of errands."

"Thanks, Emily. I'm in no rush." He nodded his thanks.

She returned to the counter and popped open the cash register drawer to start counting and bundling the bills as Wren began unloading the dishwasher and drying the cups to stack back onto the shelf. Soon the pair of them had fallen into an easy pattern of talking and singing along to the music.

Kate strolled through the Village humming to herself as she walked, enjoying the afternoon sunshine. There had been a lull in the afternoon trade, so she had taken the opportunity to walk the previous day's takings to the bank. Now the day was winding to a close and people's thoughts were moving on from coffee and cupcakes to food, which, Kate thought, was exactly the way it should be.

She was looking forward to dinner with Michael this evening, partly because she was curious to see what sort of a cook he was, but mostly because it meant they had a whole evening and the following day to spend together. She remembered her surprise the first time she had seen Michael's home. It had been one thing to discover he was a successful author, another thing to walk into the luxurious surroundings that his success had afforded him. Even more surprising, however, was Michael's admission that he preferred spending time in her home, rather than his.

"Your place is warmer," he had admitted.

"I won't argue with that; the air conditioner doesn't work very well." She'd laughed, trailing her fingers along one of the bookshelves as she tried to take it all in.

"Your place feels like a home, this is—" he'd waved a hand to indicate the apartment as he tried to explain, "—just space, you know?"

Kate had gazed at him in wonder. "Then who decorated it?" She'd looked at the tasteful floor rugs, the carefully placed lamps and pictures.

Michael had shoved his hands into his pockets, shoulders hunched forward. "Mom helped," he'd admitted. "When I bought the place, she offered to help out because she didn't want it to look too much like a bachelor pad."

"Have you added much over the years?" She'd walked toward him and wrapped her arms around his waist.

"The books," he'd answered, indicating the wall of bookshelves with a quirk of his brow. "Just one or two."

"Just one or two," she'd agreed, and then had looked away.

Michael had reached up to tilt her chin so she was looking at him. "What's going on in that head of yours?"

"Well," she'd begun, "do you like spending time here?"

"I didn't used to," Michael had said, leading her over to a sofa and pulling her down beside him. "But now that you're here, it's different."

"Maybe the trick is to make it an environment that you want to be in," she had suggested before he'd silenced her with a kiss. They had been somewhat distracted after that.

Since that conversation, Michael had been peppering her with questions, wanting details about the bakery and her apartment. He had inspected the fox print and drink coasters hanging in their frames side by side, the large oriental urn at the back of the store containing a mix of umbrellas that had been painted by Wren and were available on a "take one, leave one" basis for customers when it rained. Even the Buddha-hand ornaments that stood on her bookshelf at home had been studied and discussed after dinner. Nothing escaped his notice.

She crossed the street at the light and glanced down the sidewalk to see the red canvas canopy fluttering in the mild breeze. Even after all this time, she sometimes still wanted to hug herself at the thought of owning her own business. It was a never-ending slog, but she liked being independent and being able to do with the store what she wished. Not that ownership or lack thereof had ever stopped Wren from putting her own stamp on things. Between the two of them, they had given the bakery a style that was entirely unique. The charm seemed to beguile the customers as well, as after five years they had acquired a loyal clientele.

As she reached the door, she stood aside to let a couple of customers exit with a smile, and then went inside. Out of habit, she glanced over at the counter first to see Wren and Emily laughing between them as they worked, and then she saw Michael relaxing at a table. When he saw that she had seen him, his smile matched hers as she walked over.

"Hey," she greeted him as she bent down to give him a soft kiss.

"Hey, yourself," he replied, running his hands over her hips and cupping the back of her thighs to pull her closer. Kate leaned against his side, her warm body flush against his, and slid her hand around the back of his neck. "How's my girl?"

"Getting better all the time," she replied, feeling herself relax under his touch as his thumbs rubbed lazy circles over her jeans. She nodded toward the *National Geographic* on the table. "Checking out the boobs?"

"I am now," he said, nuzzling his face into her side and making her laugh.

"I meant in the magazine."

"Ah, my mistake." He gave her a lazy smile. "No boobs there. I've been reading while I was waiting for you, but now that you mention it ..." He pulled her closer and kissed her again, longer this time.

"Hey, you two, break it up," Wren called from the counter.

"Like you can talk," Kate shot back, laughing as Wren ducked out of sight. "I caught her and David together in the kitchen last week, wrapped around each other," she said in response to Michael's curious expression.

"Ah," he said with a grin, "it sounds like the two of them are going well."

"Very, but Wren still can't quite work out what's going on. She's used to bad boys, so David is a bit of a shock to the system." She smiled at the small woman who was working with her back to them now. "He's keeping her on her toes, and I think that's good for the little dynamo."

"David seems happy," Michael observed, thinking of his friend's smile whenever he mentioned Wren.

"So it's all good," Kate replied, trying to ignore the little voice in her head wondering how long it was going to last. "Are you okay to wait while we finish up?"

"Sure. Is there anything I can do to help?" Michael asked, still holding her close.

"It looks like the girls have everything under control," Kate said, "but I'd better pitch in and do my bit, and then we can go." She smiled and walked behind the counter to join in.

Fifteen minutes later, Michael waved off Wren and Emily as Kate tugged the door closed, and then pulled on the roll down security door, which she locked. Kate added her voice to the chorus of farewells before checking the lock again, and then straightened up to take Michael's hand. They set off toward Michael's and had gone half a block before Michael shook off her hand and snaked his arm around her waist.

"Do you want to stop off for a drink on the way back to my place?"

"Not unless you want to," Kate replied. "I'm just looking forward to kicking back on your sofa and taking my shoes off."

"Hmm." Michael kissed the top of her head. "High maintenance, huh?"

"That's me," Kate sighed, which turned into a small yawn. "Sorry."

Michael looked at her in surprise. He was still feeling energized from his afternoon of writing. The words had been bubbling in his head all the way home, and he had been distracted enough to give the cab driver an unexpectedly generous tip as he had snatched up his bags and made his way inside. The cold food items had been quickly stashed in the refrigerator before he had made his way to his desk and pulled up his chair. For a brief moment, he had stared out the window again, before the words had risen up in volume and pulled him back to the page. By the time the words had slowed to a trickle, he had discovered that it was almost time to go and meet Kate. He had snatched up his keys again, cursing that he hadn't allowed himself time to start the dinner prep, and reassured himself with the thought that the evening held no time constraints.

"Are you okay?" he asked, noticing for the first time that she was looking pale.

"I'm fine, just a bit tired," she replied, leaning into him a little more as they walked. "I'm looking forward to dinner, though. What are you cooking?"

"You'll find out soon," he said. "Although to be honest, I haven't started cooking anything yet. I got some ideas while I was out shopping earlier, so I've been working all afternoon." He gave her an apologetic look. "Sorry."

"For what?" she looked up at him in surprise. "You're sorry you were writing? Michael, it's what you do. It's a part of who you are."

❧

"Here you are," David said, sliding into the stool beside Wren where she sat at the bar and giving her a quick kiss. "How was your day?"

"Good." Wren smiled. *Play it cool.* "Better now that my weekend has officially started."

"Well, I think we'd better celebrate that with something nice," David said. "How about I take us somewhere for dinner?"

Wren glanced around the bar. "What's wrong with here?"

"I thought we were celebrating," David said. "We can do better than a bar somewhere."

"It's okay." Wren shrugged. "I don't need special."

"Well, I think you do, and I'm paying so let's go," David said in a quiet but firm tone. He put his hand over hers and gave it a gentle squeeze. "Come on, Wren, let me spoil you a little." Wren opened her mouth to protest. "No strings," he said.

She nodded and sipped at the last of her wine. Setting the glass down, she turned to David.

"Ready?" he asked.

"As I'll ever be," she replied, and slid off the stool. He held the door for her as they exited the bar, and then offered her his arm. "Are you always this much of a gentleman?"

"It's how I was raised, to give women respect," he replied, drawing her hand through the crook of his arm and holding it close.

"Oh, yeah," Wren said, feeling out of her depth. "So the whole act was drilled into you, huh?"

David looked at her in mild surprise. "Not at all. Mom and Dad set the standards and showed me by example." He shrugged.

"It must've been nice," Wren said, not noticing how wistful she sounded, "growing up like that."

"It worked for me." David smiled. "Now, what do you feel like for dinner?"

"What do you feel like?" Wren countered.

"I'm the one spoiling you, remember? If you could eat anything you wanted, what would it be?" David glanced away from their path and looked at Wren, who was deep in thought.

"You know," she said slowly, "I think right now I want a martini, and anything beyond that I'm putting myself in your hands."

David smiled and rubbed her hand as they walked on. "I'll remember that."

❧

Kate gave a groan of contentment as she sank down onto the sofa. "I'd almost forgotten how good it is to sit down."

"I didn't think your day had been that bad," Michael said, reappearing from the kitchen with a bottle of wine and two glasses. Kate shifted her feet enough for him to sit down on the sofa beside her, and he then set out pouring their drinks. "Here's to Saturday night," he said, offering her a glass. Kate accepted it, and they chinked their glasses together in a toast to the weekend.

"Oh, that's so good," Kate said after she had taken a sip, and then leaned back on a cushion.

Michael rubbed her calf with his hand. "How about you relax, and I'll go get dinner started."

"I love it when you talk dirty." Kate yawned. Michael gave a short chuckle and brushed a kiss on her forehead as he got up. Kate reached up to trail her hand down his thigh, letting her arm drop back to her side as he moved away. Setting her glass down on the coffee table, she curled up on her side and pulled the cushion into a comfortable place behind her head. Her position gave her a partial view of the kitchen, and she caught glimpses of Michael as he moved around, selecting pots and starting the oven. She yawned again, her eyes fluttering closed, and then she saw nothing at all.

❧

Wren looked around her in amazement as she draped her napkin across her lap. "I can't believe I haven't seen this place before."

"You like it?" David smiled at her reaction. He'd ushered her into a cab for a trip to the Red Cat Martini Bar. "I know it doesn't look that fancy, but when you said you wanted a martini, this place was the first one I thought of."

"It's all good," Wren murmured, having found the drinks menu. "Oh, my God, you weren't kidding. Martini ahoy."

David laughed and caught the eye of a waiter. "I think we're going to need drinks to start," he said. Wren looked up and smiled at him, her eyes shining.

He was very pleased with his choice.

❧

Michael stood at the foot of the sofa, smiling down at the sleeping Kate. He had a choice: wake her up or let her sleep. He considered the options, and then moved to bend over and kiss her cheek.

"Kate, honey…" he whispered, and reached out to trail a finger across her cheek, smiling as she sighed and shifted a little before blinking her eyes open.

"Did I fall asleep?" she asked, her voice groggy.

"Something like that," he replied, amused at her dazed expression.

"I'm sorry," she said as she struggled into a sitting position. "That was rude."

"Not at all," he assured her, sitting on the coffee table across from her and rubbing her knees. "It's nice that you feel comfortable enough here to relax like that, and besides," he went on, "dinner's ready."

Kate's eyes widened at that. "How long was I asleep?"

"Nearly two hours," Michael said, grinning at her dismay. "Like I said, don't worry about it. If you're still hungry, I can serve it up."

"Oh, I'm hungry," Kate said as she stood up. "Let's eat. What's on the menu?"

"Come see." Michael picked up her wine glass and led her to the marble kitchen counter that he had cleared and set for two. Gesturing for her to take a seat at one of the leather stools, he handed Kate her wine glass and set about serving. Kate sipped at her wine, enjoying the pepper of the Shiraz, and twisted a little in her seat to peer at what Michael was doing.

"Is that…" she paused, not quite believing what she had glimpsed, "…rack of lamb?"

"It is." Michael flashed a grin over his shoulder as he slid the lamb onto a platter. A moment later, he set the plate down on the counter with a flourish. "Rack of lamb, hasselback potatoes, and a green herbed salad."

Kate stared at the platter and then back at Michael. "Where did you grow up, Stepford?"

Michael choked back a laugh as he began to serve. "Thank my mom. She was determined that I wasn't going to end up as another woman's problem, so she made sure I learned how to cook properly." He slid a portion of lamb onto Kate's plate and indicated that she help herself to the vegetables. "Then I had a few years of trial and error cooking for myself."

"And it seems to have worked," Kate said, scooping up some salad. "Your mom sounds wonderful and terrifying all at once. My mom's idea of home cooking was macaroni and cheese made from scratch. Jack ended up doing most of the cooking."

"Is that why you're a good cook yourself?"

"Pretty much. I started helping Jack out when I was old enough, and then Paul and I became self-sufficient early on. It was a big help later when …" Her expression flickered before she shook off the mood and continued, "when we moved here."

The mood in the kitchen dimmed for a moment before Kate shook her head and lifted her glass with a smile. "Here's to a wonderful meal," she said.

Michael picked up his glass and chinked it against hers. "Here's to us," he replied, his eyes never leaving hers as he sipped.

☙

David watched as Wren set her glass down with a sigh. "Good?"

"Oh, so good," Wren said, smiling at David. "My first blueberry martini, and it's wonderful."

David propped his elbow on table and rested his chin in his hand, gazing at Wren as she relaxed further. They had enjoyed their drinks, talking about their week. Wren had told him about some of the customers she'd had, the quotes, and cupcakes, and David had entertained her with student excuses and questions. He watched as Wren's polite reserve that had flickered to life when he had met her after work began to dim, and then fall away to ashes. Her face became animated and her laughter came freely. She had engaged in a spirited debate over the latest Radiohead album, and had worked her way through three martinis in the process.

"We'd better get you something to eat soon, otherwise you're not going to be able to walk out of here," David observed, noting that the hand holding his own drink wasn't too steady either.

"You know," Wren said suddenly, "I'm having a really good time."

David's eyebrows went up at the unexpected statement. "Well, that's good to know."

"I mean really. I'm having a really good time. With you," Wren said, cocking her head. "Why is that?"

"Uh, I'm not too sure what you mean."

"You're a strange one, David Watson," she said, wagging her finger at him. "You're this quiet guy that really gets on my nerves, and yet other times, it's like this." She fished out the blueberries on a toothpick skewer and ate them with relish, narrowing her eyes at him as she chewed. "So what's the deal?"

"No deal." David shrugged.

"Bull."

"No bull." David fixed her with a steady gaze. "I like you."

❧

"You like?" Michael asked, kissing her as he picked up her dinner plate.

"Would licking my plate clean be going too far?" Kate replied as she topped off their wine.

"It'd be one way of complimenting the chef," Michael said as he stacked their plates in the dishwasher drawer and slid it shut, "but I'm sure you'll think of something."

"I can't believe I fell asleep and missed the floor show of you getting that incredible meal ready," Kate commented. "I would've loved to see you in action … uh, you know what I mean." She giggled into her glass when Michael raised an eyebrow.

"Actually, there wasn't that much to see," he said, picking up his glass and leading her back to the sofa. "Once I got it all ready, I did some more writing while you slept."

Kate sat down on the couch, curling her legs up and leaning into Michael's side. "I'm sorry I was such poor company."

"Quite the contrary," Michael said, putting his arm around her shoulders and pulling her closer still so that she ended up half-reclined across his lap.

He had called out a question to her from the kitchen and when he got no answer, had walked into the living room to see her curled up and asleep on the sofa. He had simply stood there for a long moment, watching her sleep, taking in her deep, even breaths and the way her hair spilled across the cushion. He had gone about the dinner preparations as quietly as possible, and then took his seat at his desk and worked for an hour before waking her. He had given the words free rein and now they had subsided for the evening, content.

"So, any other plans for this evening?" Kate asked, shifting more comfortably against him.

"I took the liberty of getting a movie for the evening, in honor of our first accidental date," he replied. "Pass me the remote?"

Kate leaned forward, plucked it off the coffee table, and handed it to him with a questioning look.

"You've probably seen this one, but I'm really hoping you don't mind a re-run."

Kate watched the screen as the opening credits began. "*The Fabulous Destiny of Amélie.*" She turned to Michael with a smile. "It's one of my absolute favorites."

"Are you sure you're okay with this? I can change it," he began, and was waved to silence.

"Don't you dare." Kate curled herself up against him, resting her head on his shoulder. Michael tipped his head to rest against the top of hers, taking a deep breath and inhaling her scent.

"By the way," he asked after a moment, "what perfume do you wear?"

"Mmm?" Kate was distracted in part by the movie, but Michael proved to be a headier distraction: the warmth of his body, the rise and fall of his chest, the way his fingers traced absent-minded patterns against her arm.

"You always smell so beautiful. What is it that you wear?"

"Allure by Chanel," Kate replied. "Although I'm surprised I don't smell like the shop most of the time."

Michael nudged at her neck with his nose,, and she obligingly tilted her head so that he could leave a trail of kisses. She shivered as he inhaled with obvious pleasure.

"You always smell like cake and sunshine to me," he whispered. "It's beautiful, just like you."

"Careful there, mister. Them's kissin' words." Kate smiled.

"Let me know what else I have to say, then," Michael said, nipping at her earlobe and making her jump.

"I'll keep you posted," Kate replied with a drowsy smile.

They went back to watching the movie, entwined in each other's arms. Saturday night ticked on, and neither of them had to go or be anywhere other than with each other. Kate was glad she wasn't going home tonight.

❧

"So I guess I'll see you again soon?" David smiled down at her. They had lingered over dinner and a few more drinks before deciding to call it a night. Having caught a cab, Wren had insisted they get out and walk the final block because she wanted some fresh air, and had giggled up the steps to the front door of her building, aided by an amused David.

"How someone as small as you can drink so much I'll never know," he muttered.

"Years of practice," she quipped.

"You didn't answer my question, though. Can I see you again soon?" David gently trailed a finger through Wren's bangs, getting her hair out of her eyes.

"Sure," Wren said, offering him a dazzling smile that had been amplified by a few martinis.

"Okay, then, I'll call you tomorrow." David kissed her forehead, his lips lingering for a moment, before turning and heading down the steps.

Wren watched him go, twisting her keys in her hand. "Hey, David," Wren called, making him stop and turn around with a smile.

"Yeah?"

"Can I ask you something?" She stood, uncertain at the top of the stairs. David climbed back up the stairs to stand in front of her.

"Sure."

Wren reached up to trace a finger around one of his shirt buttons, staring fixedly at his chest. "How come you haven't made a move on me yet?"

"I thought I had been," David replied. "We're dating after all."

"Yeah, but…" Wren tipped her head to look up at him. "Don't you want more?"

David looked at her and swallowed hard. "Oh, I want," he said, reaching up to cup her shoulders with his hands.

"Then why…" Her voice faltered. "I'm no angel, but I thought…"

"Wren," David interrupted, "I'm an all or nothing kinda guy. When I kiss you and mean it, I'm going to keep wanting to kiss you. I'm going to want you in my life all the time, and I want to know that, before I start, you feel the same way too."

Wren stared up at him, confused.

"I've been giving you space, Wren, because I don't know what you want," David said, his thumbs rubbing her arms where he held her. "Do you?"

"I'm not sure," Wren admitted at last, "but I'm getting a better idea all the time." She paused and then went up on tiptoe to press her lips against his.

❧

The music swelled, the credits rolled.

"I love that movie." Kate gave a contented yawn.

"It's a keeper," Michael agreed. "That director really does some trippy stuff. I can see why you like him now."

Kate yawned again. "Sorry, I'm not much of a date tonight."

"You've been working all day; I think you're entitled to feel tired." Michael smoothed back her hair and kissed her temple.

"So have you," Kate said in a drowsy tone, and was jolted by his snort of laughter.

"Yeah, right, sitting on my butt at a computer isn't quite the same."

"It's still work," Kate said. "But in the meantime, how about we take this conversation elsewhere?" She uncoiled herself from Michael's side and sat waiting. Michael took her hand and together they walked to the bedroom.

"You know," Michael began as he flicked on the bedside light, "this feels kinda weird."

"Why's that?" Kate said, taking off her watch and putting it on the bedside table.

"Well, I guess I've always tended to stay at your place. Don't get me wrong," he went on hastily. "I love having you here. It just feels different to be settling in for the night at my place instead of yours."

"Only because you haven't finished making this place a home yet," Kate replied, "but you're getting there." Kate had explored the apartment after dinner, exclaiming over the comic book collection that Michael had set out on one of the bookshelves, the Spider-Man action figure, and a few framed photos here and there.

"True." Michael hesitated, watching as Kate kicked off her shoes, and then unzipped her jeans and stepped out of them, standing there utterly unselfconscious in her boy-short underwear and T-shirt before she pulled back the blankets and got into bed. "Uh," he said.

"Michael, it's okay." She smiled to reassure him. "For what it's worth, it feels a tiny bit weird to me too, but that's only because we're not used to it. So tell me, Michael, what's your normal bedtime routine?"

He thought for a moment before he spoke. "I brush my teeth, get changed into something to sleep in and then get into bed." It sounded so simple, so dull. And yet now there was Kate, and that made everything different.

She nodded. "Well, I'll tell you what. You go ahead and do that, and I'll be right here when you get back."

He gave her a sly grin before moving off into the bathroom. He brushed his teeth and pulled off his jeans, leaving them in a pile on the floor. His sleep pants were hanging on a hook on the back of the bathroom door, and he pulled them on. He never bothered with a shirt. When he got into bed, his heart was in his throat, and he turned to face Kate.

"Hi," she said with a quiet smile.

"Hey," he replied, reaching out with one hand to pull her flush against him. With his other hand, he framed her face as he dipped his head and kissed her. What began as a languid exploration of each other's mouths became something more urgent.

"So," Kate breathed when they separated, "still feeling weird?"

"Hell, no," Michael replied, kissing her neck, trailing a path of kisses down her chest between her breasts. "Feeling pretty good actually."

"So I see," Kate replied, throwing her arm over her eyes as she moved against him. His hands caught her by the hips to hold her still as he moved lower.

"Michael," she groaned.

But he was incapable of speech.

❧

Wren woke up and rolled over to stare wordlessly at the empty space in the bed beside her. She bit her lip and hugged her pillow tightly, wondering if he'd left a note, and tried to ignore the burning in her eyes. She sniffed and rolled onto her back, scrubbing at her eyes with the heels of her hands.

It didn't matter. She'd be fine. She was always fine.

Her head jerked as she heard the toilet flush. David appeared, scratching his stomach above the waistband of his gray boxer briefs.

"Hey," he said, his voice husky with sleep. He padded across to the bed and crawled over the mattress onto his side. Settling his head on his pillow, he reached out and hauled Wren over to him. Rolling onto his side, he pulled her into his chest and slung a muscled leg over her thighs, pinning her against him. He snuffled a little into her hair, making her giggle, before she felt his lips ghost against her skin. Wren gave an experimental wriggle of her hips against his and felt his immediate reaction. David's fingers tickled her sides, making her give a breathless laugh.

"Need more sleep," he whispered, "and then we'll take up from where we finished off last night."

Wren closed her eyes and went back to sleep, feeling content.

❧

Michael woke up and glanced at the bedside clock; they'd both slept late. Rolling onto his side, he looked at Kate who was curled up beside him. She shifted as he stirred beside her and moved her hips slightly, her eyelashes fluttering.

Michael inched closer, running his hand up her thigh, caressing her, enjoying the feel of her skin beneath his hand. Kate's eyes fluttered again as his hand slid higher, dipping and exploring. She wondered if he knew she was awake; but he knew for certain when he shifted away to prepare, and then returned to move her thigh higher and slide into her. She sucked in a breath and arched her back against his chest, her head back, eyes closed as she savored the feeling of having him inside her again. For a moment they lay joined together, neither saying a word, and then Kate very gently rocked back against him.

He slid his palm, fingers splayed, over her stomach, holding her against him. Kate moved to place her hand over his, catching her breath as he moved into her deeper still. The familiar heat began to build between them, and they went with it. There was no sense of urgency, just unhurried loving that neither of them wanted to rush. Michael propped himself on one elbow behind her, leaning close so that he could nuzzle the curve of her throat. Kate reached up blindly behind her, threading her fingers through his hair to hold his face close. He picked up their rhythm and held her tight, her back against his chest as her body clenched tightly around him, pulling him along with her release.

Afterward, Kate lay enjoying the feeling of Michael's body against hers, and then shifted a little as Michael made a reluctant groan and began to move away. The bed felt cold the moment he moved away from her and walked toward the bathroom to clean up. She must have fallen into a light doze, because she jolted awake again when Michael climbed back into bed beside her.

"Hey." His breath tickled her ear. "Want some breakfast?"

"Well, I guess you've worked up an appetite," Kate agreed, turning her head for a kiss.

Michael chuffed with laughter and kissed her thoroughly, cupping a breast that he stroked into responsiveness until she broke away with a laugh.

"You know, now that you've said it, I'm getting hungry."

"Me and my big mouth," Michael groaned.

"Mmm." Kate kissed him, nibbling on his lower lip. "And all those lovely things you can do with it. I think I want pancakes."

"We'll have to go out. I didn't get much beyond the fixings for dinner," Michael said in an apologetic tone.

"Fine by me. I need coffee too," Kate agreed. "You get the shower going."

"You don't want to come with?"

"Oh, I do, but then I'd miss the view of watching you walk butt nekkid into the bathroom."

"Ah." Michael nodded. "I see your point." He got out of bed and stretched, his bed hair curled every which way. He looked glorious. Kate lay back in bed and admired.

"I'll be there in a minute," she said, yawning.

Michael headed into the bathroom and turned on the shower taps. He had just stepped under the spray when he heard his phone ring. "Son of a..." he cursed, and heard Kate laugh.

"You want me to get it?" she called out as she glanced at the call display. "It's someone called Alistair."

Michael hesitated. "He's my editor, but he's usually smart enough not to call me on the weekend. Tell him I'll give him a call back," he said. "Are you going to join me in here sometime soon?"

"Give me a second," Kate called, and then clicked to answer the call. "Hello?"

There was a startled pause. "Uh, is this Michael's phone?"

"Sorry, yes, it is. He can't get to the phone at the moment, but he said for me to tell you that he'd call you back," Kate supplied, rolling onto her back and giving a full body stretch.

"Who have I got here?"

"Kate," she replied, sitting up. She could hear a lot of splashing from the shower, and wanted to get in there.

"Kate," Alistair said, his voice brightening as he made the connection. "You're Cupcake Kate, the inspiration Michael mentioned?"

"That's me," she replied, plucking at the bed sheet, "and you're Michael's editor, right?"

"Right. I must say it's nice to talk to the person I've been reading so much about," Alistair went on. "Has Michael shown you what he's been working on? I think we're going to have another hit on our hands."

Kate stilled. "Excuse me?"

"The book he's working on. He's not sure about it, but between you and me, it's his best work yet."

"Really?" Kate said in a faint voice. "And what's it about?"

Alistair paused, aware that the conversation seemed to be stalling. "Uh, well, maybe Michael should be the one to—"

"Alistair," Kate interrupted him in a calm voice, "I'm not angry. Just give me a snapshot of what it's about."

"Kate," Alistair tried to regroup, "I'm the one that's shot my mouth off here. I think we both know that Michael doesn't like to talk about his work very much, so he's not going to be very impressed with me if I'm the one who tells you that he's writing about—"

"Me," Kate answered.

<h1 style="text-align:center">Chapter 16</h1>

<h2 style="text-align:center">Confessions and Revelations</h2>

Kate finished the conversation with an apologetic Alistair and then disconnected the call. Moving with deliberate slowness, she set the phone back down on the bedside table and drew her knees up to her chest, sitting quietly in thought. The splashing from the shower paused and Michael's voice floated out to her.

"Kate? Are you joining me?"

"In a minute," she called back, wondering whom the voice belonged to: it didn't sound like her. She took a deep breath and got out of bed, walking toward the bathroom and peeling off her T-shirt. Pausing beside the shower, she shimmied out of her underwear and shot a quick look at the mirror, relieved to see that she looked calmer than she felt.

A muffled thud drew her attention to the shower door, and she smiled to see that Michael had wiped a panel to peer through at her, the flash of his smile making her heart give an unsteady thump. She opened the shower door and stepped into Michael's embrace. Looking over his shoulder, she saw that the panel he had cleared was beginning to fog up again, but she could still see through to the other side. Reaching around behind his shoulder, she wiped the patch clear again.

"What are you doing?" Michael said, nuzzling against her neck as he lathered the soap before rubbing his frothy hands up and down her sides.

"Seeing clearly," Kate replied simply, and then turned her face toward his for a kiss.

After making love, they toweled each other dry, stopping for kisses often. Michael paused while patting the water off Kate's legs to look up at her.

"You're very quiet," he observed, and then went back to his ministrations.

"What would you like me to say?" Kate replied.

"Dunno." He shrugged, and then stopped as a thought struck him. "What did Alistair want?"

Kate stilled.

"He wants you to call him later," she said at last. "He sounds happy with what you're working on."

"Mmph," Michael snorted, more interested in the progress he was making up Kate's thighs. He paused as he planted a soft kiss at the apex of her legs before continuing with the towel up the soft, flat plane of her belly. "Right now, I don't much care what he thinks. He's in trouble, I know that much. He never calls on the weekend, so I don't know what's prompted him to start now."

"I guess he was just excited," Kate said in a soft voice, reaching down to comb his wet hair with her fingers. "He said he'd been reading."

"Ah," Michael said, getting up from his knees to stand in front of her, dropping a kiss on each breast as he continued.

"He thinks it's your best work yet," Kate continued, watching his reflection in the mirror. Michael nodded, reaching out to brush the strands of her wet hair off her shoulders, moving the towel across her back in gentle arcs. "Michael, can I ask you something?" Kate said in a quiet voice.

"Mmm?" he said, brushing the towel down her back.

"Will you tell me more about your story?"

"I've already told you a bit about it," he said, discarding the towel now that she was dry and wrapping his arms around her, pulling her against him. He rested his chin on her shoulder and looked at their reflection. "What did you want to know?"

"I don't know," Kate admitted, and then hesitated. The phone call had left her feeling exposed enough already without her having to revisit it standing there naked. "Nothing that can't wait, but right now how about we chase up some breakfast?"

"Pancakes coming up. I know just the place," Michael said, giving her a tight hug and then steering her toward the bedroom where she had left her bag of clothes. He grinned at her as she reached for her bag and pulled on some clean underwear while he got a pair of boxer briefs from his dresser and pulled them on. "There's a great diner not far from here."

"Sounds good," Kate replied as she tugged up her jeans and reached for her bra. As she fumbled with the clasp, she looked up to see Michael watching her as he tugged on his T-shirt. "What?"

"Nothing," Michael replied. "I just like watching you."

Kate looked at him with a faint smile. "It's a boob thing, isn't it?" she said after a pause. "You like watching my boobs while I get dressed."

"Maybe," Michael conceded after a diplomatic pause.

"You're such a guy," Kate said reaching for her T-shirt. "Tom's just as bad."

"Tom?" Michael stopped in the act of reaching for his shoes. "Who's Tom?"

"He's an old friend," Kate replied, glancing at him as she gathered her damp hair into a ponytail before giving up and leaving it loose.

"An old friend who has a thing for your boobs?" Michael took a step closer and put his hands on her hips. "This sounds interesting."

"Tom's my ..." Kate reached up and gave Michael a quick kiss. "Well, let's just say it's complicated."

"More please," Michael said, smiling as Kate gave him another kiss. "So," he ventured when they came up for air, "how complicated?"

"Not *that* complicated," Kate said, putting her arms around Michael's waist and hugging him. "It's in the past, but he's still in my life."

"Uh-huh," Michael said looking puzzled. "Well, I have to say this sounds like new territory."

"No big." Kate shrugged. "I'll tell you later."

"I'll make a note of that," Michael joked, watching as Kate's face clouded before she took a breath and gave him a bright smile.

"I'm sure you will," was all she said, stepping back from him and looking around for her shoes.

When she was dressed, Kate got to her feet and smiled. "Come on, Forrester. I need coffee or I won't be held responsible for my actions."

"Better not keep my girl waiting," Michael said, grabbing his keys and taking Kate by the hand.

The two of them had walked for a block before Michael realized he was the one carrying the conversation while Kate contributed here and there. He tightened his arm to draw her closer to his side, and she glanced up at him with a quick smile as they kept walking.

"Kate, is everything okay?"

"Mmm?" She pulled her gaze away from the buildings they were passing and looked at Michael. "I'm okay, why?"

"You just seem a little quiet," Michael pressed. Something was wrong; she wasn't behaving like his Kate.

"Sometimes I wake up ready to seize the day, and sometimes it takes me a bit longer to get going," Kate said. The conversation with Alistair was starting to eat away at her. She was going to have to raise the subject with Michael soon, but she didn't know how. She had been about to ask him back at his apartment, but knew that the conversation was one that had to be held on neutral ground. She feared having to ask him questions, worried about what the answers might be. She sighed, feeling sad that what had promised to be a relaxing Sunday now had the potential to become something else entirely. She didn't like confrontation, but it was something that was going to have to happen sooner or later.

Michael kissed her temple as they kept walking. "You've had a hard week, so I'm not surprised you're still feeling tired."

Kate nodded. Perhaps that was it; she was just tired and over-reacting. Still, Alistair's slip on the phone before he had realized Kate was unaware of the direction of Michael's latest work was cause for concern. She had nothing to hide, and yet the thought of her life being laid bare on the page was disconcerting to say the least. And then there was the fact that Michael had chosen her as the subject. It made her wonder about the nature of their relationship, and it raised even more questions that led her back to her only frame of reference: Thomas.

She yawned, covering her mouth with her hand and resting her head against Michael's chest as he rubbed her shoulder.

"Poor baby," he said. "We're nearly there so you'll have a coffee soon."

"I'm going to need it," she said with feeling.

They reached the diner and were lucky enough to find a small booth available. Kate poured over the menu with perhaps more attention than it warranted, grateful for the diversion as she tried to collect her thoughts. Their order was placed and, much to her relief, promptly delivered. Kate wrapped her hands around the cup of coffee and took a slow sip.

"Good?" Michael said when she put the cup down and began on her pancake stack.

"Not bad," Kate said carelessly. "They use a different coffee blend here, but at this time of day, I'm beyond caring. It's all about the caffeine as far as I'm concerned."

Michael smiled, his eyes crinkling as he watched her pour a generous drizzle of maple syrup over her short stack. He forked some of his own pancakes and glanced out the diner window as he chewed. It looked like it was going to be a nice day: the weather was mild, and the streets were filling with people out to make the most of their Sunday. And here he was with his girl, having breakfast. He felt happier than he had in a long time.

"Michael, I've got to ask you something, and I don't know what you're going to think," Kate said, putting down her cup and leaning forward over her elbows.

Michael nodded and scooped up another mouthful of pancakes. "I'm listening."

Kate traced a finger along the handle of the small jug that held the maple syrup. "Are you writing about me?"

Michael's chewing slowed down and he swallowed with effort before putting down his knife and fork. He looked up to meet Kate's eyes and saw that she was looking at the jug. He reached over and gently took her hand, watching as she met his gaze with some trepidation.

"What makes you ask that?"

"Alistair." She gave him a steady look. "He was talking about your story and then let slip something about feeling like he knew me already."

Michael nodded slowly.

"So it's true then?" Kate said after a brief silence.

"In part," Michael admitted, "although I wish you hadn't found out like this." He rubbed the back of his neck with his free hand, and looked at Kate with concern.

"Michael," Kate began in a gentle voice, "I'm not mad. I'm just ..." She broke off and stared around the diner before looking back at him. "I don't really know what I feel right now. I haven't been in this kind of situation before."

That got Michael's attention. He moved his plate to the side and reached over to enfold Kate's hand in both of his. "What sort of situation do you think this is?" His mouth was going dry. Of all the reactions he thought he might get when Kate eventually found out about the book, he never dreamed she would be this uncomfortable.

Kate squirmed under the intensity of Michael's gaze. "Michael, I don't talk myself up, and for the most part, I like to think that I make my way through life pretty much invisible."

"Kate, you've never been invisible to me—" Michael began, but Kate opened her mouth to speak again and he stopped.

"I don't know what it is exactly that you're working on, but if it's as good as Alistair thinks it is then I'm really pleased for you, truly. But I'm just thinking that maybe you could've said something to me before now." Kate's gaze dropped back to the tabletop as she considered her own words, and then looked back up at him with an apologetic shrug.

"I ..." Michael began and then stopped, clearing his throat before continuing. "I'm sorry, I ..." He grimaced. "God, this is awkward."

"You think?" Kate offered a wry grin.

"I don't quite know how to explain myself," Michael said, rubbing his thumb over Kate's hand, although he wasn't sure who the gesture was meant to reassure. "As a writer, I'm used to writing from life, so everything around me becomes inspiration, that is ..." he paused, "... when I'm able to write, in any case."

"I can understand that," Kate replied.

"I'm not sure you do. Before I met you, I hadn't written anything for months," Michael went on slowly, his forehead creasing as he thought before speaking; he wanted no room for any misinterpretation. "And then you somehow triggered the words inside me, I don't know how—I don't know if I even want to know—but when you appeared in my life all of a sudden, it was easy." He began speaking faster now, words bubbling at the back of his throat.

"You're saying I did that?" Kate gazed at him in disbelief.

"I'd like to think so," Michael replied with feeling. "So when you say you feel invisible, to me nothing could be further from the truth."

Kate's face warmed under the spotlight of his gaze as the pair of them sat silent.

"Do you want to read it?" Michael said suddenly. "If you want to, it's yours."

"You know," Kate said at last, "I don't think I do." Now it was Michael's turn to be surprised. "It's not that I'm worried; I've got nothing to hide," she went on. "But I don't think I'm ready to read it yet."

"If you're sure," Michael said, cautious now.

"Maybe later, just not right now is all," she said in a gentle voice.

"And you're really okay?" Michael lifted her wrist to his lips to brush a kiss over it.

"I think so," she conceded, "but it was a bit of a shock this morning."

"I'll bet," Michael agreed. "Which reminds me that Alistair and I are going to have to have a conversation about that."

"Is he in trouble?" A smile tugged at Kate's lips, a real one this time.

"Just a bit," Michael said in a soft growl, nibbling at Kate's wrist, making her jump.

"I'm sure it was an honest mistake. He sounded very sorry."

"Oh, I'll make him sorry," Michael replied, angling his hand so that he could kiss the soft pad of her thumb. "He upset my girl."

"Hmm, well, don't be too hard on him; it was going to come out sooner or later," Kate remonstrated. "And let's not forget your part in all this."

"True." Michael broke away from kissing her hand to consider this. "Kate, would it help if I said I was sorry?"

"Are you?" Kate raised an eyebrow.

"Of course," he said, stung by her doubt. He met her gaze, measure for measure, and sighed. "Well, maybe in part. How does that make me sound?"

"It depends on how you back it up," Kate replied, nodding for him to keep talking.

"Am I sorry that I'm writing about you? No, I'm not. You gave me words again, and for that, I'm grateful. Am I sorry I didn't tell you about more about my work? Yes." He dipped his head, looking up at her through his lashes in contrition. "I'm sorry. I never meant to hurt you."

"You know," Kate said slowly, "sometimes that can hurt most of all."

"What can?" Michael was confused now, thinking he may have done far more damage than he'd been led to believe.

"Hurting someone by omission can be just as bad," Kate replied, her eyes distant.

Michael's chest felt hollow with anxiety. "Kate, you know I never consciously set out to hurt you."

"I know." Kate shook their joined hands for emphasis. "It's okay, Michael. The look on your face when I raised the subject was enough to tell me that." Kate rolled her shoulders, trying to shake off the mood. "I guess some of this conversation has reminded me of something else."

"Anything you want to talk about?"

"Not here," Kate replied, pulling a face. "Maybe later, but I'm going to need some fresh air after this."

"Sounds good," Michael said, signaling for the check. "Are you sure you're all right?"

"A little bit fragile maybe," Kate answered. "But I'll be okay."

They settled the check and stepped outside into the sunlight, Michael keeping Kate close to his side as they walked along the pavement. Kate tilted her face toward the sun, closing her eyes as she took a deep breath, hoping Michael wouldn't let her stumble.

Paul cursed as he tripped over the piping that was stacked in his hallway, and limped a couple of paces before shaking his head and searching for his cell phone. Flipping it open, he scrolled through his stored numbers and dialed.

"Babycake," he said by way of greeting, grinning as he heard the delight in his sister's voice that was almost enough to make him forget the pain in his big toe. "Listen, I've still got that copper piping here. Is today a good day for me to install those magazine racks we talked about?" He paused, waiting for Kate to consider the spontaneous offer. "Cool. I've still got keys to the store, so I'll go in this afternoon and get it done. If I need any help, I'll give Tom a call."

They spoke a little longer before Paul got off the phone and limped into his bedroom to sit down on the bed and examine his foot. His toe still hurt, but it didn't look serious. If nothing else, the injury had given him the motivation to get the job finished. He yawned and stretched, feeling the tendons in his shoulders stretch and pop, then fell back onto the mattress as he took a moment to relax before galvanizing into action.

Still lying on his back, he lifted his leg and pulled his foot toward his chest to inspect his toe again. Thinking about the pipes in the corridor, he wondered how he was going to get them to the store without too much fuss. He considered his options, and then reached for his phone again, hoping he had enough charm for a Sunday morning favor. If all else failed, he was sure he could negotiate payment by way of man's international beer economy.

"Paul," Kate explained with a smile as she snapped her phone shut and slipped it back into her bag.

"What's he doing?" Michael said, happy for whatever reason had put a smile on her face.

Kate put her arm through his again once her phone was safely stowed and kept walking. "He got some old copper piping off a retired plumber, and he's going to use them to make some magazine racks on the wall in the shop. The bookcase we've got in there is filled to capacity, so Paul came up with the idea of the racks," Kate explained and she stopped as she inspected some shoes in a window display before walking on.

"Does he need help?" Michael asked before he could think about what he was saying.

"You know how to do that stuff?" Kate said, looking at him in surprise.

"Some," Michael said. "I don't think I'd be at Paul's standard, but I could help with the heavy lifting. Is he going to be doing it by himself?"

"He said if he needed a hand he'd give Tom a call," Kate said carelessly.

"There's that name again," Michael pounced, his curiosity growing now.

"Huh?" Kate was distracted from the shop windows. "What name?"

"Tom, you know, Boob Guy," Michael explained, cupping a hand toward his chest for emphasis, which made her laugh. "Where does he fit in?"

Kate gave him a sidelong look and saw nothing but open curiosity on his face. She should have known that sooner or later it would come to this. It seemed to be a morning for confrontations and revelations, and to think that she had been so excited when Paul suggested she start giving herself weekends off work.

"Tom's ..." She waved a hand in a vague motion. "He's complicated," she sighed.

"You said that," Michael prompted. "Have you two got a lot of history?"

"I guess you could call it that," Kate conceded, thinking that the word "baggage" would fit just as well. She gave him an uncertain look. "How much do you want to know?"

"Whatever you want to tell me," Michael said. "Does it impact on us?"

Kate thought about this for a few more paces before shaking her head. "I don't think so. That is, I mean … I guess I don't think it will." She stumbled over her words, shaking her head in frustration as she searched for the right thing to say.

Michael gave her a soft smile. "Is that a definitely maybe?"

"That's a good way of putting it," she agreed.

Michael mulled over her explanation, wondering what kind of history could be a possible hindrance between himself and Kate. He arranged his expression into one of calm curiosity, hoping it would encourage her to keep talking. His ability to be a quiet listener had worked well for him in the past, and he hoped it wouldn't let him down now. Kate sighed and pushed her hair away from her face, a gesture he noticed she did when she was thinking about something difficult. He uncoupled his arm from Kate's and slid it around her waist, pulling her warm against his side, providing as much silent encouragement as he could.

"Tom is from my hometown," Kate began, keeping her gaze on the pavement ahead of them. "We went to different schools, but Jack and I were like extended family to his." Kate gave him a wry grin. "So I guess that's where the history started. Tom and I met on the playground, and we grew up together. He dated, I dated, and then we ended up together after graduation."

"Childhood sweethearts, huh?" Michael commented.

"Kind of," Kate nodded. "We both ended up at the same college and we hooked up," Kate said. "I don't know if it was two homesick and lonely hearts finding each other, or if we were just acting on something that had always been there. Being with Tom was just—" she waved her hand as she searched for the right word, "—easy, I guess."

"And perhaps convenient?" Michael suggested with caution.

Kate shot him a measured look. "That too," she allowed. "But there was a lot of feeling there."

"I don't doubt it," Michael said. "You're not someone a guy takes for granted."

Kate wrinkled her nose at him in amusement. "You'd be surprised."

"Don't sell yourself short," Michael argued. "So go on. What happened with you two?"

"Well, here's the thing," Kate said, and she was silent for a few more paces while she gathered her thoughts. She pushed her hair off her face and puffed out a sigh before continuing. "Tom and I were pretty serious for those couple of years in college, and then ..." She pushed at her hair again before giving a nervous laugh. "This is ridiculous. I don't know why I'm nervous about this."

"Don't be," Michael urged in a gentle voice. "You don't have to tell me if you don't want to."

"It's okay." Kate ran her fingers through her hair and then grimaced when she realized she was giving into a nervous habit and stuffed her hand into her pocket. "So Tom and I were together, and then one day he told me that we, uh, weren't compatible anymore."

"That sounds pretty harsh," Michael commented.

"Oh, it gets better," Kate agreed. "It turns out we were incompatible because I wasn't a gay man."

"You weren't—" Michael began and stopped as he processed what she had said. "Oh."

"Exactly," Kate sighed. They reached an intersection and stopped at the curb, waiting for the light to change. "So there you have it: the history of Tom and Kate."

"Hang on, back up a minute," Michael said. "Had Tom always known he was gay?"

"He says with the benefit of hindsight that he had his suspicions. Getting away from home gave him an opportunity to reinvent himself, but being with me for the first couple of years was like a security blanket," Kate replied. The light changed, and they crossed the street. There was a cool breeze blowing into their faces, and Kate closed her eyes as she took a deep breath, consciously releasing the tension in her shoulders. She could feel the comforting weight of Michael's arm around her waist and their denim-clad thighs rubbing against each other as they walked.

"Right." Michael considered this. "And how were things once he came out?"

"Well, I guess I was in shock at first. It was about a year after Jack ..." She checked herself and then continued, "after the accident. When I finally told Paul, he wanted to find Tom and beat six types of shit out of him."

"Paul was ..." Michael raised an eyebrow.

"Protective of me, not homophobic," Kate confirmed as Michael nodded. "He didn't like seeing me hurt, but once things calmed down we were okay. I got through college and Paul and the three of us ended up in New York."

"Who came here first?"

"Paul did. He finished college two years before me. So by the time I got to town, I had somewhere to stay for a year before I found my feet, and things went from there. About two years after I got here, Tom hit town and he's been in my life ever since."

"It must have been hard, going it alone like that," Michael mused, and was surprised when Kate gave him a surprised look.

"It never occurred to me," Kate commented. "I guess I was so used to being in a small family in a small town, and doing things for myself, that it just felt like I was doing the same thing, just with a few more people around me." She squinted down the street. "Not to change the subject, but where are we going?"

"The park," Michael said simply. "After that conversation, I think you need some unconditional love from the dogs, as well as me."

Kate looked up at Michael. "Thank you."

"You're worth it," Michael said in reply, pulling her close to kiss her forehead.

Chapter 17

The Evil Twin and the Angry Jogger

By the time they left the park an hour later, Kate's eyes were peaceful. Michael had watched the way her face had lit up as various dogs had bounded over to investigate them where they stood by the fence at the dog run and the way she had laughed at the smaller dogs whose enthusiastic tail wagging threatened to knock their little bodies off balance.

"I didn't realize how much I needed that until we got there," Kate commented, snuggling into Michael's chest as they stood at the light.

"I remembered you saying that you went there when you wanted to feel better," Michael explained, rubbing his hand over her lower back. "Is there anything else you feel like doing today?"

"Why do I feel like I'm getting spoiled?" Kate said, smiling up at him as they crossed the street.

"You're the one with the harder work schedule; I'm just trying to make your free time really count," Michael said.

"Would you mind awfully if we call in at the store? I'd really like to see what sort of progress Paul's making in there."

"You're the boss," Michael replied as they set off toward the village.

"That's what people keep telling me," Kate said, and then in response to Michael's look added, "Private joke. I'll explain later."

As they neared the store, they could hear the steady thumping of rhythmic base through cheap speakers that were clearly being pushed beyond their limits.

"That has to be Paul. He likes his music loud," Kate explained with a grin. She hadn't seen Paul for three weeks now and was looking forward to catching up.

She opened the door and stopped in surprise. Paul was there, with Thomas in tow, and they were in the midst of lifting a row of piping up to the wall, singing along to Paul's Rolling Stones CD with lusty voices. Both men were shirtless and made for an impressive display of muscle in motion. Paul looked over Thomas's shoulder and gave a loud whoop when he saw his sister standing in the doorway. He dropped the pipe and headed toward her, ignoring Thomas's shout of protest as he tried to stop the copper length from hitting the floor.

"Babycake," he greeted her, gathering Kate into a sweaty hug despite her attempt to cringe out of the way. He looked past her to see Michael hesitating at the threshold and extended a calloused hand. "And you must be the Michael I keep hearing about. I'm—"

"Paul," Michael supplied, shaking the proffered hand with a broad grin. "Otherwise known as Brother Bear, right?"

Paul's eyebrows went up at that, and he looked down at the still squirming Kate. "You've brought him up to speed on the basics, I see." He released Kate, giving her a gentle shove back toward Michael, a grin nearly splitting his face in two as she wiped her face with both hands.

"Oh, God," she declared in a disgusted voice. "Bear, that was too gross for a Sunday morning." She plucked at her T-shirt and fluffed at her hair, feeling as if she had been doused in sweat. Paul chuckled in response.

"Ah, c'mon, just having fun," he said, reaching out to ruffle her hair as she ducked out of the way.

"Hey, Kate," Tom called, having put down the pipe and wiped himself down with a towel. "C'mere and give me some sugar." He held out his arms and frowned when Kate hesitated before stepping forward for a quick hug. He stared at Michael and made a move to hold on to Kate for longer, but she wriggled out of his arms and stepped back toward the door where Michael was standing.

"Tom," she said, "I'd like you to meet Michael." She met Michael's eyes, silently pleading for understanding. Cursing inwardly, she realized that although she had told Michael about Tom, she hadn't told him that Tom was still very much a fixture in her life.

After a brief pause, Michael stepped forward to shake Tom's hand. "Tom, Kate's told me about you. It's a pleasure."

"I'm sure," Tom murmured, blatantly assessing and then dropping Michael's hand and turning back toward the pipes as if he had lost all interest in the exchange. "Come on, Paul. I don't have all day to get this done."

"It's looking really good," Kate said after an awkward pause, stepping forward to have a closer look. The wall Paul had chosen had a wooden lintel that ran the length of the space about three feet off the floor. It would make a perfect 'rest' for the magazines, once the pipes were bolted in to hold them flat against the wall. "You're doing a great job, guys."

"You know what would really help us get this done quicker though, right?" Paul shot his sister a pleading look. Kate sighed and looked at her watch, and then at Michael.

"Is that all you ever think with, your stomach?"

"I'm sure he makes the occasional exception," Tom replied in a dry tone, earning a snort from Paul.

"If I'm going to do any baking, it's going to have to be something quick," Kate warned, and then turned to Michael with an apologetic look. "I'm sorry. I—"

"No need for that," Michael broke in smoothly. "Look at the work these guys are doing; they're going to need rewarding." He took her by the hands to gently tug her toward him and gave her a soft kiss. "I can see that you've got some catching up to do. How about I leave you guys to it, and I'll see you later."

"Are you sure?" Kate shot a sidelong look at Tom who was making a show of ignoring them.

"I'm sure," Michael repeated, kissing her again. "Call me, okay?" He smiled at her, and then waved to Paul. "Great to meet you guys. We'll catch up again soon."

"You know it," Paul called. "Tom? Michael's leaving."

Tom turned his head slightly and grunted, making Paul sigh loudly as Michael looked taken aback. "Ignore the bitch, Michael," Paul said. "It was nice meeting you."

"Likewise," Michael said, looking uncertain as he glanced at Tom's back. He turned to Kate and offered her a genuine smile. "I'll see you later."

"Will do." She smiled. Following him to the door, she stopped him for another kiss before watching him walk away. Turning back into the store, she pointed a stern finger at Tom. "Mind telling me what all that was about?"

"What?" Tom didn't meet her eyes, choosing instead to focus his unnecessary attention on the work Paul was going.

"Don't give me that," Kate replied. She could hear the waspish tone in her voice but was unable to stop it.

"I'll second that," Paul commented, picking up his hammer drill. "You were a complete prick."

"What is this, 'pick on me' day?" Tom said, shrugging off Paul's criticism.

"Only when you deserve it," Paul replied, lining up the drill carefully with the mark he'd made on the wall and getting back to work.

Tom muttered to himself as he angrily snatched up a gym towel from Paul's bag and wiped himself down before pulling on his shirt. Paul stopped drilling and turned around with a resigned look on his face.

"Listen, if you're going to be like that, why don't you take your attitude elsewhere," he suggested. He pointed at Kate. "And you should go with him. You guys need to have a talk." Kate and Tom looked at each other and then back at Paul. "Go on," Paul said, shooing them despite the fact he was still holding the drill. "Get out of here and be nice."

"But what about—" Kate began.

"It's cool. I can finish up here myself," Paul said. "You guys have got some talking to do."

"Paul, man, listen," Tom began awkwardly, stopping when Paul waved him off.

"Tell your story walkin'," Paul said in an even tone as he turned back to the job at hand.

Tom looked at Kate who shrugged. "Guess we've been told." She offered him a wry smile. "So how about it, Tom? Shall we go get a coffee?"

He looked at his watch. "Screw that, it's after noon. I'm up for something stronger."

Paul watched them go. "About time," he muttered. He didn't envy the conversation they had ahead of them, but these things had to be done. He turned back to the wall and began to drill.

Michael closed the door behind him and tossed his keys onto the kitchen counter. He was home sooner than he'd planned, and quite alone. After only just discovering the history between Tom and Kate, he hadn't expected to meet the man in question on the same day. Even more of a surprise had been the naked hostility Tom had shown when he had realized who Michael was.

Kate had looked uncomfortable, and Paul seemed decidedly unimpressed by Tom's behavior, going so far as to call him out on it when Michael was leaving. Michael hadn't liked the look of concern on Kate's face when he had decided to leave them to it, but he could tell from Tom's behavior that there was a whole subtext to that relationship which needed to be addressed. He had spoken to Kate with as much reassurance as he could muster, and he had caught an eye flicker from Paul that indicated the big man understood his actions. He hoped so. It was good to know he had Paul in his corner. He stopped by his desk, frowning as the thought occurred to him. Was there going to be a battle for Kate's affections? He hoped not.

Kate was aware of the war between her head and her heart as she walked along the street with Tom, who was now trying to make light of the situation. He whispered outrageous fashion police comments in her ear as they passed people who met with his disapproval, and he draped his arm around her shoulders with the ease of long familiarity. She shrugged it off, and then sighed when he gave her a hurt look and let him take her hand instead. She knew this conversation with Tom had been brewing for some time now, but all she wanted to do was run in the other direction. The direction that she knew Michael had taken.

Tom led her across town to one of his favorite bars. It was very hip and stylish, and at this time of day the music was kept to a tolerable level. Kate nodded and made the right responses as Tom beamed and saw that they were ushered to a secluded table. Kate took a seat and looked at some of the more fashionably dressed clientele. She felt frumpy and underdressed in her old jeans and comfortable fitted tee. She didn't realize how refreshing she looked: her cheeks flushed from the outdoor air, and her hair held back from her face with her sunglasses, which she had rammed up onto the top of her head. Compared to some of the more conscientious consumers in the bar, she looked completely and unselfconsciously natural.

Kate may not have noticed the attention she was getting, but Tom did. He slid his chair closer to hers to denote a subtle ownership, but not so close that any welcome male attention toward himself would be deterred. Once their drink orders had been taken and delivered, Tom leaned back in his chair and gave Kate a long stare.

"So, what's the problem, Kate?"

"I was hoping you could tell me," Kate answered. "What was all that back there?"

"What was what?"

"You know what I'm talking about. That was the first time you met Michael and you totally froze him out."

Tom took a long sip of his wine, and made a show of setting his glass back on the table, taking his time before answering. "I don't like him."

"You just met him," Kate protested.

Tom shrugged. "It was enough to get a general impression."

"Well, tough. You're going to have to get used to him because he's going to be around for a while," Kate said, taking too big a mouthful of her own wine and choking slightly. She wasn't used to trying to be forceful, but the false courage provided by the wine seemed to be working. It also gave her something to do with her hands.

Kate put her glass down and put her head in her hands. "Tom, what the hell are we doing?"

"About what?"

Kate gave him a hard look, unable to tell if he was being deliberately obtuse, or had no idea what sort of an impact he was having.

"We started out as one thing, and now we're something completely different."

"Not so different," Tom pointed out. "We've always been friends, after all."

"True," Kate agreed, "but sex wasn't always part of the equation."

"It isn't now either," he argued.

"This is also true," Kate said, "and look where it's gotten us." She took a sip of wine and tried to think. "I bet our families never saw this coming." She remembered Jack and Gwen laughing with Tom's father over pictures of the two of them throughout childhood.

"Are we really in that much of a mess?" Tom rested his folded arms on the table and leaned across to Kate. "Be honest."

"Sometimes I think no," Kate said slowly, "but today, I'd have to say a definite yes." She gave him a wry smile to try to soften the blow. "It's hard enough staying friends with someone you've got a sexual past with, let alone having the goalposts moved so comprehensively."

"I guess," Tom said, staring at the tabletop as he mulled over Kate's words.

"C'mon, Tom," Kate said in a coaxing tone, "you've got to admit that coming out was a bombshell for everyone involved."

"I know it was a bombshell." Thomas reached out to take one of her hands. "But what could I do? I had to follow my heart."

"I know." Kate scrubbed her face with her free hand. "It was a bombshell, all right. I think I'm still carrying some of the shrapnel." Thomas's worried expression deepened, and Kate sighed. "God, none of this is coming out right."

"Coming out seems to be a recurring issue with us," Thomas deadpanned, getting a weak laugh from Kate.

"I just..." Kate tried to speak again and stopped. "Tom, you know I love you, but things are different now. *We're* different now."

He stared unhappily into his glass. "I know."

Kate reached over and covered his hand with hers. "And Michael's different. Surely you can see that."

"I guess," he replied, then looked up with a challenging stare. "Do you love him?"

"I, ah..." Kate was taken aback by his interrogatory tone. "I think I do."

"And have you told him?"

"Not yet," Kate replied, sipping at her wine. Maybe they needed to get something to eat; she could feel the wine going straight to her head.

"So you can say it to me, but not to him," Tom said with just a hint of satisfaction.

"I wasn't aware that it was a competition between the two of you," Kate chided.

"Well, I was here first," Thomas added.

"And now you're suddenly twelve years old," Kate said, exasperation creeping into her voice now. "You've got to cut this out. You do it every time."

"Do what?" Tom was all innocence.

"Every time a new guy arrives on my horizon, and I'm not saying that's a regular occurrence," Kate added, holding up an admonishing hand as Tom opened his mouth to interrupt. "You check them out, announce that they're no good, and start crowing as soon as they're gone."

"Well, they're not. I've known you long enough to know what's good for you, Kate. We all do," Tom said, finishing his wine and signaling for another.

"No, I don't think you do," Kate said, her fingers whitening on her glass stem. The conversation was heading in a direction she didn't like, and she felt her stomach twist with anxiety.

"Excuse me?"

"Tom, we've got a long history and it's seen some pretty big changes over the years, but enough's enough. You've got to let me move on."

"What do you mean?" Tom replied. Now it was his turn to look worried.

Kate set her glass aside and ran her fingers through her hair, lifting it off the back of her neck before rubbing her face. She felt terrible. Now that it was finally happening, she was becoming aware that this was a conversation that had been building up for years.

"Tom," Kate began in what she hoped was a gentle voice, "what I'm trying to say is that it feels like you've had me all to yourself for a long time. That might work for you, but it doesn't work for me. It's like you get the best of both worlds: you're dating and having a great time, plus there's our friendship. Why can't I have that too?"

"You do. You've dated other guys," Tom protested.

"And have I had your support every step of the way?" Kate sipped her wine again, watching him carefully. Tom was silent. "You know you're in my heart, but you just can't have *all* of it anymore."

Tom mumbled something unintelligible into his wine glass.

"Sorry, what was that? I don't speak Merlot," Kate prompted, earning a sheepish look from Tom.

"I said I don't see why we can't share."

"Oh, I think Michael can share. It's you I have my doubts about after this afternoon's effort," Kate said.

The pair of them sat staring at each other before Tom broke the silence with a loud sigh.

"Fine," he said. "If that's what it takes."

"I can't make you do what you don't want to, but if you're going to cause problems, Tom, then I think it's time you let me go."

"Oh, you did *not* just say that," Tom said, his face flushing with a combination of anger and shock.

"I did," Kate said, feeling the struggle of the conversation take its toll as her cheeks began to flush.

"Is this because I hurt you when I came out?" Tom said, his eyes narrowing. "It's taken you a while, Kate, but if this is payback then—"

"God, no," Kate protested. "C'mon, give me some credit. I'm trying to say that if you want relationships *and* our friendship, then you have to extend me the same courtesy."

"But I have," Tom replied, slouching back in his chair.

"C'mon, Tom, have you really?" Kate kept her tone as even as she could, but all she wanted to do at this point was curl up, go to sleep and wake up when it was all over.

Tom was silent while he considered her words. "Maybe not, but I *have* talked you out of a few bad shoe choices," Tom allowed at last, startling a laugh out of both of them.

"True, and I'll always need help in that department." Kate smiled. "At least until they come out with a pair of Converse that go with a cocktail dress." She laughed again as Tom gave a theatrical shudder and made the sign of the cross to ward off fashion evil. They looked at each other and began laughing again, although the hilarity was out of proportion to the joke.

"So," Kate ventured once their laughter had begun to subside, "are we good?"

"We'll see," Tom sighed. "I guess so. It's just going to be hard, you know?" Tom stared unhappily into his wine. "I've gotten so used to having you all to myself, I figured that whatever happened it'd always be you and me."

"You know I'll always be here," Kate said, reaching over to pat his hand, and was surprised when Tom took her hand in a fierce grip.

"I'll share, but I'm not happy about it. Still, if he can prove that he's good enough, then I'll go along with it." Tom delivered this pronouncement with an air of martyrdom, giving Kate an arch look as she smiled into her glass. "Going by the look on your face, you seem to think he's worth it."

"He is." Kate nodded, the knot in her stomach loosening now that the conversation was taking a friendly turn.

"Hmm, well, prejudice aside, given he's taking you away from me," Tom mused, "I have to say that he's gorgeous—that hair, those eyes." Tom's eyes took on a wicked glint as he continued, "high and tight in the back too."

"Tom." Kate laughed at this, and Tom grinned at the look of embarrassment and delight on her face.

"Speaking of taking away, though," Tom mused, "how come he bailed earlier?"

"You were a total bitch queen for a start," Kate said bluntly. "Who'd want to stick around for that?"

"True," Tom said with a reminiscent smile. "I was in fine form."

"I don't know that you should be patting yourself on the back for that little display. Paul was looking pretty pissed at you too."

Tom blanched. If there was one friend he treasured as much as Kate, it was her big brother. Paul was perhaps the only person in New York City other than Kate who could rouse Tom out of bed to help with some manual labor on a Sunday.

"Point taken," he said, looking chagrined. "I'll buy him a beer later."

"He'll like that," Kate assured him.

Michael flickered his fingers over the computer keyboard, and then sighed and deleted the sentence. He gave the laptop a light shove and kicked back in his chair, staring at the screen. He didn't know what he was writing. He wasn't even in the mood to write; he was just trying to occupy himself as a way to kill time until he heard from Kate again. He needed to find something to do. Getting up from his chair, he wandered over to his bookshelf, selecting books at random and then putting them back when they didn't appeal.

He huffed out a sigh and stood with hands on hips, staring dejectedly around the apartment. Used to his own company for so long, he now found himself missing Kate's. He had no idea what he was going to do with the afternoon that stretched interminably ahead of him.

Half an hour later, he slouched lower on the sofa, staring at the television, trying to work out what the movie was about, and then realized he didn't particularly even like it. Reaching for the remote, he scrolled through some more cable channels before giving up in disgust. There was nothing he wanted to watch, so he switched the TV off and got up, scuffing into the kitchen. A minute later he slammed the refrigerator shut. He didn't want anything to eat, either. He stood in the living room, hands on his hips again as he stared at the floor. What he really wanted was Kate, and she wasn't here because she was back at the store with another man. Not just another man, but an ex-boyfriend with whom she'd had a committed relationship.

So what if the guy was gay now; it wasn't helping him feel any better about the situation. And what had he done? Reaching up to rub the back of his neck with one hand, Michael ran his fingers through his hair and growled under his breath. The first sign of any conflict and he'd turned tail and fled, which was playing right into the other guy's hands. And what if Kate had wanted him to stay? Michael groaned this time, rubbing his face with his hands in frustration. She hadn't begged him to stay. If anything, she had looked just as uncomfortable as he had felt. Should he have asked if she wanted to leave with him? No, she'd stayed. Paul seemed to be the emotional stabilizer in the store, so perhaps he'd keep things on an even keel.

Or not.

Michael didn't know Paul's history with Tom, which in itself was no surprise given he'd only just heard about the man today. He grimaced at the turn the day had taken. He and Kate had woken up in each other's arms and were delighting in the thought of a whole day together stretching before them. That feeling had lasted as long as it had taken for Alistair to call. Kate had dealt with the surprise far better than he had expected. When it came to his previous relationships, Michael was used to the opposite: pouting and endless questions about why the current woman in his life *wasn't* featured in his work.

He shook his head as he thought of some of the women in his past. They had all been beautiful and intelligent to be sure, and yet strangely insecure and hungry for some kind of immortality in the reflection of Michael's words. He had never delivered, and they had inevitably moved on. Their disenchantment at their inability to inspire had been combined with Michael's less than stellar social skills and impossible working hours. He knew it was foolish to blame that sole factor on the breakups, but there were at least two ex-girlfriends who had longed to be considered his literary muse.

He'd never needed a muse until he met Kate. Her appearance in his work had been quite unexpected, but once she was on the page, it became impossible for him to write anything else. By the time he had begun to wonder if he should tell Kate what he was working on, they'd seemed to have passed the point of no return. Kate had asked him a few questions about his work before he had been ready to discuss it, and then the subject had been dropped. He had entertained the brief fantasy of presenting Kate with a finished copy of the book, watching the surprise and delight dance across her face as she realized what the story contained. All it had taken to ruin all of that was for Michael's phone to be out of reach when Alistair called.

Punching the wall with frustration, Michael stalked toward the bedroom and stripped off his T-shirt. He might as well go for a run. He shoved down his jeans and kicked them aside as he walked into the bathroom to grab his shorts off a hook on the back of the bathroom door. He changed with quick, angry movements, slamming the apartment door after him with unnecessary force.

"So when do you think you'll be seeing him again?" Tom asked, his voice only slightly muffled by the potato wedge he had just stuffed into his mouth.

"Today, I hope," Kate replied, licking some sour cream off her fingers. After two glasses of wine, she had started to feel a bit wobbly, so she'd insisted that they get something to eat.

"Don't let me stop you," Tom urged, holding up his empty glass to signal a passing waiter, and then gave Kate a questioning look. "Glass or bottle?"

"Might as well make it a bottle," Kate said in a resigned tone. Given the rate he was drinking, it would work out cheaper. She felt a pang of sympathy for Tom now. He drank like this when he was nervous, so the conversation had obviously had more of an impact on him than she'd thought. "Tom, are you seeing anyone?"

"Not right now," he admitted, reaching for another wedge.

"But what about that guy you—" she began, stopping when Tom shook his head vehemently.

"Uh-uh, Momma's boy," he said with a tone of finality.

"Right." She considered this. Tom's dating history since he had come out had certainly been a moving feast, but there hadn't been many relationships in the intervening years that had lasted more than a couple of months at best. "Anyone on the horizon?"

"Nope," he said, "and while the hunt for Mr. Right continues, I've still got you."

And with that simple comment, Kate had an epiphany. Even though they had ended the sexual side of their relationship, she was still very much Tom's girlfriend. She was his go-to girl when he wasn't in a relationship of his own, which is why he preferred it when she was available. Anger roiled in her chest at the thought of being Tom's beck and call girl to satisfy his thirst for company. She looked up and was arrested by the look of stark longing on his face: Tom was watching a couple on the other side of the bar, laughing and enjoying themselves.

Tom looked back at her and raised an eyebrow, his expression shuttered once more.

"What?"

"Did you hear what you just said?" Kate said.

"No, what?"

Kate repeated his words back to him. Tom stared at her for a long moment.

"Fuuuuck," he sighed at least. "Okay, point taken."

"Wow." Kate nodded.

"That's putting it lightly. You know, Kate, I never meant... I guess that..." he broke again and snorted at his fumbling. "Would it, I mean, that is to say..."

"Oh, just say it," Kate said.

"Security blanket," he blurted.

Kate blinked. "Okay," she said at last. "I'll need a little more information than that."

"Kate, we've known each other most of our lives. Hell, even when you moved to the big smoke, I wasn't too far behind. All this time you've been my security blanket. Even when I knew I might be gay, I thought if I could make it in a relationship with you, everything would be okay." He swallowed. "But I only ended up lying to the both of us."

Kate's throat felt tight, and all she could do was nod for him to continue.

"You've always been there for me, and it's something that I never wanted to end."

"It doesn't have to," Kate suggested. "You just have to stop being such a bitch."

"Look at yourself every twenty-eight days and say that." Tom snorted, prompting a choked laugh from Kate.

"To be fair, though," he went on, "I've been your fallback as well. Remember all those times you wanted to go out, you were dateless and didn't want to go alone?"

"True," Kate agreed. "I guess over the years, we've each been as bad as the other."

"Yeah." Tom nodded. "Still, this is *you* that I've hurt. You're not other people to me; you're *Kate*." He reached over to take her hand. "And I'm sorry that I didn't talk about Michael with you more. I knew, the last time we spoke, that he was maybe something special, but I guess I wasn't ready to face up to it."

"Well, you faced up to it today," Kate said, holding up her glass of wine.

"I guess you can teach an old dog new tricks after all," he replied, chinking his glass against hers. "So," he continued after they had sipped their wine, "what do you think he's doing now?"

"Actually, I'm not sure. We had talked about going to the market, but I'm not sure he'll do that now. Maybe he'll do some work."

"Sounds boring." Tom pulled a face. "Why don't you give him a call? Judging by the way he was looking at you earlier, I'm sure he'll come a-runnin'."

Michael had set a good pace for his jog, but the more he thought about Alistair and Tom, the angrier he got. He picked up the pace, running faster now.

Alistair had upset Kate, Tom had been an insulting prick, and here he was running laps in a damn park because he had wimped out of the equation. Furious at himself, he ran faster still, ignoring the pain as his muscles and lungs began to burn.

Two circuits later he saw the park entrance in the distance and began to slow his pace. By the time he stopped, he was gasping for breath. He bent over double with his hands braced on his knees, gulping down air and trying not to throw up. He felt like shit. After a long time, he felt able to stand up without passing out. He limped over to a nearby bench and did some cool-down stretches. He wondered what Kate was doing, and fumbled in his pocket for his phone, quickly realizing he didn't have it. He cursed under his breath as he left the park, resolving to call her as soon as he got home.

He needed to see his girl, and then he'd feel a lot better.

"Voicemail," Kate announced, putting her phone down on the table. "He's either busy or he's gone out and forgotten it."

Tom put a hand over his heart. "Is such a thing even possible?"

Kate gave him an amused look. "Yes, it's true—there are people out there that can actually function without a cell phone."

"Next you'll be telling me there isn't a Santa," Tom protested.

"He'll call when he gets back to his phone," Kate said, ignoring Tom as she shot her phone another glance. She hoped he was okay. She groaned and put her head in her hands. "Crap, shit, fu—"

"Whoa there," Tom said. "What brought that on?

"I've just realized," Kate groaned, her head in her hands, "I only just told Michael about our history this morning."

"Yeah, and?"

"And then we show up at the store and you're there acting like..." Kate glanced at Tom, who had enough self-preservation to look chastened. "... the way you did. And then he leaves and I take off with you. How does that look?"

Tom considered that. "Hate to say it, kiddo, but not good."

Kate gave him a solemn nod. "Not good at all."

"So, it's getting serious?"

"Think so," Kate confirmed, sipping at a Coke. The wine had proved too much and she had moved onto something soft, much to Tom's disgust.

"Well, that's good. So long as he treats you right, I promise to be on my best behavior." Tom nodded. "Think he'll put a ring on your finger?"

Kate laughed, and then jumped as her phone rang. "Well, my phone is ringing; does that count?" She snatched it up and smiled when she saw Michael's name on the screen.

"Hey," she greeted in a soft voice.

"How's my girl?" Michael asked, his heart in his throat. Although the walk home had cooled him down from his run, his pulse was jumping.

"All good," Kate answered, "but I miss you. What are you doing?"

"I went out for a run and forgot my phone," he admitted, smiling when he heard her gurgle of laughter.

"I told Tom that's what must've happened. How are you feeling now? Do you want a recovery drink?"

"That sounds good. Where are you?" Michael nodded when she told him the name of the bar. "No problem. Give me time to shower and change, and I'll see you soon."

"Promise?"

"I'm on my way," Michael said. "And Kate?"

"Yeah?"

"Are you sure everything's okay?"

"I'm sure. It's all good, you'll see."

"See you soon," Michael promised, and was still grinning when they hung up. He loped toward the bathroom.

Kate snapped her phone shut and beamed at Tom. "He's on his way."

"He'd be crazy not to," Tom said.

❧

Michael paused in the doorway, looking for Kate as his eyes adjusted to the light. He'd showered and changed in record time, sprinting down the stairs and into the first taxi he saw.

Tom saw him first and nearly choked on his next mouthful of wine. He had been so ready to dislike him at the store that he hadn't paid him any attention. Now that he and Kate had cleared the air, he was feeling slightly drunk and quite at ease with the world.

"Holy shit," he muttered. "Are you absolutely, one hundred percent sure he's straight? Because if there's any margin for error at all, I'm *so* there."

Kate twisted in her chair and waved when she saw Michael. Glancing back over her shoulder, she shot Tom a smug smile.

"Figures." Tom watched as Michael's face lit up with a grin when he saw Kate and strode through the crowd toward them. It didn't escape Tom's notice that a couple of other bar patrons had noticed Michael as well. Michael was oblivious to all of this as he made a beeline for where Kate was waiting, bending down to kiss her cheek as he grabbed a vacant chair and took a seat.

Michael's smile dimmed to wary courtesy as he nodded at Tom. "Hello again."

"Be nice," Kate warned Tom in an undertone as he extended a hand toward Michael.

"Michael, I believe you met my evil bitch twin earlier. Allow me to introduce myself, I'm Tom," he said with a smile that was equally cautious.

"Evil twin, huh?" Michael's lips curled into a more genuine smile this time.

"You'd be amazed how much he gets around," Tom said with a solemn nod.

Kate sniffed the air, found it was friendly, and was pleased. As Tom and Michael fell into conversation, she smiled into her glass. She sat back in her seat, smiling when Michael unconsciously moved his seat closer so that he could drape his arm around her shoulders. A waiter approached their table to take Michael's drink order, and while he was occupying himself with the menu, Tom caught

Kate's eye and winked. Kate felt as if a weight had been taken off her shoulders. It was still early days, but the initial steps had been taken.

"So, Michael," Tom was saying, "I know Kate and I have cleared the air, but there's just one thing I have to say to you before we move on and put all this behind us."

"I'm listening." Michael nodded.

"Hurt her, and I will beat you to death with one of her industrial baking trays," Thomas said in a matter of fact tone. Michael looked at him in askance, and he shrugged. "A vague disclaimer is no one's friend."

"It won't happen," Michael said in a firm voice. "I know what I want."

Tom gave an imperceptible flinch at the obvious barb in Michael's answer, before swallowing hard and holding up his glass in a toast. "I believe you," he said at last.

Kate looked at Michael, who simply leaned forward and kissed her.

"So do I," she answered.

Kate watched as the two men took the first tentative steps of friendship toward each other. Wariness was evident on both sides, but for the time being, any animosity or insecurity was put aside for the sake of the woman that sat between them.

"All good?" Tom asked Kate in a quiet voice when Michael went to the bar. She looked up to see Tom watching her with caution.

"All good."

"You look happy with this guy," he said after a pause. "He seems to really care about you."

"I hope so," Kate said, glancing over to where Michael stood at the bar.

"As long as he treats you right, I won't interfere," Thomas offered. "But I can't say I'm not jealous as hell."

Kate felt something in her chest relax at last. It felt as if the worst had been confronted and dealt with and now she could move on.

Chapter 18

Procrastination and Pizza

Wren kept her head down and focused on her footsteps, making a game of not stepping on any cracks in the pavement. Next she amused herself by counting dogs and seeing how many businessmen were wearing colorful ties. Fishing in her bag, she sighed as her hands came up empty, and crossed to the other side of the street as she saw the familiar booth ahead.

"Hey, Betty," Wren greeted the elderly woman as she approached the newsstand.

"Hey, yourself," Betty replied with a gimlet smile. "I suppose you're after the usual."

"You know it." Wren nodded, digging out some bills from her wallet as Betty slid a copy of *InStyle* magazine and a pack of gum toward her.

"Good weekend?" Betty made conversation as she dug out some coins.

"Not bad." Wren shrugged.

"And that young man of yours, how's that going?" Betty slapped the change into Wren's outstretched hand and leaned her hip against the counter.

"Who told you?" Wren gave her a look of amazement.

"No one had to." Betty winked. "But that's some love bite you've got on your neck there, kid."

Wren slapped a hand to her neck and moaned.

"Other side," Betty cackled, enjoying the younger woman's mortification as Wren switched her hand to the other side of her neck, and then gave it up as a lost cause. "Looks like you've been having a good time."

"I guess so," Wren replied as she stuffed the magazine into her tote bag and unwrapped the gum to pop a piece into her mouth.

"You *guess* so?" Betty shook her head. "Damn girl, youth is wasted on the young." She folded her arms and rested them on a pile of *Newsweek*. "What's he like?"

Wren thought for a moment. "Persistent."

"He'd have to be," Betty observed. "You're like a fart in a bottle."

Wren arched an eyebrow at that. She'd been called many things in the past, but this was a new one.

"You like him?" Betty asked as she served another customer.

Wren nodded, keeping her chin close to her chest. She was loitering now and feeling like a kid being called out at school, but Betty's calm assessment and no-nonsense questions made her feel curiously better.

"I didn't hear you," Betty said, and then, "Not you. Four fifty," to another customer.

"Yes," Wren said in a louder voice.

"Good." Betty nodded. "Then get off your bony ass and do something about it."

"I have," the younger woman protested.

"I don't mean sex." Betty waved a dismissive hand. "Although Lord knows it gets the job done. Men are like linoleum, lay them right the first time and you can walk all over them for the rest of your life, *but,*" she went on as Wren laughed, "you need someone that'll treat you with respect, keep you on your toes and give you the best sex you've ever had."

"Oh, well, when you put it that way, it sounds almost too easy." Wren snorted.

"So what does he do, this young man of yours?" Betty ignored Wren's easy dismissal.

"He's a teacher at NYU," Wren replied. Then at Betty's silent prompt for more information she added, "Specializing in American history."

"So he's smart then?"

"Oh, yeah," Wren said, remembering their latest argument about consumerism.

"And passionate," the older woman went on. Wren sighed and nodded. She was never going to live the love bite down.

"Like you're smart," Betty mused, "and I'm guessing you can more than stand your ground in the sack."

"Betty." Wren coughed back a shocked laugh.

"Relax, kid." Betty laughed. "When you've chalked up as many years as I have, it gives you a certain level of free speech." She considered Wren for a long moment. "How long you been scared of this guy?"

"Who said I was scared?"

"You're not exactly standing here in the flush of new love. What is it you want?"

Wren sighed, feeling incredibly weary of the whole situation. "I wish I knew."

Betty shook her head slowly and slid another pack of gum toward Wren. "You'd better make up your mind, because guys like him don't grow on trees. If there's one thing we women are good at, it's looking a gift horse in the mouth. You're being treated with respect and kindness when you're used to being used and abused, and that's got you scared. You know what my mom used to tell me when I was dithering over my Earl?"

"What?" Wren stepped closer as the older woman beckoned, and then her eyes widened as Betty muttered to her in an undertone. Passing customers glanced up at the laughter, some of them wondering how such a small woman could laugh so loud.

Bidding her a fond farewell, Wren made her way to work with a broad grin on her face. Betty had given her the makings of a great quote, and she couldn't wait to see how Kate was going to come up with a cupcake for this one.

❧

"Morning, Wren." Kate smiled, her cheeks pink from her morning walk. The seasons were starting to turn and the air was getting cooler.

"Morning, boss."

"Wren, don't call me boss."

"Sorry, boss."

"Good weekend?" Kate asked as she pushed the front door open and went inside.

"Not bad," Wren called over her shoulder, carrying her bag in one hand as she shrugged off her coat. "Yours?" She stopped in her tracks and turned slowly to stare at the new installation. "Oh, wow," she gasped. "They look fantastic."

"Don't they," Kate agreed with a pleased smile.

"When?" Wren asked as she crossed the floor to run a hand along the polished copper piping. Paul had done a great job; his craftsmanship and attention to detail had done the store proud.

"Sunday," Kate replied, looking pleased with Wren's reaction, and then she looked closer at Wren and gave her a knowing smile. "Good weekend?"

"Great," Wren replied, putting her coat and bag away before stopping to gather up an armful of magazines.

"And how's David?" Kate said in a too-innocent tone.

"He's good," Wren said casually.

"So I see," Kate replied as she filled the jug with milk and kicked the refrigerator door closed with her foot.

"What?" Wren looked at her, puzzled, and then reached up to touch the love bite on her neck. "I knew I should've worn a scarf," she groused.

"Right, because that would be so subtle," Kate teased. "When did the two of you hook up?"

"Saturday," Wren allowed, dumping the pile of magazines on the counter and leaning against it as Kate went to work on the coffees.

"Morning, guys. Wren, you've got a love bite on your neck," Emily called as she walked through the store, past the counter and into the kitchen.

"Everyone has to know?" Wren protested as Kate laughed.

"Honey, it's right there where we can all see it." Emily reappeared, tying on her apron.

"Just because you two haven't got any," Wren mumbled in mock anger at the two smirking women.

"That you can see," Kate rejoined, her eyes crinkling with amusement.

"How about you, Emily? Anything to report about Bookstore Brad?" Wren studied her closely.

"Uh..." Emily's face began to warm beneath their scrutiny. "Well, that is to say..." She waved a hand, aware that her face was getting warmer by the moment.

"His place or yours?" Wren asked matter-of-factly.

"His," Emily replied promptly and then gazed at her in horror when she realized what she'd let slip.

"Ah-*ha*," Wren said. "I *knew* you two would get together." She looked from Kate to Emily. "So how about that? All three of us are getting laid."

The three women looked at each other for a moment, before laughing and exchanging high-fives.

"We should all get together and have a drink after work sometime," Emily suggested. "I know that Brad would love to meet Michael, but not," she added hastily, "in a groupie kind of way."

"Michael and David go way back, so they'll be fine, and David seems to get a kick out of meeting new people all the time," Wren speculated. "How about it, boss?"

"Sounds like a plan." Kate nodded.

"Maybe you could give Paul a call as well," Wren suggested, "and how about Tom? Do you think he can share you for a change?" She was taken aback when Kate pulled a face.

"Early days," Kate cautioned, "but he has agreed to play nice for now."

Wren gaped at her. "They've *met?*"

"Yup." Kate finished making the coffees and carefully moved the cups across the counter. Emily was stacking the last of the magazines onto their new rack, but Wren swooped onto her cup with all the reverence it deserved.

"Ahh." Wren nodded sagely after her first sip. "And how did that go?"

Kate concentrated on stirring some sugar into her cup. "About as well as could be expected."

"Ouch." Wren winced. "Was Tom up to his old tricks?" Wren had seen Tom give prospective beaus the cold shoulder in the past to devastating effect. She had wondered why Kate put up with it, but had rationalized that she did not know the secrets of the friendship between the two. "How did Michael take it?"

"Okay, I guess, but it was a lot for him to take in. Things ended up well enough." She smiled at this as she remembered the night before.

It had been late in the afternoon when Michael and Kate arrived back at her apartment. Kate had slung her bag onto a chair and sprawled on the couch. After a moment's hesitation, Michael had followed. Kate had smiled at his approach and curled her legs up to allow him room, and then shifted around to snuggle up against him with a small sigh, fisting her hands in his shirt to bring herself closer still. Michael had stretched out his legs to rest his feet on the coffee table, and put his arm around her shoulders, combing his fingers absently through Kate's hair as he tipped his head back to stare at the ceiling.

"Big day," he'd said at last. Kate's eyes had been closed and Michael's voice was a deep rumble in his chest.

"You could say that," Kate had sighed. She'd rested her head against Michael's chest and traced the pattern of his T-shirt with a lazy finger. He'd dropped a kiss onto her forehead, and then gave a sigh of contentment as he'd rested his head against hers. Running his hand in calming circles on Kate's arm, on impulse, he'd run his hand down her side and up under the hem of her T-shirt. Encouraged by her quiet hum of pleasure, he'd shifted slightly and kept stroking her skin, his fingers circling and becoming more insistent as her skin flushed under his touch.

Kate had reached up to pull his head down to hers, her breathing becoming shallow. Michael had kissed her lightly once, and then returned for more. His hands shifting to her hips, he'd moved her along the couch so that he could rest himself between her legs as he'd urged them open. Kate had needed no prompting, flushed now, very warm. Pushing up the base of her T-shirt, Michael had pressed a soft kiss against the flat plane of her belly.

"Michael, please…"

"I know." He'd bent his head to her skin again. Sitting up, he'd reached out to smooth a strand of hair off her face while she'd watched him.

Kate had hardly moved, hardly breathed. *What did he see?* she'd wondered. *Did he see a character for his book, was he fantasizing about someone else, did he see her?* Again she'd found herself wondering what it was she had to offer. She had given all she had to Thomas, which turned out to be not nearly enough. The pain of that was receding as time went by, although in her lonelier moments, she found that the scar was still fresh. Since then she had worked to shroud herself in her bakery, in her friendships and independence to bury her fear that she would only ever be perceived as a means to an end. She wanted to be the destination and not the journey. She wanted to be loved and adored.

"You are so beautiful," Michael had muttered. His insecurities from the afternoon had come flooding back. "Kate, tell me what you want. What can I do to make you mine?"

Her only answer had been to pull him down for another kiss before struggling off the couch and leading him to the bed.

"Earth calling Kate…"

Kate blinked and looked up to see Wren regarding her with her head cocked to one side.

"Are you okay, boss?"

"Sure." Kate remembered to smile as she pulled a waiting cup toward her and poured in the milk. "I was a million miles away."

"So you were saying the evening ended well enough, but does that mean things got off to a shaky start?"

"Yup." Kate nodded.

"How about Paul?"

Kate's face softened as she thought about her big brother. "Bear was wonderful. He took to Michael straight away and then gave Tom and me a verbal spanking and kicked us out of the store to go have a talk."

"Hang on, I'm confused. Where was Michael?"

"He took off to let Tom and me sort things out," Kate clarified.

"As in, he chickened out?" Wren frowned. That didn't sound like the Michael she knew.

"Not at all. He just wanted to give us some space, but I don't think he was too happy about it."

"You've lost me again. What was Tom doing here?" Wren sipped at her coffee, trying to process what Kate was telling her.

"Sorry, I'm all over the place. Bear wanted to get the job done quickly, so he called Tom to give him a hand. Michael and I were out having brunch and decided to stop in to see how it was all going and…" She waved a hand. "Michael was polite, Tom was a total bitch," Kate began and then paused to sip at her coffee, winking as Emily came in to take her cup. "And then Tom and I went to have a long talk, and Michael tried to kill himself jogging."

"I hate coming in at the tail end of a conversation," Emily commented as she strolled up to the counter, making the other two women laugh.

"The boss was just giving me a summary of her weekend," Wren explained.

"Which included gay men and death by jogging," Emily said, still looking none the wiser.

"Kate's main men met each other over the weekend," Wren explained. "Bear was fantastic as always, Tom was the bitch queen from hell, and Michael was the shy, retiring type."

"Oh, I wouldn't say *shy*," Kate mused, thinking back to how Michael managed to put Tom in his place and stake his claim on her at the same time. "He's a man that knows what he wants."

"About time you hooked up with one like that," Wren muttered, and then looked up to see Emily and Kate regarding her with surprise. "What? Just sayin'," she continued in a defensive tone.

"Wow," Emily commented. "Sounds like we all had quite a time of it then."

"What can I say?" Kate waved her cup. "Life is never dull." She swigged back the last of her coffee and set the cup down as she gave Wren a speculative grin. "Speaking of which…" she said in a meaningful tone.

"This one's going to get you," Wren said, leaning across the counter to pick up her stub of chalk. She collected the chalkboard and propped it on a chair to write up the quote, and then turned it around with a flourish to reveal her words.

> Procrastination is like masturbation;
> in the end you're just screwing yourself.

Emily gave a whoop of laughter, and Kate chuckled before her gaze turned inward and she walked slowly toward the kitchen. Wren watched her with satisfaction. She could almost taste victory.

⁓

Michael was thinking about food when he let himself into his apartment. Kate's early morning starts had meant he was home earlier than usual and so he had gone out for his morning run. Now that he had jogged off the Indian meal indulgence from the night before, he was ready for breakfast.

He had abandoned his phone on the kitchen counter when he'd gone out, and now he snatched it up as it started to vibrate against the marble countertop.

He inspected the display and considered rejecting the call, but then thought better of it. Kate had dealt with her issues head on, the best he could do was follow her example.

"Alistair," he said briefly as he kicked off his running shoes, "you have some explaining to do."

"I know," came the sighed admission. "Would it help if I said I was sorry?"

"It might," Michael grunted as he flicked his phone onto loudspeaker and tossed it onto the bed so that he could take off his shirt. He listened to Alistair's apologies with half an ear as he peeled off his running clothes. He wanted a shower and he didn't feel particularly well disposed toward listening to apologetic babble. The damage had been done, but the damage control had been swift, no thanks to Alistair. He sniffed at his tank top, and after making a face, balled it up and threw it toward the laundry hamper. It missed and fell to the floor. He'd pick it up later.

Alistair was still talking. Michael leaned over the bed and snatched up the handset.

"Alistair, can I call you back?"

Alistair stopped mid-sentence and stared at the receiver. It had been a while since Michael had offered to call him back.

"Sure," he said after a moment's pause.

"Won't be long," Michael replied, and disconnected the call.

Alistair listened to the disconnected tone. Michael wasn't one to talk on the phone very much so the fact that he had offered to call Alistair back spoke volumes. Alistair sat and rubbed his chin. He just couldn't work out if it was good or bad.

❧

"Good, huh?" Wren had popped her head around the kitchen to see Kate leaning against the counter deep in thought.

"Almost too good," Kate replied. "You might have me on this one."

"Ha." Wren turned to give Emily a victory fist bump.

"Hang on." Kate held up a cautionary hand. "I haven't thrown in the towel yet."

"Maybe not, boss," Wren taunted with a wide grin, "but the clock's a-tickin' and customers will be here soon—" She broke off as Kate snapped her fingers and turned toward the mixer. "You haven't," she gasped.

Kate looked up and gave her a conspiratorial wink, and she pulled the mixer forward on the counter and then started to measure sugar into the bowl.

"No," Wren all but wailed, "I thought I really had you on this one."

"We'll see," Kate replied in a placid tone, hoping she had enough white chocolate.

Wren pushed herself away from the door frame and headed out to finish setting up for the morning.

"Any clues?" Emily paused on her way out to stock up the sugar packets on the tables. "I promise not to consort with the enemy," she vowed, holding up her pinkie.

"No clues yet," Kate muttered as she watched the butter and sugar mix to a creamy consistency. "I'm winging it this morning. I think she might really have me this time."

"Your secret is safe with me." Emily smiled and went about her duties.

✑

"Michael, I had no idea that Kate didn't know," Alistair began as soon as he answered Michael's call.

"It's okay." Michael sounded resigned but not angry. "It's something I should've told her myself, so we're both to blame."

Alistair blinked; he had expected more fallout than this. Perhaps Michael breaking through his writer's block had been beneficial in more ways than one.

"So," he began with caution, "how's the writing going these days?"

Michael gave a dry chuckle. "Alistair, you're as tenacious as a pit-bull. I really haven't missed these conversations at all."

"I'll take that as a compliment," Alistair replied in an equally dry tone, "but no avoiding the question, Forrester—how's the writing?"

"Good," Michael allowed. "Better than good," he added after a moment's pause. "I'm averaging about a thousand words a day."

"How much more time do you think you need?" Alistair asked as he moved forward in his seat and propped his elbows on the desk.

Michael told him.

"So soon? I'll let them know," Alistair said, his eyebrows raised in surprise. When the call ended, he hung up his phone and leaned back in his chair, staring at the notes and doodles he'd scribbled in his diary. After his conversation with Kate the day before, he had been sure the situation had been heading for disaster. Now he found himself in the position of reviewing his Gantt chart and wondering what sort of marketing push they were going to come up with for Michael's latest creation.

Kate set the last cupcake creation on the tray and twisted it slightly so that it was in line with all the others before giving a slight nod of satisfaction.

"Wren," she called, "brace yourself."

"Hang on," Wren answered. "Be there in a minute."

"That's what she said," Emily replied, earning a few laughs of appreciation from their morning customers.

Carefully scooping up the tray, Kate carried it out of the kitchen and toward the display cabinet. Wren appeared to slide the door open, so that Kate could set the tray down with all the reverence the cupcakes deserved.

"All right," Wren said in a weary tone. "Let's be having it." She had picked up the small chalkboard and stood waiting.

"*Time Flies When You're Having Fun*," Kate dictated. "Chocolate cherry butterfly cakes with white chocolate wings."

Wren wrote quickly, and then set the chalkboard onto its easel with a dejected sigh.

"One day," she vowed as she shook Kate's hand to concede defeat, "one day."

"It's good to have a goal," Kate assured her.

"Penny for your thoughts?"

Wren blinked. It was late in the afternoon now and she had paused in the act of resupplying the sugar packets, thinking about David.

"Want to talk about it?" Kate gave her a gentle smile.

"I don't know." Wren pushed her hair away from her face and then shifted her weight from one foot to the other, aware that she was fidgeting and unable to stop it.

"I told you mine," Kate prodded. She gave the store a quick glance. The day was drawing to a close now and the pace of customers was beginning to slow down. "Come on, we're getting ready to close so we've got time. Spill." Taking Wren by the elbow, she steered her into the kitchen. "Emily, can you hold the fort?"

"No problem," Emily assured them. She had come a long way from the days when she had been nervous about making coffees.

Kate urged Wren to sit on the solitary high stool in the kitchen. "So, what's up? Is it David? Is something wrong?"

"No ... I don't know," she said as she wiped her sweaty palms on the thighs of her jeans. "It's just all harder than I thought."

"What is?" Kate asked.

"Being with someone," Wren said, picking at a thread on the beaded patch that adorned one knee of her jeans. "What's it like with you and Michael?"

Kate was nonplussed with the question. It wasn't something she often stopped to think about. "It's … well, I guess it's …" she searched for the right word, "… easy isn't quite right, but it's comfortable."

"Right," Wren sighed. "So it's just me then."

"Oh, Wren, no." Kate rushed in to reassure her. "You know I wasn't sure about Michael for a long time, but we just took things slow and …" She smiled just thinking of him. "He was always there for me."

"Uh-huh." Wren nodded. "Go on."

"Like David seems to be there for you."

"Tell me about it," Wren said with an air of gloom. "Every time I turn around lately, there he is."

"Maybe it's a sign," Kate said with a gentle smile. "How do you feel when you see him?"

Wren considered the question for a moment, thinking of the way David's smile had lit up his face when he saw her. "Good," she answered at last, not noticing that her entire demeanor had softened when she thought of him.

"Well, then, that's a start," Kate offered with a gentle smile. "Wren, you don't have to label what the two of you are straight away. Just take it as it comes and see how comfortable you feel."

"I guess." Wren nodded. "I'm so used to doing my own thing that it freaks me out a little."

"If you're happy when you're with him, then focus on that," Kate advised. "And whatever follows will be worked out in time by the pair of you."

"Door's closed, boss." Emily appeared, wiping her hands on a dishcloth. "So that's us done for the day. Got any plans tonight?"

"Not that I know of," Kate answered. She and Michael hadn't made any plans for the week now that she thought of it. Feeling a buzzing in her pocket, she dug out her cell phone. It was Paul.

Dinner? xP

She grinned and typed out a response.

Sure. Where? xK

The response came so quickly she knew he had to be waiting for her reply.

Pizza + beer = happy bear. Meet u at shop. xP

"Looks like I'm catching up with Paul." She smiled. "He's probably wanting to check up on me after the weekend to make sure everything's okay."

"As far as protectors go, you can't get much better than him," Emily commented. "He's pretty good value."

"Yeah, he does good," Kate acknowledged with a proud smile. "Jack told him to look after me, and I guess he takes that pretty seriously at times."

"Well, you're all each other has, don't forget," Emily said.

Wren paused on her way past and gave a slight cough for dramatic effect. "Hello, I'm standing right *here*."

Kate laughed and threw her arms around her. "And, of course, I've got you," she said. Emily caught her eye and made her lower lip tremble. "*And* you," she added, reaching out to haul her in for a hug as well.

"Just so we're clear on that," Wren said, squeezing Kate for emphasis. "Bear's all well and good, but the sisterhood will always be here too."

"Damn straight," Emily seconded.

"And that's always good to know," Kate said, her voice muffled as she hugged her two friends.

❦

Michael glanced at the time display in the upper corner of his laptop screen and then looked back at his work; he had made good progress today. Alistair would be more than pleased when he saw the volume that he had managed to produce over the last few months. *When it rains, it pours,* he thought with a smile. Months with nothing to show for it, and then the floodgates had opened. As long as his editor could make sense of it all, then he'd feel confident about his work. He sat and rubbed his top lip while he re-read what he had written, wondering when Kate would want to read it. She had said little after their discussion. Perhaps the very fact that she was the source of his inspiration was still sinking in. He was sure that her curiosity about it would only be a matter of time. Words stirred in his mind as he sat thinking about her, and he looked at the keyboard for a moment before he smiled and began to type again.

Standing up from his desk, he wrapped his arms around his shoulders to give himself a squeeze before stretching his arms up and over his head, feeling his muscles pop. The action pulled his T-shirt up, and he stood absently scratching his abs while staring out the window. It was late afternoon; Kate would be closing up shop soon and they hadn't talked about they might be doing that evening. He picked up his cell phone and dialed the number he knew by heart.

"Hey," he greeted her in a soft voice. "Doing anything this evening?"

"Hi," Kate replied, and he could hear the smile in her voice. "Paul just messaged me wanting pizza and beer tonight. I think he's doing his Brother Bear after Tom unleashed the bitch on the weekend."

"Sounds fair." Michael laughed. He wondered if Kate noticed she tended to adopt Paul's syntax when she spoke. "Should I leave you to it?"

Kate paused. "No, I'd like you to get to know him better. How about I run a couple of things past him and let you know where we'll be?"

"Sure, but no pressure okay? If you need family time, I'm cool with that."

"Thanks, babe," Kate replied. "I'll be in touch soon, 'kay?"

"Okay. Have you had a nice day?"

"It's getting better all the time," she assured him.

Michael put his phone down and strolled toward the bathroom. If he didn't see Kate tonight, he was sure he could keep working. Still, it would be good to see his girl. He got into the bathroom and shucked off his jeans, pausing when he saw Kate's toothbrush and a tube of mascara sitting on the bathroom counter. He had a toothbrush and deodorant at Kate's place now, and these small domestic touches made him smile.

❧

"I don't have to ask who that was," Wren commented. "Just hearing his voice makes you go all goofy."

"Takes one to know one," Kate retorted, swatting Wren on the rump as the smaller woman passed her to empty the water jugs in the industrial sink behind the counter.

Kate started tapping out a message to Paul on her phone.

Can I bring Michael or do you need Bear time? xK

Her phone beeped a few minutes later with his reply.

No prob. How about Bear time gets 30 min head start? xP

Kate smiled at her brother's response.

Sounds good. C u soon xK

As expected, Paul got in the last word.

Not if I c u first! xP

Kate groaned at the old joke and put her phone back in her pocket.

"Is that good or bad?" Emily asked as she untied her apron and folded it carefully.

"Definitely good, and a bit mysterious," Kate answered. "Michael's coming out with Bear and me tonight."

"Sounds good. Hey, can I play show and tell?" Wren chimed in, and at Kate's nod, she unbuttoned her little black waistcoat and pulled it open to reveal a smiling fox print on her T-shirt. "What do you think?"

"I think it was made for you." Emily grinned. It was true; the fox even had dark brown—almost black—grinning eyes that reminded both women of Wren.

"Funny you should say that," Wren replied, buttoning up the waistcoat again.

"You made it?" Emily gaped.

"Yep, the shirt and the print. You like?"

"I love," Emily enthused. "I've got to put an order in."

"Me too," Kate agreed. Wren smiled beneath their praise, soaking it up like a drug.

"I've said it before and I'll say it again," Kate said, "you've *got* to start selling your fashion somewhere. Hell, you can even sell it here if you like, but you've got to get your work out there."

"We'll see," Wren conceded. The idea excited and terrified her all at once.

"So will you, once it starts flying off the racks," Kate said. "You'll have fans everywhere. Speaking of which ..." She raised an eyebrow toward the doorway.

David had reached the bakery and had stopped to read the quote of the day. He was still laughing as he stepped inside.

"There's my girl," he said with a chuckle as he walked toward her to pull her in for a kiss.

Wren ducked her head under his chin and looked oddly shy at his obvious pleasure at seeing her. Kate and Emily exchanged a glance and went about their final duties for the day.

"You ready to go?" David murmured, running his hands on her back.

"Soon," Wren said, "I've just got to—"

"No, you don't," Kate broke in. "I've got it from here. I'm waiting for Bear so you two can take off. That goes for you as well," she added, turning to include Emily.

"Are you sure?" Emily began. "I was just about to—" She broke off as Kate pulled the dishtowel she had slung over her shoulder and began to twirl it meaningfully. "We're going," she squeaked. She had learned from experience that Kate could snap a dishcloth with deadly accuracy.

"What?" Kate said as David laughed. "It's good to be the boss."

"No argument from me." David held his hands up in surrender.

He leaned against the counter and made idle chitchat with Kate while Wren hung up her apron and gathered her things. When she appeared, he helped her on with her coat and then put his arm around her shoulder as they made their way out of the store and called out their farewells.

"Had a good day?" David leaned down as he spoke, his breath chuffing against her hair.

"Yep." Wren nodded. "You?"

"Can't complain, not when I've got you at the end of it." He grinned.

Wren smiled back. She wasn't used to this. She wasn't used to having someone to talk to, to wake up with. For all her conquests, Wren was used to being alone; she had never shared her life with anyone, and yet with David there was a strange sense of familiarity, as if she had known him for years.

"Got any plans for tonight?" he asked.

"Uh ..." Wren stalled. She had wanted to sketch some designs. "A few, but I guess we can—"

"Babe." David gave her a gentle squeeze. "I just want to eat and watch television, so if that's something I can do in the background of whatever you're doing, it's all good."

Wren squinted up at him. "Really?"

"Really," he said with a solemn nod before he grinned at her confusion. "Why, you think I need to be entertained?"

"Maybe," she replied. They had stopped at the light now. "I don't know how this works," she went on with a shrug.

"It's pretty straightforward. You just wait for the light to change to green and cross when everyone else does."

"Not that." She gave an exasperated snort. "This whole girlfriend gig."

"Mmm?" David was kissing her temple and appeared to be half-listening.

"I'm serious." She dug her elbow into his ribs and he gave a grunt of surprise.

"So I gather," he said. "All right, so let's talk. What's the problem?"

Wren kept her head down. She hadn't wanted to have this conversation and now she was going to look foolish. David gave her a gentle nudge, signaling he was waiting for her to reply.

"Idon'tknowhowtobeagirlfriend," she said in a rush.

"You want to run that by me at half speed?" David gave her a curious look.

Wren huffed in annoyance.

"I *said*," she repeated, "I don't know how to be a girlfriend."

David's forehead wrinkled as he frowned in confusion. "Yeah, and?"

"And that's it," Wren muttered. "I don't know how all this shit works."

They walked on a few paces in silence before David sighed and slowed down. He looked over his shoulder before steering Wren over to lean her against a building, bracing his hands on either side of her face.

"Wren, this isn't some sort of job description you have to aspire to," he began, and then cupped her chin in his hands to turn her gaze back to him when she tried to look away. "No, listen. I want *you*, Wren. Just the way you are."

"But you don't really know me," she replied.

"So the joy will be in finding out." David shrugged.

Wren mulled this over, and David watched the different emotions flicker across her face.

"Wren, I like you, and I want to be with you. That's all that matters, and the rest we'll make up as we go along."

Wren could feel a tightness in her chest, that had perhaps always been there, soften and release at his words. She sighed and felt her shoulders loosen as she relaxed under David's steady words and gaze. David was still cupping her face, his thumbs brushing over her cheeks.

"Okay," she said at last. "I'm game if you are."

David's hands slid down to the nape of her neck as he leaned in closer and kissed her, his mouth warm and open against hers. Wren wrapped her arms around him and pulled him closer still.

Chapter 19

Brother Bear and That Word

Kate was tidying up loose ends around the store when she heard a quick tattoo on the store window. She looked up and saw Paul letting himself in, closing the door after himself and flipping the sign on the door to CLOSED.

"Hey," Paul greeted her as he crossed toward her with a grin. "How's my favorite sister?"

"Good," Kate said as she stepped into his hug before returning to the counter to collect her bag where it sat waiting. "You?"

"Yeah." Paul stretched and gave a quiet groan. "I've been better." He rolled his shoulders and then his neck with a slight wince as his muscles protested.

"I'm sorry." Kate returned to his side with a guilty look. "All that extra work yesterday wouldn't have helped."

"If I didn't want to do it, I wouldn't have offered," Paul said in a mild tone as he propelled her toward the door with a light touch on her back. "Plus I had Tom there to help."

"Hmmm." Kate sounded dubious at that, making him laugh.

"Granted he made a fuss over getting dirty, but he was pleased with the way it was going when you and Michael showed up." Paul paused outside as Kate reached for the security grill.

"Right," Kate commented over her shoulder as she locked the door. "And look how that worked out." She finished locking up and stashed her keys inside her bag. "Tom's evil bitch twin came to the party, Michael went home and you got left with all the work."

"Not that much. We were nearly done," Paul replied as he draped a brotherly arm around her shoulders. "And you and Tom had some business to attend to."

"That's what you're calling it?"

Paul gave an expansive shrug. "It sounds better than hissy fit," he said, looking down at her as she gave a rueful smile. The pair of them began to walk across the Village. Kate hadn't asked where they were going, instead trusting that Paul's need for pizza would mean he had already decided their destination well in advance. "So," Paul began when they paused at the light, waiting to cross the street, "Michael. How's all that going?"

"All that?" Kate looked up at him, noticing yet again the height difference between them, the top of her head barely reaching his shoulder. The light changed and they began to cross the street along with the rest of the crowd. Paul drew her close to his side in an instinctively protective gesture as the pedestrians from the other side of the intersection drew near.

"You know," Paul said, giving her a quick glance before returning his attention to negotiating a clear path. "Did you guys have a talk too? He left you and Tom to it, but I'm guessing he was wondering what the hell was going on."

"You guess correctly." Kate sighed. She felt tired again. It seemed all she was doing was talking lately and it was wearing her down. Not for the first time she realized how easy it was at times to be single. Now it felt that by putting herself on the dating radar, she had somehow entered a minefield of emotions.

Paul didn't miss the sigh. "Everything okay?"

"Yeah, we're fine. Everyone's fine," Kate answered as she hitched the strap of her bag on her shoulder.

"Fine as in 'Fucking Insecure Neurotic and Emotional' type fine, or okay?" he ventured after a brief pause.

Kate snickered at this.

"I mean we're *good.*" She emphasized the last word, watching as Paul gave a sage nod. "Tom and I talked it all out, and then Michael joined us at the bar for a drink and the boys played nice."

"Really?" Paul tried not to look too surprised at this. "That's gotta be a first."

"I know, but ..." Kate considered this as they kept walking, and then frowned as she looked further down the street. "Where are we going by the way?"

"Lombardi's," Paul answered. "And don't change the subject."

"Hang on, I said I'd let Michael know where we'd be," Kate said, slowing her pace a little as she dug in her bag and then began to tap out a message to Michael on her phone.

Paul glanced down and saw what she was doing. "You want to stop and do that?"

"No, you steer and make sure I don't trip over anything," Kate said absently as she kept composing the message.

Paul nodded and tightened his arm around her shoulders, whistling tune-lessly as they walked.

Michael looked at the word count of the document and gave a low whistle. For someone with writer's block for a few months, he had certainly managed to redeem himself. Alistair would definitely be pleased with this. Or not. Michael paused as he considered this. It was certainly a break from his usual style of writing, although the sheer volume of this would give Alistair enough to work on for a while. With luck they would be able to work their way toward a mutu-ally agreeable finished product. He looked away from the screen as his phone beeped with an incoming message.

Pizza at Lombardi's cnr Spring & Mott – see you soon? xK.

Michael smiled and wrote a reply.

No probs. Let me know when. xM

He relaxed in his chair and waited for her response, rubbing an absent hand over his chin and feeling the rasp of stubble against his fingers. His phone beeped again and he smiled when he read her message and then flicked the phone back onto his desk where it landed on some paperwork with a dull thud. For a moment he considered shaving and then remembered with a grin that Kate enjoyed his scruff on occasion. Glancing at the laptop screen again, he began to re-read the afternoon's efforts, his smile fading as a small voice in his head wondered what Kate would make of it. He sighed and rubbed his face again. There was nothing for it but to wait and see. He'd come this far.

"Are we there yet?" Kate teased as she slipped her phone back into her bag.

"Nearly," Paul said. "You hungry?"

"A little," Kate conceded.

"You know, it wouldn't kill you to eat a bit more," Paul commented. It hadn't escaped his attention that Kate had shivered each time a cold gust of wind had swept against them. She had been working too hard again, and he could see that she had lost a couple of pounds. She had inherited their mother's slight build and any loss showed. Turning his attention back to the street and looking ahead toward the pizzeria, he resolved to ask her more about her relationship with Michael. Not for the first time, he wished Jack were still alive. He knew Kate would have borne Jack in Papa Bear mode with more grace than she would an inquisitive older brother, no matter how well intentioned.

"Don't fuss, Bear. I'm okay." Kate shook her head at him. It hurt her to see the worry in his eyes; she preferred to see him happy. She cast about for a distraction.

"On to more important things," she said, "pizza. Have you thought about what you want?" She knew her ploy had worked when Paul laughed.

"Kat, dinner's a done deal. I've been thinking about it all afternoon."

By the time they were crossing Houston, they were indulging in a good natured squabble about toppings.

"Definitely sausage," Paul said, "and plenty of peppers."

Kate gave him a look of amused tolerance. "Like you could possibly consider anything else," she said. Ever since their teenage years, Paul had been known for his devotion to pizza. "Just don't forget I want mushrooms."

A while later they were settling themselves at a table, Kate stashing her bag between her feet and accepting a bottle of mineral water from a waitress with a smile of thanks while Paul opened the beer he had ordered and took an appreciative swig.

"Good?" Kate asked with a smile when he set the bottle down on the table with a sigh.

"There are times when hard work means a hard earned thirst." He sighed. "And today is one of those days." He looked at her and then started to fidget with the label on the bottle. He raised an eyebrow at her. "So, getting back to business, you said that you and Tom played nice yesterday when I kicked you out of the store. How did it go?"

Kate sipped at her water while she considered his question. "As well as could be expected," she said at last. "Things got a little bumpy."

"I bet they did," Paul said, folding his arms and leaning slightly toward her. "But it's a talk that's been a long time comin'."

"Yeah." Kate nodded.

"You're both as bad as each other sometimes, you know that, right?" Paul pressed on.

This time Kate's nod was slower.

"I'm not saying that you two can't be friends, but c'mon, Kat, sometimes it hasn't been too healthy."

Kate couldn't look at him now. She traced the beads of condensation on her bottle and drew on the tabletop with a wet fingertip. Paul said nothing further. Instead he sipped at his beer and waited for her to say something. Finally she looked up and gave him a watery smile.

"You're right," she admitted at last, "but we talked about it." She reached over and picked up Paul's beer bottle, raising an eyebrow at him and taking a swig after he nodded.

"So what did you talk about?" Paul prodded as she set the bottle down.

"All the stuff that has been building up for a few years: his sabotage, my passivity, our love lives—together and with other people." She thought for a moment and shrugged. "Guess it was all the stuff that needed to be said to clear the air."

"What about Michael?"

"We talked about him too." Kate nodded.

"No, I meant how was Michael with it all? He took off pretty quickly."

"Yeah," Kate agreed. "He left us to talk it out, but came and had a drink with us later on."

Paul gave a slow considered nod of approval. "Gotta give props to the man for showing up after Tom let the bitch off the leash."

Kate laughed at Paul's choice of phrase. "I know, right? He was really good, and Tom behaved himself too."

"I'm glad to hear it." Paul nodded. "Michael seems like a nice guy, if that smile on your face is anything to go by." He grinned. "And that blush." His grin broadened as Kate groaned and put her hands to her face in a futile attempt to hide the color in her cheeks. "Wow, getting serious, huh?"

"I think so," Kate conceded.

"You think so … what?" Paul prodded. "You've fallen in …" He waved an expressive hand for Kate to fill in the blank, and when she said nothing, he lifted his bottle to his lips and took a long sip. He kept drinking, widening his eyes at her before releasing the bottle from his lips with a soft 'pop' and setting it down. "What?" he said.

"You know." Kate reached over and fidgeted with the paper label on the beer bottle for a moment.

"So," Paul went on, "you haven't said it?"

"Not to him," Kate answered. She had all but admitted it to Thomas.

"So when?" Paul asked as he watched Kate turn her water glass in small circles on the table.

"When the time is right," Kate said at last, looking up when she saw Paul's grin. "What?"

"Kat, there's no such thing as the right time. You're talking about feeling safe enough to say it."

Kate sipped at her water again and, realizing she wanted something more, flagged a passing waitress to order a Coke. She turned back to see Paul watching her, his face impassive as he waited for her answer. There was nowhere for her to go, no way she could bluff her way through the conversation. No matter how hard she tried to stall, he would simply wait her out. He had done it before.

It had been Paul who had sat waiting by her hospital bedside after the accident with Jack, waiting for his only sibling to wake up so that he could tell her that they were orphans. He had been the only person besides Kate listed as next of kin, and had made the journey from upstate to keep vigil by her side. He had watched and waited for her grief to burn down to ash before telling her she had to leave home and make a life for herself.

"You're no good here, Kat," he had said one day.

Kate still remembered the way he had said that, his body looming large in her bedroom doorway, his boot scuffing at the hallway carpet.

She had been sitting on her bed going through an old photo album after another quiet dinner when Paul had appeared at her door and made the announcement.

"Bear, I'm fine—" she had begun, and had stopped when he slowly shook his head.

"See, Babycake, that's where you're wrong," he had said in a gentle tone. "I've been watching you," he'd continued as he stepped into the room and took a seat beside her on the bed, "and you're just going through the motions of living."

"Bear—" Kate had begun again.

"No, Kat, this isn't living, and it doesn't honor Mom and—" He had stopped and swallowed hard. "Dad. You *know* they wouldn't like this, so you've got to make a life for yourself." He had reached out and put a gentle hand on her shoulder. "Go back to college, Kat, get your degree, and make a good life for yourself. You know that would make them proud. You won't be alone."

Now Paul sat waiting again, watching Kate smile her thanks as her Coke was delivered to their table, checking her wristwatch to see how much longer it would be before Michael arrived.

Kate looked up and saw Paul regarding her with a steadfast gaze.

"Kat," Paul said, reaching out a gentle hand, "he's not Tom."

"I know." Kate nodded. "I'm just scared, you know?"

"Oh, I know," Paul said, giving her hand a soft squeeze before leaning back in his seat. "But sometimes you just have to throw yourself wholeheartedly into something, or not at all."

Kate cocked her head as she gazed at her brother.

"That's quite a philosophy you've got going there," she said.

"It was Mom's," Paul said easily, making Kate smile. Their mother had been a free spirit compared to Jack's more conservative nature, but had managed to impart life lessons along the way.

"Mom could be a flake at times." Paul shrugged. "But her words kinda stuck, I guess, and it's a philosophy that works for me. Anyway, you want to finish your life feeling like you've had one helluva ride, or regret that you didn't do more when you had the chance?" He leaned forward and grasped Kate's hand again. "We both know that life can finish anytime, so why hold back?"

"I guess," Kate muttered, thinking of Michael. She glanced at her watch again and then looked up as Paul straightened in his chair and waved with a broad smile. Kate turned to follow his gaze, and Paul watched as his sister's face lit up with a smile of recognition.

Michael had been standing in the doorway scanning the dinner crowd when Paul's whoop had caught his attention. Paul's wave barely registered before Michael's attention swung to Kate's smiling face beside him. Walking over to the table, he stooped down to brush his lips against Kate's before leaning over to shake Paul's proffered hand.

"Good to see you again, Paul." Michael smiled and then pulled out the spare seat beside Kate and sat down.

"Likewise." Paul gave him a cordial grin. "It's good to see the cause for Kate's smiles lately."

"Is that so?" Michael relaxed into his seat, grateful that he was going to be spared any conversation about his writing career.

Kate shot Paul a look that had her brother fumbling for the menu. "So," he began in a slightly-too-jovial tone, "who's for pizza?" Paul peered around the room for a waitress so that he could get their order placed as quickly as possible. Michael slipped his arm around Kate's shoulders and drew her close.

"Smiles, huh?" he whispered, dropping a kiss on her forehead.

"That's Bear for you," Kate replied. "Either all protective or gooey matchmaker. When he's this happy, there isn't much middle ground."

"You didn't answer my question," Michael replied, watching as she bit her lip before smiling again. Michael looked into Kate's warm brown eyes and thought again how much he needed her.

Kate looked at Michael and realized how much she had wanted to be with him this evening. She was about to answer when Paul directed a question to Michael about pepperoni and the two of them fell into discussion about the pros and cons of sausage pizza. She watched as Michael and Paul worked their way through the usual dance steps of conversation as they negotiated their way toward common ground. Of course, sports was the universal leveler, although they surprised each other with their mutual interest in books and music.

She smiled as she felt Michael's hand rest on her back and begin to make lazy circles as he continued to converse with Paul. She leaned into his touch and felt content to simply watch him: his strong jaw line as he spoke, the way his eyes crinkled with amusement, and best of all, the way he glanced at her from time to time. The pizzas arrived and the conversation continued.

Kate licked some grease off her fingers, laughing as Paul told them a story about his day, and then happened to glance over at Michael. His eyes were watching her lips as they sucked and pulled at her fingertips one by one as she licked them clean. She licked her bottom lip slowly for good measure and watched his eyes grow darker still. Paul continued talking, and so she leaned back in her seat and rested her hand on Michael's thigh and rubbed her thumb against the rough denim. She heard his breath hitch for a moment before he remembered himself and laughed on cue as Paul's story reached its conclusion.

Kate could feel the heat of Michael's body against hers. All she wanted to do was run her hand up under his shirt and across the hard planes of his chest as she pressed herself against him.

If she did that, he would touch her like only Michael could touch her. He knew all her sweet spots, the places on her body that made her sigh and arch against him, to find some release from the need that was spiraling up from her core. Somehow she was able to smile and keep talking, smiling as Paul kept getting distracted by the game on the wall mounted TV, all the while realizing she wanted nothing more than to feel Michael's mouth on hers. She shifted a little in her seat, trying to ease the sudden ache.

"Don't do that." Michael's words were a hot whisper against her ear, tickling her neck and making her give a delighted shudder. "Oh, God, don't do that. I don't think I can stand much more."

Kate felt a rush of pleasure at his murmured plea. *I did that. I make him feel like that.*

She turned her attention back to Paul who, she realized with a guilty start, was gazing at her expectantly.

"Uh …" she stammered, "sorry, what were you saying?"

"Miles away, huh?" Paul asked with a knowing smile.

"Something like that," Kate admitted, although the distance had been much closer than Paul had given her credit for. Michael was, after all, right beside her.

"I was saying that we ought to call it a night soon, given you and I both have early starts tomorrow."

Kate nodded, sliding her hand further up Michael's thigh and grinning as he clamped his hand over her wrist to stop her from going further still.

"Guess it's easier for you creative types," Paul said. "You can set your own hours so you can be your own boss."

"Oh, I don't know," Michael mused, "if the ideas aren't coming, then there's nothing to do, and nothing can be a lonely place if you're relying on it for a living."

"Guess I hadn't thought of it like that," Paul commented. "Is that the voice of experience?"

"Oh, yeah," Michael sighed. "There's nothing worse than waking up and realizing that you're living in an inspiration wasteland." Releasing Kate's wrist with a warning look, he settled his arm around Kate's shoulders in a bid to shift his attention away from the warmth of her hand resting on his thigh.

"Everyone's their own worst critic," Kate added. "And being your own boss can be a different kind of pressure in itself."

"C'mon, Kat, you love your store," Paul commented as he finished his drink.

"Oh, sure, I do now, but those first couple of years were hard."

"Were they?" Michael looked at her, curious. She hadn't told him much about the early days of the bakery, and however tired the day made her, she still managed to make it look easy.

Kate shot him a tired smile. "There were months when Cup o' Noodles for dinner was considered haute cuisine. When the business was still getting off the ground, money was pretty tight."

Michael felt a twinge of guilt at how his career and financial success had all but dropped in his lap.

"But you kept at it," Paul commented, giving his sister a proud look before looking at Michael. "Man, I wish you could have seen it. That store was a roach hotel when Kate found it. Hey, Kat," he went on as his face lit up with remembered amusement, "remember the shouting match we had when you said you'd found the venue?"

"You guys fought?" Michael looked surprised.

"Definitely." Kate nodded, although the smile on her face belied her words. "Paul was still deep in business school territory then, so he crunched the numbers and was sure I was headed for financial Armageddon."

"Michael," Paul sighed, "let me just give you a tip right now. You might think you know stubborn, but that woman you've got there redefines the word."

Kate scoffed at that, making both men laugh.

"Seriously, we had some knock-down fights about the store, but she would *not* budge."

"I just knew I was right," Kate commented in a serene tone. "So all I had to do was get you on my side and I couldn't possibly fail."

"You must have been pretty determined," Michael commented.

"Oh, she was." Paul nodded. "You know," he went on in a doleful tone, "sometimes she wasn't happy until she'd made me cry."

The table erupted into laughter at the notion of the diminutive Kate towering over the enormous, jovial man, Paul included.

"All right, so she broke me down using her power of persuasion," Paul added, "and more sweat and elbow grease than I would've thought possible."

"It wasn't *that* bad," Kate chided in a gentle tone.

Michael watched the interplay between brother and sister, noticing how they were both smiling as they recounted the story for his benefit. Although the period had obviously been one of high stress, they were both genuinely pleased with its eventual success.

"No, but you have to admit it wasn't that great either," Paul replied. Then turning to Michael, he said, "The place was a tiny Asian food store. Great concept, but it just didn't seem to fit where it was. The lease was up and the owners decided to move on, which is where our girl stepped in." Paul relaxed in his chair, watching the memories flicker across Kate's face.

"What got your bakery idea across the line with the owners?" Michael asked, reaching up to twine a strand of hair around his index finger. He was soaking up the story, filing it away for future reference.

"Babycake pitched some woo," Paul said with a cheeky grin.

"Oh, there was a whole lotta woo goin' on," Kate agreed.

"Kat started sending cupcakes to the leasing agent and the owners. She got someone to draw up some concept boards of what she wanted the store to look like. You name it, she pretty much did it." Paul shook his head at Michael.

"It seems to have worked," Michael commented, releasing the strand of hair and combing his fingers through the silken lengths. "They must have been happy with your vision."

"They're still happy." Kate smiled. "Remember that high tea you saw in the store weeks ago?"

Michael sifted through his memories, flicking through scents, sounds, and images. "Balloons and little girls?"

"That's the one." Kate was pleased at his recollection. "The birthday girl was the grand-daughter of the owner."

"You've got that kind of relationship with them?" Michael was surprised at this.

"We don't get in each other's way," Kate clarified, "but when the store opened after the renovations, I sent them some cakes and a letter expressing my appreciation. They stop in once or twice a year to see how things are going."

"That's really … nice," Michael said at last. "It's something you don't hear about much these days."

"That's Kate," Paul answered.

Michael nodded. That was his girl.

❧

Paul and Kate stood by the door watching as Michael settled the check. There had been a protracted argument over who was paying for dinner, which Michael had settled by simply picking up the check and strolling over to the register without another word. Paul had gaped at his retreating back for a moment before startling Kate with a face-splitting grin.

"I like him."

"That's all it takes?" Kate gazed at him in disbelief. "Whatever happened to overprotective Brother Bear that saw off the other guys I've dated?"

"None of them bought me pizza." Paul shrugged.

"I never thought I'd see you become so easy," Kate commented. "Throw some food into the equation, and you can't even pretend to play hard to get."

Paul ignored her sass. "None of them made you smile the way he does. Face it, Kat. You're going to have to say it sooner or later." He stepped forward and wrapped his arms around Kate. "So are you going to?" he whispered into her ear.

"Yes," she whispered back. "But not until I'm ready."

"Okay," Paul said, giving her a squeeze before stepping back. "Just don't be scared. I'm with you."

"I know." Kate offered him a smile. "And it's appreciated."

Michael turned from the counter, stuffing some change into his pocket and reached for Kate's hand with a smile. He drew her to his side, waving off Paul's thanks for dinner with an easy grin as he ushered them outside.

"So..." Paul clapped his hands and rubbed them together briskly, smiling expansively at everyone. "This was good; let's do it again." He reached out and shook Michael's hand. "Michael," he said, "good to see you again."

"Likewise." Michael smiled. "And I agree. Let's catch up soon."

Kate managed to keep the surprise off her face. This was the first time Paul had volunteered to spend more time with someone she was dating. Even better, it seemed to be entirely mutual between the two men.

Kate snuggled into Michael's side as they walked. The wind had picked up during the evening, and she was feeling the cold a little more than she cared to admit. She made a mental note to dig out some of her warmer coats to wear to work. Her arm was around Michael's waist and so she felt the tremor of silent amusement.

"Penny for your thoughts?" she asked.

"Just thinking about Paul's turn of phrase," he replied. "*Pitching woo.* I like it." He thought about the large, gentle man who had watched him through fatherly eyes, and smiled again at Paul's vernacular. Michael had listened and admired the sibling bond between the brother and sister all evening, and for the first time began to understand what it was he had missed out on by being an only child. Paying for dinner tonight had been a spontaneous gesture, one that he was well within his means to make, and yet he couldn't help but feel that Kate and Paul were far richer. Words bubbled in the back of his mind.

By the time they reached Kate's apartment block, the words were louder, and his fingers twitched. Michael knew from experience that the words would simply gather momentum until the sound became a roar, and he would get no rest until he had poured the words onto the page.

"Do you want to come up?" Kate turned to lean into his chest and he put both of his arms around her to hold her close.

"I'd like nothing more," he admitted, "but I've got to do some work tonight."

Kate nodded her head against his chest, and he dipped his head slightly so that he could inhale the fragrance of her hair. He had noticed her shivering a little on the walk home, and he held her to his chest: a combination of wanting to keep her close and just plain wanting her.

"Okay," Kate said at last. He could hear the disappointment in her voice, and it stabbed through him, but he had to write. He didn't want to lose his words again, not when he had at last found so much. "I'll miss you in my bed." She sighed.

For a moment, Michael forgot to breathe. He thought about persuading her to come back to his apartment, but decided against it. He would be poor company until he had gotten the latest vein of words out of his system.

"Not as much as I'll miss you," Michael said, tilting her head to give her a soft kiss.

He saw her to her door and waited until she had closed it with considerable reluctance. When he got back outside, he crossed to the other side of the street and looked up at her apartment. The words tumbled over themselves in his mind as he tried to keep the memories fresh, rejoicing in and resenting the rush of creativity all at once. He stood alone trying to think unexciting thoughts while his body ached for her, watching until at last he saw her bedroom light go out.

Kate blinked against the sudden darkness of the room, and then rolled over onto her side, trying to get comfortable enough to get to sleep. She had wanted him to spend the night, but she had seen the distant look in his eyes and known that she couldn't compete with his words. She shifted in the bed, kicking against the sheets that felt too constrictive over her feet and then reached up to pull a spare pillow against her chest. She wrapped her arms around it and took a deep breath, realizing that she could detect a trace of Michael's scent.

Perhaps Paul was right. Nothing in life was certain; that was a lesson that she had learned the hard way. She had no way to predict the future, no way of knowing what life had in store for her. Perhaps there would never be a right time to tell Michael she was falling in love with him. Curling herself around Michael's pillow, she felt her body ache and wished he were there beside her. She rolled over and gazed at the bedside table where she had left her phone. Perhaps she could call him back to her. For a moment she began to reach out and then arrested the gesture, her arm half-extended before she turned back to the pillow with a sigh.

She wondered what he was writing and then told herself again that she didn't want to know. The conversation with Tom was very fresh in her mind. She was glad they had aired their grievances yesterday; it was time for their college relationship to mature into adult life once and for all. A part of her would always love Tom, just as a part of her would always hurt. Her thoughts wandered from Tom back to Michael, and she sighed again. Perhaps it was best if she didn't read what he was writing. Some secrets were better left unsaid.

Michael walked home deep in thought. Snippets of the evening conversation flickered through his mind, setting off an unconscious trail of word associations that lead his attention back to his work. He sighed and shoved his hands deeper into his coat pockets. He really didn't know how Kate would feel about the book when it came out, and again he wondered if he should encourage her to read it. Her refusal had surprised him at first. He had offered the manuscript to her on the spur of the moment, and now he realized how much he needed her to read it and to understand.

But she didn't want to read and he couldn't force her. Perhaps in time she would be ready. All he could do was wait and wonder. He wished he knew how she felt about it. In the meantime, he knew how he felt about her.

He loved Kate; he was sure of that now.

When he had left her at the store to deal with Tom, his chest had felt hollow and the empty feeling hadn't dissipated until he had seen her again. It was a feeling he was experiencing more and more these days. He had only been just beginning to realize that when he had entered her store. He had stepped into her world, and she had been steadily binding him to it ever since. She left him feeling satisfied in a way that no amount of words had been able to accomplish.

He wanted to tell her how he felt, perhaps when the time was right.

Michael walked on, words swirling in his head.

Chapter 20

Tiaras and Winter Warmers

Kate nodded a greeting as she approached Wren, who was waiting underneath the store canopy, rubbing her mitten-clad hands together.

"Morning, boss," Wren called out as she gave a quick salute.

"Wren, don't call me boss," Kate replied as she produced the door keys from her pocket and unlocked the roller door.

"Sorry, boss." Wren blew a bubble and stamped her feet in an attempt to keep warm while Kate rolled up the security grill.

"Been waiting long?" Kate asked as she unlocked the front door.

"Longer than usual," Wren admitted. "Stayed at David's last night and woke up early is all."

"You had *another* sleepover?" Kate glanced at Wren as she opened the door and stepped aside to usher the smaller woman inside. "Keep this up and I'll start to think you guys are getting serious."

Wren snorted as she headed toward the kitchen, shrugging off her coat as she went. "Talk to David about it," she quipped as she hung up her coat and began to tie on her apron. "He's the one that keeps pushing the issue."

"How so?" Kate had flicked on the coffee machine and was now stowing the shop keys on their usual hook before removing her coat. She rubbed her hands briskly against her upper arms in a bid to warm up quicker, making a mental note to wear more layers tomorrow.

"*He* thinks we're dating," Wren said as she picked up the chalkboard and hefted it onto a nearby table for better writing access.

"Right," Kate said as she flicked a lever to measure coffee into the filter.

"Hey, guys." Emily let herself into the store, her cheeks reddened from the chill outside.

"Hey," Wren called over her shoulder as she picked up her stub of chalk.

"So what would you call it?" Kate asked as she kept her attention on the espresso filter running into the two cups.

Wren stopped and considered Kate's question. "Actually, I don't know," she admitted at last, "but I don't know that we're *dating*."

"What'd I miss?" Emily re-appeared from the kitchen, tying on her apron.

"Wren here isn't sure she and David are dating," Kate said in a droll voice.

Emily stopped and looked at Wren with disbelief. "You're kidding, right?"

"What?" Wren shrugged. "It doesn't seem that serious."

"Right," Emily said as she got out a third cup and slid it toward the coffee machine where Kate was standing. "Have you been seeing anyone else?"

"No, she isn't," Kate answered for her. "And from what I hear, neither is David."

"How did you know that?" Wren turned around to look at Kate.

"Michael told me," Kate said with a smug smile. She removed the two cups from the machine and added the third, refilling the coffee filter with practiced movements and reaching for the milk jug.

"Right," Wren said. She had the feeling she was losing ground in the conversation, but wasn't entirely sure how.

Kate shot her a quick look and then went back to making the coffee as she thought about what Michael had told her a few days ago while they were getting dinner ready at her apartment. From what Michael could tell, David was more serious about Wren than he had been about any other woman in quite some time.

"What about you and Michael?" Wren asked, pulling Kate's attention back to the present.

"What about us?" Kate replied, stirring some sugar into her coffee.

Wren pushed herself away from the counter and took a few steps toward the table where the chalkboard waited, before she answered.

"Well…" She scrawled absently on the chalkboard, frowning when she realized she had doodled David's initials and wiped the board clean with her hand. "The two of you seem tight. You're practically living at each other's homes, you spend every free moment you have together, you've met his parents and he's met Paul." Wren gave her an expectant look.

"And?" Kate looked at her.

"Have you told each other how you feel?"

"Not in so many words," Kate hedged, "but I think we both know."

"Boss, even Lincoln said 'to assume is to make an ass of you and me.' I don't think you should keep taking things for granted," Wren huffed.

Kate coughed to cover her laugh. "Spoken by the woman who can't admit she's dating."

"It's always different when it's someone else," Emily commented in a sage tone from her position at the counter where she was pulling out the tubs of sandwich fixings for the day. She paused when she saw both women looking at her. "Or easier to call, just sayin'," she went on with a slight shrug.

"The Oracle speaks," Wren muttered in a not-so-quiet undertone.

Emily paused in her task and strolled over to the counter to collect the proffered coffee with a smile. "I just want you two happy, but you're going to have to accept what's in front of you and admit what it is that you want."

"Uh-huh." Wren nodded, looking dubious now. "And that's what you did with Bookstore Brad?"

"Yup." Emily gave her a Cheshire cat grin of satisfaction. "And things have never been better."

"Really?" Kate was intrigued now. "You just came out and said it?"

Emily gave the matter some thought. "Well, there was some give and take on both sides really, but the time came where we told each other how we felt. Trust me, when you finally give words to how you feel, it's really ..." She paused to search for the right words.

"Terrifying?" Wren suggested.

Emily shook her head. "I'd go with 'liberating.'"

"Mmph," Wren snorted with a dubious expression as she rubbed chalk dust off her hand.

"It's only terrifying if you let it be," Emily replied. "Seriously, what's the worst that can happen?" She shrugged again and returned to her work.

Wren said nothing.

Kate carried her cup into the kitchen and switched on the industrial oven to pre-heat. She set her cup down and looked at her tiny kitchen space. Everything was as it should be. The stainless steel counters gleamed, and the large clear plastic tubs of flour and sugar were tightly sealed and stacked. As always, she felt a rush of pleasure at her workspace. She wondered what Wren was going to come up with today, and walked out of the kitchen to see her friend staring at the fox collection on the wall. Rolling the stub of chalk in her fingers, she seemed lost in thought.

Kate watched her for a moment, and then picked up one of the other coffees and carried it over.

"Here you go." She offered the cup.

"Hmm?" Wren snapped out of her reverie and accepted the coffee with a slight smile. "Thanks, boss, I was miles away."

"So I see," Kate said as she strolled back to the counter to pick up her coffee. "Everything okay?"

"Yeah," Wren replied and then shrugged. "Maybe."

"Talk about it?"

"Not first thing in the morning." Wren shook her head. "Maybe later. I've got to do my quote."

"Okay, but I'm here and ready to listen any time you want to spill." Kate's gaze flickered to Emily who was hard at work making a large tub of salad. "You know, the Oracle might have had a point."

"I know," Wren sighed. "But I'm scared. You?"

"Sometimes," Kate admitted. "Paul had a similar conversation with me a few days back."

"Bear's in love?" Wren's eyebrows went up at this revelation as Kate nodded.

"Not yet, but I think he'd like to be if he could find the right woman."

"Are you saying he's a lonely heart? Not possible," Wren scoffed. "Bear loves the planet."

"It's one thing to be the big lovable guy, but it's another to put your heart on the line," Kate cautioned. "I think that's what he was trying to get across to me."

"Noted." Wren nodded. She took a long sip of her coffee, and the two women stood in a moment of companionable silence. "Of course, in the meantime, there's always shopping."

Kate smiled over the rim of her coffee cup. "That's your cure-all?"

"Of course." Wren looked shocked that Kate could think otherwise. "I always feel better after I've gone out looking at beautiful things. In fact, I—" She broke off and stared at Kate as a smile began to tug at her lips. She bent over the chalkboard and began to write, finishing the quote with a flourish and a few artful stars and hearts. Kate strolled over to see what Wren had written and laughed. Another day had begun.

⁓

Michael's day started earlier than usual after a less than satisfying sleep. He hadn't slept well the night before, which he noted was happening with increasing regularity whenever he and Kate didn't spend the night together. He had woken alone, gripping his pillow as he jolted into wakefulness. After staring at the ceiling for half an hour, he finally gave in to the inevitable and rolled out of bed. By the time he had changed into his running gear and hit the pavement downstairs, it was six a.m. The chill in the air kept him shivering until he had warmed up enough for the early morning run to feel even halfway bearable.

The ranks of morning joggers in the park had thinned as the season had grown colder, but those that still ran exchanged nods as they passed each other in silent solidarity. Finishing his cool-down stretches, Michael jogged at a slow pace back toward his apartment, and along the way passed a pedestrian just in time to have to endure a heavy exhalation of cigarette smoke. His nose wrinkled in disgust at the rank smell, and he marveled again that he had ever found the habit satisfying. It had been six months since he had quit, a fact of which he was inordinately proud.

Showered and dressed after his run, he set his coffee machine and took a seat at his desk, opened his manuscript document on the laptop and began to check it against the annotated version that Alistair had sent back. He began typing, stopping only when the smell of the fresh percolated coffee wafted through the apartment enough to catch his attention. He padded barefoot toward the kitchen and poured some coffee, adding cream and sugar to his liking before sipping it and carrying it back to his desk. Sinking back down into his chair, he took another sip and then set the cup down with mild regret. Kate's coffee tasted better, but in the meantime this would have to do. The last passage on the screen wasn't reading well, and he frowned over the words and kept working at it until they arranged themselves into a more pleasing pattern.

The cell phone lit up as the handset began to buzz and vibrate against the desktop. Michael shot it a brief look and kept typing. The phone stopped ringing and the apartment was silent again except for the tapping of Michael's fingers on the keyboard. After a moment the phone beeped to indicate a voice mail message had arrived. Michael kept working.

The phone began to ring again.

Michael's lips tightened in irritation before he turned from the laptop with a sigh and picked up the handset to answer the call.

"Forrester," he answered. "What is it, Alistair?" Michael kept his focus on the screen as he scrolled through the text in front of him.

"How did you know it was me? I'm not even calling from my number."

"Only you can make my phone sound so insistent," Michael admitted, startling a laugh from his editor.

"Well, at least I know I'm good at something," Alistair replied, and Michael could hear the smile in his voice. "I'm calling to see if you got my revisions."

"I did," Michael said. "I'm working on them now."

"Already?"

"No time like the present," Michael admitted. Normally he preferred to wait until his work was finished before he let anyone else's influence intrude on the work, but Alistair had raised some interesting questions.

"I think I'm flattered. So you thought they were okay?"

"Some were," Michael allowed. "Others were taking things in a direction I wasn't happy with, but you've given me some ideas to work on."

"That's … I'm glad to hear it's going well."

Michael said nothing.

"Michael?"

"Sorry, what was that?" Blinking, Michael returned his attention back to the conversation.

"I said I was glad to hear it's going well."

"We'll see," Michael grunted. He wasn't one to get his hopes up in advance when it came to his work.

"Listen, it sounds like you're busy, so I'll check in with you later. I was just calling to see how things were progressing."

Michael leaned back and swiveled the chair slightly so that he was gazing out the window. The weather was getting progressively colder, and he noted that today the city looked gray in the pale morning light. He wondered if Kate was keeping warm, knowing she walked to work every day. There wasn't much of her and he wondered if she had a good winter coat to withstand the weather. Perhaps he could do something about that.

"Okay," he replied in an absent tone. The more he thought about Kate, the more he wanted to go see her. "Thanks for calling."

He dimly heard Alistair say goodbye before disconnecting the call and reaching out to drop the phone on the desk as he kept gazing out the window. The phone clattered on the hardwood floor, jolting Michael back to the present. He had been so wrapped up in thoughts about Kate he hadn't realized his reach had fallen short of the desk. Stooping over, he picked up the phone and checked the time. Scrolling through his contact list, he selected a number and dialed, leaning back in his chair and fiddling with a pen as the phone rang. It was still relatively early, but he knew at least one of his parents ought to be home.

"Hi, Mom," he said when the call was answered.

"Michael," his mother replied warmly. "How are you?"

"Good, all good here. How're you and Dad?"

"Missing you, of course. How's Kate?"

"Actually, she's the reason I'm calling." Michael flicked the pen back onto the desk and began scrolling up and down the screen for something else to do.

"You have my complete and undivided attention." There was a slight scrape in the background and Michael knew that Susan had just pulled out a chair to take a seat at the kitchen table. His father always laughed when she did that, saying she was hunkering down for serious business.

Michael laughed. "Mom, don't panic. I said it's all good. I just wanted your advice on something."

"Don't propose on Valentine's Day," she responded promptly. "It's too cheesy."

"Okay, so that wasn't where I was going, but I appreciate the advice all the same." Michael scratched his chin, listening to his stubble rasp beneath his fingertips.

"You said advice," she replied in a mild tone, "you didn't say what *for*."

"Only because you didn't let me finish," Michael rebuked her but smiled as he spoke.

"All right, so what's the situation?"

"The weather," Michael said promptly.

"Oh, honey," Susan sighed. "By the time you're just talking about the weather, there's something seriously wrong. Have we taught you nothing?"

Michael rubbed his forehead. His mother was being deliberately obtuse which was something she did from time to time when he hadn't been in touch often enough for her liking.

"You win," he sighed. "What's this conversation going to cost me?"

"Sunday lunch with the two of you." Susan had the answer so readily that he knew she must have been thinking about inviting them for a while now. "Come early so we've got plenty of time. No need to bring anything."

"I'll check with Kate and let you know," Michael allowed with a slight smile. "Can we talk now?"

"Of course, now that we've taken care of business, I'm prepared to play nice."

"I appreciate it," Michael said in a droll tone, "but I really was calling to talk about the weather."

"Really?" Susan sounded taken aback now. "In what context?"

"Getting Kate a winter coat." Michael sat waiting as his mother gave the situation some thought.

"I'm assuming she already has a duck down one," Susan ventured after a pause.

"Sure," Michael replied. He'd caught a glimpse of the puffy sleeve of it in Kate's wardrobe the last time he'd been over. No self-respecting New Yorker was without a coat that could withstand the wind chill factor once winter tightened its grip on the city, "but I'm thinking something of middle ground would be good."

"Okay." Susan was thoughtful now, and Michael smiled at how seriously she was taking the proposition.

It had been a month since Michael had introduced Kate to his parents. They had been well aware that he was dating, thanks to an injudicious comment David had made to *his* parents, thus setting the lines of communication aflutter between the two families. Susan had phoned Michael, ostensibly to see how he was but fishing for information. Bowing to the inevitable, Michael had suggested his parents meet Kate and a lunch invitation and promptly been issued.

Kate had been charmingly nervous, and his parents had worked to put her at ease. Their approval of her had only deepened upon the discovery that she had a degree in English literature. Michael had breathed a quiet sigh of relief that his mother hadn't immediately hauled out his books for literary show and tell. By the time their lunch had concluded, there seemed to be a genuine fondness growing between them that had Michael smiling all the way home.

Returning his attention to the present, Michael realized his mother had asked him question that he hadn't caught.

"Sorry, Mom, I didn't catch that," he apologized.

"I was asking you what other coats she has," Susan repeated.

"I haven't gone prowling through her closet if that's what you're asking," Michael retorted. "But we were out a couple of weeks ago and what she was wearing didn't look warm enough."

"Lucky you were there, huh?" his mother replied, and he could hear the smile in her voice.

"Yeah," he conceded, "but getting back to the question, what do you recommend?"

"You're after a mid-winter coat, so something fully lined and something that isn't black. Kate likes color," Susan concluded. She had visited the store a couple of times and the vibrant aprons and artwork-covered walls had given her a good sense of Kate's style.

"I'm going to need more information than that," Michael admitted, making his mother laugh.

"Michael, go to Saks, find the women's fashion department, and then go to the coat section and get someone to help you."

"Really? Just like that?"

"Just like that," Susan confirmed. "You've got the money, and they want the sale."

"If you say so," Michael replied, trying to keep the dubious tone out of his voice.

They talked for a while longer before Michael excused himself and ended the call. He set the phone down on his desk again and stared out at the gray weather. He wanted to make sure Kate kept warm.

Kate blinked as she opened the oven door and the rush of warm air hit her face. Grabbing a couple of dishcloths, she pulled the trays of golden cupcakes out of the oven. Moving quickly she set them down on the waiting cooling racks and transferred another two trays into the oven to cook.

"Smells good in here," Emily commented with an appreciative sniff as she popped her head around the doorway. "Nice and warm too."

"How is it out there?" Kate asked, jerking her chin toward the storefront. "Everyone okay?"

"It's fine," Emily assured her. "I don't think we'll need to start using the heaters just yet."

"Okay, as long as it's comfortable."

"Sure, boss." Emily nodded, laughing as Kate gave her a look of fond exasperation. "By the way, those muffins you made are popular this morning."

"Really?" Kate looked pleased. She had been in an experimental mood so had whipped up a tray of cranberry and orange muffins with a demerara sugar crust to hold off the morning rush before the daily cupcakes were ready.

"Really," Emily confirmed with a nod. "I think you might have to make those again." She gave the cooling cupcakes a curious look and then glanced back at Kate. "What's today's special going to be?"

Kate shook her head. "Work in progress, Emily. You know the drill."

"Okay." Emily held up her hands in surrender and withdrew.

Kate gave the cupcakes a gimlet stare as she pulled the mixer toward her to start making the frosting. Pouring in a generous measure of powdered sugar, she added a scoop of soft butter as she switched on the mixer. "Tiaras," she muttered to herself as a faint idea began to stir. "Tiaras and shoes." Leaving the mixer running, she turned and opened a drawer, eyeing the collection of inch-tall pots sitting in a neat row. She hadn't used the contents before; perhaps today was the day.

Wren spooned some milk froth into the waiting cups and quickly drew a leaf pattern into the coffee. Emily grinned at her as she picked up the coffees, transferred the cups to their saucers and carried them out to the waiting customers.

A quick glance confirmed that all the orders had been filled, and she held up an empty cup to Emily as she approached.

"Oh, please," Emily sighed as she rounded the counter. "The first one barely touched the sides."

"Another heart starter comin' right up," Wren replied as she cranked the coffee measure again. She turned to face the kitchen door. "You okay in there, boss?"

"Sure," Kate answered. "Be right out."

"Coffee?" Wren called back.

"Yup."

Emily leaned against the counter and watched Wren get to work. Her own coffee skills had improved considerably since she had started, but she didn't think she moved with the confident grace that Wren did. The small woman moved seamlessly from one task to the next, shooting Emily a couple of sidelong glances as she worked.

"Okay," Wren said at last. "I give up. What's on your mind?"

"You and David." Emily had the answer so readily that Wren knew it had been on her mind for a while.

"What about us?" Wren kept her attention on the espresso coffee that was filtering into the cups.

"Just…" Emily paused and fidgeted with a pen before taking a deep breath and continuing. "Just how long do you think you can keep downplaying what you've got with him?"

"Huh?" Wren added a third cup and tried to feign ignorance.

"You heard me. You can shrug off David all you want, but the man is *good* for you, Wren. If you lose him, you've got no one to blame but yourself."

Wren paused and brushed some hair off her face as she tried to collect her thoughts.

"That's a bit harsh, don't you think?" she replied in a mild tone.

Emily huffed out a breath and, to Wren's surprise, nodded her agreement. "It is, but maybe it's the kick in the pants you need."

"Mmph." Wren shrugged and began to frappe some milk. "If you say so."

"I do say so," Emily said more quietly. "Wren, you're happier than I've seen you in a long time. Why can't you admit it?"

Wren said nothing. Emily waited her out.

"Maybe sometime," Wren said at last when she finished frothing the milk.

"When?" Emily pressed, and was startled to see the look of vulnerability on Wren's face.

"Soon," Wren replied. She knew that Emily was right; the moment was coming and it excited and exhilarated her all at once. David was a patient man, but even Wren knew that he wouldn't wait forever. She sighed, letting her shoulders slump as she finished making the coffees and slid Emily's cup toward her.

"You know, for someone who puts so much work into making everyone else happy, why can't you accept some happiness of your own?" Emily said as she took a sip.

"Self-preservation," Wren quipped. "It worked for Mom, so I thought I'd try it too."

"Hmm, and how happy is she?"

Wren was silent and sipped her coffee.

"Look," Emily said quietly. "I won't push you any further. This is a conversation that you and David need to have, not us."

"Thanks," Wren said, surprised at this sudden reprieve.

"Just do yourself a favor and talk to him about it. You might be surprised at his reaction."

"Okay." Wren nodded, turning as she heard her name called from the kitchen.

Kate appeared carrying a tray and a broad smile. Wren and Emily exchanged a glance and stepped out of Kate's way to let her pass.

"Oh, wow," Emily gasped, "is that—"

"Yup." Kate nodded, pleased.

"You're kidding, right?" Wren gaped. "I didn't even know you had that stuff."

"Babe, we've only just begun," Kate replied as she set the tray down in the counter and tweaked Wren's nose. "Is that my coffee?"

"Sure," Wren said automatically, her eyes not leaving the cupcakes. "Boss, they look spectacular."

"They sure do," Emily agreed. "What are they called?"

Kate smiled. "I thought you'd never ask. Wren, Get your chalk."

"Got it." Wren picked up the stub and reached for the small chalkboard that sat waiting on the counter.

Kate dictated, Emily laughed, and Wren wrote with a sigh.

"You like?" Kate asked when Wren had set up the chalkboard on its easel.

"You win," Wren replied, as she exchanged a high five with Kate.

"Let's see how long they last," Emily replied as she nodded toward the door. All three women glanced up to see customers heading indoors, drawn by the smell of fresh coffee and baking.

Hours later, Kate waved off another customer with a smile and leaned back against the counter behind her with a mild sigh. The day had been a busy one, and now things seemed to be winding down. She pushed herself away from the countertop and strolled toward the display case to bend in for a quick inventory.

"Stock seems to be holding," Emily commented as she walked past with a tub of cups and plates to be stacked into the dishwasher.

"Which is good. I don't know that I'm in the mood to bake more this afternoon," Kate replied as she slid the Plexiglas door closed and straightened with a mild wince. She hadn't slept very well the night before, and her back still felt a bit stiff. The best nights for sleep and pleasant dreams seemed to be when she was with Michael—a fact she had only realized when she had woken up clutching the pillow that held so much of his scent.

"You're looking a bit tired. Are you okay?" Emily paused in her stacking and gave her friend a concerned look.

"I'm fine," Kate assured her. "I think I'm just burning the candle at both ends."

"The store does keep you busy," Emily agreed, "but what about the home front?"

"Mmm?" Kate pushed some damp hair off her forehead and reached beneath her apron to tug down her T-shirt. She was going to have a long shower when she got home, whenever that was.

"You're dividing your time between your place and Michael's. That must get a bit tiring."

"Sometimes," Kate admitted. There were evenings when she found herself wanting a favorite book to re-read, only to discover that it was at her apartment and Michael didn't have a copy. Michael had given her free rein at his apartment, but there were times when she found herself wanting her own things. Michael's kitchen was impressive, but she found a certain level of comfort in baking with her mother's bowls and equipment. A sentimental approach perhaps, but one that provided a certain amount of tranquility that was reassuring at the end of the day. "But I'm okay."

"And Michael?" Emily pressed.

"He's fine," Kate replied, opening the refrigerator and reaching in for a bottle of sparkling mineral water. She offered it to Emily who shook her head, and then opened it and took a long swig, wiping her mouth with the back of her hand. "Michael can work anywhere."

"But he'd rather work at his place?"

"I guess." Kate shrugged, not noticing the contemplative look on Emily's face.

"So if he's okay and you're tired, we need to work out how to cut you some slack," Emily continued.

"Don't fuss so much. I told you I'm fine." Kate smiled.

"Yeah? So what happens to the store if you get hit by a truck?" Emily regretted her words the moment she saw Kate's face blanch. "Oh, God," she babbled, "poor choice of words, boss, I—"

"Relax, Emily." Kate waved off Emily's remonstrations. "It's just a figure of speech."

"Yeah, but you've experienced it literally," Emily said, her expression overcome with remorse. "What I meant to say was—"

"Seriously," Kate interrupted again, "it's okay. You were talking about a backup plan, am I right?"

"Something like that." Emily gave a weak nod, inwardly cursing herself for her carelessness.

"Well…" Kate wiped some condensation off the bottle and rubbed her damp hand on the back of her neck, hoping the cold would revive her a little. "You've jumped the gun on what I wanted to talk to you about, but I guess now's as good a time as any."

"For what?"

Kate gave Emily a tired but fond smile. "To talk about you being second in command if you're interested."

Emily gaped at her.

"Finally, the Oracle is speechless," Wren commented as she stepped out from the kitchen. She glanced at Kate who was watching Emily's reaction with quiet pleasure. "I take it you told her?"

"I've just started to," Kate replied.

"You knew?" Emily managed at last as she glanced at Wren. "And you didn't tell me?"

Wren gave her a smug smile by way of answer.

"I thought you didn't do suspense?"

"Actually, it's something we talked about a while ago, but we had to wait and see how things worked out for you and the store," Wren answered. "Not to mention that the boss lady here threatened me with grievous bodily harm if I gave away so much as a peep." Wren glanced at Kate. "Now how about you two take this conversation to a table, and let me know when Emily says yes."

Kate picked up her bottle of water and draped a comradely arm around Emily's shoulders.

"She sounds like she means it," Kate said, "so let's go."

"It's okay," Wren said soothingly to Emily who was still looking surprised. "I'll bring you a soy chai to soothe your nerves."

"Bossy little thing, isn't she?" Emily commented as they headed toward a table.

"You're only just telling me that now?" Kate muttered as she took a seat. "Now, about the offer…" She paused to take another swig of water and then leaned forward in her seat to begin talking.

Wren began to frappe some milk and stirred in some chai syrup, glancing over at the two women with a smile from time to time. She knew that Kate was doing the right thing and was pleased for both of her friends.

"So here's the offer," Kate began, "and feel free to turn it down, but I'm offering you more work, more responsibility and a bit more money."

"Right." Emily gave her an uncertain nod. "But shouldn't you be having this conversation with—"

"Wren?" Kate finished for her. "She and I have already talked about this, and it's not what she wants. You, on the other hand, have got a good approach; you like baking and I think this could be good for both of us."

"But, Wren…" Emily paused and swallowed before continuing. "I mean, she's been with you from the start. Shouldn't she be the one who takes this on?"

"Have you not seen my stunning fashion creations?" Wren chimed in as she set down a cup in front of Emily. "Honey, you know fashion is my thing, not cupcakes. Sure, I can make a mean bagel, but that's the extent of my kitchen prowess. You, on the other hand, are a natural." Wren smiled as she said this, her hands smoothing down her apron lovingly as she spoke, twining some of the fluttering ribbons around her fingers. "Sorry to interrupt, but that's just my humble opinion."

"Humble." Kate snorted as she swatted at Wren's rump. "Yeah, right."

"I'm going," Wren protested as she retreated to the kitchen.

Kate was laughing as she turned back to see Emily looking thoughtful. "So, what are your thoughts?"

"When you say more work and responsibility, what would I be doing?"

"We can work that out, but I'd imagine it will be opening up for me on occasion, cupcake production…" She paused as Emily gave a mild squeak. "What?"

"You want me to make the cupcakes?"

Kate reached out to pat her hand. "All the recipes are written down. You'd be surprised just how easy they are."

"It's not the baking that worries me, it's the *competition*," Emily replied, making Kate laugh.

"Wren has promised to go easy on you," Kate assured her. "You'll be fine."

"Okay." Emily shrugged.

Kate looked puzzled.

"Okay, as in, okay, I'll do it," Emily clarified.

"Really?" Now it was Kate looking surprised. "I thought I'd have to sweet talk you for longer than that."

"Meh." Emily sipped at her chai. "Wren probably told you I was a sure thing, and what have I got to lose by giving it a try?"

"You go, girl," Kate said as she raised her bottle of water in a toast. "Here's to you."

"No, here's to us," Emily said with a smile as cup and bottle clinked together.

Wren watched them from her position at the kitchen doorway with a wistful smile. The chance to manage the store had been offered to her, but she had refused it. She knew that in her heart of hearts the bakery wasn't the right path for her, but the prospect of job security had been enough temptation to give her pause. It had been David who had helped steer her back on course.

"Wren," he had said at last when she had finished explaining the scenario a few evenings earlier, "would that make you content?"

"I don't know." Wren had stared down at her risotto. She had arrived home to discover David cooking in her kitchen. "I guess."

"That's not enough of an answer," he'd chided her gently. "Think about it."

"I know I have a lot of fun there during the day. Kate makes the store a happy place to be."

"Sure, she does," David had agreed. "But being happy can come and go; contentment is a kind of core happiness that lasts a lot longer."

"Right," Wren had allowed cautiously. David was having another one of his "moments" as she now thought of them: moments when he seemed to take her happiness very seriously indeed, and urged her to think about what it was that she wanted and why. She wasn't used to being challenged like this and found it deeply unsettling and provocative. She'd found herself looking at the crease between his eyebrows and wanted to smooth it away.

"Would making cupcakes make you as happy as you are when you've finished another one of your couture creations?" David had persisted.

Wren had paused at that. "No," she had ventured at last.

"Then you know what it is that will make you content, and you go for it."

"And that's why you threw away a journalistic career to go back into academia?" she'd challenged. "Because the financial rewards must be huge."

David had thrown his head back and laughed, confusing her all the more.

"Oh, you know I didn't do it for the money. I just realized that life is too short to have an average day at work."

"Right, and what does your landlord say?"

"My landlord is fine." David smiled. "You know I wouldn't do anything stupid, but I wanted to feel proud of what I do."

"And teaching comatose students makes you proud?" Wren was curious.

"They're not comatose by the time I've finished with them," David had retorted, aware that Wren had not yet discovered that he had a reputation for being unconventional in his approach to his subject. "And I'm working to get published soon, so that'll bring some more dollars in."

"You've covered all the bases then," Wren had replied in a dry tone.

"Got to, if you're going to be realistic about it. If you're doing what you love, it'll never feel like work again."

Wren stood behind the counter, watching Kate and Emily as they made plans for the future. Taking David's words to heart, she had acted on her heart's desire and turned down what she had known was a good opportunity. She wanted to be content with her decision, and now she knew what she had to do.

Michael was about to enter the store when he remembered to check the chalkboard hanging outside. He stepped back a pace to scan Wren's quote of the day and grinned.

> With the right pair of shoes and a tiara,
> I could rule the world.

He could just imagine Wren writing that and wondered how Kate was going to match it; he stepped inside, eager to find out. He glanced around to see a few of the tables occupied by customers, but for the most part the café seemed quiet. He walked to the counter and peered at the cupcake display, smiling when he saw the daily special.

> Everyone's a princess: *strawberry shortcake*
> *with white chocolate frosting and Regal Red edible glitter.*

Edible glitter? Now he'd seen everything. He turned from the counter with a grin and that's when he saw Kate and Emily sitting at one of the side tables having a quiet talk. Emily saw him first, and Kate turned in her seat to see who she was smiling at.

"Hey, you," she called as her face lit up with a smile of recognition.

Michael felt an answering smile of his own, walking toward the table and dropping the shopping bag at his feet to give her a long kiss.

"Phew." Wren walked past them with a comment as she moved out to collect some empty cups "And there I was thinking someone had turned the heat up, but it's just you two."

Emily muffled a laugh of her own and got up to move away. "Take a seat, Michael. I think the boss and I are done."

"Funny girl." Kate broke away from the kiss to laugh, but kept her fingers twined in Michael's hair as he nuzzled her neck. "So how's my guy?" She turned her attention back to Michael.

"Better now. How's my girl?"

"Much, much better," she said, rubbing his stubble with the tips of her fingers and gently biting his earlobe.

Michael felt a jolt of heat start in his belly and start to drill down. "Kate," he warned in a rough whisper as he dragged a chair over to sit as close to her as possible, "don't start what you can't finish."

"Can't?" she asked softly as she ran her tongue along his lower lip.

"Won't," he amended with a shudder as she pressed her soft body closer, hitching one of her legs over his thigh.

Kate continued her gentle assault for a moment longer, and then broke off with a sigh of regret. "You're right," she admitted. "Don't want to scare the customers off."

Michael looked over his shoulder to see a few of the customers regarding them with quiet amusement. "I don't think they're scared, but you might have given a couple of them ideas," he commented, and smiled as she ducked her head against his shoulder with a quiet snicker. "Had a good day?"

"Real good." She smiled. "I just told Emily my dastardly plan."

"How did she take it?"

"I think she's in shock, but she's accepted the offer."

Michael twisted in his seat. "Congratulations, Emily," he called, grinning when her "Thank you" carried back to him from behind the counter.

"That was a big step you've taken, handing the reins over to someone else like that," Michael commented.

"Bear said the same," Kate agreed, "but he thinks I'm doing the right thing."

"If Paul gives it the nod, then that's good enough for me. In fact, I think you deserve a reward." He lifted the Saks bag onto the table in front of him and gestured for Kate to open it.

"What have you done?" Kate asked, straightening up in her seat to peer into the bag. All she could see was tissue paper.

"Got you a present," Michael replied with an expectant grin.

Mystified, Kate reached into the bag to pull out the contents. Tissue paper rustled and fell away to reveal a cherry red cashmere coat. Kate gazed at it for a moment before clutching it to her and rubbing the collar against her cheek as she gave Michael a delighted smile.

"For me?"

Michael was very pleased with her reaction. "I didn't want my girl to be cold when I'm not around," he said in a low voice, leaning toward her to give her a kiss.

They both looked up as Wren gave a low whistle. "Michael," she said as she walked toward them, her eyes not leaving the coat. "I'm impressed. That's the new Kenneth Cole wing collar trench."

"Huh?" Michael gave her a blank look.

"I think that means it's good," Kate said by way of translation as she reached up to give Michael a kiss of thanks.

"Better than good. It's one of this season's hot looks," Wren added as she reached out for the coat. "May I?"

"Sure," Kate said as she handed the coat over.

Wren took the garment by the shoulders and gave it a quick shake so that it hung properly and after turning it this way and that for inspection, held it out for Kate to put on. "Come on, let's see it on you," she commanded.

"Here?" Kate glanced down at her apron and jeans.

"Why not? Come on." Wren jiggled the coat for emphasis.

"You might as well. David's told me what she's like when she's on a mission," Michael whispered into Kate's ear, making her giggle.

"Preaching to the choir," Kate said in an undertone, untying her apron and handing it to Michael before turning and slipping her arms into the waiting coat sleeves.

Emily strolled out from the kitchen to see Kate trying on her gift and grinned. Crossing the store, she indicated the apron in Michael's hands.

"Give that to me and I'll hang it up," she offered. "I think she's done for the day."

Michael handed it over with a smile of thanks, and Emily retreated to the kitchen again. Wren helped her pull the coat on and then made her turn around, fussing over her as she made sure the coat was sitting properly before reaching for the belt.

"I think I can manage—" Kate began, only to be shushed by Wren as she quickly knotted the belt and stepped back with a nod of satisfaction.

For a moment, Wren and Michael just stared at her, making her blush a little under their scrutiny. Kate ran her hands down the front of the coat, loving the feel of the soft fabric beneath her touch. The coat fell to mid-thigh, which Wren assured Michael was perfect.

"How does it look?" Kate said after she decided they had been quiet long enough.

"You'll do." Michael smiled. The red cashmere was a perfect foil for her dark blond hair and pale skin, and her lips curled invitingly as she smiled back. He took up the silent offer and leaned forward for a soft kiss.

"It's gorgeous," Wren said approvingly. "Now all you need is something to keep your head warm and—" She broke off as Michael reached into the shopping bag again.

"You mean something like this?" Michael held up a smaller tissue-wrapped bundle.

"There's more?" Kate was feeling very spoiled. Again the tissue paper was dispensed with to reveal a gray cashmere cap that fit softly onto her head like a beanie, along with a matching scarf.

"Forrester," Wren said once Kate had been accessorized to her satisfaction. "I like your style."

"I can't take all the credit," Michael admitted at last. "I spoke to my mom about where to go, and then the saleswoman at Saks picked out a few to choose from."

"You didn't talk to me first?" Wren tried to look affronted. "I think I'm hurt."

"I only just got the idea this morning," Michael explained, "but trust me, next time I get an idea, I'll be sure to call."

"Good." Wren nodded. "You guys look pretty cozy now. Why don't you take off?"

"Huh?" Kate looked surprised.

"What, you think Emily and I can't lock up for the day? You're standing there all rigged up and gorgeous; go enjoy yourselves."

"But—" Kate began, blinking as Wren snapped her fingers peremptorily at her.

"No buts, we'll call this a training run," Emily joined in. "Give me the keys and then you two can go."

"What, you're drunk on power already?" Kate teased.

Emily laughed but stood firm. "You were saying that you wanted to check out some winter warmers, so why don't you just go do some research or something if calling it that is going to make you feel better."

"Winter warmers?" Michael looked interested at this.

"The boss here likes to have a winter drink menu. We were talking about getting some fresh ideas this morning, so I think this is your cue to take her out for some research," Emily replied.

"Winter drinks, huh?" Michael looked thoughtful. "You know, I think I know just the place." He'd glanced at a menu in passing when he had left Saks, and on the basis of Emily's conversation knew that it had to be just what Kate was looking for.

"You are *so* bossy." Kate laughed at the two determined women before her. "Wren," she appealed, "a little help?"

"Sorry, boss." Wren grinned. "New boss has a point: you're outta here."

"So it's mutiny, huh?" Kate replied.

"You should be getting used to it by now," Wren quipped. "Really," she went on to Michael, "Emily and I gang up on her all the time these days."

"So I see." Michael grinned. "And who am I to argue?" He gave Kate another kiss. "Get your bag. We've got research to do."

Kate retreated to the kitchen to get her bag, and Michael congratulated Emily again on her promotion.

"Thanks." She gave him a shy smile. "It was quite a shock."

"It's well deserved," Michael assured her. "Kate has been thinking about it for a while."

"It's a great opportunity." Emily nodded. "She really is something."

Michael looked up as he heard Kate laughing at something Wren had just said. She was still laughing as she rounded the corner from the kitchen and walked toward him to take his hand.

"She sure is." Michael smiled. "C'mon, let's go research."

"See you tomorrow," Kate called as Michael tugged her toward the door.

"Not too early," Wren answered. "We'll open up."

❧

Michael took her to the Flatiron Lounge, an art deco bar that was warmly lit and already getting busy for the evening with the after-work crowd.

"Look at those red leather lounges. I'm warming up just looking at them," Kate marveled as she stepped inside.

After a brief wait they were seated side by side at a booth, and Kate was poring over the menu as she unwound her scarf and gloves.

"Wow," she said after a considered pause, "their mixologists here really know their stuff." Her eyebrows went up in surprise. "Jasmine-infused vodka with white peach puree?" She gave Michael a happy smile. "We're going to have to come back here when I don't have to work the next day."

"Which could be sometime soon now that you've got more backup," Michael said as he settled himself more comfortably and put his arm around her shoulders.

Kate leaned into him and kept reading, and then sat up straight, tapping the menu decisively. "Sold. I've just found what I want."

"What's that?" Michael leaned forward to check the menu.

"Cocoa Chanel," Kate read for him. "Valrhona hot chocolate mixed with Herradura Reposado Tequila and served with a floater of loosely whipped cinnamon cream."

"Cocoa Chanel?" Michael chuckled with quiet amusement as he remembered his afternoon.

"Am I missing something?"

"When I was at Saks this afternoon, I smelled you, or rather, your perfume. I followed the trail and it let me to the Chanel counter." He had smiled at the thought of Kate's scent trail leading him throughout the store, and wondered, not for the first time, if argon had any scent of its own. The more time they spent together, the more their breaths mingled, the more the immortal molecule continued to bind them together. It was an invisible bond that he never wanted to break.

"Ah." Kate nodded knowingly. "My *Allure*."

Michael leaned in to give her a soft kiss, and when he pulled away, Kate smiled at the intensity of his regard as their breaths washed softly over each other. "It certainly is," he agreed.

Chapter 21

The L Word

Kate finished her cocoa and swiped some of the cream off the rim of her cup with a finger and licked it off.

"How was it?" Michael asked as he watched her over the rim of his cup of affrogatto.

"Just as good as the first," Kate replied, and scooped up some more cinnamon cream on her finger and held it out to him. "Want some?"

Michael dipped his head toward her hand by way of answer and gently sucked the cream off her finger, kissing the tip of it as he withdrew.

"I see what you mean," he said. "Do you want another?"

Kate had another lick of cream and then pushed her empty cup away with a regretful sigh.

"I think two is my limit," she said as she leaned against his shoulder, nestling against him as he pulled her closer. "I'm actually kinda tired."

Michael set his cup down so that he could check his watch. "It's just past seven," he commented. "Do you want to do something for dinner?"

Kate played with her spoon aimlessly as she considered his offer and then glanced up at him. "I don't think I'm hungry." She lifted a hand to her throat as she swallowed.

Michael watched as she rubbed her throat and sipped at a glass of water with a slight grimace. "Is everything okay?"

Kate looked surprised. "Sure, the day was good." She patted her collar of her coat and gave him a pleased smile. "And I adore my present." Her smile faltered. "I guess I just feel a little off."

"Hmm." Michael stroked her face with the back of his fingers. "You've been working pretty hard; maybe you're burning out."

"Like you can talk," Kate scoffed. "You've been putting in some ridiculous hours yourself."

"True," Michael conceded. "But sitting on my butt is different than what you do."

"I guess we're busy in our own way," Kate commented, shrugging off his comment.

"Just as well I'm here to make sure you look after yourself, then," Michael teased, and then was startled to see Kate looking at him with her eyes watering. "What's wrong? Sweetheart, are you—" He broke off as Kate's face crumpled and she sneezed three times in quick succession.

"Guh," she said, groping for a napkin and blowing her nose. "That was unexpected."

"That's it. I'm taking you home," Michael said as he signaled for the check. Kate was looking a little flustered now, and he began to rub her back with one hand as they waited. The check was delivered, and Michael spared it a cursory glance, pulling out his wallet and tossing down a few bills as he stood up.

"No, I'm okay," Kate protested as she wiped her eyes. "If you want to get something to eat we can—" Her words were cut short by another sneeze.

"You were saying?" Michael started to laugh as he helped her to her feet.

"I don't know what the hell is going on," she muttered as he allowed him to steer her toward the bar. "I felt just fine earlier."

"So what happened between then and now?" Michael asked before stopping her at the door to make sure she was bundled up against the cold before ushering her outside.

"Nothing." Kate shrugged. "I had a talk with Emily about the new arrangement."

"And it all went well?" Michael put his arm around Kate's waist, hooking his thumb on the belt of her coat as they walked.

"Better than," Kate confirmed. "She's excited and scared, but I think she'll be great."

"And Wren is okay?"

"Oh, sure." Kate nodded, swallowing and wincing against the slight pain. "Managing the store is something she never wanted to do, so she's good."

Michael nodded as he listened to Kate talk. She had been worried about broaching the subject of the store with Wren and had talked it over at length with Michael. Wren certainly had more experience with the store than Emily, but it was obvious that her natural creativity would eventually lead her into a world beyond the bakery doors. They paused at the traffic lights, and Michael glanced down in concern as Kate sneezed again.

"That definitely doesn't sound right," he commented as she blew her nose with a groan.

"There's a right way to sneeze?" Kate quipped as the light changed and they crossed the street.

"Oh, sure," Michael replied. "Dad and I made it a point to sneeze in a manner we saw fit."

"Really," Kate said with amused skepticism.

"Yup." Michael winked at her and then moved his attention back to the sidewalk as he navigated them through the pedestrian traffic. "Practically anyone can say *ah-choo* when they sneeze, but Dad and I worked on different sayings."

"Such as?" Kate blinked and, feeling fatigued, leaned against Michael a little more.

"Well, there was *wa-hoo*," Michael began. "That's always a classic, and *wee-ha*. Of course," he went on in an off-hand tone, "Dad went through an Al Pacino phase after *Scent of a Woman* came out, so all of his sneezes sounded like *hoo-ah* for a while there."

Kate shook with laughter, and Michael quirked an eyebrow at her in mock disdain.

"You mock our time-honored efforts when the best you can manage is some kind of cat sneeze?"

"A what?" Kate rubbed at her nose; it had started to tickle again.

"You haven't noticed? You come out with a kind of—" He broke off and performed a serious of soft high-pitched *ish, ish, ish* sounds.

"You're telling me I sneeze like a cat?" Kate managed when she'd stopped laughing.

"I am," Michael said as he gave her a fond look. "And I, for one, think it sounds cute."

"Fine," Kate said, waving a hand with resignation. "I'm the girl with the cute sneeze, whatever."

"More than that," Michael said as he pulled her close to kiss her temple. "You're *my* girl with the cute sneeze."

Kate considered that and nodded. "Works for me. So where are we sleeping tonight: yours or mine?" she asked as they kept walking.

"Tricky," Michael mused. "Your place is closer, so I'm happy to go there—"

"Your place." Kate decided while he thought aloud, making him glance at her in surprise.

"Really? I thought you'd want to go home if you weren't feeling well."

"You've got a king size bed," she admitted with a sheepish grin, "*and* a bath."

"Ahh, now we get to it." Michael nodded sagely. "You only want me for my bed and bath."

"I guess you had to find out some time." Kate sighed. "Now take me home."

"Yes, ma'am," Michael answered, grinning to himself as Kate tried to muffle another cat sneeze with minimal success. They exchanged a quick sidelong look but said nothing as they kept walking.

The first thing Michael did when they arrived at his apartment was to run Kate a hot bath. A quick rummage in the bathroom cupboard produced a bottle of bath foam that Kate had purchased, and she settled back into a sea of foam with a sigh of satisfaction as soon as the water was to her liking.

Some time later, Michael peered at Kate around the bathroom doorway. "Do you think you'll be up for something to eat after you're done soaking?"

"I think so, but nothing big," Kate replied after a considered pause. "You know," she went on as she scooped up a handful of foam, "there's plenty of room in here for two."

"Oh, I'm well aware of that," Michael said as he crossed the room to kneel beside the tub and gently kiss her shoulder, "but you're not well."

"I could feel better," Kate said in a hopeful tone, turning her face toward him for a kiss that quickly became heated.

"I think," Michael growled when he managed to pull away at last, "you need some rest before I have my way with you."

"I feel rested now," Kate argued as she reached out a wet hand to grab a fistful of his T-shirt.

Michael put up a half-hearted resistance at best before his tongue licked inside her mouth as he cupped her face in his hands. Her skin felt warm to the touch, and he looked at the flush in her cheeks and beads of sweat dotting her forehead.

"Baby, you're hot," he said in concern.

"Flattery will get you everywhere." Kate smiled as she evaded his hands and nipped at his throat.

"Uh." Michael's eyes fluttered closed for a moment as her breath puffed against his neck. "Wait, no, I meant you could be running a fever."

He drew in a shaky breath as he watched a clump of suds slide down her arm and rest against her naked hip that peeked out of the water. He shifted slightly and slid a hand down her arm and across her body so that he could cup a breast, his thumb rubbing over the rosy tip. Kate closed her eyes and relaxed in the bath, curling up slightly in pleasure. Michael watched her as she opened her eyes and gazed at him, the tip of her tongue darting out to moisten her lips.

"Sure you don't want to join me?" she asked as she ran a damp finger along his forearm.

"No," he admitted as he dipped his head to kiss her again. This time when he broke the kiss they were both looking flushed. "I'm going to get you something to eat," he said, his voice sounding hoarse now. "And you're going to get into bed and get comfortable."

"Okay." Kate smiled, although her bottom lip was sticking out a little.

Michael cocked his head and regarded her demure acceptance for a moment.

"Are you pouting at me?" he asked.

"Maybe a little," she admitted. The tequila in her cocoa had been minimal at best, but the combination of a little alcohol on top of feeling tired and then a hot bath had her feeling more than a little silly.

"Just when I think you can't get any cuter," he muttered. He got up and yanked a fluffy towel off a nearby hook to leave beside the bath. "Take your time. I'll be about twenty minutes."

"Will do." Kate lifted a leg out of the water and gazed at her foot to see how wrinkled she was getting before relaxing back into the water with a splash. She could dimly hear Michael moving in the kitchen, the run of a tap and the clank of what sounded like a saucepan. A small part of her wondered what he was up to, but she dried her hands and picked up the magazine she had found on one of Michael's bookshelves earlier. It was a copy of *Vanity Fair;* a couple of years old by the looks of it, but the articles looked interesting.

She flicked through the pages, giving them a cursory glance. Her mind felt too fuzzy to handle anything too intellectual at the moment; most of the articles looked to be beyond her tolerance levels for the evening. The magazine was glossy and the advertisements catered to the wealthy, but an Annie Leibovitz portfolio of Hollywood actors soon distracted her. The bath water had cooled slightly, but her skin was still flushed. She wiped some stick tendrils of hair off her forehead and kept reading.

"Hey." Michael's soft voice interrupted her, and she blinked up at him owlishly as he leaned against the door frame, his arms folded over his chest as he regarded her with a slight smile. "You done?"

"Sure," she replied, startled when her voice came out sounding like a tired croak.

"Come on, let's get you to bed."

Kate stood up with a slight wobble and stepped out of the tub into the towel that Michael held out for her. He rubbed her down with gentle movements, wrapping her up in it and giving her another kiss as he steered her toward the bedroom.

"Get changed, and I'll get your snack."

"Why are you being so good to me?" Kate asked, the question bubbling out of her without any conscious thought.

"Because I can," Michael said in a mild tone. "Because I want to."

"Really?" Kate stood at the foot of his expansive bed, naked but for the towel she held clutched around her damp body. Her hair had half-fallen out of the sloppy knot she had tied it up in, and it straggled around her shoulders, making her look like a wet dandelion. Michael didn't think he'd ever seen her look more vulnerable.

"Really. You just make yourself comfortable, and let me take care of the rest."

Another smile of reassurance, and he was gone.

Kate stood in the bedroom blinking at his retreating back, and then turned to look at the bed. Even when she and Tom had been dating, he'd never fussed after her like this. The bed had been freshly made by the looks of it; the comforter was a beige waffle-weave bordered with white sheets, and there were enough pillows to make a fort. She crossed to the dresser and opened what she thought of as her drawer to grab some clean underwear and an old T-shirt of Michael's that she liked to sleep in. Retrieving the magazine from the bathroom, she climbed into bed. The sheets were crisp and cool against her warm skin, and she settled herself against the pillows with a sigh.

She could still hear Michael banging things in the kitchen and wondered again just what he was up to. Flicking some damp hair off her neck, she thumbed her way through the magazine to the last photo she had been studying. She let her gaze dwell on the couture gowns worn by a group of A-list actresses posed amidst an elaborate set of chaise lounges, packing crates, and Afghan rugs. Lost in a study of plush fabrics and body language, she looked up at the sound of movement nearby to see Michael padding toward her with a small ceramic bowl in his hand.

"Here you go," he said. "I know it's simple, but it's what I want when I don't feel good."

"Mashed potatoes?" Kate surveyed the bowl with surprise. The mash was creamy and topped with cracked pepper and a generous curl of butter. She smiled when she realized that Michael had drawn the shape of a heart in the mash with the fork that accompanied the bowl. She looked up at him with a smile of thanks, and suddenly the words that she had been hesitating over were there. "I love you."

Michael looked at her and a slow, pleased smile spread across his face.

"If I'd known mashed potatoes would earn that kind of declaration, I'd have made it weeks ago," he commented as he sat down on the bed.

Kate looked down at the bowl in her hands and then gave him a tremulous smile. "I guess it's been a while since I've been looked after like this."

Michael leaned closer and gave her a kiss.

"It's no less than you deserve," he said. "And I love you too." He straightened and gestured to the bowl. "Now, eat."

Kate picked up the fork and took her first mouthful. The potatoes were creamy and delicious. "Wonderful," she said at last. "Just what I needed."

Michael smoothed her hair with one hand. "It's the best I could do on short notice. What you really need is some of Mom's soup."

"Gwen used to make great chicken soup," Kate said in between mouthfuls. "It's been a long time since I've had mom-cooking."

"Speaking of which, the folks want to see us again for lunch sometime." Michael kept stroking her hair as he spoke.

"Yeah?" Kate gave him a glance and kept eating. The mash was warm and smooth, which felt soothing against her sore throat. Even more soothing was the feel of Michael's hands as he stroked and combed her hair with his fingers.

"Yup." Michael nodded and kept talking. "It was a part of the deal I made with her this morning."

"Deal?" Kate glanced at him, careful not to disturb his hand; she wasn't ready for him to stop just yet. In fact, he could keep doing it forever as far as she was concerned.

"Uh…" Michael looked a little embarrassed. "I called her this morning to ask her where I could get you a good coat," he explained.

Kate laughed, which turned into a cough. "You know, that's kinda cute."

"Kinda lame," Michael admitted. "A grown man asking his mom where to go shopping for his girlfriend."

"I bet she was happy to help out, though," Kate said with a smile.

"You have no idea." Michael smiled at the memory of Susan's happy voice as she rattled off her instructions. "It's the first time I've asked her about that kind of thing, and she and Dad love you."

"Do they?" Kate flushed a little at this.

"You know they do." Michael gave her a smile.

Since meeting Kate, Susan and Charles welcomed her with open arms into their home at every possible opportunity. Aside from the fact that they had a love of literature in common, Kate's natural warmth and her obvious affection for Michael had endeared her to them all the more.

Michael's previous girlfriends had been charming in their own way although they were more career-hungry than Kate, who seemed more content with her bakery and friendships than she was in scaling the profit ladder. They had also derived a certain satisfaction from dating a known author, and delighted in taking him to various corporate functions where they could introduce him. By contrast, Kate had known nothing about his success and seemed quite content to keep it that way. Even the discovery that Michael was writing about her had done little to upset her equilibrium; at least it seemed that way on the surface.

Kate's reluctance to read his published works was a matter that Michael dwelled on from time to time. He didn't care if she read them or not, but her refusal to read the incomplete manuscript despite his offers—a rarity to anyone that knew how protective Michael was of his writing—and despite knowing she was featured, had him puzzled. Other women would have pestered him senseless had they known they were going to be immortalized in the printed word. He didn't need Kate to read his work for his own satisfaction or her approval, but it bothered him that his words seemed to be building some sort of invisible barrier between them.

"Well, they're kinda cool too," Kate admitted. She finished her meal and set the fork down in the bowl with a clink and a sigh.

Michael reached over to take the bowl from her and set it on the bedside table before taking her in his arms and resting back against the pillows. The pair of them lay there together in silence until Kate spoke.

"You know, I think Jack and Gwen would have really loved you too."

Michael said nothing but kissed her temple by way of reply. He recognized her hesitant words for the accolade they were. Kate rested her head against his shoulder and gave a soft sigh as Michael kept stroking her hair. After a time, her breathing evened out as she slid into sleep. Michael checked his position and decided he would be comfortable enough for the time being; he didn't want to move and risk Kate waking up. He glanced at his watch and saw that the evening was creeping toward ten o'clock.

Words bubbled in his head, and a slight inclination of his head gave him a partial view of his desk in the living room where he could see the glow of his laptop screen. He glanced down at Kate sleeping against him. Her hair was beginning to dry, and he smiled to see the soft curls springing out from her temple. Kate mumbled something under her breath and settled against him with a soft chuffing sigh. She felt warmer to the touch now; he was sure that she had a fever. The words were still there, and he rolled them around until he had shaped them into a pleasing construct. He repeated the phrasing to himself a few more times until he knew he would remember in the morning and then let them subside.

He drifted off to sleep, feeling content.

"G'morning," Michael whispered. "I love you."

"Iloveyoutoo," Kate mumbled as she reached out and fumbled to pull his face toward hers for a kiss.

"How are you feeling?"

Kate cracked an eye open to see Michael hovering over her with a look of concern, and then blinked and rubbed her eyes, which felt as if they were full of sand. Her body ached and her skin felt hot and parched in a way that had her longing for another bath. Inventory over, she grimaced at Michael.

"Bad?" he asked as he put a hand on her forehead. "You were running a fever all night."

"I was?" She frowned at that. She couldn't remember the last time she had been sick.

"Yeah." Michael smiled. "You kept me warm all night."

Kate pushed her lank hair off her face and plucked at her shirt. As grimy as she felt, Michael didn't seem to care. He kept his arm around her as he lay on his side with his head propped in one hand, his legs entangled with hers. Glancing over Michael's shoulder, she saw the curtains shift a little in the breeze.

"You opened the window? In this weather?" She looked at Michael in surprise.

"You told me to."

"I did?" Kate shook her head against the pillow. "I don't remember that." She had the dim memory of waking up a few times but that was all. "Did I say anything else?"

"What kinda guy would I be if I repeated what you say when you're out of it?" Michael protested.

"A *live* one." Kate tried to growl and ended up coughing instead.

"Still not saying." Michael grinned.

Kate shook her head in exasperation but closed her eyes and curled her body against his like a sleepy kitten.

"I guess you telling me I had to open the window because you were on fire tipped me off," Michael mused out loud.

Kate gave a sleepy chuckle. "Really?"

"Uh-huh. You got a bit cranky." His shoulders shook with silent amusement. "You kept trying to get out of bed to open the window, so I did it for you."

"I'm ignoring you now," Kate told him, her eyes stayed closed but her lips curled in a smile.

"Really?" Michael nuzzled her clavicle.

Kate sighed as she felt Michael's lips ghost across her skin. Seconds later her eyes flew open and she sat up so abruptly Michael's nose bumped on her chest.

"What's the time?" She looked at the bedside clock and groaned. "I've got to get to work."

"I don't think so." Michael winced and rubbed his nose as Kate kicked away the sheet and tried to stand up. She had just gotten to her feet when her head thumped with pain, making her sit down just as quickly as she had gotten up.

Kate put her head in her hands. "This isn't happening," Kate muttered. "I haven't been sick in years."

"You are now." Michael observed that Kate's attempt to start the day had left her ashen-faced and shaking. "Give me your phone. I'll call Wren."

"I'll have to call Emily." Kate shook her head. "Wren doesn't have any keys."

"She hasn't?" Michael glanced at her. "How long have you guys been working together?"

"I know." Kate nodded her agreement. "I've offered, but she kept saying no."

"That doesn't make sense," Michael commented as he retrieved Kate's phone from the living room.

"Her argument was that she kept losing her *own* keys, so she didn't want the stress of losing the store keys as well."

Michael snorted. "For someone called Pocket Rocket, she's awful scared sometimes."

"I know," Kate sighed and scratched her head. "I'll take a shower and get going. I just need to let Emily know I'll be late."

"Like hell." Michael shook his head. "You're staying right where you are."

"Oh, really?" Kate glared and rubbed her eyes again. Her head was feeling stuffy and her nose was tingling. "And what's going to stop me?"

Michael was about to speak when Kate broke into a sneezing fit. Kate sneezed five times, annoyed at the interruption and aware that she was indeed sounding like a cat, but seemed unable to do anything about it. She accepted a tissue from Michael with what she hoped was a dignified silence and blew her nose.

"You were saying?" Michael asked in a mild tone as he proffered her cell phone.

"How about I start late?" she bargained.

"How about you talk to Emily and see what she thinks?" Michael asked.

"And then what?" Kate eyed the phone with a wary expression.

"And then if she tells you to stay at home, you stay in bed, I call Mom, and knowing her, she'll come over with some soup."

"I can't." Kate shook her head. "This sort of thing doesn't happen."

Michael took her hand. "Kate, it's happening now, and maybe it's because it can."

"Huh?" Kate gave him a blank look.

"Think about it; you've got Emily *and* Wren. You've got support for moments like these."

"But it's only the day after Emily and I talked about it," Kate's wail came out sounding like a croak.

"Just call Emily and see what she—" Michael began.

"What if she freaks out when—" Kate started.

"Sweetheart, *call* her." Michael gave her the phone. "Enough with the what-ifs."

Emily hurried toward the store, her breath misting in the cool air. She saw the red canopy in the distance and could make out a pacing figure beneath it—it had to be Wren.

"Hey, B2," Wren greeted her as Emily reached her.

"B2?" Emily shot her a curious look as she sorted through the store keys to find the right one for the security grill. Wren reached over and pointed at the correct key and then helped her open the doors.

"Boss Two?" Wren suggested.

"At least you didn't call me Number Two." Emily grinned. "But it still feels weird."

"Not to me." Wren shrugged.

"You sure?" Emily looked at the smaller woman. That Kate had asked Emily to take more responsibility rather than Wren had been a point of worry all night.

"Yup," Wren answered with a clear expression, and Emily's confidence lifted a little.

"So where's Kate?" Emily asked as they both walked toward the kitchen to put away their bags and get ready for the day. "I'm usually the last one here."

"Don't know," Wren said, pausing in the act of switching on the coffee machine to look at the clock. "She should be here by now."

The two women exchanged a glance as the phone rang. Emily reached for the receiver.

"Good morning, Take the Cake," she greeted, and then, "Kate!" Her face broke into a relieved smile that faltered as she listened to Kate. "You sound *terrible.*"

Wren took in Emily's look of concern, before turning without a word and walking into the kitchen. By the time she returned carrying a small notebook, Emily was replacing the receiver and looking worried.

"What's the verdict?" Wren asked, although she already knew.

"She's sick," Emily said in a flat tone as she gave Wren a look of trepidation. "So I told her to stay home." Emily gulped. "I guess it's just us today."

"Looks like," Wren replied as she held up the notebook.

"What's that?"

"The recipe bible," Wren said as she handed it over. "I'll help get you started."

Emily flicked through the pages. Some of the recipes were written in Kate's handwriting and others she didn't recognize. She looked up at Wren, feeling scared now.

"Where should I start?" she asked with a dry mouth.

"Jack's Favorite," Wren advised. "It's a simple butter cake recipe."

"Really?" Emily sounded hopeful now.

"It's how Kate got started." Wren smiled and put her arm around the taller woman's shoulders to steer her into the kitchen. Emily stood in the kitchen, looking around with wide eyes.

"You've helped Kate out before," Wren said soothingly as she switched on the oven. "And you know where everything is and how she does it. You've made muffins; this isn't any different."

"Wren, I'm making the *cupcakes*," Emily said as she walked toward the counter and pulled the mixer toward her.

"It's just another product," Wren replied. "We'll be fine." She slapped Emily's rump on her way out of the kitchen. "I'll get us some coffee and get to work on the bagels. We've got an hour and a half before we open, and we can get it done."

"Can we?" Emily raised an eyebrow.

"We have to." Wren grinned. "And you know how I like a challenge."

"True." Emily couldn't help but smile back.

Emily read the recipe again, looking at Kate's notations as the quantities had grown over the years. It looked easy enough. Emily glanced at the oven and nodded as she saw the thermostat increasing. She knew she'd better get started.

Wren paused from frothing the milk and smiled when she heard the mixer start up. They were going to be fine. An hour later, Wren had powered her way through the bagel preparation and was setting out some savory muffins that Kate had made the previous afternoon. She stopped and surveyed the display cabinet. Levels of stock were looking good; there was just one thing more that she needed.

Emily appeared beside Wren, looking pleased and nervous. "Want to come see?"

Wren gave her a flat look.

"Okay." Emily laughed and threw up her hands. "Stupid question. Come look."

Wren followed her into the kitchen and checked out the finished product.

"Nice, very nice." She nodded slowly.

"Thanks." Emily sighed with relief. "I was worried that—" She broke off. "*Shit.*"

"What?" Wren was wide-eyed at the sudden change in mood. "What's wrong?"

"We've done this all wrong," Emily said. "What's the quote for the day?"

"Hell, I nearly forgot." Wren put a hand to her forehead. "I'll think of something now, and then see what you can come up with to name those." She pointed to the waiting cupcakes. She darted out into the store to grab the chalkboard and stared out the store window to the traffic outside, her mind racing as she waited for inspiration.

"Hey, Emily," she called. "What's the main ingredient in those things?"

Emily appeared with one of the trays and slid them into the cabinet. "If you're including the frosting, I'd have to say sugar or butter. Why?"

"Thanks." Wren scribbled for a moment and then turned the board around.

Emily read it and laughed.

What whiskey or butter can't cure,
there's no cure for.

"Now it's your turn," Wren said.

"What do I do?" Emily said as she looked from the cupcakes to the chalkboard.

"Think of a cupcake name that matches the quote and you're done," Wren replied as she carried the chalkboard outside to hang it up. "You'll get the hang of it in no time."

"If you say so," Emily muttered under her breath. She leaned against the counter and crossed her arms as she studied the cupcakes. "Whiskey and butter," she murmured to herself.

Wren returned inside to see Emily making them another coffee, her face a mask of concentration. Wren gave her a quick pat on the back as she passed and busied herself filling up the water jugs, dropping in slices of lemon before carrying them over to a small table for customers to help themselves. Emily finished making the coffee in short order and handed Wren her cup as she returned behind the counter.

"Thanks," Wren said as she took a sip. "So, got a name?"

"I have." Emily smiled.

"Great." Wren swooped on her piece of chalk and grabbed the smaller chalkboard and gave her an expectant look.

Emily took a sip of her coffee and then dictated, watching as Wren wrote down her words. When Wren held out the chalkboard, both women studied it for a moment.

Miracle Cure: *Vanilla butter cupcakes with chocolate butter frosting.*

"You know, I think we're going to be just fine."

"Here." Michael set a steaming mug on the bedside table. "I know it's not the standard you're used to, but I'll get us something later."

"S'fine," Kate said as she reached for the cup. Michael set down a glass of juice as well.

"You need to keep up your fluids," he parroted and then pulled a face. "Mom called, so I'm just repeating what she told me. She's stopping by with lunch later."

Kate sipped at the coffee, and then slumped against the mountain of pillows that Michael had stacked up around her.

"I feel pathetic," she admitted.

Michael leaned over and gave her a kiss. "I don't know, you feel pretty good to me, babe. Kinda toasty."

"I'm going to be an impatient patient," she warned him.

"Okay." Michael nodded. "You want to sleep some more?" he asked as he watched Kate struggle to keep her eyes open.

"I'm fine." Kate shook her head even as she settled herself more comfortably on the pillows. She closed her eyes and sighed.

Michael stood watching her with a slight smile on his face. Her breath hitched once, twice, and then settled into a deeper rhythm. Leaving the bedroom, Michael returned to his desk and sat down in front of his laptop. He typed for a while, and then pushed back his chair so that he could glimpse the lump that was Kate's feet beneath the covers. There were no signs of movement; Kate was sound asleep. He smiled and went back to work.

Kate slowly returned to consciousness to hear Michael talking quietly in the other room. She squinted at the bedside clock and saw that she had slept for another couple of hours. Struggling into a sitting position, she pushed her hair off her face and rubbed her eyes. She felt gritty again, so shoved the covers aside to make her way into the bathroom. She had a quick shower and changed into some fresh clothes before making her way out into the living room.

"Hey, you're looking a little better," Michael said, looking up when she appeared.

"I feel it," she mumbled as she sat down on the sofa and then curled up on her side with her eyes closed. It felt good to be out of bed, but she couldn't find the energy to do anything. She heard Michael get up from his desk but didn't pay it any heed.

"Lift up," Michael instructed.

Opening her eyes, she saw Michael standing in front of the sofa with a pillow he had retrieved from the bed. She propped herself up so that Michael could slide the pillow under her shoulders and then lay back down, smiling her thanks when he covered her with a light blanket.

"You want something to drink?" Michael asked as he brushed her check with the back of his fingers.

"Mm-hmm." Kate nodded, her eyes fluttering closed again. She was still feeling light-headed. It felt as if her center of balance had somehow moved six inches away from where she lay, leaving her with the curious sensation of feeling as if she was not properly anchored within her body. Closing her eyes, she let herself drift.

Michael went into the kitchen and returned with a glass of water, which he set down on the coffee table in front of her.

"We can expect a soup delivery soon," he said as he took a seat on the arm of the sofa.

"Your mom doesn't have to do that," Kate said in a drowsy tone as she blinked at him slowly. She felt guilty over the level of attention she was getting for what appeared to be a mild head cold.

"Just let us take care of you," Michael soothed. "We want to, okay?"

"If you say so," Kate said, "but don't you think you're too far away to do that?"

Michael took the hint and eased himself onto the sofa. Kate shoved the pillow aside and burrowed against his chest. In contrast to her body heat, Michael felt deliciously cool. Settling her head on his shoulder, she looked up at him with a sleepy smile. Michael bent his head and kissed her out of reflex.

"Hey," he whispered, "love you."

"Love you too." She smiled.

Now that the words had been said, they wanted to say them often, as if making up for lost time. Keeping his arm around her, Michael reached for the

TV remote and flicked it on, scrolling through the channels to see if there was anything worth watching.

"See anything you like?" he asked as he kept his gaze on the screen.

"Not on TV," Kate murmured, running her hands up his chest.

"I had no idea you were such a horndog when you're sick." Michael smirked at her as her fingers traced idle figure eights on his shirt.

"You never know—" Kate waved a hand in an entirely vague gesture before returning to Michael's shirt, "—it could be a great way to break a fever."

"Mmm," Michael mused, closing his eyes as Kate kissed his jaw and ran a hand over his thighs. "Don't forget we're getting a soup delivery."

"Yeah," Kate replied, "but I bet your mom's soup can't do this." She gently bit his bottom lip before coaxing his mouth open with her tongue and dipping inside.

Michael's hands floated up to hold her in place as they kissed and stroked each other in all the ways they liked best. By the time they broke apart, Kate's face was flushed and her eyes dilated as she gazed heavy-lidded at him. She looked, Michael realized, almost as if she was drunk. Her movements were slow and deliberate as if she had to concentrate on what she wanted to do.

"Damn." Michael's soft curse sounded shaky as he looked at his watch. "And Mom's on her way here already. It's too late to put her off."

Kate didn't take her gaze away from his lips as he spoke, and she leaned in to kiss him again the moment he stopped speaking. This time the kiss was not as gentle as their mutual desire grew.

"Honey, you're not well." Michael's breath was ragged now. "Are you sure this is a good idea?"

"I've never been more sure of anything," Kate replied. She shifted her weight and threw a leg over his thighs so that she straddled him. Michael's hands automatically shifted to cup her bottom, so that he could lift and pull her closer against him. They both gave a quiet moan as their cores came into contact through their clothes.

"Jesus." Michael had time to mutter before Kate fisted her hands in his hair and pulled him to her for another kiss. His hips lifted slightly as she ground down on his lap, and he shifted his hands to run them up and under her T-shirt as he gave in and accepted what she was offering. "Need this *off*," he growled as he pulled at the soft fabric.

Kate broke away from him long enough to pull the T-shirt up and over her head. As her arms lifted, he leaned forward to pull the rosy tip of one of her breasts into his mouth. The T-shirt was tossed aside as she clutched his head to her. She couldn't sit still. Her hips rose and circled against his as she all but whimpered in her need to get him closer still.

"I need," Kate stuttered, trying to get the words out when all she wanted to do was kiss him. "Off." She tugged at his shirt, pushing him back against the sofa so that she could fumble it up and over his head.

Michael looked at his watch and then at Kate.

"Maybe traffic will be bad," he bargained.

"Could be," Kate agreed, licking and nipping at his chest before pausing to look up at him. "Now?"

"Now," he agreed.

Somehow they made it to the bed and fell onto it in a tangle of limbs that were immediately kicking off the last of their clothes. There was no murmured sweet talk, no gentle exploration; it was all need. Michael lunged for the bedside drawer and produced a foil packet, the contents of which were fitted with shaking hands as Kate tongued and kissed his skin. Rolling her onto her back and holding his weight above her, Michael stopped and gazed at her for a long moment.

"Kate," he began, "I…"

"I know." She nodded and pulled his face toward hers. His hips flexed forward as her legs wrapped around him, and he sank into her warmth. They both sighed and felt their bodies adjust to each other, before he flexed his hips again, withdrawing and returning over and over.

"More," Kate groaned as she jerked her hips to meet his thrusts. "Michael, I can't, I—"

"What? Tell me," Michael whispered in her ear before kissing her throat. "You've got to tell me."

"I feel like I can't get close enough to you," she muttered. Her hands were splayed across his shoulders, pulling him closer still.

"I know." Michael was trying to touch and kiss as much of her as he could as their bodies curled and thrust against each other. "Me too."

Kate felt hot, the fever raging through her body as her system fought to restore her equilibrium, and all the while she surged toward Michael. She felt light-headed and could hear her ragged breathing as she struggled toward release. Something had to give; it just had to. Opening her eyes to gaze at Michael, she could barely see him; the fever was eating her up from the inside out. Michael's body felt cool and strong, and she clutched him as she tried to keep her awareness in check.

"Close," Michael managed as he slid a hand beneath her shoulder to give a firmer grip. Kate's only response was to nod and mumble something incoherent as she tightened her legs around his hips, her heels digging into his thighs and urging him deeper. Michael felt the familiar tightening as his body gathered its release. He broke away from kissing Kate to look at her before his body shook with its climax. At the same time, Kate's breathing hitched, the fever broke and sweat popped and beaded over her skin.

Michael sighed and nuzzled Kate's neck, careful to keep his weight from crushing her diminutive frame. When he had caught his breath, he carefully withdrew from her and got up from the bed to clean up as quickly as he could. Returning to the bedroom, he saw Kate sprawled amongst the crumpled sheets with a peaceful smile on her face.

"Hey," he said as he crawled across the bed and gathered her into his arms. "Where did you go?" he murmured as he gave her soft kiss. "I lost you somewhere."

"Whaddya mean?" Kate slurred. "I was here the whole time."

Michael's chest shook with suppressed amusement. "You know what I mean."

"Relax, lover boy." Kate patted his thigh. "Just because you don't hit the jackpot every time doesn't mean I'm not having fun." She blinked up at him and then lifted some sweaty hair off the back of her neck. "I got my release a different way, and I feel *good*."

Michael gazed at her and then rested his hand on her forehead. "You feel cooler. Did your fever break?"

"Feels like it." Kate's nod was sleepier this time.

"You need more sleep," Michael observed as Kate covered her mouth with a hand and gave a massive yawn.

"I do." She blinked. "But I want to have a shower first."

"I'll have to remember this," Michael commented. "When you get sick, you're like a cross between a mermaid and a horndog."

Kate tried to look stern as she regarded him despite her nudity. "Is that going to be a problem?"

"No, ma'am," Michael replied.

"Good, now come take a shower with me."

"Yes, ma'am," Michael repeated as he helped her off the bed. Kate staggered slightly but made her way toward the bathroom and turned on the shower. Michael glanced at the clock as he followed her. He guessed they had five or ten minutes before Susan arrived. He stepped into the shower cubicle to see Kate standing directly beneath the spray, her hair plastered against her head and shoulders as she soaped her hands.

"Come here," she said with a soft voice as she turned to face him.

Michael stood and let her soap his chest before returning the favor. It seemed only fair. Michael was dressed but still barefoot when his mother arrived.

"Thanks for coming over," Michael said as he gave his mother a kiss hello and helped her off with her coat. He had only just remembered to collect his and Kate's hastily discarded T-shirts from the living room floor and flick them into the bedroom before answering the door. "Did you drive?"

"I did. It was easier than catching a cab with what I had to carry," Susan replied as she indicated the two bags she had arrived with. "Where's the patient?" Susan asked as she saw the pillow on the sofa.

"She'll be out soon. She just had a shower," Michael replied as Susan made for the kitchen with her goodies.

Susan arched an eyebrow at her son as she took in his wet hair, watching as he had the grace to look sheepish. "I'm not asking." Susan smiled.

"Good," Michael replied, poker-faced. "Because I'm not telling."

"Fine by me," Susan replied airily as she set her bag down on the kitchen counter top. "You know, your father gets a similar look."

"When?" Michael asked without thinking and then immediately regretted it. He looked at Susan who was regarding him with a knowing smile. "Forget I said that."

Thankfully, Kate appeared in the doorway, and Susan's attention was immediately diverted.

"There you are," she said as she stepped forward to wrap her arms around Kate. "How are you feeling?"

"I'm okay," Kate replied as she returned Susan's hug.

Michael couldn't help but notice the genuine affection between the two women. He allowed himself to be relegated to the background as Susan ushered Kate back to the sofa and made sure she was settled comfortably.

"Have you eaten?" Susan asked as she pulled the blanket over Kate.

"A little. I haven't been very hungry," Kate admitted.

"Michael." Susan gave her son "the look."

"Hey," he protested from where he stood, "I tried to get her to keep her fluids up, but she slept most of the morning."

"Never mind." Susan rubbed Kate's shoulder. "We'll fix that." She paused and then took a seat on the coffee table while holding Kate's hands in her own. "I'm not here to intrude, but Michael told me you were sick, so I've brought a few things over."

"Thanks, Susan." Kate nodded as she tried to swallow the lump in her throat. "It's appreciated, really." She picked at the throw and gave Susan a watery smile. "I guess it's been a while since I've had a mom around me when I'm sick."

"How long has it been?" Susan asked in a quiet voice.

Kate did some mental arithmetic. "Coming up on thirteen years now," she replied. "Longer, I guess." She paused. "Gwen was sick for a few years before she went, so I looked after her as much as I could." She sat still, remembering. "It didn't seem right to complain about not feeling well, when she ..." She broke off and shrugged again.

"It's a terrible thing, losing your mother." Susan gave Kate a sad smile of understanding. "Charles once said that our mothers hold the memory of our lives before we know ourselves, and when they pass on, it's as if we can never be a child ever again."

"I'd never thought of it like that." Kate nodded as she considered Susan's words.

"So," Susan said with a bright smile to dispel the moment of sadness, "what sort of patient are you?"

"Not bad," Michael commented as he took a seat on the sofa and pulled Kate's feet onto his lap and rubbing her legs. "But she didn't like admitting that she couldn't go to work."

"I'm not surprised," Susan replied. "Watching a parent succumb to a terminal illness would make anything else sound petty. *But*," she said as she turned back to Kate, "you do need to look after yourself."

"God, it's not the end of the world." Kate rolled her eyes, making Susan laugh. "I think I was just over-tired or something."

"And you're recovering quickly, which is good," Susan answered, brisk now. "But you can't keep pushing yourself."

"Okay." Kate nodded as she wriggled her feet in Michael's lap. He got the message and resumed stroking her legs.

"You're resting, so you stay there and I'll get you something to eat."

Susan got up and waved Michael to stay seated as she went into the kitchen.

"You know," Kate whispered once she had gone, "I feel kinda stupid just laying here and being waited on by your mom."

"She wants to do it," Michael reassured her. "It's a mom thing to do; just go with it."

Kate looked uncertain.

"Kate, you're just outta practice. You'll be fine."

Susan called Michael and Kate into the kitchen in good time, and they arrived to discover she had produced two bowls of steaming chicken soup accompanied by slices of buttered crusty bread and a jug of water. The kitchen counter had two place settings, and as they took their seats, Susan busied herself with packing things away.

"Now," she said over her shoulder as she opened the refrigerator, "there's enough soup in here for another two meals. This container—" she showed them another sealed plastic tub, "—has got pie in it."

Michael swallowed a mouthful of soup and looked at his mother in amazement. "The one with the potato crust?"

"That's the one." Susan nodded.

"Wow." Michael looked impressed. "Even I don't merit that very often."

"Oh, stop." She swatted his shoulder with a laugh as Kate grinned.

"Susan, that's amazing, but you didn't have to go to so much tr—" Kate was waved into silence.

"Honey, just let me do this. I'd be doing the same for Michael, so it's just nice to have someone prettier to look after."

Kate snorted at this and tried to convert it into a cough without much success. She kept spooning her soup and studied Michael who was unshaven, wearing an old T-shirt, sporting wet hair and teasing his mother. He looked glorious. Kate dunked a chunk of bread into her soup and scooped it into her mouth. Tired as she was, she felt content.

❧

Emily looked at the wall clock, and then checked the cake supply in the display cabinet. To her delight, the cupcakes had been selling well, and she was feeling quietly confident. Wren returned to the counter with a tub of plates and cups, and Emily opened the dishwasher to help her stack them inside. It was early afternoon and they had gotten through the main rush of the day. There had been periods of stress, but between them they had coped.

"All good?" Wren asked as she straightened with a slight grimace. She glanced around the store and swooped into a downward dog pose. She held the pose for three exhalations before flowing through to upward dog and then carefully stepped back up into a standing position.

"Feel better?" Emily smiled as Wren washed her hands. Over the last few months, she had gotten used to Wren and Kate's spontaneous yoga and had started to attend a few evening classes near her apartment.

"Yeah." Wren rolled her head from side to side. "Guess it's been a hard day."

"I know." Emily looked guilty. "But it'll get better."

"Not you, Emily, you're fine." Wren shook her head. "I think we just got used to it being three of us, instead of two."

"I don't know how you and Kate did it," Emily admitted.

"Now that you're here, neither do I," Wren said with a tired smile. "Now, how about we call our boys and tell them they're taking care of us tonight?"

"Good plan." Emily nodded.

"I thought so." Wren smiled with satisfaction.

Emily reached for the cordless phone and handed it to Wren. "Hey, do you think Kate will be in tomorrow?"

Wren took the handset and looked thoughtful, tapping one foot as she considered Emily's question.

"How did she sound?"

"Awful," Emily replied.

"I think we'd better plan for her not to be in, just to be on the safe side," Wren advised. "Why do you ask?"

"I had an idea earlier, something else I could bake for the morning crowd."

"Go for it." Wren shrugged.

"Just like that?" Emily wiped her suddenly clammy hands against her jeans.

"Why not? Kate put her faith in you; how about you try doing the same thing?" Wren began to dial.

"If you say so." Emily nodded. She was thinking fast now, wondering how many to make, but her attention was caught by Wren's dialing. "Who are you calling?"

"David's voice mail at work. He'll be in class now," Wren replied.

Emily leaned against the counter and folded her arms, watching as Wren cooed a brief message into the phone about getting dinner that evening.

Wren disconnected the call when she had finished and handed the phone over to Emily who was still watching her with a quiet smile.

"What?" Wren said, and when Emily said nothing, she looked down at herself. "Do I have something on me?" She touched her hair. "Something in my teeth?"

"Uh-uh." Emily shook her head. "So," she went on in a casual tone, "you called David at work."

"Yeah." Wren gave her a blank look. "What about it?"

"And you knew his schedule." Emily ticked the facts off on her fingers. "You knew his extension to get his voice mail."

"Right." Wren nodded slowly.

"He has a key to your apartment, and you have a key to his," Emily went on.

Wren bit her lip and waited, but all Emily did was raise an eyebrow at her and then began to dial.

"What?" Wren said. "Emily, *what?*"

"Just sayin'." Emily shrugged as she listened to the phone.

"You haven't said anything," Wren protested.

"Haven't I?" Emily said, and then, "Hey, Brad."

Wren picked up a damp cloth and began to wipe down the counter, her mind racing as Emily spoke to Brad, making plans, joking and exchanging easy warm endearments. By the time she got off the phone, her expression was tranquil.

"You two sound really good," Wren commented as she flicked out the cloth before rinsing it out under cold water and hanging it on a rack to dry.

"We don't sound any different than you and David," Emily commented as she set the handset back in its holder and began to head into the kitchen. After a moment's thought, she opened the refrigerator and checked the contents before flicking on the industrial oven. What the hell, she'd try out her idea.

"You really think so?"

Looking up, she saw that Wren had followed her and stood leaning against the kitchen doorway, her expression uncertain.

"Sure." She smiled. "Now, what do you think about a breakfast muffin?"

Wren grinned and any introspection for the afternoon dissipated in the wake of her natural curiosity. "I think you'd better tell me more."

❩

"Not even a hint?" Kate wheedled from her position on the sofa.

"Nope," Michael called over his shoulder as he walked back into the kitchen to get her some more juice.

"How about just a little taste?" she tried again.

"Give it up, Shannon," Michael replied as he reappeared and set the glass down on the table in front of her. "You're just going to have to wait until we're ready for dinner."

Susan had stayed and talked over a cup of coffee as Michael and Kate finished their lunch and then had gone on her way. They had stood in the doorway to wave her off, Michael's arm around Kate's waist as Susan waved to them as the elevator doors closed. Michael had led Kate back inside and gotten her comfortable on the sofa.

"I feel much better than this morning," Kate said. "Maybe I could just go into the store for an hour to—" She stopped when she saw the look on Michael's face and back-pedalled. "Maybe not," she amended.

"You're right. You're not a good patient at all, are you?" Michael observed.

"No," she said, giving him one of her little guilty smiles that he loved. "But Paul is even worse."

"Oh, really?" Michael sat down beside her and pulled her into his arms.

"Really," she said snuggling against him.

"Well, if he's gets sick, I'm not cuddling *him*," Michael stated. He settled her in his arms and reached for the remote to see what was on the movie channel.

Kate leaned against him and gazed at the screen. "You know," she said at last, "this is really nice."

"What is?" Michael said in an absentminded tone as he scrolled through the list of movies available.

"Being self-employed," Kate replied. "I mean, it's stressful, but being able to take a day like this without thinking about a boss, it's—" She shot him a look. "Maybe you don't know what I'm talking about."

"We go about it differently, but I know what you mean," Michael said. "Here's one. Have you seen *The Hangover?*"

"No." Kate's attention returned to the screen. "But I've heard good things about it."

"Done." Michael selected the movie, and they both settled back to watch.

They were both chuckling at the movie an hour later when the words woke up and stirred in Michael's mind. He had pushed them aside for a few hours, but now they were back and wanting attention.

"A tiger in the bathroom?" Kate was giggling now. She had eased herself down so that she was lying on the sofa with her head in his lap.

Michael leaned his head on the backrest and closed his eyes as he willed the words to go away, but it was no good. Another wellspring had been tapped, and the words would go on and on until he could silence them on the screen. He couldn't afford to lose them now, not when he was so close. He leaned forward, brushing Kate's hair aside from her ear.

"Sweetheart," he began in an apologetic tone, "I need to get some work done."

Kate rolled onto her back and gazed up at him. "You gotta write?" When he nodded, she got up into a sitting position and gestured at the TV screen. "We can watch this later," she said as she reached for the remote.

"No, it's okay," Michael answered. "Leave it on, I won't be long."

"Don't you usually work with peace and quiet?" Kate asked, and when Michael hesitated she had her answer. Reaching for the remote, she switched off the TV and tossed the controller onto the coffee table. "You go do what you gotta do, and I'll have a nap or something."

"I won't be long," Michael repeated as he gave her a soft kiss.

"No problem." Kate grinned. She got up and made her way into the bedroom.

"You don't have to leave the room," Michael protested as he stood beside his desk.

Kate paused in the doorway and smiled again. "Come get me when you're done," she invited.

Michael took a few paces away from his desk so that he could watch as Kate shucked off her yoga pants and crawled into the bed. She seemed comfortable enough with the situation, and yet he paused before taking a seat at his desk and opening the manuscript file on the laptop. He sat there for a moment with his fingers poised on the keyboard, and then began to type, slowly at first, and then with increasing speed.

Kate cocked her head in the bedroom, listening to him typing and then turned her attention back to the magazine. She felt rested enough, and she had flicked through most of it already. Michael had plenty of books in the living room, but she was reluctant to intrude, especially when she had only just gotten into bed. Rolling onto her back, she stared up at the ceiling and huffed out a quiet breath. She was in the middle of reading a really good book, but it was back at her apartment. Rolling back over, she leaned over the side of the bed and picked up the discarded magazine, flicking through the pages with a desultory hand after a quick glance at the clock. Michael had said he wouldn't be long.

An hour later, Kate closed the magazine with a soft yawn. She had read articles about politics, the economic situation in Iceland, a Proust questionnaire, she had even re-read the puff piece about the latest Hollywood sensation, and she could hear that Michael was still typing. She leaned over the side of the bed again and peered around for her bag that she had left at the foot of the bedside table. Retrieving her iPod, she put in her ear-buds and scrolled through until she'd found the meditation podcast. Getting comfortable once more, she closed her eyes and let the gentle voice guide her away.

At his desk, Michael kept typing, and the words kept coming.

Chapter 22

Black Holes and Invisible Girls

Something had awoken her. Kate opened her eyes and saw that the room was dark. The mattress dipped again, and she turned her head to see Michael easing himself into bed.

"Sorry," Michael whispered as he moved closer to curl his body around hers. "I didn't mean to wake you."

"What time is it?" she asked in a drowsy voice as she shifted back a little and lifted an arm so that Michael could slide a hand around her waist and pull her closer still. At some stage during sleep, her ear-buds had come loose, and she fished about in the bed to pull them out and stuffed them under her pillow.

"Sometime after two," Michael admitted after a careful pause.

Kate rolled over so that they were face to face. "You wrote for that long?"

"I didn't mean to, but the words kept coming," Michael apologized, leaning forward to give her a soft kiss and then rested his forehead against hers.

He hadn't meant to work for so long. When at last he had leaned back in his chair and discovered he had a stiff back, he had looked at the time and realized he'd left Kate alone all evening. Shutting everything down for the night, he had made his way into the bedroom to see Kate fast asleep with a discarded magazine on the floor beside the bed.

Kate gave a sleepy hum of pleasure and tucked her head under his chin as she fisted his shirt in one hand, listening to the steady thump of his heart. She could smell the slight dampness of his skin and realized that he had showered before joining her.

"I'm sorry." Michael kissed the top of her head. "I really didn't think—"

"S'okay," Kate mumbled as she began to slip back into sleep. "But we're going to have to do something … about …"

The room was quiet and still while Michael waited.

"Something about what?" he prompted in a whisper, but his only answer was Kate's steady breathing. Moving carefully so as not to disturb her again, he settled his arm around her waist and stared sightlessly into the darkened room, wondering what she had been about to say before sleep claimed him too.

When Michael woke up the next morning, it was to the steady swish of turning pages. Cracking open an eye, he saw Kate sitting propped up against her pillows with a comic book on her knees. The bedside lamp was on, giving her face a golden hue. Her face was intent as she read, so it took a few minutes before she realized that Michael was lying awake beside her.

"Hey." He smiled and moved closer to rub his leg against hers.

"Hey," she answered, carefully leaning down to give him a kiss.

"What time is it?" he asked as he rubbed his eyes with the heels of his hands. His voice sounded raspy with sleep.

"Sorry." Now it was Kate's turn to sound guilty. "My body clock is still on work time, so it's a little before six."

Michael groaned and rolled over so that he could snuggle his head on her lap. Kate held the comic book out of the way until he was comfortable, and then rested it on his shoulder.

"What are you reading?" he mumbled into the covers as he snaked an arm around her hips. He could feel the warmth of her thighs and his body reacted accordingly.

"New Mutants," Kate replied as she went back to her reading. "I haven't read these in years, and I found some on one of your bookshelves when I was up earlier."

"They're good," Michael mumbled again. His eyes felt heavy, and he chuffed out a content sigh as Kate began to stroke his hair while she read. He woke some time later when Kate shifted, and he lifted his head to see her regarding him apologetically.

"I have to get up," she whispered. "Gotta get to work."

Michael frowned at this. He'd liked having her with him yesterday and wanted to make it up to her for leaving her to her own devices all evening. "How are you feeling?"

"Okay, maybe a little tired," she answered after a quick self-inventory. "But much better than I was."

"Stay another day," Michael said as he dropped his head back onto her lap and squeezed his eyes shut, trying to hide his grin as Kate gave a gurgle of laughter.

"Easy for you to say," she protested, "but you know the drill. I own the store, I run the store."

"You've got backup," he rejoined, hooking her legs with one of his and holding her tight. "And you don't want to force yourself back to work too soon or you'll just burn out again."

"Mmph." Kate snorted although she had to admit Michael's argument had a certain amount of merit. "How about I go in and see how I'm feeling?"

"You'll get caught up and then you'll be exhausted by the end of the day."

"Maybe, but I've got to go in all the same." She squirmed and wriggled until Michael released her with a mournful sigh. Struggling out of bed, she swayed for a moment and almost fell back onto the mattress before she righted herself and walked into the bathroom with a determined air. Michael watched her go, and thinking of the tight ache in his groin, sighed again. He burrowed into her pillow and breathed in her scent. The shower started, and Michael lay listening to the sound of the water running until he drifted back into a light doze. The next time he opened his eyes, Kate was standing in front of his closet, looking at his shirts in thoughtful consideration.

"Something you need?" he asked, admiring the lace covered swell of Kate's breasts as she turned toward his voice.

"A shirt," she commented. "I just need a fresh one, and I've realized I need to do laundry."

"Something you could do if you weren't going into work today," Michael commented from the bed as he rolled onto one side and propped his head on his hand.

Kate shook her head and kept searching until she found what looked to be an old college shirt. She tweaked the sleeve enough to pull the shirt out slightly and, without looking back, asked, "May I?" She heard the sheets rustle a little as Michael sat up to see her selection and agreed with a slight chuckle.

"No objections at all," Michael said.

Kate slipped it on over her head and, seeing it fall almost to her knees, began to roll and twist the excess fabric into a knot that sat in the small of her back. The sleeves were rolled up as well, and then she darted back into the bathroom to check her reflection. Satisfied that she looked presentable enough, she walked back into the bedroom to see Michael regarding her with the kind of bare-chested, lazy grin that could surely be the downfall of saints. Her mouth went dry.

"See something else you like?" He raised an eyebrow.

"You could say that." Kate managed at last as she tried to pick up her bag and keys while at the same time finding it very hard to tear her gaze away from him. She caught her purse strap on the third try and started to back away into the living room.

"No kiss?" Michael looked disappointed.

"I think we both know what will happen if I go anywhere near that bed. I know that look in your eye, Forrester."

"And I know that look in *your* eye, Shannon," he countered.

"Maybe so," she acknowledged, "but I really do have to go in today."

"Fine," Michael sighed, and then threw back the sheet and got out of bed.

Kate's eyes were drawn to the tell-tale bulge in his pajama pants, and she swallowed before resolutely turning her back and heading for the hall closet where Michael had hung their coats. She was just about to pull on her new coat when Michael appeared to help her into it. As soon as the coat was settled on her shoulders, he pulled her back against his chest and held her there as he did up the buttons he could reach and knotted the belt. Positioned as she was, she could feel his arousal against the small of her back and the warm puffs of his breath against her neck. She closed her eyes and chanted, *Duty ... Responsibility.*

"Have you eaten?" he asked as he gently propelled her around to face him.

"I'll have something at the store," she reassured him, watching as a small line appeared between his eyebrows. "Don't fuss so. I'll be fine."

"If you're sure," he said, trying to keep the doubt out of his voice.

"If I feel unwell, I'll leave," Kate offered as she lifted the strap of her bag over her head so that it crossed her body and rested against one hip.

"And you'll call?" Michael pressed.

"I'll call," she said soothingly as she stepped forward and wrapped her arms around him. Now that she was bundled up for work, she felt safe enough to hug him, although the feel of his warm bare skin beneath her fingertips had her closing her eyes and reminding herself about duty once more.

"Mmm." Michael snuffed her neck. "You smell so good."

"So do you," Kate countered as she rubbed her cheek against his chest. "But I've *got* to go."

"Heartbreaker," Michael sighed as she turned toward the door.

"Oh, hush." She smiled and offered herself up for another kiss before she stepped through the door and closed it behind her.

After she had gone, Michael leaned against the heavy wooden door for a moment before strolling back to bed, yawning and scratching his hair as he went. The bed seemed bigger than ever now that Kate wasn't in it.

Kate waited until the elevator doors had closed before slumping against the rear wall and puffing out a loud sigh. Michael had looked so *good* and had smelled even better. There was something about his natural musky smell that her body responded to every single time. Watching the floor numbers count down, she dug in her coat pockets and drew out her gloves, pulling them on and settling her scarf around her neck. The doors opened with a soft chime, and she strode across the foyer and out into the gray morning.

There were already people on the street making their way to work or wherever, dressed up in grays and blacks for the most part. For a moment, she felt conspicuous in her warm red coat, but when a passing woman eyed it and gave Kate a quick nod of approval, she felt flattered and pleased all at once.

❧

Emily rounded the corner and squinted ahead, her eyes widening in disbelief. There was no one waiting. She'd done it: she'd managed to be the first one there. She picked up her pace, but then huffed with amused disappointment when she saw a small figure sprinting along the pavement from the other direction. By the time Emily had reached the store, Wren had gotten her breath back and was endeavoring to act casual.

"Morning, boss," Wren said from her casual stance against the wall.

"Nice try, Wren, but I saw you *running* not a moment ago." Emily laughed as she got out the keys and unlocked the security grill.

"Running? Moi?" Wren gave her a wide-eyed look before giving up and helping Emily with the grill. "David and I got to talking this morning, and it made me a little late."

"Talking?" Emily raised an eyebrow at this as she unlocked the main door and pushed it open.

"Yes." Wren pursed her lips and gave a prim nod. "*Talking*."

"If you say so," Emily said as she waved for Wren to enter the store, "you were talking."

"Shut up, boss, and make me coffee," Wren retorted.

The two women hung up their coats and bags and were waiting for the coffee machine to warm up when Kate arrived, flushed but pleased to be back.

"Hey," Wren said in mild surprise, "I wasn't sure if we'd be seeing you today."

"Oh, I can feel the love." Kate grinned as she good-naturedly nudged Wren with her hip as she walked past her into the kitchen.

"You know what I mean," Wren called after her. "How are you feeling, boss?"

"I'll live," Kate called back. Her coat was carefully hung up, and she grabbed at her apron and tied it on as she walked out into the front of the store. "How was yesterday?"

Wren and Emily glanced at each other and shrugged.

"Fine," Emily said. "No problems."

"Really?" Kate was surprised.

"What, you didn't think we could handle it?" Wren stepped aside from the coffee machine and gave Kate a meaningful look as she slid three empty cups across the counter.

"Not that," Kate corrected her as she stepped up to the machine and slipped into the routine of making the morning coffee. "But I feel bad about not coming in."

"Sometimes the best way to learn is under pressure." Emily shrugged. "I won't lie. I was terrified for a while there, but we managed okay."

Emily leaned back against the workbench and watched Kate make the coffee with practiced ease. She had been exhausted when she had arrived home the night before, but Brad had been pre-warned and had looked after her all evening—and the next morning, now that she thought about it with a slight flush. The day had certainly been tiring, but she had felt a rush of pride on her way home that she had risen to the challenge so well.

"Well …" Kate emptied the coffee filter with a few sharp bangs and gave it a quick rinse before accepting the jug of milk that Wren passed her and began to steam it. "As long as you were okay. How was business?"

"Good, no different really," Wren replied. "Emily here made some Jack's Favorite cupcakes, and the day went well."

"Good to hear." Kate smiled with relief.

"Everything's cashed out and in the safe out back," Emily added, "so you can check it later before you do the bank drop."

"Sure," Kate answered. She slid two cups toward the waiting women. "But for now, what I'm really wanting to know is …" She arched an eyebrow at Wren who reached for her chalk.

"Oh, I'm well ahead of you on that one," Wren retorted. She sipped at her coffee and leaned against the counter, looking pleased with herself.

"Okay." Kate tasted her coffee. Michael was right; her coffee was much nicer than the stuff he had at home. She made a mental note to take a bag home for him soon. "Don't let me rush you."

"By the way, boss," Emily interrupted with a slight smile. "That's a … uh … nice shirt you've got on there."

"What, this?" Kate glanced down at herself. "It's one of—"

"Michael's, we know," Wren chimed in.

Kate looked from Wren to Emily and then back again. "How did you know that?"

"Likes to mark his territory, does he?" Emily went on, her smile getting bigger.

"Huh? I don't know. It's just a shirt I grabbed from his closet this morning. Why?" Kate twisted her neck to see if there was any printing on the back. Emily stepped toward her and ran a finger along the bold letters that were printed across the shoulder blades.

"Forrester," Emily read aloud. "Guess it's a shirt from his college days."

"You're kidding." Kate turned and gaped at her. "So I'm walking around branded?"

"Yup." Emily nodded. "He didn't say anything?"

"Not as such," Kate admitted as she remembered Michael's knowing smile. "I guess he didn't have to."

"He knew you'd find out soon enough." Emily grinned. "I think it looks cute."

Wren snickered until Kate cleared her throat and nodded at the chalkboard.

"Impatient, are we?" Wren said as she grabbed the chalk and walked over to pick up the chalkboard where she'd left it in its usual place beside the door. Laying it down on a nearby table, she wrote quickly and added a few flourishes when she was done. Giving a nod of satisfaction, she carried it over to the counter to show Kate and Emily who were finishing their coffee.

If you reach for the stars,
your lungs will collapse from lack of oxygen.

Kate narrowed her eyes and looked thoughtful, and then her expression cleared. "Got it," she said as she snapped her fingers. "Wren, are you going easy on me?"

"No," Wren protested. "I thought I was being clever. Damn. I'll get you one day."

"Ha," Kate retorted as she went into the kitchen to start baking.

Emily smiled and shook her head at the friendly rivalry between the two women as she collected the empty cups and put them in the dishwasher. Wren returned from outside, looking happy, and stopped to straighten up the magazines and books before making her way back behind the counter.

"What's next?" she asked Emily as she began filling the water jugs.

"I'll do some bagels and wraps. Can you check the tables?"

"Sure." Wren nodded at Emily's suggestion, and when the jugs were filled and set out, she grabbed the plastic tub that held the sugar and sweetener packets and began her rounds. The mixer started up in the kitchen as the store became a hive of activity. When the first batch of cupcakes was in the oven, Kate reappeared, wiping her hands on a dishcloth before stopping at the CD player and opening the folder that sat beside it. It was a pleasant morning, and she wanted to prolong the mood with some music. The CD player whirred to life, and then the store was filled with the sound of steady guitar strumming as the mellow voice of Feist filtered out of the speakers.

⁂

Kate set down the baking tray and turned to close the oven door, blinking as the rush of warm air hit her face. Turning back to the counter, she surveyed the cupcakes that sat cooling, pressing a cautious finger against a couple of them and nodding in satisfaction as they sprang back. These cupcakes were going to be a little more work than she usually did, but Wren's quote had been too good to resist. Kate went to the storage shelves and selected a large jar of her favorite raspberry jam that was then spooned into a bowl and stirred until smooth. Setting the bowl aside, Kate started to make the frosting to match, humming to herself as she walked, pausing occasionally to yawn against the back of her hand. It felt good to be back in the store, but she envied Michael his sleep in.

By the time she carried the finished cupcakes out toward the display case, she had started to feel better and nodded gratefully when Emily held up an empty cup in silent query.

"Wren," she called as she set the tray into the counter, "c'mon, girl."

"Be right there," Wren called back as she delivered a coffee to a waiting customer. She returned promptly, wiping her hands against her jeans, and grabbed her chalk. "Okay, shoot."

"*Black Hole Cupcakes*," Kate announced as Wren scribbled. "Chocolate cupcakes with a rich, raspberry center and dark chocolate frosting."

"Oh, God," Emily whimpered as she looked at them. "I don't think I'm strong enough."

Kate laughed and reached back into the cabinet to pick up a cupcake and hand it to Emily. "Don't torture yourself. Just bite into it carefully."

Emily peeled off the paper cup with all the reverence the cupcake deserved and took a cautious bite, rolling her eyes appreciatively as the raspberry jam and chocolate cake oozed into her mouth. Kate and Wren both watched her reaction.

"Good?" Kate said at last.

"Mmmmph." Emily nodded.

"She likes it," Kate commented in satisfaction, turning around just in time to see Wren swipe one.

"What?" Wren said in a defensive tone as she picked the raspberry garnish off the top and popped it into her mouth. "It's only fair."

"I'm not judging," Kate said, holding her hands up in surrender. "I had one in the kitchen." She regarded the two women as they both ate, and then walked over to the coffee machine to get another coffee ready.

"You're having another one already?" Wren asked in between mouthfuls.

"I'm still tired," Kate commented as she got out the milk.

"You know the caffeine doesn't kick in for at least an hour. Anything you feel at the time is just a placebo effect," Emily commented as she licked her fingers clean of jam and crumbs.

"Don't spoil the magic." Kate swatted at her. "I need it." Before she could stop it, she yawned again, ducking her head toward her shoulder to try to hide it.

"So just out of curiosity, boss," Wren asked in a mild voice, "what the hell are you doing here if you're still tired?"

"I'll be okay." Kate shook her head and blinked before returning her concentration to the coffee that was filtering into the cups.

"Right." Wren shook her head. "So if you're feeling that great, how come you look like shit?"

"Hey," Kate objected, "that's a bit harsh."

"Sorry." Wren held up her hands in a placatory gesture. "I'm just saying that you look exhausted, and one day off isn't going to cut it." Wren walked toward her and gave Kate a hug. "Come on, boss, you haven't had a break since I've been here. Don't you think it's about time you started to be a bit gentle with yourself?"

"If you won't, I'm sure Michael will," Emily chimed in when Kate paused.

"Are you guys trying to get rid of me?" Kate joked, feeling self-conscious.

"Kinda." Emily shrugged. "But it's for your own good."

"Yeah," Wren added, "I'd hate to have to call Paul."

Kate whipped her head around to glare at the smaller woman. "You wouldn't," she accused.

"Wouldn't I?" Wren matched Kate stare for stare. Kate broke her gaze first.

Kate watched the coffee drizzle into the cups as she steamed the milk and sighed quietly to herself. Perhaps the two women had a point. Paul had certainly been pushing her to hire some additional help and take some time off. The arrival of Emily had been a welcome boon to the business, but Kate had still found it very difficult to step away from the store that she had steadily built up from scratch. Other employees had come and gone, but Wren had stayed with her for over two years now, and Emily provided just the kind of stability that Kate had been looking for. Of course, being single for the most part had made it easy to pour all of her energy into the store. With no partner making demands on her time, there was no need to compromise. The store was also a very convenient excuse when people wondered aloud why she wasn't dating. And then Michael had come along.

Kate poured the milk into the cups and topped them off with some froth. A customer approached the counter, and she picked up her cup and stepped away as Emily stepped forward with a bright smile. Sipping at her coffee, Kate retreated into the kitchen, still deep in thought. When the customers had been dealt with, Emily followed Kate into the kitchen.

"So, boss, what's it gonna be?" she asked as she folded her arms and leaned against the doorway.

Kate had pulled herself up to sit on the counter and sat sipping at her coffee, legs crossed at the ankles as she swung them back and forth, lost in thought.

"I dunno." Kate shrugged.

"Okay, I'll make this simple for you," Emily replied. "What do you want to do right now?"

"Um…" Kate considered the question. "Well, I guess I ought to—" She broke off as Emily shook her head.

"Not what you think you should do, what do you *want?*"

Kate stared into her cup for a long time and then huffed out a long sigh. She thought some more, swinging her ankles and feeling like a lost child before she looked up at Emily.

"I think I want to go home."

"Then go." Emily nodded.

"Just like that?" Kate blinked.

"You're the boss," Emily said, "and you know Wren and I will be fine. If we need something, we'll call you."

Kate stared into her cup again, and then swigged back her coffee.

"It's not like you're going to be doing this every day," Emily reasoned. "You're not a hundred percent, so why don't you just give yourself a bit of time so that you can get better?" When Kate said nothing, Emily grinned and continued, "Go on; get outta here before I change my mind."

Kate looked up at this and grinned. "Just listen to you, one day in charge and now you're kicking me out."

"I can't argue." Emily nodded. "I feel drunk with power."

Wren peered around the doorway and looked at Emily. "Have you told her to go yet?"

"Just did," Emily replied as she stepped toward Kate and took the now-empty cup.

Kate slid down off the counter and began to untie her apron. Sensing movement outside, Wren looked out into the store and then gestured to Emily.

"Boss, we're on." She nodded her head toward the front.

"Coming," Emily said and then moved toward to give Kate a quick hug. "We'll be fine. You go home and take a nap, or get a cuddle from your boy. Do whatever it takes to feel better, and we'll see you tomorrow."

Kate looked past Emily out to the customers at the counter. "Maybe I could help out first with—"

"Kate, *go*. I'm sure there're other things you could be doing."

Gathering her things, Kate pulled on her coat and made her way toward the front of the store. Pausing at the door, she looked back at the counter: Wren and Emily looked like they had everything under control. She stepped outside, wrapped her scarf around her neck, and began to walk home, wondering what Michael was doing and resolving to call him when she got home.

Kate let herself into her apartment, hung up her keys and then dropped her bag onto the armchair as she surveyed the room. It felt good to be back in her own home, but compared to the space and light at Michael's, everything seemed to be a little darker and smaller. The air was still, and so she lit her aromatherapy lamp and added some drops of orange oil and ginger to scent the room. Everything around her was just as she liked it, and yet she was alone. Years of being alone—or keeping herself alone if she was going to be honest—had been just what she had wanted. Now she found herself missing Michael's companionship. Sighing, she walked into the bedroom and sat down on the edge of the bed, feeling listless. She wanted to call Michael but felt silly for thinking about it. After all, she had only left his apartment a few hours ago. Falling backwards, she stared up at the ceiling wondering what Michael was doing.

Michael stashed the dry cleaning ticket in his wallet, stepping aside with a polite smile to allow another customer into the store. A gust of cold air whistled down the street, making him tug up his coat collar and stuff his hands into his pockets as he walked. A flash of color and movement caught his eye. Glancing across the street, he saw a woman flicking a long red scarf around her neck. The color made him think of Kate, and he wondered how she was feeling. Michael smiled and tucked his chin into his chest as he kept walking. After his run, he had reviewed the previous night's work before calling a very surprised Alistair and telling him to expect the completed manuscript within the week. The rest of his morning had been spent running a few errands, and now he found himself with a free afternoon. He'd go see his girl. As he crossed the street, he felt his phone vibrate in his back pocket and fished it out. Tapping the screen, he scanned the message and gave a short laugh before he turned around and broke into a light jog.

Kate was curled up on the sofa dividing her attention between her book and the talk show on television when she heard the intercom buzz. Pushing the magazine aside, she sat up and half-walked, half-skipped toward the door, hoping that it would be Michael.

"Hello?"

"It's me." Michael's voice crackled through the speaker.

"It's open." Kate hit the button, and then unlocked her door before returning to the sofa. She didn't bother with the magazine now; she sat looking at the door unable to hide the silly grin that was spreading across her face. There was the rapid shuffle of feet on the stairs, and then the door was pushed open to reveal a flushed and slightly out-of-breath Michael.

"That was fast," she marveled as he shrugged out of his coat and took off his scarf before making his way over to the sofa.

"I was already downtown," Michael explained as he put his hands on the arm of the sofa and leaned over to give her a long kiss. "So when I got your message, I came straight over."

He sat down beside her and pulled her to him, smiling when he realized she was still wearing his shirt. Kate had changed her jeans for a pair of leggings and now she wriggled around to sit on his lap.

"I felt kinda stupid sending that message," Kate admitted as she curled a hand around the nape of Michael's neck.

"Why's that?" Michael was running his hand up Kate's thigh to hold her closer to him, their heads getting closer as they spoke.

"Well, I was at your place this morning. Being apart for just a few hours shouldn't leave me acting like a damn teenager." She nipped at his bottom lip.

"Meh." Michael shrugged.

"Meh?" Kate gave him an incredulous look. "'Meh,' said the *writer?*"

Michael dug his fingers into her sides, where he knew she was ticklish, to make her squirm. "Hey, that's sass. Are you sassin' me?"

"Maybe a little," Kate managed as she tried to evade his hands without much success.

"Right then, I guess I'll have to see what we can do about that," Michael growled, grinning as he watched the color rise in Kate's face while she gasped and squirmed again. She was torturing him as well; the movement on his lap was causing the usual reaction. He knew she had noticed when she stopped moving and regarded him with a slow smile. He raised one of his hands and gently traced the slight smudges beneath her eyes. "How are you feeling?" he asked in a soft voice.

"Tired, but I'll live," she said, closing her eyes and leaning into his touch. He trailed his fingers down her cheek and onto her neck. "Having yesterday off was actually kinda good." She cracked an eye open to look at Michael. "But don't tell them I said that."

"Your secret is safe with me," he assured her, pulling her closer.

"Mmmm," she said as she settled against him and rested her head against his chest.

Michael's stubble rasped against Kate's hair as he rubbed his chin against the top of her head in a gentle caress.

"So whatcha been doin'?" he asked.

"Nothin' much," Kate said, almost slurring the words in her relaxed state. "Errands, cleaning—" she yawned, "—stuff."

"Sounds exciting," Michael observed.

"I know. I'm not much fun," Kate apologized.

"You don't have to be." Michael kissed her hair. "You've been ill."

"Or just over-tired," Kate muttered. "Emily gave me a lecture this morning."

"Just Emily?"

"And Wren," Kate added. "The two of them ganged up on me, which is why I'm here." She waved a hand at the TV.

"Maybe they've got a point. It wouldn't hurt to be a bit easier on yourself."

"Any easier and I'd be in a coma," Kate scoffed, "but actually..." She considered. "It's nice being at home during the day. Kinda like skipping school or something."

"Did you ever do that?"

"Me? Never." Kate yawned again. "I was always the good girl, you know, the really boring one."

"Oh, I don't know. They say it's the quiet ones you have to watch," Michael said in a thoughtful tone. "I bet not many of your classmates ended up in New York."

"No," Kate admitted, and Michael could feel her smile against his chest. "Most of them stayed at home and married the guys that they'd gone steady with in school."

"And you? Could you have done that?" Michael stared at the TV while he listened to Kate, curious as to her answer.

"I had a couple of boyfriends, nothing serious," Kate replied. "Anyway, I left town to go to college and then..." She broke off and gave an odd little smile.

"And then what?"

"Tom," Kate admitted after a long pause. "And then there was Tom."

"Right," Michael said after a slight pause of his own.

"And look how that turned out." Kate gave a nervous laugh.

"Yeah, about that," Michael began. "Have you heard from him lately?"

A small worry line appeared between Kate's eyebrows, and Michael immediately regretted the question.

"I got an email from him last week." Kate focused on Michael's shirtfront again. "He's seeing someone. It seems to be going okay."

"And are you?" Michael kept running his hand up and down Kate's thigh in a soothing gesture.

"Sure." Kate nodded, but didn't lift her gaze.

"Then that's all that matters to me," Michael said as he kissed her forehead.

Kate looked up in surprise. "That's it?"

Now it was Michael's turn to shrug. "I don't see why not. You and Tom have a history. You're still friends, but as long as he's not after my girl, it's all good."

Kate's shoulders shook slightly as tension she wasn't aware of carrying began to subside. "That simple, huh?"

"Yup." Michael slapped her rump and leered at her, smiling at her gurgle of laughter. "I'm a simple man." Kissing the side of her neck, he nuzzled her cheek and continued, "It must have been a hell of a shock, though."

"Well, yeah," Kate admitted. "We were friends and then lovers. Tom helped me get past the shock of losing Jack and settle back into college. We were really good for each other."

Michael gently began to stroke Kate's hair, saying nothing, just letting her speak.

"But when he worked things out, we went our separate ways. He never set out to hurt me, but he couldn't deny what he was. I knew he still loved me, but he just couldn't see me—" she broke off and waved her hand in an entirely vague gesture, "—*that* way."

Michael wrapped his arms around Kate and held her closer as she kept talking. Her voice sounded dreamlike as she spoke from the past.

"So I guess after that, I stopped dating for a long time. Wren and Paul kept at me to put myself out there, but I just couldn't do it. Being friends was easier, so I just decided that I felt safer being invisible."

Her voice trailed off, and they sat together in silence for a long time. Michael tried to imagine the level of hurt and rejection on such a fundamental level and failed. Now he began to remember the way she ducked her head when complimented, and how she always reacted to his attraction to her with pleasure and surprise, and perhaps a little fear, as if she thought it was too good to last.

"Kate…" Michael's throat was tight, and he had to clear his throat before he continued. "You're not invisible to me."

"I know." Kate nodded, still staring at the television.

"Hey." Michael gave her a slight shake. "Look at me."

Kate's gaze moved with painful slowness until she was looking into his eyes. He could see the silvery track marks of her tears on her cheeks as she stared at him in silence.

"You're not invisible to me. You never were, and you never will be."

Kate's lips curled into a slight smile; somehow he always knew what to say. She moved so suddenly Michael was surprised when she sat up and fixed him with a long stare. "And while we're on the subject, you have to promise me something."

"I'm listening," Michael said, surprised by the ferocity of her expression.

"You have to tell me if you're ever seeing someone else, or if you ever *want* to. I won't go through that again."

"Okay." Michael nodded.

"Promise?"

Michael nodded again. "I promise. Kate," he continued in a quiet tone, "all I see is you." He leaned forward and gave her the softest of kisses. "Only you."

Kate's expression softened as Michael kept peppering her with kisses, and she laughed, kissing him back until neither of them was capable of speech at all.

❧

"Cat got your tongue?"

Wren was pulled out of her reverie by David's soft voice, and she looked up to see him regarding her over the top of his reading glasses. Tonight they were at David's apartment, and she had been sitting at the table, twirling some hair around a finger while she stared off into space, lost in thought.

"Sorry." She offered up a sheepish grin. "I was miles away."

"I could tell when I asked you what you wanted for dinner, and you didn't say anything." David smiled. "That's gotta be a first."

"Mm-hmm," Wren mumbled as she glanced down at her notebook that she had covered in random sketches. Ideas were coming thick and fast this evening, and she was trying to get them all down.

"Okay." David hauled himself up off the sofa and tossed the paper he'd been reading onto the coffee table. "History can wait. What's going on?"

"Nothing," Wren said as she flicked the notebook over to a blank page and started to scrawl her initials over and over.

"Right." David paused and glanced down at the page before giving her a skeptical look. "I'll order something."

"Do you ever cook?" Wren asked as she watched him saunter toward the phone and the collection of menus. His 501 jeans were riding low on his hips, and she admired the view as he lifted one side of his T-shirt to scratch his ribs. He moved with the kind of careless grace that she envied.

"I've been known to." David nodded. "I'll even cook for you some day."

"Really?" That had Wren putting her pencil down and regarding David with amazement. "And when's that going to happen?"

"When we're celebrating," David replied as he sorted through menus and held one up with a quizzical air. "Tempura?"

"Why not." Wren waved in agreement. "Celebrating what?"

"Guess we'll have to wait and find out," David replied, stopping to drop a kiss on the end of her nose as he carried the phone back to the sofa.

It was too much. Wren got up from the table and followed David, sitting back patiently while he placed an order, leaning forward to put in a request, and smiling when he nodded and ordered extra pickled ginger before she could say anything. As soon as he got off the phone, she pounced. "What? Celebrate what?" She began to tickle him, giggling as David tucked his legs up into his chest in a bid to fend her off.

"Celebrating you, idiot," he gasped before she let him go.

"Huh?" Wren was shocked into stillness. "What am I going to be doing?"

"What we talked about this morning," David replied, pushing his hair out of his eyes and giving her a look of fond exasperation. "You can pretend you've forgotten about it all you want, but I haven't."

"Well," Wren huffed, "there's a lot to consider and—"

"And nothing," David interrupted. "You've gotta take a chance on yourself now and then, sweetheart."

Wren stared at David in amazement. "I wish," she said at last, "that I could see myself the way you do."

David stared back at her for a long moment and then pushed his glasses back up his nose. "You'll need a prescription," he drawled.

Wren gave a hoot of laughter that turned into a shriek when David lunged forward to push her back against the sofa cushions and began to tickle her in retaliation. Gasping with laughter, she looked at David's broad smile as he pouted at her in mock sympathy while she writhed and squirmed in a futile bid to get away. She felt as if she was seeing clearly for the first time in her life.

❧

"Find anything?" Michael appeared at Kate's shoulder and put a hand on either side of her hips, peering over her shoulder as she chopped some bacon.

"Enough for a Spanish omelet," Kate replied, turning her head for a quick kiss before she returned her attention back to the ingredients.

"Nice," Michael said as he nuzzled her neck for another kiss.

"What, the omelet or my neck?" Kate smiled.

"Um, the middle one," Michael muttered as he nibbled her earlobe.

"Good choice." Kate smiled.

Michael sighed and rested his chin on her shoulder, softly grinding his hips against her bottom.

"Thank God, you don't do that in the store," Kate said through her smile. "I'd never get anything done." She could feel Michael's lips curl into a tomcat grin against her neck. "Back up there, babe. I've got to finish this."

"Woman," Michael sighed as he released her. "You've got nerves of steel."

"I wouldn't say that," Kate said, moistening her lips with her tongue as she poured the egg mix into the pan and waited a moment before adding the other ingredients. She shot a sidelong look at Michael and cleared her throat. If he kept looking at her like that, dinner was going to be a burnt offering at best.

Michael strolled back into the living room and occupied himself by checking out Kate's bookshelves. The books were in no apparent order that he could discern, and he found himself smiling as he saw Tudor history interspersed with travel, Spanish poetry beside Tolkien, even true crime beside…he leaned in closer and turned his head to read the narrow spine.

"*The Teach Your Chicken How to Fly Training Manual*," he read aloud slowly, stepping back and shaking his head. "Kate," he called toward the kitchen, "this chicken book here—"

"It's from an art exhibition. Keep looking. There are some good ones."

"M'kay," Michael murmured, giving the occasional grunt of amusement while he explored the bookshelves.

"Dinner," Kate announced a short while later as she set down the bowl and plates before returning to the kitchen to get the omelet.

"Find something you like?" Kate said as she sat down.

"Where the hell do you find these?" Michael looked away from the bookshelves, his face bright with curiosity.

"Secondhand bookstores, friends, Bear." Kate shrugged.

Michael looked at her bookshelves again. If this was the kind of variety that she liked, then no wonder she had been hard pressed to find something to read at his place. An idea niggled at him, but he set it aside to discuss later.

"I've got to go book shopping with you sometime," Michael commented as he put the book aside with slight reluctance and then noticed dinner. "Wow."

He nodded at the dinner offerings. "For someone cooking on the fly, that looks fantastic."

"Wait until you've tried it," Kate cautioned.

"It'll be great," Michael said as he poised his fork over his plate, and it was.

Kate was relegated to the sofa after dinner while Michael cleared everything away, so she flicked through the cable channels until she found something she wanted to watch. Stretching out on the sofa, she stuffed a plump cushion behind her head and gazed at the screen. She could hear Michael moving around in the kitchen, and she smiled to herself as she heard him opening various cupboards, muttering quietly as he worked out what went where. He appeared just as the next show was starting.

"What's on?" he asked as he sank down with a sigh and hauled Kate against him.

"*True Blood*," Kate replied as she wrapped an arm around him.

"Which is?" Michael raised an eyebrow at her.

"Vampire porn," Kate replied as she gave him a quick wink.

"You're kidding, right?" Michael looked at her in disbelief as the twangy country theme song started. The room was silent for a few minutes. "Jesus," Michael breathed out, "where the hell did you find this?"

"HBO," Kate replied. "Now shut up and watch."

"Right," Michael said, his gaze not moving from the screen, "yes, ma'am." And so he watched, and the more he followed the story the more he became aware of the warm, soft body pressed up against his side.

It seemed that Kate wasn't immune to the eroticism on the screen either. Her hand was drawing a lazy pattern on Michael's thigh, slowly spiraling up and down until he began to squirm. Two could play at that game, however, and he very slowly worked his hand up Kate's shirt so that he was gently cupping a breast. Kate arched and shifted so that she was leaning into his touch.

"Is this show on DVD?" Michael whispered into Kate's ear, catching her earlobe between his teeth in a soft nip.

"Uh-huh." Kate squirmed and offered herself up for more.

"Then what the hell are we doing here?" Michael whispered between open-mouthed kisses on her neck.

"Good point." Kate tried to sit up but only succeeded in falling back against the cushions as Michael scrambled to his feet.

Had he been asked later, Michael would have been completely unable to recall how he and Kate transitioned from the sofa to the bedroom. One thing he did remember was Kate turning her back to him, and how he was arrested by the sight of his surname printed across the shirt. Running his hands up and under the cotton, Michael eased the shirt up and off Kate's body, then pulled her close and kissed everywhere that the letters had been. They fell onto the bed in a tangle of limbs, delighting in each other as all the layers of cotton and denim were discarded. Licking and kissing her shoulders, he cupped her breasts in his hands and pulled her against his chest. Kate submitted at first, but her need for friction had her turning and pushing him onto his back, straddling him with a soft growl as she set out to do some exploring of her own.

Michael squeezed his eyes shut, tangling his fingers in her hair as her tongue swirled around him, lapping and sucking as she teased him to the brink before stopping and regarding him with a sly smile. Matching her smile, Michael wondered where this vixen had come from and grabbed her by the shoulders to pull her up beside him.

"My turn," he said in a hoarse whisper, pushing a knee between her thighs as he pressed her slight body against the mattress. Kate whimpered and arched her back as Michael's chest hair rasped against her sensitive skin, as he took his time exploring her topography. Frustrated at his leisurely pace, Kate hooked one of her legs around his hips to pull him closer.

"Uh-uh." He shook his head with a smile, and then took her slim ankle in a firm grip with one hand while he trailed his other hand over her sternum in a soft, teasing pattern. He twisted and shifted slightly to read the scrolling letters on her ankle. "What does this one mean again, *Suscipio Tripudium?*"

Kate shifted and groaned when Michael held her in place, giving her a look of quiet patience while he waited for her to answer.

"Receive Joy," she volunteered at last as she reached for him. "Please, Michael."

"Can't let my girl down," he murmured as he dipped his head toward her skin again, and Kate snatched convulsively at the bed sheet as his tongue dipped inside her, and she breathed out a keening sigh. Michael lifted his head to regard her for a moment. "Oh, I like that sound. Let's see if you can do that again."

"Quit . . . toying with me, Forrester," Kate said.

But Michael was too busy to say anything for quite some time. When he at last moved up her body and slid into her, they were communicating by taste and touch, already knowing each other's sweet spots as they stroked and curled their way toward bliss.

"Only you, Kate." Michael rested his forehead against hers as their bodies moved in unison.

"Only you," she agreed, hooking her other ankle around Michael's hip, giving as much joy as she received.

Chapter 23

Reviews and Bacon

Michael woke as he felt a tickle start on his chest and cracked his eyes open to see Kate curled up against his side, her fingers swirling in sleepy patterns on his bare skin. Turning his head, he pressed a soft kiss against her hair and smiled when she shifted to give him a bleary smile before snuggling and closing her eyes again. He wasn't surprised at this reaction. Sunday mornings were Kate's only opportunity to sleep in, and she always made the most of it.

He was awake now but didn't want to move for fear of disturbing Kate, so he contented himself by studying the bedroom, his gaze stopping as he focused on the large print of Klimt's "The Kiss." The gold detail in the picture had been picked out in foil, and he watched as the soft light in the bedroom made the picture glow. The room was quiet and still in the early morning light. Kate sighed in her sleep and shifted closer to him—an almost impossible feat given their bodies were already entwined. Glancing across at the window, Michael saw that it was snowing outside, and as he watched the snowflakes flutter down outside, he felt warm and secure with Kate in his arms, knowing that he wanted more.

An hour later, he smiled as he felt a soft kiss against his shoulder and glanced down to see Kate blinking sleepily up at him.

"Hey, you." He smiled.

"Mornin'." Kate yawned and rolled onto her back and arced into a cat-stretch, laughing when Michael swooped down to kiss her belly where her T-shirt had ridden up. "Nice try but your aim's off. Get up here," she suggested.

"Yes'm," Michael said obediently before giving her a quick kiss. "Sleep well?"

"Yup," Kate replied as she draped a languid arm around his neck to hold him to her, "but the waking up bit is much better."

"You won't hear me arguing," Michael muttered as he kissed her again, running his tongue along her bottom lip before dipping into her warmth.

❧

After a leisurely shower and change, Michael sniffed at the air as he walked into the kitchen, pushing his still-wet hair off his face. He nuzzled Kate who was getting some coffee cups out.

"Smells good," he said as he planted a quick kiss on the side of her neck.

"I thought you'd like it." Kate smiled at him as she got out the milk. "It's the same blend I use at the store."

"Great." Michael watched as she picked up a small stainless steel jug and began frothing some milk on the home-sized espresso machine. "Don't you get sick of that?"

"What, making coffee?" Kate glanced at him over her shoulder while she worked before returning to attention to the task at hand. "Not at all. Not when it gets me my morning heart starter."

"Fair call," Michael agreed, turning around in surprise when the oven timer pinged. "You baked?"

"Nope." Kate grinned. "Warming up some muffins that Emily made. I didn't get a chance to try them at the store, so I brought some home." She nodded toward the oven mitts on the counter. "Do me a favor and take them out?"

"Sure." Michael carefully took the tray out and rested it on the stove top, and then gave the muffins an appreciative sniff. "What are they?"

"Cranberry and orange, with a demerara sugar crust," Kate answered as she poured the steamed milk into the waiting cups and then spooned on some froth. "Here you go," she said as she passed Michael a cup. "Sugar's over there." She jerked her chin to indicate the sugar bowl as she busied herself putting some muffins onto a serving dish. Grabbing her coffee and the plate, she carried them out into the small living room, setting the dish down on the coffee table and returning to the kitchen for the butter.

"Okay." Michael searched the bottom shelf of the coffee table to pull out a bundle of papers and magazines. "What have we got?"

"There should be yesterday's *New York Times* and a few copies of *Vanity Fair*," Kate said before she sipped at her coffee. "I'm not sure what else you'll find there."

"Hmmm." Michael scanned the newspaper and realized he'd read most of it already. He thought of the weekend newspapers that would be waiting at his apartment and suppressed a sigh.

"Sorry." Kate interpreted his look and gave him an apologetic smile.

"Huh?" Michael glanced at her and shook his head while he broke off a piece of muffin and spread some butter on it before taking a bite. "No big deal."

Kate reached over for the other half of Michael's muffin that he had buttered and left on the plate, biting into it with relish as he gave her an indignant look. Michael helped himself to another muffin and settled back on the sofa while Kate switched on the TV and turned to a news channel. He contemplated the muffin in his hand while he chewed. "You know … these are really good."

"I know." Kate nodded over her cup at him. "She's flexing her muscle a bit in the kitchen. It's good."

"You don't mind?"

Kate looked at him in surprise. "Why would I? Sure, I do the cupcakes, but it's great to have some backup now."

"I just thought because the store was yours, you'd want things to stay, you know …" he shrugged, "… exclusive."

Kate gave him a fond look. "It's just baking, Michael, not rocket science."

"I know." Michael waved off her amusement. "But given the time you've put into the store, I didn't know how protective you'd be."

"Ah, now I get where you're coming from. The hallowed recipe book is mostly up here." She tapped a finger against her temple. "And the basic ones are kept in the store."

"Gotcha. Just checking." He looked down and brushed some crumbs off his T-shirt, and then he picked up his cup and drained it. When he lowered the cup, Kate was regarding him with amusement. "Have I told you how much I love your coffee?"

"Uh-huh." Kate nodded as she chewed.

"Have I told you how much I love you?"

Kate smiled and sipped at her cup. "Uh-huh."

"And," Michael swallowed hard and then continued, "have I told you that I think we should live together?"

Kate, who had been about to take another bite of muffin, paused and set it back down on the plate. "That bit you've kinda kept quiet," she said as she regarded him with calm eyes. She didn't seem surprised at his words, and Michael felt a rush of relief as he looked at her calm expression.

Michael rubbed the back of his neck with one hand. "So, uh, how about we talk about it?"

"How about we do that," Kate agreed in a soft voice.

&c;

Wren sneezed and slapped away the hand that had been fluttering over her top lip.

"Guh." Her voice was muffled as she rolled over and stuffed her face into the pillow to evade David's hand. "Get away from me."

"That's not what you said last night," David rumbled as he hooked a leg over Wren and pulled her against him. "Especially when you were about to—"

"God." Wren pushed herself away and glared up at him. "Do you have to be such a morning person?" she snapped before thumping her head back into the pillow.

"Babe," David replied in a mild tone. "I wanna take us out for breakfast."

"Fine," Wren mumbled. "Later."

"It's later now," David objected. He was silent as Wren kept her eyes resolutely closed before he reached out to rub her back. It was time to utter the magic words. "There's gonna be coffee," he said in a wheedling tone.

It worked. Wren huffed and then turned her head to give him a long hard stare.

"Fine," she said at last. "You go shower. I'll be in there soon."

David beamed at her, and then threw back the covers to make his way into the bathroom. "Don't be long," he called over his shoulder.

Wren mumbled something into the pillow. It was not "have a nice day."

An hour later saw Wren and David waiting to cross the street, wrapped up in coats and scarves. David stamped his feet on the sidewalk a few times to keep warm, as Wren folded her arms over her chest against the morning chill and squinted across the street.

"Where are we going again?"

"Somewhere with bacon and pancakes," David said as he put his arm around Wren's shoulders, pulling her alongside him as the light changed and they began walking again.

"And coffee," Wren reminded him.

"And coffee," David agreed. "You know, when we met I seem to recall you being really peppy."

"That was in the store. There's *coffee* in the store. *Lots* of coffee," Wren snapped.

"You'll have some soon," David replied.

Wren gave him a quelling look, trying to retain her tired and grumpy mood and failing when he flashed her a grin that revealed his dimples. He seemed to be very pleased with himself.

David chaffed Wren's upper arm with his hand as they walked, humming under his breath. He had a surprise for her this morning and getting her out for breakfast was a means to an end. The previous evening had been a late night for them both, although neither of them had been worrying about that at the time.

"I could've made pancakes at home," Wren grumped.

"There's just no joy in you until you've had a coffee, is there?"

"Not when I thought I could have a sleep in." Wren sighed.

"You can nap this afternoon, and anyway, I've got a surprise for you," David replied, giving her an enigmatic grin when she looked at him.

"What kind of surprise?" Curiosity had her feeling more alert now.

"The kind where you're gonna have to wait and see," David answered, laughing when she stuck her tongue out at him. The distraction had been enough to dissipate her morning grumbles, but she wouldn't feel completely human until she had coffee. Fortunately they arrived at the café soon enough. David laughed when Wren placed her coffee order before she even sat down. Soon he was sitting back with a smile, watching Wren as she picked up her cup and sipped at it with reverence.

"So," he began, "I wanted to—" He broke off as Wren held up an imperious hand for silence. When she had consumed half the cup, she nodded at him for continue. "You weren't joking," he said in a mild tone.

"When it comes to coffee, I'm never joking," Wren said as she knuckled her eyes and shook her head as if to clear it. "Okay, you can talk now," she instructed.

"Gee, thanks," he said in a dry tone. "So here's the surprise," he said as he passed her a copy of the weekend newspaper. "It's something I cooked up a while back."

❦

"When?" Kate asked when Michael had finished talking.

"Um, I'm not sure. Whenever you think you could—" Michael began, stopping when Kate shook her head.

"Not when I could move; I meant when did you have this idea about us living together?" She had finished her coffee and was sitting with her legs tucked beneath her, leaning against the sofa back with her head resting on one hand, listening quietly to Michael's reasoning.

"A few weeks back," Michael admitted.

"And you didn't say anything back then?"

Michael shook his head. Kate was being very calm about this. He wasn't sure what he had expected, but her quiet acceptance made things seem almost too easy.

"I guess it just didn't feel like the right time," he said.

"Mm-hmm," Kate said in a thoughtful tone as her gaze turned inward. Michael would have given everything he had to know what she was thinking in that moment. "I'm going to get us some more coffee, and then we're going to continue this conversation."

"Okay," Michael replied, uncertain. She wasn't angry, but she wasn't turning cartwheels of excitement. He didn't know what to make of the situation; was her answer going to be yes or no? He watched Kate as she got up and moved past him to walk into the kitchen with their cups before he gave a quiet sigh. The conversation didn't seem to be going in quite the way that he'd hoped. He was startled, therefore, when Kate suddenly reappeared in front of him and straddled his lap to give him a hot and hard kiss.

"And just so you know," she said softly, "my answer is yes, and I'll be right back."

Michael sat blinking on the sofa as Kate disappeared back into the kitchen, a slow smile of delight spreading across his face.

"So how are we going to do this?" Michael asked when Kate returned with some fresh coffee.

"Not sure. I'm new to this, too," Kate said as she handed him his coffee and then carefully curled up on the sofa beside him. "I'll need to talk to Paul."

"Why's that?" Michael kept a careful grip on his cup as he rested it on his thigh and watched Kate as she sat twirling some hair around her finger while she thought.

"Well, he and I always talk big life stuff through first, plus there's this apartment."

"You own it?" Michael was surprised.

"Kinda." Kate shrugged and sipped at her coffee. "The bank owns it more than I do. Paul's the money brains in the family, and he's the one that insisted I get this a few years back."

"How did you find it?" Michael looked at the apartment with new eyes. Kate was in a good location, and although the apartment was tiny, its charm compensated for the lack of space. Apartments like these didn't last long on the market.

"I was renting it when the owner decided to sell, so the day I found out, Paul and I had a long talk and put an offer in that afternoon," Kate explained with a proud smile. "It didn't even hit the market before it was sold."

"I'm impressed." Michael nodded slowly as he considered her answer. They were both used to leading very independent lives, so there was more to be considered than he thought. "But what does that mean if you move to mine?"

"You mean, you don't want live here?" Kate gave him a shocked look.

"Uh…" Michael hesitated. He certainly liked the atmosphere of Kate's home more than his own, but the apartment was *tiny*.

"Relax." Kate nudged him. "I'm kidding."

"Right." Michael relaxed.

Kate cocked her head and regarded Michael with a thoughtful expression. "You know…you're as nervous about this as I am."

"You're nervous?" Michael laughed now. "I thought you were being really calm."

"Check it." Kate reached across for his hand and held it against her chest so that he could feel her drumming heart.

"I stand corrected," Michael said, rubbing her skin with his thumb.

"I'll talk to Paul," Kate continued, "and we'll talk it through. I can sublet this and keep it as an investment property." Kate looked around the room with a wistful smile. "I've got too many good memories here to let it go entirely."

"And I wouldn't expect you to," Michael assured her. "We can sort out the details later. Right now, I'm just glad you said yes." He set his cup down and nodded at Kate to do the same. When her hands were free, he reached over to pull her onto his lap. "Hey," he whispered, rubbing his nose against hers, "love you."

"Love you too." Kate smiled and gave him a kiss before pulling back and regarding him with a mixture of excitement and trepidation. "So, we're really going to do this?"

"Looks like." Michael nodded.

"It's been a long time since I've done this," Kate mused.

"It's a first for me," Michael confessed, giving Kate a rueful smile as she gaped at him. "Yeah, you heard that right."

"Never?"

Michael shook his head.

"Never ever?"

"I guess it was a case of not the right person, not the right time," Michael suggested with a wry smile.

"So what happened to change your mind?" Kate marveled.

"Simple. I met you," Michael said as he pulled her in for another kiss. "So what do you want to do, call Paul?"

"Uh…" Kate's mind was reeling now. She felt daunted by Michael's impressive show of faith in their relationship. Living together was the next logical step, she knew, but it was intimidating, even though she was delighted that Michael was willing to commit to her so much. "How about we get out of here?"

"You want to go out there?" Michael gestured toward the window where they could see a glimpse of gray skies and the occasional flurry of snowflakes.

"Why not?" Kate shrugged. "We could always go to your place and start to talk things through some more. It's where we're going to be living after all."

"If that's what you want," Michael replied, a smile tugging at his lips.

Kate looked at Michael, his hair sticking up in damp curls and whorls, a rumpled T-shirt and his old jeans riding low on his hips. She could feel a pressure expanding in her chest, a bubble that was waiting to burst into pleasure or fear of the unknown, she couldn't tell. She took a deep breath.

"It is. It really is." She smiled, and with that, the bubble in her chest subsided and the pressure was gone. "Let's get outta here."

Wren looked up when David deposited the newspaper on the table in front of her. "Read that and see what you think." He grinned.

Wren grabbed the newspaper and scanned the title. "Food and Review," she read aloud. "I don't get it, what am I ... oh!" Her eyes widened, and she began scanning the pages, flipping through it quickly until she stopped with a short squeal of excitement.

David leaned back in his seat and watched her with an indulgent smile. He already knew what the article had to say; his former colleague had emailed him a draft before it had gone to print.

"Was this you?" Wren gave him a smile of delight when she had finished reading.

"I didn't write it, but—" David began and stopped when Wren got out of her seat to give him a kiss that was eighty percent exuberance and twenty percent caffeine. "Wow," he said when he came up for air. "Remind me to surprise you more often."

"Let's not get too excited," Wren cautioned him as she took her seat, but despite her words, her eyes were dancing with excitement. "I usually only like surprises if I know about them in advance."

"But then it's not a—" David was waved to silence by an impatient Wren.

"Back to the article," she said, tapping the page for emphasis. "How did this happen?"

"Don't you remember me buying some cupcakes weeks ago? That's how I got your number."

"Oh, yeah." Wren stared off into space with a little smile. "I remember that, but how come it took them so long?"

"Babe, there's more than a few restaurants and cafés in this town, and the writer had to wait until she had the right angle for a cupcake feature."

"Hmm, I see she's reviewed a couple of bakeries." Wren gave a sniff of dismissal as she scanned the section again. "But they're not as good as *ours*," she said proudly.

"She knows her stuff," David replied with a pleased smile.

Wren read the article again, smiling.

Cupcakes used to be the domain of children's parties, but not anymore. These miniature works of art have enjoyed a renaissance of popularity, and it seems that cupcakes are here to stay. For the cupcake fan, there are bakeries aplenty in New York, offering all manner of frosted wares to tempt even the most jaded palate. For the aficionados, there are the mainstay bakeries such as Magnolia Bakery (be prepared to wait in line, this bakery has enjoyed a cultish following since its appearance on Sex and the City) and Cupcake Café that do a nice trade in personalized-photo, bite-sized masterpieces. Once in a while, however, along comes along something special.

Take the Cake is a small café bakery in Greenwich Village that charms visitors as soon as they walk through the door, usually laughing at the Quote of the Day, which is prominently featured on the chalkboard outside. Either this store hasn't made up its mind what it wants to be when it grows up, or it has a quirky sense of style designed to bemuse and beguile. I'm going with the latter.

The store is an eccentric mix of gallery, bookstore, and bakery. The walls are covered with a collection of original art and found objects. There are racks filled with a collection of vintage books and magazines for customers, even an umbrella stand for those unfortunates caught out by the weather. The marble counter, brass fittings, and mismatched wooden tables and chairs makes it feel as if you're sitting down in the kitchen of a grandmother you never had. All of this, however, is only the trailer to the main attraction: the cupcakes themselves.

Don't be fooled, some of these cupcakes carry a real sugar punch, but oh, what a way to go. For those of you that are sweet enough already, there are cupcakes that deliver a bite; bitter chocolate and raspberry, chili chocolate, lemon meringue, and even— heaven help me—gin and tonic cupcakes. The names of the cupcakes themselves are just as eye-catching: 'Lemon Afterglow,' 'Woodstock After Burn,' and even 'Vegan Rehab,' all the result of an ongoing war between the baker and barista who try to outsmart each other every morning with their cupcake/quote war. These two have been battling it out for two years now with no end in sight, but the customers are the ultimate winners, and to the victors go the spoils.

Take the Cake offers the usual lunch offerings of wraps and bagels, and a delicious Zuma blend coffee that will make your ordinary filter coffee experience seem like a forgettable one night stand. The service is quick, the cupcakes are bliss, and the coffee is hot, so forget what you think you know about children's party snacks and high-end designer bakeries, and Take the Cake.

"Wow," Wren whispered to herself and then looked up to see David watching her with an intent expression. "You've read this already?"

"Yup, and I believe *that*—" he nodded his head toward the page, "—is what we, in the industry, call a rave review."

"Did you have anything to do with it?" Wren narrowed her eyes as she considered this. If there was any hint of favoritism, she was going to find out.

"Nothing beyond taking some cupcakes to the Food Editor and telling her to send someone your way," David explained. "The rest of it was up to you guys."

Wren looked at the article again and traced a gentle finger over the words with a smile.

"Does Kate know?" she asked as the thought occurred to her.

"She will if she gets the weekend paper," David answered.

"I don't think she does." Wren frowned.

"Michael will have it," David assured her.

"Maybe she's at home," Wren suggested as she reached for her phone.

"Or maybe she's not," David said as he glanced at his watch. "It's not even ten yet. Any idea if she likes to sleep in?"

"Oh," Wren said, "yeah, she does." She considered her options before brightening and began to compose a text message. "You're sure Michael gets this paper?"

"Sure, I'm sure," David replied and then gave a slight frown. "At least he did while I was writing for them."

"You stopped working there months ago," Wren accused. "What if he's canceled his subscription?"

"If he has, they can go out and get one," David said in a soothing tone. "Which they will once they find out the bakery is featured. It'll be okay."

"I hope so," Wren fretted, biting her lip. She wanted Kate to find out *now*. "Oh, to hell with it, if she gets mad, the worst she can do is fire me," she muttered as she began to dial.

"Damn, it's cold. What the hell were we thinking, leaving your warm apartment?" Michael tried to grumble but was feeling too good to even pretend to be complaining.

"Don't know." Kate shrugged. "Jack used to call it a rush of shit to the brain," she added, looking up with a grin as Michael laughed.

"I've got to remember that one," he said, chuckling, and then stopped as he saw a yellow cab approaching. "We're in luck," he added and waved his arm up and down. "Come on." He picked up the pace as the cab approached.

"We're only a few blocks away," Kate protested in a half-hearted voice.

"Maybe, but you're cold and tired, so we're getting out of this weather," Michael retorted, reaching for the door of the cab as soon as it stopped and raising an eyebrow as another intrepid New Yorker tried to beat him to it before he bundled Kate inside. "Come on, sweetheart, let's get you home."

Kate slid across the back seat with a smile at Michael's words and waited for him to climb in beside her. Michael gave the address and the cab took off with a lurch.

"So what did Wren want?" Michael asked after he had gotten himself settled. They had been leaving Kate's apartment when Wren had called, babbling excitedly about some sort of surprise.

"I'm not sure, but do you get the paper delivered?"

"Just the weekend edition. It'll be with the doorman," he answered. "Why's that?"

"There's something for us to read, but she wouldn't say what," Kate said with a puzzled air.

"Which paper?" Michael asked, and when Kate told him, it was his turn to look thoughtful. "That's where David used to work," he said, and then shrugged. "Sorry, I've got no idea."

"We'll find out soon enough," Kate assured him. "When we get home." She smiled as she said it, and then looked out the window. Was she really doing the right thing? Only time would tell, but she found herself needing to talk to Paul now more than ever. Decision made, she pulled out her phone again.

Need Bear time xK

She didn't have to wait long before she got a response.

Everything okay? xP

Kate smiled. She could picture the look of concern on her brother's face.

Yes. Need my big bro for talk tho xK

Michael gave her a curious look but said nothing.

Anytime, anywhere xP

Kate was about to reply when another message came in.

With food xP

She laughed and glanced over at Michael.

"It's Paul. I told him I wanted to discuss something, and I think he's negotiating dinner."

"Would you expect anything less?" Michael smiled.

"Oh, hell, no." Kate grinned and returned her attention to the phone.

2day sometime? xK

Paul was quick to respond.

Sure. Call when ur ready. Sure all ok? xP

She smiled at his question and sent back some reassurance before stowing her phone back in her coat pocket.

"That's got him curious as all hell," she commented as she turned to Michael, "but I'll call him later to arrange a time and tell him then."

"Do you think he'll be okay with it?" Michael asked. He knew how tight the bond was between the two siblings and didn't want to be the cause of any unrest, particularly after the situation between Kate and Tom.

"Sure." Kate glanced at him in surprise. "As long as I'm happy, he's fine." Looking at Michael's pensive reaction, she leaned in closer. "Relax. Paul likes you because you make me happy."

"And if I don't?"

"Well, then..." Kate tried to look solemn. "I guess you've got a problem."

"True, but there's one thing I'm really curious about," Michael mused.

"What's that?"

"What had Wren so excited on a Sunday morning."

Sitting in Michael's living room, Kate sat on the couch with the paper held loosely in her hands, her face slack with surprise. "I can't believe it; we've been reviewed."

"And it's a good one," Michael added, reading over her shoulder.

"Did you have anything to do with this?" Kate turned her head to look at him, watching as his eyebrows went up in surprise.

"Me? No, it might have something to do with Watson, though. That's the paper he used to work for," Michael commented as he scanned the article again, smiling as he read the comment about the cupcake/quote war. "This is really good."

"I know." Kate nodded her head slowly, wondering what the review would mean for business. She had the sudden sensation of things moving and changing around her outside of her control, and for the first time she realized what a cloistered life she had created for herself. Paul would always be there for her—she knew that now—but Michael was an entirely different matter. He had chosen her, worked to get to know her, and now she couldn't imagine her life without him. And now the business she'd worked so hard to establish was on the brink of greater success than she'd dreamed of.

"I'm going to get us some coffee. You want anything?" Michael said as he got up from the sofa.

"I'm fine," Kate said in an absent tone as she read the article again.

"Okay." Michael trailed his hand across her shoulder as he walked past her to get to the kitchen, and Kate gave him a brief smile at the gesture.

She sat on the couch for a moment, and then got up and walked into the bathroom. Her skin felt dry and taut from the cold outside, and she grabbed a facecloth to run under some warm water before scrubbing her face. Looking at her reflection, she saw her cheeks were flushed with high spots of color and her eyes were a little dazed.

It had been an interesting morning. What had started out as a relaxing Sunday had turned into a life-altering conversation about moving into Michael's apartment, and now the store had made a prominent appearance in a widely-read newspaper review section. She stared at the bathroom counter, at her spare toothbrush, and visualized her perfume bottles sitting there. Turning slowly, she took in the rest of her immediate surroundings, looking at the vast expanse of walls and wondering where she would hang her pictures. Leaving the bedroom, she walked out into the living room and studied Michael's bookshelves. She had a lot of books too, but there looked like there would be enough space for her collection. She swallowed hard as the realization hit her; she wasn't just going to be sharing space with someone, she was going to be sharing her life.

"Hey." Michael's soft voice came to her from the other end of the room.

Looking up, she saw Michael standing there with two mugs of fresh coffee, and she realized that she still hadn't brought him some of her coffee blend from the store. She'd do something about that soon.

"Everything okay?" Michael moved toward her, pausing to set the cups down on the coffee table before he crossed to her. "You look like you're freaking out a bit."

"I'm fine," Kate said in a voice that only trembled a little. "I think things are just sinking in. Today has been …" She paused and licked her lips. "Unexpected."

Michael put his arms around her and pulled her to his chest. "I know," he said as he kissed her hair.

Kate put her arms around him and ran her hands up and under his T-shirt, so that she could feel the warm hardness of his back. Michael kept talking and his voice was a soothing rumble in his chest.

"We don't have to do this any faster than you're comfortable with, okay?"

Kate gave a silent nod.

"I want you here, Kate, I want to live with you, I want to …" He stopped, realizing he had nearly overstepped the mark.

Kate pulled back so that she could look up at him.

"You want to what?"

"Later," Michael promised. "You want to call Paul?"

"Oh," Kate's eyes widened. "I nearly forgot." She began to pull away to get her phone, stopping when Michael clamped his arms around her.

"Kiss?" he said in a hopeful voice, smiling when she gave a short laugh and gave him a quick peck. He let her go then, watching as she walked over to the hall closet to get her phone out of her coat pocket. This morning had progressed very quickly indeed. "Get Paul over here if you like," he suggested in an offhand tone.

"You sure?"

"Why not? Maybe we can do something for dinner." Michael shrugged. "I've got a few things here. I'm sure we can come up with something. You go do your thing. I'll check my email."

While Kate spoke to her brother, Michael fired up his laptop and wasn't surprised to see a number of emails from Alistair. It appeared that his editor had already gotten to work on the drafts Michael had been sending through and was now eager to see the final manuscript. Looking over his shoulder, Michael saw that Kate was deep in discussion, wandering around the apartment as she spoke and gradually making her way to the bedroom. It looked like she may be a while.

He sat drumming his fingers on the desktop for a moment before opening the manuscript document sand scrolling through to re-read the sections that Alistair had raised a few questions about. He could see the other man's point; some sections of it needed revising. Culling, even. Another moment's consideration, and then he began to type. He stopped when he heard a whoop of laughter from Kate. When her conversation resumed, he went back to work. Used to working in relative silence, Michael found the murmur of Kate's voice in the background to be strangely soothing, and he listened to the indistinct one-sided conversation awhile before he got back to work.

Michael was frowning at the screen, rubbing his forefinger across his lip as he sat deep in thought, when he was jolted by a touch on his shoulder.

"Sorry." Kate had jumped in fright herself, not expecting Michael's reaction. "I called your name a couple of times, but you didn't hear me."

"Mom used to scold me about my habit of switching off." Michael swiveled in his chair and looked at Kate who was standing in front of him, shifting her weight from one foot to the other. "How's Paul?"

"Good." Kate gave a fond smile. "We've talked it over, but he's still keen on being fed." She made a wry face. "No surprises there."

"I thought you were going to catch up, so you could talk about it?" Michael was surprised that the matter seemed to have been dealt with already.

"I know, but he made some good suggestions and seems okay with it all," Kate said as she dropped her cell phone onto one of the living room armchairs, making a mental note to see if her own armchair was going to match. Glancing back, she could see that Michael had turned back to his laptop and was typing furiously. She stood watching him for a moment, wondering what to do, before she padded over to him again and nuzzled his neck. "Hey," she said, "if you want, I can go back to my place and leave you in peace."

"What?" Michael pulled his attention away from the manuscript and looked at her in shock. "Hell, no. Shit." He pushed his laptop away from him and stood up to pull Kate toward him. "I'm sorry. I got in the zone again. I'm just used to doing my own thing."

"You know…" Kate pursed her lips, standing in Michael's arms as she looked up at him. "We're going to have to talk about that side of things."

"What, my work?" Michael frowned down at her. "Is it a problem?"

"No, well, not really," Kate amended. "I guess I just don't know what to do around you when you're working. I don't know if I'm intruding, or if you need total silence, or …" She broke off and shook her head. "Maybe I'm over-thinking things, but this apartment has been *your* space for a lot longer than I've been on the scene. I think we're both going to have some adjusting to do."

"We'll get through it," Michael promised her. "As long as we keep talking."

"Hmm." Kate was thoughtful now, feeling as if they had just hit the tip of the iceberg. Somehow she didn't think things were going to be as easy as Michael made out. Casting about for something else to say, she glanced over at the coffee table. "Our drinks have gone cold. How about I make us something else?"

"Sure." Michael watched Kate as she collected the cups, and then looked back at his laptop. He was nearly finished, just a few more minutes and … He watched Kate's departing back as she walked into the kitchen and thought about their morning so far. Turning back to the desk, he snapped the laptop shut with a decisive click. Alistair wasn't expecting to hear from him for a few days, and there were other things to discuss. More important things, he decided, as he followed Kate. When he got there, Kate was sitting up on the counter with her ankles crossed, swinging her legs slowly while she waited for the stovetop coffee pot to brew. "So," Michael said, "is Paul coming over for dinner?"

"If you want." Kate gave a tentative nod, which stopped Michael in his tracks.

"If I want?" he repeated, surprised at her phrasing. "What's going on?" He walked toward her and gently uncrossed her ankles, standing between her thighs and cupping her bottom so that he could pull her toward him. Kate gave a slight smile and draped her arms around his neck, her fingers curling through his hair.

"Dunno." Kate's answer was a mumble this time. "It feels weird, is all."

"What, inviting him over? Kate…" Michael rested his forehead against hers. "This is going to be your home too."

"But you started working," Kate argued. "I didn't want to interrupt."

"Kate, I work at home anyway." He sighed, realizing that they were getting to the crux of the problem. "You don't have to tip-toe around me."

"I guess I just worry about disrupting things," Kate admitted. "You work so hard and—"

"And so do you," Michael replied. "But you saw how I switched off earlier."

"True." Kate gave a reluctant smile at this. "But you don't do that all the time, surely."

"Wanna bet?" Michael teased. "You give Mom a call. She used to complain that she could have had Whitesnake blaring out of the sound system and I wouldn't have heard a thing."

"Whitesnake?" Kate was shocked. "Susan likes Whitesnake?"

"With a passion," Michael sighed. "Why do you think I was so keen to get my own place?"

"Seriously?" Kate's smile had turned into a smirk. "I mean, c'mon."

"And don't get me started on Dad's Johnny Cash collection."

"Oh, God." Kate started giggling as she pictured Michael's academic parents. "And I thought Jack's Elvis devotion was hard going."

"Why do you think I'm so good at tuning out? It's a survival instinct." Michael growled as he nuzzled her neck. "So here's the thing," Michael said as he pulled back and looked at her, his playful expression fading to something more serious. "When I'm working, I tune out noise, but don't ever think that I'm ignoring you. My work's important the same way that yours is, but that doesn't mean that you're less important to me." He reached up to cup her face, trying to will her to believe the sincerity behind his words. "I love you and I want you here," he said. "I really want this, and I hope that you want it too."

"I want." Kate swallowed. "But I'm not going to lie; it kinda scares me shitless too."

"Living with me scares you?" Michael watched her carefully, trying to gauge her reaction.

"No." Kate ran her hands down his shoulders in an attempt to reassure him. "Not that. I guess it's the part about giving up my apartment." She gave him an anxious look. "You know what it's like when you live alone, everything is just the way you like it, and now we're both going to have to ... compromise." Kate rolled the word around in her mouth as if she was trying to get used to it.

"Yeah, I know, but do you see that as good or bad?"

"Neither," Kate said after she had considered the question. "Just different."

"Well, then, we'll adjust." Michael smiled and hoped she didn't notice that he was just as nervous as she was.

"We'll compromise," Kate agreed.

Chapter 24

White Russian Appreciation

"Morning, boss," Wren called out as Kate approached. She had only been waiting a short time, but the wind chill was enough to have her hopping from one foot to the other in a bid to keep warn.

"Wren, don't call me boss," Kate said as she fumbled in her coat pocket with gloved hands for the keys.

"Sorry, boss. Did you see it? Tell me you saw it," Wren demanded as she helped Kate roll up the security door.

"I saw it." Kate nodded as she unlocked the main door and pushed it open. Stepping aside to let Wren through the door, she glanced down the block and saw Emily approaching at a quick pace. She raised an arm in a leisurely wave and smiled when Emily acknowledged her before going inside.

Wren shuddered as she pulled off her heavy overcoat and struggled with it into the kitchen so that she could hang it up. "Get that coffee going, boss. I need warming up."

"Yes'm." Kate nodded as she flicked the coffee machine on as she walked past it before following Wren into the kitchen. "Emily is nearly here too."

"Cool," Wren replied. "Did you read it?"

"Sure did." Kate grinned. "We're finally in print."

"Can you believe it?" Wren was glowing with excitement. "David surprised me with it yesterday. Did you know?"

"Kinda," Kate admitted, and then looked up with a smile as Emily walked into the room, dropping her bag onto the counter and unwinding her scarf from her neck.

"Hey, guys." Emily smiled. "Anyone here read the paper on the weekend?"

"You read it?" Wren looked up from tying on her apron and gave the other woman an expectant look as Kate brushed past her on her way to the coffee machine.

"After your call? Of course, I did. Brad went out and got the paper as soon as I told him. How did you find out?"

"David drove me nuts until we went out for breakfast, and he grabbed the paper when we were at the café," Wren explained before glancing at Kate. "How about you, boss?"

Kate gave her an amused look as she poured the frothed milk into the cups, sliding two cups over to the waiting women before she finished making her own.

"Well, of course I'm beyond ecstatic at the review. I just can't believe David did this without even telling Michael," she murmured.

"I can't believe David didn't tell anyone," Emily pointed out in a mild tone.

"Well." Wren thought about that before continuing, "At the very least he could have told *me*. I mean I'm his..." she floundered at this, waving her hand as she opened and closed her mouth without saying anything. Emily and Kate watched her with interest.

"Girlfriend?" Kate suggested.

"Love of his life?" Emily added.

"Ohh, I like that one," Kate commented as she toasted Emily with her cup.

Emily gave a modest nod. "Thanks, I'm quite pleased with that one myself." They both looked at Wren who had the grace to blush.

"Okay, okay." She flapped her hands at them, hoping the color in her cheeks wasn't too much of a giveaway. "Moving on."

"Really?" Kate looked disappointed. "I thought the conversation was just getting interesting."

"Whatever." Wren rolled her eyes as she sipped at her coffee.

"So..." Emily leaned against the counter with her hip. "What *do* you call David?"

To Kate and Emily's mutual delight, Wren squirmed.

"Well," she hedged, "I guess, that is to say—"

"Oh, just tell us already," Emily said with a laugh.

"All right." Wren chugged back her coffee and set the cup down with a flourish. "I call him my *boyfriend*."

"Well done." Kate burst into applause as Emily swooped on the smaller woman to give her a congratulatory hug.

"What's the big deal?" Wren asked Kate over Emily's shoulder, who was laughing as Emily began to waltz them both around the limited space behind the counter.

"You finally admitted it," Emily sang. "I'm so proud."

"Oh, shut up," Wren said as she disengaged herself. She smiled as she waited for Emily and Kate to finish their coffee so that she could collect their cups. She rifled through her chalk collection to pick out the color she wanted.

"She's back to business," Emily observed with a wink to Kate. "I guess that means the fun's over."

"Excuse me." Wren held up the chalk. "But I think we're just getting started. And *you*—" she turned to point at Kate, "—had better get busy, because after that glowing review, I think we're going to get slammed today." She turned and stalked over to collect the chalkboard, laying it across a table so that she could write. When she had finished writing, she carried the chalkboard over to the counter to show Kate who read it with a smile.

Appreciate me now, avoid the rush!

By the time Wren returned from hanging the chalkboard up outside and brushing the chalk dust off her fingers, the mixer in the kitchen was already going. Emily watched Wren set to work filling up the glass jar beside the coffee machine with marshmallows as she started to make up the wraps and bagels for the lunch time crowd. She turned when she heard her name called from the kitchen.

"Yeah, what's up?" Emily said as she peered around the kitchen doorway.

Kate pushed some hair off her face with the back of her hand as she looked up from the mixer.

"I took home some of your muffins for the weekend," Kate said, "and they were so great I was wondering if you could make some more."

"More?" Emily gaped at her. "It was just a recipe that I found online and thought I'd try. Are you sure?"

"Yup," Kate said as she added some more flour to the mix. "Michael loved them and they sold well." She gave Emily a quick grin. "So I say go for it. As soon as I've got the cupcakes done, the kitchen's all yours."

Emily gaped at Kate as she thought of all the new customers that would be coming into the store today, and her grandmother's words echoed in her mind: "You don't get a second chance at a first impression." She had been browsing through cupcake blogs and recipe sites one evening when she had found the muffin recipe. Brad enthusiastically reviewed a test batch, and his response had given her the confidence to make some for Kate. Making some for customers somehow felt entirely different.

"How are my girls?" Kate stuck her head out of the kitchen long enough to see how Emily and Wren were coping with the morning rush.

"We might need you out here soon, boss," Wren called over her shoulder as she kept making coffees with her usual brisk efficiency. "Things are getting busy. How are you truckin' back there?"

"I'll be right out," Kate answered as she ducked back into the kitchen and picked up the piping bag to finish frosting.

Wren's predictions about the review had been right; the increase in business so far had been steady and showed no signs of slowing down. Emily had been coaxed into the kitchen to make a batch of her cranberry and orange muffins, which seemed to be walking out the door with accompanying takeout coffee just as much as the cupcakes usually did. Kate finished icing the latest batch of cupcakes and set the frosting aside, pausing to roll her neck and work out some kinks.

"Boss," Emily called, "we've got people wanting to know what your answer to the quote is."

"Coming," Kate answered back as she carefully hefted the tray of cupcakes and carried them out into the store. "Wren, assume the position."

"Gotcha," Wren answered as she snatched up the chalkboard and a piece of chalk.

"Okay," Kate began, pitching her voice a little louder so that the waiting customers could hear. "In response to the delightful Wren here—" she grinned as Wren bobbed a curtsey, "—we have *No Time Like the Present:* White Russian cupcakes with a cherry garnish." Kate gave Wren an expectant smile. "Get it? Russian, as in 'rush in'?"

"That one was too easy," Wren commented as Kate put the cupcakes into the display cabinet and stood back as Emily promptly sold one.

"Maybe you're getting soft," Kate said as she patted her shoulder. "How about I spot you here?" She nodded at the coffee machine.

"Would you?" Wren shot her a relieved smile. "I've got a few jobs that need doing before we get too busy."

"Get going," Kate urged her. "I'll do this. How about you, Emily? Are you okay?"

"I'm fine," Emily said as she handed over some change with a smile.

Wren darted out from behind the counter to collect some empty cups and wipe down the tables that had been vacated. There was enough of a lull in customers for Emily to finish making the bagels and for Kate to rearrange the display cabinet stock.

"Do you think we'll have enough?" Emily said as she slid another tray of turkey and ham wraps into the cabinet, nodding toward the cupcakes. "They're the star attraction after all."

"We'll find out soon enough. Just keep an eye on things and let me know if I need to make more," Kate advised. She held up an empty cup and at Emily's enthusiastic nod began to make them all another coffee.

❧

Michael had gotten up at the same time as Kate so that they could have breakfast together before she went to work. He looked at the gray weather outside and sighed before deciding against jogging, wondering if he ought to look into gym membership for the colder months. After fortifying himself with another cup of regrettable coffee, he sat down in front of his laptop and looked at his revisions from the previous afternoon.

A couple of hours later, he realized he had been writing for the sake of it rather than following his established storyline. Cutting and pasting the unnecessary words into a spare document, he scanned the final chapter and realized with a mild sense of anticlimax that further work was unnecessary.

He blinked as he realized that the manuscript was complete, and after a brief hesitation, emailed it to Alistair. Watching the email send, he swiveled in his chair as he stared out the window again, and then with a herculean effort, got up from his laptop and walked away. It was out of his hands now, and it was time to find something else to do.

Michael was standing in front of his bookshelves, shifting some of the contents around in order to make room for some of Kate's things when the phone rang. It was his editor, Alistair.

"Michael," Alistair greeted him. "I got your email, and I have to say I'm surprised."

"You are? What's wrong?" Michael's mind was racing.

"You've finished, and so far I like what I see."

Michael walked over to his desk and sat down, his face slack with surprise.

"How are you feeling about it?" Alistair went on.

"Good," Michael said at last. "I think," he amended. "I finished it earlier than expected, so I guess that's a good sign."

"Early for you, but you missed your deadline by four months," Alistair reminded him. "Still, it's good to see you got back on the wagon." Alistair wasn't going to press the issue. Michael's books had generated a vast and loyal readership, so there was no question of its marketability.

Michael grunted a non-committal response as he toyed with a pen on his desk. His months of writer's block were a painful, but thankfully receding, memory. He looked at his email screen again so as to reassure himself that the final manuscript had finally left his hands.

"Listen," he began, "I agreed with some of your recommendations on the earlier draft, but not all. I changed what I thought suited the text, and the rest I've left with your mark-up comments, so let me know what you think when you get to it."

"I'll be reading it this week," Alistair assured him. When Michael had advised that the manuscript would be arriving, the editor had breathed a quiet prayer of thanks and cleared his schedule as much as possible for the week. "So you'll be hearing from me soon."

"When has that ever changed?" Michael smiled.

Alistair sat up straighter in his office chair as he grinned, looking out the window of his high-rise office. He was enjoying this conversation more than he was prepared to admit. "Just playing to my strengths, Michael. You write, I pester."

"And you do it very well," Michael replied.

"Finishing your work obviously agrees with you. Is this a good time to talk about what you might be working on next?" Alistair picked up his pen and began to doodle on the pad in front of him. He wrote Michael's name and put a question mark next to it as he spoke.

"Give me a break," Michael protested. "I've just finished the last one. Anyway, I've got a few things to organize here before I can start writing again."

"Another project?"

"No, it's to do with Kate," Michael admitted. "You know, the one you met on the phone."

Sitting alone in his office, Alistair cringed.

"Oh, *Kate*," he said. "Right, we've met."

"Yes, you have, although you'll get a chance to meet her in person when the book comes out."

"Based on what I've been reading, I look forward to it," Alistair replied. "She sounds like an incredible woman."

Michael finished his conversation with Alistair and set the phone down, spying his empty coffee cup as he did so. Picking it up, he carried it into the kitchen, setting it down on the sink as he opened the dishwasher and began to stack the dinner plates from the previous night. True to form, Paul had arrived with a healthy appetite for someone else's cooking and plenty of questions. Fortunately, there had been enough provisions in the refrigerator for Michael to make a big pot of chili, and when told what dinner would be, Paul had offered to bring the corn chips and sour cream.

Kate had busied herself in the living room, setting the table and catching a news show after commenting that she was woefully behind on current events. Paul had remained in the kitchen and hoisted himself up onto the countertop where he'd sat and peppered Michael with questions about the forthcoming living arrangements.

"You know I won't let her sell the apartment, right?" Paul had asked before taking a swig of his beer.

"I wouldn't expect her to," Michael had pointed out in a mild voice as he stirred the chili and tapped the wooden spoon on the rim of the pot before setting it down on the chopping board. "But if she ever wants to, it's her decision."

"Ours," Paul had clarified. "We're both investors in the property." He'd regarded Michael for a moment before continuing, "Listen, man, I'm not trying to be the bad guy here, but she's my little sister. I've gotta know she's going to be okay."

"She will be," Michael had said as he sipped at his beer. "She and I have talked it through, and she's talked to you. What else do you need to know?"

"Nothin'," Paul had admitted as he rubbed the back of his neck and surprised Michael with a sheepish grin. "Sorry, I guess I've always looked out for her, and it's kinda hard to let that go."

"No problem." Michael had shrugged. "Sometimes I wonder what it would have been like to have a brother or sister to relate to, the way you guys do."

"Wasn't always easy," Paul had confessed with a rueful smile. "We've had our moments. But once Jack and Gwen were gone, we suddenly realized we were all we had." His expression had become pensive for a moment. "For a while there, I figured she and Tom would—" He'd broken off with a sigh, and then looked at Michael. "But we all know how that turned out."

"Was it that bad?" Michael had risked the question. He hadn't wanted to pry, but with Paul in an expansive mood, he couldn't resist the opportunity.

"How much has she told you?" Paul had given him a shrewd look.

"She told me how he came out, how it all happened."

"Man." Paul had stared down the neck of his beer bottle and had shaken his head before having another swig. "She was philosophical at the time, but yeah, it was bad. She just retreated into herself for a long time."

Paul had thought back to the months after Tom had come out. Kate had put on a brave face when she was in public, letting her guard down only in the presence of Paul and friends whose discretion she trusted. She'd thrown herself into her studies and withdrawn from socializing. Paul hadn't realized what had been happening until one of her friends had emailed him to give him the basics of the situation. He'd flown her to New York for a weekend, and she had seized at the opportunity to escape. By the time she'd returned to college, she still felt vulnerable but strengthened by her brother's reassuring presence in her life. Mercifully, Tom had maintained a low profile, respecting his friendship with Kate enough not to flaunt his newfound lifestyle in front of her.

Paul had watched as his sister forged a new life for herself, throwing herself into the endless variety that New York had to offer, but all the while maintaining a careful distance between herself and anyone that got too close. Watching her as the years progressed, Paul had lamented Gwen's passing anew, wishing that Kate had someone to talk to. When Michael came on the scene, Paul had watched his sister slowly blossom.

"Still," the big man had continued, "everyone moves on, and the store has been really good for her." He'd given Michael a meaningful look. "I've watched her go from strength to strength, so if she's ready for what you're offering, then more power to her."

The chili had bubbled in the pot again, and Michael had turned to give it a quick stir before glancing at his watch; dinner would be ready soon.

"Thanks, Paul," Michael had said. "She means the world to me."

"Likewise," Paul had said, holding up his beer bottle in a silent toast.

Michael had grinned and clinked his bottle against it before pitching his voice loud enough for his girl in the next room to hear.

"Kate," he'd called, "dinner's nearly ready."

"So am I," Kate had called back and then had appeared seconds later to see Michael regarding her with a slight smile. "What?"

"Nothin," Michael had said as he gave her a quick kiss. "Just admiring the view."

"Oh, hush." Kate had smiled. "You guys look like you're having a moment."

"Hey," Paul had objected, "we were having a serious conversation here."

"I dunno. Seems like there's a bit of bromance in the air." She'd narrowed her eyes at her brother. "What were you talking about?"

Paul had been the first to blink. "Okay," he'd said as he looked at Michael, "time for chili?"

"Sure," Michael had responded as he pulled the pot off the heat. "Get the corn chips, and there's some fresh guacamole in the fridge."

Paul had given Michael a hopeful look. "How do you think that went?"

"Smooth, Paul," Michael had said with a laugh as he'd carried the pot over to the table. "Really smooth."

The evening hadn't been late, but it had been very good. The conversation had been punctuated with teasing comments and laughter, and Michael felt the warmth of a genuine friendship growing between himself and Paul. It felt good, and it felt like family.

Michael smiled to himself as he remembered Paul's cautious line of questioning last night; Kate's brother took his role of protector quite seriously, in a way that was loving but not intrusive.

He finished stacking the dishwasher and then walked around the apartment, giving it a once-over. He found that he was looking at his home in a new light now that he knew he was going to be sharing it with someone else. He was pleased to note that there was plenty of blank wall space, so Kate would have fun finding places to hang her numerous pictures and curios. His mother had helped him furnish the apartment, and they had kept things to a neutral color scheme. No doubt Kate would be adding a lot of color, and he grinned at the thought. He couldn't wait.

❧

"I'm cleaning up while we've got a moment. I don't think we can afford to wait on stuff like that today."

"Do you think we'll have enough stock?" Emily said as she slid another tray of turkey and ham wraps into the cabinet.

"I guess there's only one way to find out." Kate shrugged. "We're heading into the great unknown now, but it'll be fun."

"I think so," Emily agreed.

"Speaking of which, Michael and I decided that we're going to live together." Kate kept her tone casual as she worked, not wanting to make a big deal about it.

"Sorry?" Emily put her knife down and stared at Kate who was focusing her attention on the coffee that was trickling into the cups. "Could you say that again?"

"Say what again?" Wren paused on her way to the dishwasher, a fully laden plastic tub balanced on her hip. "What'd I miss?"

"I think the boss lady here—" Emily gestured to Kate, who was starting to froth the milk, and hid her grin, "—said something about living arrangements."

"Oh?" Wren's eyes were wide with curiosity now. She set the tub down on the workbench with a thump and served a customer while Kate finished making their coffees. "One more, boss, tall latte."

"Right," Kate said. She banged out the filter and filled it with fresh coffee that she set to percolate as she got the milk out again. Working seamlessly with Wren, the order was filled and the customer departed with a muffin and some coffee.

Emily had gone back to work clearing up the workbench where she had been making the bagels and wraps, putting the cover back on the tubs of meat and fillings that she then moved into the refrigerator. As soon as the customer had left, she and Wren both pounced back onto the conversation with Kate.

"Tell," Emily commanded as Kate handed her a coffee. "What's going on?"

"And when did this happen?" Wren chimed in as she accepted her cup from Kate with a smile.

"Yesterday morning." Kate smiled. "We're still working things out, but it's definitely happening."

"Good," Emily commented as she sipped at her coffee before setting her cup down with a smile and attending to another customer. It seemed their days of being able to relax for a coffee and leisurely chat were behind them.

"You don't think we're rushing?" Kate asked, curious.

"Nope," Emily said as she returned to the conversation. "It's a natural progression, and you guys are good together. Of course," she went on, "it makes me feel better about telling you that Brad and I have been talking about it too."

The two women turned and looked at Wren.

"We haven't talked about it," Wren answered the unspoken question, biting the inside of her lip. It was true. She and David hadn't discussed living together. They had, however, discussed marriage.

"So you and Brad," Kate said with a speculative glint. "You're going to have to tell us more."

"I could," Emily agreed with a nod, "or I could get back to work." She swigged down her coffee as another customer approached.

"She got out of that easily enough," Wren commented as Emily greeted her customer with a smile and got to work.

"Sure did," Kate replied, nodding as Emily called out the coffee order. She grabbed a takeout cup and set the coffee to percolating. "There's something else we need to talk about too."

"Which is?" Wren gave Kate a wary look.

"Our Christmas party," Kate answered as she poured some milk into the stainless steel jug and began to froth it.

"Ohh." Wren's face lit up. "Have you thought of anything?" As far as Wren was concerned, it was a welcome distraction. She avoided the topic of her relationship with David as much as possible, not wanting to jinx what was going on.

"I've been looking around at some bars we could go to," Kate said as she poured the milk into the cup and spooned on some milk froth before covering it with a plastic lid and handing it over to Emily. "And some restaurants nearby."

"Right." Wren nodded. "Guess it won't be as small as last year's get together, either."

"You're right there. For one thing, there's Emily and Brad." Kate smiled.

"And David and Michael," Wren added.

"And Paul and a date if he's got one," Kate went on. "And maybe Tom, if he wants to come along. He's dating someone, and it sounds like it could be going well."

"Really?" Wren was surprised at this. "You've heard from him?" Since Tom and Kate had what Wren now referred to as "The Talk," he had been missing in action for a few weeks.

"Not often, but we've been emailing." Kate shrugged. "And he calls from time to time. This new guy sounds ... nice."

Wren watched Kate's expression turn thoughtful. "Is that nice in a good or bad way?"

"Huh?" Kate glanced at Wren as she put the milk in the fridge. "Oh, it's good, definitely good. Tom was actually sounding relaxed when we spoke. I think he might actually be settling down."

"Sounds like everybody's doing it," Wren commented as she picked up a dishcloth and gave the counter a quick wipe. "Maybe relationships have gone viral this year." She grinned as Kate laughed. "But back to the main topic, what ideas have you had?"

"Actually ..." Kate stepped away from the coffee machine and leaned against the counter behind her as she folded her arms. "I was thinking about maybe having the party here."

"Here?" Wren looked skeptical.

"What's here?" Emily appeared at Wren's elbow looking curious.

"The boss is thinking of having the Christmas party here," Wren explained.

"We get a Christmas party?" Emily looked excited. "That's so cool."

"It's nothing huge," Kate explained, "but I was thinking that we could have it here after hours. Think about it." She pushed herself away from the counter and rounded the coffee machine to gesture out to the shop front area. "We can move some of the tables aside, do it all by candlelight with some great music."

"And we can make some good food," Emily supplied.

"Oh, to hell with that." Kate turned back to the two women with a grin. "I'm getting it catered. I don't want us working in the kitchen if it's our party. Plus if we have it here, we can kick our shoes off and have a really great time."

"You know," Wren said slowly as she warmed to the idea, "I think you might be on to something." A thought occurred to her, and she spun around to point at Kate and Emily in turn. "We'll have to work out what you two are going to wear, of course."

"I didn't think it would take you long to get to that." Emily laughed. "I suppose you already have something in mind?"

"I may have one or two ideas," Wren said with a gracious nod.

"Ideas?" Kate prodded.

"Preliminary sketches," Wren clarified. "Along with some fabric swatches."

"You started designing what we were going to wear to the Christmas party?" Emily asked in a faint voice. Wren's forward planning could be a little intimidating at times.

"Not really," Wren admitted. "But I found some great vintage fabric pieces that I bought for a song and knew they would work for you two. Why not kill two birds with one stone?"

"You're on," Kate said with a decisive nod. "But I'm paying you for them."

"Like hell you are." Wren snorted. "They're my Christmas present to you guys."

Kate walked toward her and put a friendly arm around her shoulders for a gentle shake. "Wren, I'm paying you for my outfit one way or another, so just get used to the idea."

"I won't take the money," Wren said as she put her hands on her hips.

"Tough," Kate replied in a voice that was just as stubborn. "Everyone that knows you figures it's only a matter of time before you're selling your stunning creations, so you might as well get used to the idea."

Wren looked up into Kate's warm regard. "What, you don't want me here?"

"Are you nuts?" Kate scoffed. "You will always have a job here, but I think we both know that toting coffee isn't your real passion. We're all just waiting for you to take the leap and do it."

"Huh?"

"Okay." Kate rubbed her forehead with her free hand and then gently pushed Wren toward a free table. "This is going to take a couple of minutes. Emily, are you okay for a while?"

"Yup." Emily nodded. "Go do your thing."

Kate turned back to Wren. "Sit." She pointed at a chair. Taking the seat opposite, Kate leaned forward with her elbows on the table. "Wren, I've watched your design style get better and better. You've *got* to do something about it."

"Have you been talking to David?" Wren asked with slightly narrowed eyes.

"No, but it's good to know he and I are of the same opinion," Kate replied. "Wren, I believe with my whole heart that you are destined for greater things, and what I'm trying to say here is that I'm going to support you however you want to do it."

Wren opened her mouth to protest but then paused. "What do you think I should do?"

"I think we both know I don't know enough about fashion to advise, but maybe you could talk to Paul about the financial side of things. As for getting it all made, you can cut your hours back here, so you've got more time to work at home."

"Cut my hours? But you're just getting busy now that you've been reviewed."

"Then I'll hire another worker." Kate shrugged. "And you can help screen whoever it is, unless you know another Emily." Kate smiled at Wren's dumbfounded look. "You don't have to decide now. Take your time and let me know when you think you might feel brave enough to do it." Kate stood up from the table and walked around it to give Wren a quick kiss on the cheek. "In the meantime, let's get the Christmas party organized."

Wren gave Kate a grateful smile. "You know, you're a great boss."

Kate grinned. "Wren, don't call me boss."

"Sorry, boss."

Wren sat at the table a moment longer, and then looked up as some customers began to filter into the store. Glancing up at the wall clock, she saw that it was nearly lunchtime, and she had a feeling they were going to be very busy indeed.

David looked at his wristwatch as he waited to cross the street. It was the end of the day, and he was on his way to meet Wren at the bakery to walk her back to his place. He got out his cell phone and sent her a text.

Nearly there. C U in 5 xD

He kept his phone in his hand until he heard a quiet cheep and checked the screen.

V. busy day. Look for the tired zombie xW

They got home to David's apartment where he made them a quick dinner while Wren luxuriated under a warm shower. The meal was enjoyed on the sofa in front of the television, and David leaned back and flicked through cable channels as Wren gathered their dishes and gave them a quick wash. Retrieving some notes from his rucksack, he began to flick through some lessons, listening to a news station with half an ear. Twenty minutes later, he realized that Wren was pacing aimlessly around his apartment.

"You okay, sweetheart?" he asked as he looked over the back of the sofa.

"Hmm? Yeah, I'm fine," Wren replied in an absent tone as she flicked through the newspaper. "I just feeling like doing something is all."

"I thought you were going to have an early night?" David commented from his position on the sofa. He was a little surprised to see her looking so alert. She had all but sleepwalked home under his guidance, but now that she had eaten, she seemed to have a new rush of energy.

"So did I," Wren said in an absent voice as she read the local cinema offerings, "but I feel too wired to sleep. Let's go see a movie."

"O-kay," David said in a dubious tone. "Whatever you want is fine by me."

"Well, what do you feel like seeing?" Wren asked, her gaze not moving from the screen.

"Whatever you feel like." David shrugged as he scratched his chest through his T-shirt and went back to his lesson plan for the rest of the week.

"C'mon, there must be something you want to see."

"Nope, I'm easy," David said as he kept reading.

"Look, just pick one and we'll go," Wren said in exasperation.

"And I've already told you, I don't care what we see." He looked up to see Wren standing in front of the table, casually flicking through the movie listing.

"David." Wren stamped her foot. "I'm telling you to pick one." She thrust the newspaper into his lap and headed into the bathroom.

"What are you doing?" David called after her.

"I'm getting ready to go out," she called back. "Assuming you make a decision."

David watched her go with a slight smile. He honestly didn't care which movie they went to see, but it amused him to see her so bothered by his easy-going approach to the situation. For someone that was used to being in control, she didn't respond to uncertainty very well at all, but she needed to relax a bit. He pushed his glasses up his nose and looked at the movie offerings again.

"Okay," he said as he pitched his voice so that she would be able to hear him from the bathroom, "we'll go see the French one."

"Fine," Wren said. "But I'm choosing the snacks."

"Done," David answered. He got to his feet and looked around for some shoes. "Walk or cab?"

"You're just not able to make decisions today, are you?" Wren said as she breezed past him and reappeared holding his Doc Martin boots. "Here." She handed them over along with a pair of socks.

"How did you know I wanted those?" David said as he accepted the boots.

"Because I know you better than you think I do, and don't think—" she tapped a finger on his chest, "—that I don't know that you're pushing my buttons."

"Aw, c'mon," David tried to protest, but his grin gave him away.

"I knew it." Wren threw her hands up in disgust and went to collect her coat and scarf while David pulled on his boots. "Just tell me why?"

"Because it does you good to get all riled up sometimes." David finished lacing up and then strolled over to accept the coat that Wren held waiting.

"Can't think why," Wren muttered as she pulled her scarf on and around her neck with quick, angry movements.

"Well, for one thing…" David stepped closer so that he could slide his hands around her waist and pull her back against his hips, "…you're really hot when you're mad."

"Am not," Wren retorted as she ducked her chin to hide her smile.

"Yes, you are," David whispered, giving her earlobe a gentle nip before sliding his hands up to cup her breasts. "You are the sexiest, most exasperating woman I've ever met."

Wren's eyes fluttered closed, and she wavered between annoyance and arousal.

"Damn you, Watson," she growled. "Get your coat and let's get out of here before we miss the movie."

"Yes'm." David grinned before he made a soft growling noise and sank his teeth into her neck, backing away with a laugh as Wren wriggled and squirmed out of his grasp.

"That's just cost you some Junior Mints, smart guy," Wren said, although the smile on her face completely undermined her threat.

"Totally worth it," David said with an unrepentant grin as he finished pulling on his coat and followed Wren toward the door. He looked at her clothing and realized that they were going to have to pay a visit to her apartment soon to retrieve some more clothes. They clumped down the stairs together hand in hand, and David held the door open for her as she stepped outside with a wince into the cold night air.

"Oh." Wren turned to David suddenly and put a hand on his chest. "I can't believe I didn't tell you the news."

"Which is?" he asked, amused at the delighted smile on her face.

"Michael and Kate are going to live together." She grinned.

"Really?" David's eyebrows went up at this. Michael hadn't mentioned it to him, although he knew that Michael had been keen to finish his manuscript as soon as possible. The weather had kept them both from jogging, and he immediately made a mental note to call his friend soon to catch up. "Sounds like things are getting serious."

"Has he gotten serious like this before?" Wren asked as they walked and David scanned the traffic for a vacant cab.

"Not that I recall," David said, "although the opportunity has certainly been there." He glanced down at Wren. "How about Kate?"

"Dunno." She shrugged. "I don't think she's lived with another guy since Tom."

"Ah." David gave a sage nod. Wren had filled him in on that aspect of Kate's history. "Interesting."

"You could say that," Wren replied after they had walked on in a thoughtful silence. "Do you think they can do it?"

"Why not?" Now it was David's turn to shrug. "They've got as much chance as anyone." He gave her a sidelong look. "Even us."

"Yeah, right," Wren scoffed, and then looked up to see that David was still regarding her with a thoughtful air. "You're serious?"

"Sure, you know we've talked about this."

"Well, yeah," Wren said, floundering now. She had gone from introducing what she thought was a hot new piece of gossip to finding herself in uncharted territory. She had mapped out her life well enough so far but found, when it came to matters of the heart, she was completely lost.

"And?" David gently guided her back to the conversation. "What's your snappy comeback this time?"

"I can't believe we're talking about this again," Wren muttered. She withdrew her hand from David's arm and stuffed her hands into her coat pockets, hunching her shoulders against the chill.

"C'mon," David cajoled as he put an affectionate arm around her.

"I've told you before," Wren huffed in irritation. "I grew up getting told not to get married and not to have kids, and here I am."

"Mmm." David nodded. Wren's childhood was a touchy subject. "And you know I'm not going to push, *but*…" He paused to make sure he had her attention. "I'm not going anywhere."

"So I see," Wren replied as her hand crept out of its pocket to reach out for David's. He immediately clasped her hand in his own and gave it a gentle squeeze. The rest of the conversation remained unspoken and yet they walked on in perfect understanding.

℘

"I just don't get it." Kate sighed, flopping onto the bed and gazing at Michael as he shucked off his jeans and pulled on a pair of track pants.

She felt exhausted; every muscle in her body ached and she felt a hundred years old. Now that she was home, instead of resting, all she could think of was how much she had to do. That and how good Michael looked, of course. She was distracted from her thoughts of packing as she admired the play of muscles in Michael's legs as he pulled on his change of clothes. She had called him to suggest they meet at her apartment, but instead he'd surprised her by arriving at the bakery not long after closing time, in a cab that he had kept waiting with the meter running until she was ready to go. She had bundled up the day's takings, which had exceeded her expectations, and stashed them in the store safe before locking up and stumbling into the cab and Michael's open arms.

"You don't get what?" He walked over to the bed and crawled toward her.

"How I can have regular culls and yet *still* end up with so much stuff that has to move." She rolled onto her side and propped herself up on one elbow. "I'm having my doubts, Forrester."

"About moving?" Michael frowned as he turned his head to gaze at her.

"Not about moving," she assured him, and he managed to hide his relief. "Just the logistics." She waved her free hand at the room. "I mean, I work six days a week. I just don't see how I'm going to get this done."

Michael stared up at the ceiling for a moment, gathering his thoughts before looking back at Kate. "Well, I know one thing you could deal with so that you don't have to take it with you."

"Oh?" Kate was miles away as she tried to think of where she could get some more packing boxes. "What's that?"

"The elephant in the room," Michael said simply, and held his breath as she turned to look at him. "I've finished the manuscript. Why won't you read it?"

Michael held her gaze until she blinked and looked away. The silence stretched between them, and he found himself counting their breaths, wondering about the argon flowing between them. Such a simple thing: an inert gas that was used in fluorescent lighting. And yet it had been there in the vows and sighs of ancient lovers and the battle cries of Waterloo. Now it was floating between himself and Kate, and he watched her take a deep breath as she blinked and looked at him with worried eyes.

"What if…" She licked her lips and started again. "I'm scared that…" She blinked and cleared her throat. "It's just that…" Her hands twisted the hem of her shirt until Michael reached over and covered her hand with his. The warm of his hand seeped into her skin and soothed her.

"Say it," he urged her.

And suddenly it was that easy.

"I'm scared that I won't like it," she confessed.

❦

"There," Wren said as she dropped down into her seat and set her soda down in the cup holder. "That wasn't so hard, was it."

"No," David sighed as he sank down into his seat. He stowed his soda and rested his candy on his lap before reaching over to pull Wren closer. She took the opportunity to snuggle against him and open his box of Junior Mints at the same time.

"So," Wren began in an off-hand tone, "Kate sat me down and told me that I need to start doing something about my fashion."

"Really?" David glanced down at Wren, who kept her gaze firmly on the screen. "What did she say?"

"Just that I ought to take a chance and make something of it." Wren shrugged, holding the box of candy to David who shook some into his hand.

"Like I've been saying," David commented.

"Yup." Wren nodded. "She had some good ideas."

David waited, but it seemed she wasn't going to elaborate unless prodded.

"And?" he prompted. "What sort of ideas?"

"About how I could go part-time so that I'd have time to design. You know, supportive stuff like that."

"How did you feel about it?"

"I don't know," Wren admitted. "Flattered, scared, all that stuff." She frowned. "But I don't know if I can afford to go part-time. Until I start selling, my income can't really take a hit, not with rent to pay."

"You know we've talked about that," David said as he nudged her shoulder.

"I know." Wren looked up at him and wrinkled her nose. "I just..." She broke off and sighed. "It's a lot to take in. Can you give a girl time to think things through?"

"Sure." David nodded.

Wren blinked up at him for a moment, and then offered a hesitant smile. "So, this could all be really happening?"

"If you let it." David smiled.

"Wow." Wren blinked as a wave of excitement and fatigue washed over her. Rousing herself, she reached over and plucked a Junior Mint out of David's hand and popped it into her mouth. "Mmm," she said as the chocolate began to melt on her tongue. "Now I'm starting to feel relaxed."

"Right," David said with amusement. "We just had to go outside into the freezing cold to catch a cab downtown to a cinema so you could tell me your big news of the day and I could buy you exorbitantly priced candy."

"But it's making me feel better," Wren said in a small voice.

David looked down to see Wren peering up at him from where she had her head resting on his shoulder, and sighed.

"Then it's a good thing," he said in a gentle voice, and Wren smiled before snuggling against him with a quiet sigh as David rubbed his hand up and down her shoulder in a soothing rhythm.

The lights dimmed as the trailers began to screen, and Wren was asleep before the film's opening credits had even finished. David noticed this with a mild sigh and shifted slightly to get comfortable, resigning himself to watching a movie that he knew nothing about while his girl slept soundly against his shoulder.

❧

Michael blinked at Kate and felt himself relax. At last they were finally talking about the subject that they had been skirting for months, and it wasn't as bad as he thought it would be.

"That's what had you worried all this time?" He reached out and brushed some hair off Kate's face with a gentle hand.

Kate sighed and leaned into his touch before blinking sleepily at him.

She gave him a wry smile. "Well, that and the fact that Alistair told me a bit of what you were writing about."

"Right." Michael's lips tightened.

"Are you mad that I found out that way?" Kate ventured as she watched his expression.

"Yeah, a little," Michael admitted. "I wanted to show you myself without someone blurting it out, but somehow it just never happened. I wanted to," he went on, wanting to reassure her now. "I never wanted to hide it, but I was just waiting for the right time, and for some reason it just never came."

"Life's funny like that." Kate nodded. "Jack used to tell Paul and me not to wait because life isn't a dress rehearsal."

"Good advice." Michael nodded. "He was a smart man."

"He never thought so." Kate's smile was sleepier now. "He always said it was common sense, but have you ever noticed that common sense isn't common?"

Michael nodded as he ran his hand down Kate's arm and settled it on her hip as he pulled himself closer to her.

"Hmm." He ran his nose along Kate's jaw and nuzzled her neck, making her give a slow but delighted squirm.

"So," Kate ventured after they had exchanged a soft kiss, "how much am I in there?"

"A lot," Michael admitted. "But there are a lot of other characters too." He pulled back so that he could look into her eyes. "I didn't use your name, but there's enough in there for you to recognize as being you."

"Right." Kate considered this and nodded. She hadn't been able to work out what it was Michael had been writing. Of course, she could have spared herself the angst and taken him up on his offer months ago, but for some reason, she had shied away. Knowing she wasn't featured as some sort of biographical character gave a measure of reassurance that she hadn't realized she needed. "When does it come out?"

"The book?" Michael blinked at her change of tack. "Not for a while. There's a lot of work to be done. It could be anything from six months to a year."

"So long?" Now it was Kate's turn to blink in surprise. "What on earth do they have to do?"

"Well . . ." Michael took a breath and then glanced at her. "Do you really want the technical details?"

"Bring it on." Kate nodded.

"Well, for starters, Alistair will read it and send the manuscript back with his comments for revision. I might agree with some, all, or none, but it's a point for negotiation."

"But you said you'd already sent some to him," Kate pointed out.

"I did." Michael nodded. "That was when I wanted him to get a sense of what I'd been working on, but he hasn't read the whole thing."

"Gotcha." Kate snuggled a little closer to him, nudging him until he rolled onto his back and opened his arms so that she could snuggle against him with her head on his chest. "Go on."

"When I've made the revisions, the manuscript goes to a copy editor, and that person checks every word, the continuity, fact checking queries if needed, and then sends it back to the editor. Alistair then checks the comments and sends it back to me so that I can answer the copy edit manuscript."

"Mm-hmm." Kate's eyes fluttered closed. Michael felt nice and warm, and his voice was a reassuring rumble in his chest. He may not have realized he was doing it, but he was running his hand in lazy circles over her back and occasionally combing her hair with his fingers.

"So once that's done, the production department gets involved. They choose a typeface, and the typesetter prepares an original cast-off which is when we know how many pages the book is going to be." Michael paused as he thought about this. "That's when I usually freak out."

"Why's that?" Kate asked.

"I guess it's one thing to write the damn thing, but finding out it's going to be anything from four hundred to seven hundred pages is kinda daunting." Some of Michael's books weren't known for their brevity. "Then they come up with the cover art, which I have nothing to do with." Michael pulled a face at this. Sometimes he liked the cover art, other times he wondered if anyone in that department had taken the time to actually read the book, but it was out of his hands. "After that, I get a big fat package in the mail, and that's the galley proof."

"Sounds like a pirate police line-up," Kate commented, startling a rumble of laughter from Michael that set her head to bouncing up and down on his chest until his laughter subsided. Kate sighed and slid her arm around his waist as he kept talking.

"The galley proof is the typeset, unbound copy of the book, and if it's all okay, then they go into production. Then the marketing people get involved and they send off advance copies to everyone they can think of. Book reviews are usually arranged anything up to six months in advance, so Alistair has been kinda ticked."

"Why's that?" Kate lifted her head to peer at Michael.

"That damn writer's block." He smiled at her indignant expression, protective of a book she hadn't even read yet. "It threw the whole schedule out, but they're working on a new timeline now to get things up to speed."

"Well, that wasn't your fault." Kate huffed as she settled back against Michael's shoulder. "You didn't know you were going to get writer's block."

"True," Michael agreed. "But I have to say that the cure for it has been amazing and life changing."

"What was it?"

"You." Michael smiled at her look of surprise. "It was always you, Kate. I just didn't know that until I found you."

Chapter 25

Fashionable Phases of Life

"I think that's the last of it," Paul said as he shifted the stacked boxes off the moving trolley and stood wiping his face with the hem of his T-shirt.

"Oh, you're such a good brother," Kate said as she emerged from the bedroom to collect another box from the ones Paul had piled up in the living room.

"I'm your favorite brother, right?" Paul gave her a hopeful look.

"You're my bestest, most favorite brother," she assured him.

"That's what I thought." Paul grinned.

"And the fact that I'm going to be cooking for you for the next year to thank you for helping me move has nothing to do with it," Kate went on.

"Well, it doesn't have to be a whole year," Paul said after a ruminative pause. "But regular cupcake offerings will certainly be highly regarded in terms of paying off this massive debt of thanks you owe me."

"How massive are we talking about here?" Kate called as she hefted a box and carried it over to set down in front of the bookshelves.

"Oh, I'm thinking at least once a month," Paul suggested with a grin. He peered at the boxes in the pile and read Kate's handwritten label on the top. Seeing they were full of books, he gave a quiet sigh and eased them back onto the trolley so that he could wheel them over to Kate. "How about I just set these ones here, and you can unpack when you're ready."

"Thanks," Kate said in an absent voice as she stuffed a handful of books onto an empty shelf.

Paul watched her efforts with mild interest as he took the opportunity for a break.

"Aren't you going to put them into some sort of order?" It hadn't escaped his notice that Michael's bookshelves were alphabetized.

"Nope," Kate said. "I like having them in random order. It means I have to go looking, and then sometimes I find books I forgot I had." She gave him an impish grin. "Plus it's going to freak Michael out."

"If that's what you want," Paul said with a low chuckle.

"I figure it can't hurt for him to get a little ruffled on occasion," Kate went on, completely unaware that Michael had entered the apartment and was silently creeping up behind her.

"Like that, is it?" Michael said in a low voice beside Kate's ear, laughing and stepping back when she shrieked.

"Michael." Kate turned and swatted his arm as he ducked away with a grin and set down the box he was carrying. "And you …" She turned and pointed at Paul who was wearing a matching smile. "Thanks for your backup there."

Paul spread his hands in a gesture of surrender. "Hey, I'm not getting involved."

"Right," Kate scoffed as she reached for another handful of books. Michael watched as she studied the spines for a moment and then set them on the shelf, shoving them against the other books already there and holding them steady as she reached for more.

"I hadn't actually thought of it like that," Michael commented, and went on when Kate looked up at him. "The random order, I mean. I think I like it."

"Try it sometime and see what you think," Kate offered. "And it's not so random; I usually remember where they all are. My books are all like old friends to me."

"And soon you'll have a new one, right, Babycake?" Paul commented as he reappeared from the kitchen having fetched a glass of water.

"Let's hope so," Michael answered. "Paul, I'm getting another box. See you down there?"

"Sure, let me just finish this." Paul held up his glass, and Michael nodded before leaving the apartment. He turned to Kate as soon as Michael had gone. "So, he's told you more about the book?"

"A bit." Kate nodded as she reached for more books. "We had a talk about it a couple of weeks back."

"And you're telling me now?" Paul looked affronted.

Kate emptied the box and set it aside to reach for the next one. She would go back and sort through the books later, but for now she just wanted to get rid of the packing boxes. As it was, the apartment looked like a war zone, and although there was more than enough space in the place, Kate found it unsettling to see her surroundings in such a state of upheaval.

"Yup." Kate nodded.

"So how much do you know?" Paul chugged down his water and set the glass down on one of the boxes.

"Enough to wait until it comes out," Kate replied as she gave him what she knew was an infuriating smile.

"Aw, c'mon," Paul protested as she knew he would. "You've gotta give me more than that."

"Nuh-uh." Kate shook her head as she picked up a box labeled KITCHEN. "I want to be as surprised as everyone else."

"How surprised?" Paul narrowed his eyes as he watched her reaction. He was fishing for clues, however small.

"*Good* surprised," Kate confirmed and then turned to walk toward the kitchen. "You'd better not leave Michael waiting."

"Right," Paul muttered as he ran his hands through his close-cropped hair. "Good surprised? Okay, I can work with that." He headed out of the apartment sure he had heard a muffled laugh as the door closed behind him. He got downstairs to see Michael leaning against the truck.

It had taken Kate two weeks and a few mornings off work to get her things packed up. There were a few choice pieces of furniture that she would be bringing with her: Gwen's armchairs, Jack's barometer, the coffee table from the family home. But for the most part her furniture was not something she had a deep sentimental attachment to. Her books, on the other hand, were an entirely different story. Her bookshelves had been lovingly packed away, and along with her art collection, were amongst the first items to be moved. Paul and Michael had provided the muscle, and Paul had procured a truck from work to help out.

"Sorry, man," he apologized as reached the street and jogged toward the truck as he fished out his keys. "Kat and I got talkin'."

"No worries." Michael waved off the apology. "Everything okay?"

"Sure." Paul grinned. "She was telling me about the book."

"Really?" Michael's eyebrows went up at that. "So she told you about..." Michael broke off and considered Paul who did his best to look unconcerned. "Wait, she didn't tell you anything."

"Dammit," Paul groused as he tossed back the tarpaulin cover and started to pull an armchair toward him. "I thought I had you there."

"You nearly did," Michael admitted as he helped lift the chair. "But Kate told me how you guys used to play your folks against each other when you wanted something."

"Well, hell," Paul grunted again as they lifted the chair off the back. "Two against one, that ain't fair."

"Sure isn't," Michael agreed with a grin as they shuffled through the front door of the building and toward the service elevator. Michael hit the call button with his elbow, and when the elevator doors opened, they carried the chair inside and set it down. Watching Paul as he punched the button, Michael cleared his throat and straightened up. It was now or never. "Paul, there's something I've been wanting to talk to you about," he began.

℗

"Morning, boss."

"Wren, don't call me boss."

"Sorry, boss." Wren beamed. "So, how was the big move? Are you all done?"

"Mostly." Kate nodded as she unlocked the security grill and rolled it up.

"What does that mean?" Wren asked as she watched Kate unlock the front door. "Are you in or not?"

"I'm in," Kate replied. "But I've still got to go back to my place and finish cleaning it to get it ready to rent out."

"Sounds like fun," Wren commented as she followed Kate inside.

Kate flicked on the coffee machine and continued into the kitchen to wrestle out of her goose down coat.

"So how was last night?" Wren asked as she followed suit.

"Quiet." Kate laughed. "By the time we had everything moved, we were beat. Lucky for us, Michael ordered enough pizza to sink a battleship."

Kate smiled to herself as she slipped her apron on and tied it up at the back, thinking about the evening before.

The moving process had progressed well enough but it wasn't until everyone sat down to relax that the efforts of the day had caught up with them; Kate had been so tired she had barely been able to string a sentence together. Pizza had been ordered and consumed with minimal conversation, and Paul had been yawning enough to split his head by the time he had called it a night.

The sound of the refrigerator door closing jolted Kate back to the task at hand, which was getting the morning coffees going, a task she was reminded of as Wren thoughtfully grabbed the milk out and set it on the counter as a prompt.

"So after dinner," she said, resuming the conversation about the night before, "I don't think any of us were capable of doing much."

"And then what?" Wren asked as she followed Kate out to the storefront.

"Not much." Kate shrugged as she got out some cups. "We ate and talked for a while, Paul left, and we called it a night."

"I see." Wren gave a hopeful leer at Kate who looked at her for a moment before pushing her hair off her face.

"No, you don't." Kate gave a tired chuckle. "We slept like the dead, and when I got up this morning, I had to try to remember where I'd put everything."

"Really?" Wren looked disappointed. "I thought you guys would have been celebrating."

"Oh, we've been celebrating," Kate assured her. "Just not yesterday."

"Gotcha." Wren nodded, and then looked up with a smile as Emily pushed the door open and stepped in, her cheeks pink with cold. "Hey, girl."

"Hey," Emily greeted them as she breezed past to hang up her coat. "Get that coffee ready, boss. It's *cold* out there."

"Comin' right up," Kate assured her and then looked at Wren with a raised eyebrow. "Milk?"

"What do you think that is?" Wren nodded at the milk container she had set down on the counter earlier.

"I didn't even see you do that," Kate said as she reached for it. "Wren, you're *good*."

"That's what you pay me for," Wren said with a complacent sigh.

Emily reappeared, and the three women got to talking about their weekend, Kate's move and important fashion advice from Wren.

"Dresses are fine, but I'm saying you're going to want a heavier fabric this time of year," Wren instructed as she sipped at her coffee in between tasks. "I've got a gorgeous wool blend print that is going to lend itself beautifully to what I have in store for you," she went on as she gestured at Kate with her cup.

"Oh, what plans are those?" Kate looked up from her order forms.

"Let's just say it'll be a masterful blend of Diane von Furstenberg and my devious mind," Wren said in a satisfied tone.

Kate tapped her pen against the clipboard as she considered Wren's words.

"Did you understand any of that?" she asked Emily.

"Not a word," Emily assured her. "Let me know when she comes out with the English language version."

"Guys," Wren huffed, "all you need to know is that you're going to love it."

"Then that's all we need to know."

"Oh, and that you need to get boots," Wren added as an afterthought.

"What sort?" Emily asked as she looked up from her inventory of the freshly chopped ingredients she had assembled on the counter.

"Knee-high," Wren began as she ticked off the salient points on her fingers, "black or brown. You can get either, but let me know which color you go with, and the heel I'll leave up to you."

"Generous of her," Emily muttered in an amused undertone to Kate who gave a quiet snort.

"I heard that," Wren snapped. "Now pay attention. I'm only going to say this once. No accessory shopping."

"Huh?" Kate looked surprised at this.

"You heard me," Wren replied. "I'll talk to your boys. They should have some input into this, given you'll be wearing my dresses to our Christmas party."

"What sort of input do we have?" Emily objected.

Wren gave her a pitying look. "Didn't I just tell you that you could buy boots?"

"Is that it?" Emily stared at her.

"That's it." Wren nodded. "Now if you two have finished asking questions, time's a-wasting. Get back to work." She waved an indulgent hand before winking and sailing out into the store to check the condiment supplies on the tables, and once satisfied they were all right, she went to get the chalkboard.

"Wow. When she's on a mission, she gets drunk with power," Kate commented in a stage whisper to Emily.

"I can't deny it," Wren sang back. "It's like a drug." She grabbed the chalkboard and carried it over to the counter where Kate stood waiting. Wren held out her hand. "Chalk me," she instructed, grinning when Emily passed the stub of chalk over with all the efficiency of a surgical nurse. "Here goes," she said and wrote quickly.

"Any clues?" Emily said as she leaned over the counter to get a look.

"No clues needed. I'm done," Wren quipped. She dropped the chalk into its waiting cup and then swiveled the chalkboard so that the other two women could read it.

Lead me not into temptation,
I can find it myself.

"I love it." Kate laughed. "But you're getting soft, Wren. What's up with that?"

"Let's just call it an early Christmas present." Wren shrugged. "And I had a hankering for what I thought you might make when you saw this."

"Right." Kate nodded. "You better hope I have some," she said as she walked into the kitchen.

"Are you two talking in some kind of code?" Emily asked.

"Kinda," Wren conceded, "but you'll get the hang of it soon enough." She looked up as Kate reappeared in the doorway.

"You're in luck." Kate smiled before she disappeared again.

"I love it when a plan comes together," Wren said as Emily gave her a measuring stare. "What?"

"You know, you're the only one that seems to know what's going on around here today," Emily said as she paused, bagel in hand.

"Yeah." Wren couldn't conceal her satisfied snicker. "It's great."

"Right." Emily went back to work, thinking about the situation while Wren strolled to the stereo and put some more music in. "So," she ventured after a considered pause, "I'm thinking maybe you could share some of the goods."

"Huh?"

"Well, you know what we're up to these days, how about what's up with you?" Emily ventured. She kept making the bagels and wraps with her usual efficiency, but a brief glance upwards showed that Wren had paused in the act of flipping through the folder of CDs that Kate kept in the store.

"Oh, you know," Wren commented in a perhaps too casual tone. "The usual."

"Ah, so you're talking about moving in together, then?" Emily added.

"Who told you?" Wren whipped around to face Emily with a startled look on her face.

"No one." Emily grinned. "But you just did."

"Shhh." Wren frantically waved her hands in a shushing gesture. She opened the folder and grabbed a disc, put into the stereo, and pushed play. As soon as the Black Eyed Peas were pumping out of the speakers, she started talking again. "We're only—" she waved a hand in a vague motion, "—you know, talking."

"That's generally how these things start," Emily noted with a droll smile. "But what brought it on?"

"We went shopping over the weekend." Wren shrugged as she began filling the water jugs. The mixer started up in the kitchen, and Wren relaxed slightly knowing that she wasn't about to be put on the radar just yet. "I got excited over some vintage clothes, we started talking about my fashion, and he wanted to talk more about Kate's offer."

"It's a good offer," Emily replied. "You know we love you here, but, honey…" Emily downed tools to give Wren her full attention. "You've got such a talent. Why don't you see where you can take it?"

"You sound like David." Wren gave her an amused smile as she dropped slices of fresh orange into the jugs before hefting them to carry them over to the small table where they would sit for customers to help themselves. "He keeps telling me the same thing."

"Maybe we're right," Emily commented. "We'll always want you here, babe, but just ask yourself," she paused and looked at Wren, "do you still want to be here in ten years' time, or do you want to be doing something different?"

⁓

Michael took a few steps back as he inspected his handiwork and grinned at the thought of how different his life had become over the last few months. Gone were the mornings of museum-like quiet in his apartment. Now he woke to the sounds of cohabitation: quiet singing in the shower, the rustling of clothes, and clinking of plates and cups in the kitchen. Power tools shattered today's peace and quiet, and he found he couldn't be happier about it. Kate's move had gone smoother than anyone had expected, although Paul hadn't been surprised.

Earlier that morning he had woken to the sound of a soft curse, and had cracked his eyes open to see Kate looking blearily at the time on her bedside clock before she had settled back into his arms with a quiet sigh. The pair of them had stayed in bed, tangled around each other as the minutes ticked by before Kate had nuzzled his neck and moved with regretful smile.

"Stay?" he had asked in a hopeful voice. The weekend had been a rush of boxes and unpacking, and he was still looking forward to the notion of waking up without either of them having to go anywhere.

"Want to, can't," she had replied in their sleepy morning shorthand as she hauled herself into a sitting position and sat there for a moment, trying to wake up. Michael had reached up and ran his hand lightly down her back before cupping his hand on her hip. Kate had turned her head to look over her shoulder at him. "You're not helping."

"Sorry," he'd mumbled into his pillow, but he really wasn't. His lips had curled into a smile as she leaned over and brushed a kiss against his cheek, squirming away as he reached for her again.

He had dozed in bed until Kate had left for work, and after a quick breakfast, had retrieved the supplies he had stashed under the bed where he had hoped Kate wouldn't find them. A couple of hours later, Michael frowned and climbed up the ladder to jiggle what he had just fixed to the wall to ensure that it was sturdy. Satisfied, he climbed down again and put away the stepladder before returning to sweep up after himself. He looked at the walls again with a slight grin; Kate was going to love it. He glanced at the items that had been left stacked along the bookshelves and hesitated over them for a long moment. It had been his plan to have the project finished for when Kate got home, but now that he stood so near completion, he realized the pleasure should be hers. He stepped away with some reluctance and began to pack away the drill instead.

He was eager to see her reaction, but for now he was going to have to wait.

"Now?"

"Not yet," Kate called back in answer to Wren's plaintive question.

There was a very brief pause. "Okay, how about now?"

Kate choked back a laugh as she finished garnishing the cupcakes on the tray, and then stepped back with a nod of satisfaction. Wren had timed it well as the batch was ready, but she still got a kick out of making her wait. She turned toward the sink and washed and dried her hands before picking up the tray and walking out of the kitchen.

"Here they are," she announced as she appeared in the kitchen doorway.

"Finally." Wren turned and put her hands on her hips as she watched Kate walk toward the display cabinet.

"You just can't handle suspense at all, can you?" Kate commented with a short laugh as she set down the tray.

"Not when I'm hungry," Wren quipped as she got three cups off the shelf and set them down next to the coffee machine with an expectant smile. "And I just know one of those will go great with a coffee."

"Do you now," Kate drawled. "Well, I guess we're lucky there's good coffee available."

"Damn right." Wren nodded as she fished out her piece of chalk. "Okay, boss, what are these ones called?"

"I'm calling these ones *Original Temptation*, Apple Crumble Cupcakes," Kate announced as Wren scribbled furiously.

"Nice." Wren propped up the chalkboard on the waiting easel. "They'll go well today."

True to her prediction, two customers stepped up to the counter moments later and ordered coffee and temptation cupcakes to go.

"There's just no resisting those," one of the customers remarked.

"Preachin' to the choir." Wren smiled as she reached into the display cabinet with the tongs.

"Mom, you're not telling me anything I don't already know." Michael laughed as his mother huffed at him through the phone line.

"Oh, really? That sure of yourself, are you?"

"Uh." Michael sobered at that. His parents had called to see how the big move over the weekend had gone, and Michael was filling them in on the details. "Well, no, not entirely. I don't know that I'd ever think of it as a *fait accompli*."

"Good." Michael was startled to hear his father's voice on the line. "But it sounds like you have things well in hand."

"Dad?"

"Morning, son," Charles greeted him. "I heard the tone in your mother's voice and knew who she was talking to, so I picked up the extension."

"Oh, now there's a comment that's going to get you places," Susan retorted.

"Now I'm the one in trouble?" Charles objected. "How did that happen?"

"Well, you—" Susan began but broke off as Michael interrupted.

"Guys, do I need to be here for this discussion?"

"Sorry, honey," Susan soothed. "Your father gets these ideas in his head sometimes."

"It's called independent thought," his father chipped in with a dry rebuttal.

"And any other comments like that are called 'you're getting your own dinner,'" Susan retorted, making Michael laugh.

"Thanks, guys. You're making me feel really good about this."

"So what's it like, living with Kate?" his father asked.

"She only moved in yesterday," Michael pointed out, "but all signs point to pretty damn good so far."

"Good to hear," his father praised. "Just remember to agree to everything, and you'll be fine."

"Wait a minute, I don't remember you using that tactic with me," Susan pointed out.

"Uh, son, a little help?"

"I'm not getting involved," Michael vowed.

"That's my boy," Susan said in a fond tone, "taking your mother's side. Well done."

"Who said he was taking your side?" Charles objected, making Michael grin. For a smart man, his father really managed to dig himself into a hole at times.

"I did," Susan replied. "Don't you think that's the right thing for a good son to do?"

"Yes, dear," Charles sighed after a heavy pause.

The conversation degenerated into a babble of explanations and laughter. By the time Michael got off the phone, he was none the wiser about the best approach to take, although he felt more convinced that he was doing the right thing.

❧

"So have you worked out what you're going to do?" Wren asked as Kate rinsed the coffee filter before clicking it back into place.

"Yup," Kate replied and looked out at the activity in the store before turning toward the notebook she kept on the workbench beside the phone. "And you've just reminded me I have to make some calls to confirm the details."

"When do we get told?" Wren asked, her eyes bright with curiosity.

"As soon as I've confirmed things, I'll tell you guys straight away. You're going to like it so just calm down."

"Okay," Wren grumbled as she turned to the counter where a customer stood waiting. "Can you believe she won't tell me anything?" she asked the customer, jerking her thumb over her shoulder to indicate Kate's departing back.

"Tell you what?" the customer asked, distracted from his eager perusal of the lushly sugared wares in the cabinet.

"I don't know." Wren shrugged. "But I wanna know. Now, what can I get you?" Wren beamed.

"You know you're driving her nuts," Emily commented as she sidled past Kate, having cleared the tables of cups and plates.

"That's the plan," Kate replied in an absent tone as she reached for the phone. She glanced over at the door as more customers came in. The front door was kept closed in the cold weather, and Wren had switched on the overhead gas heaters which kept the room cozy without being oppressively hot. "Are you guys okay to deal with them while I make some calls?"

"Go ahead," Emily assured her. "If we need help, I'll let you know."

"Thanks, babe." Kate flashed her a grateful smile before picking up the phone and going into the kitchen to finalize some details.

The trickle of customers became a flood, and Kate was pressed back into service. The three of them were run off their feet for the next few hours until the lunchtime rush had slowed enough for them to take a short break.

"Damn." Emily grabbed a tissue and dabbed at her forehead and the back of her neck. "Where did everyone come from?"

"That review has really boosted trade," Wren agreed as she leaned forward with her elbows on the countertop and gave a long sigh.

"I don't know about you guys, but I need something to eat," Kate commented as she paused to untie her hair and pull it back into a fresh ponytail. Maybe she'd get a haircut soon, she thought, glancing over at Emily's smart bob. "What have we got that's good?"

"Everything's good," Emily said. "How about you go take a seat, and I'll bring you something."

"What about you?" Kate's forehead wrinkled with concern. "Are you going to get something to eat?"

"Listen," Wren butted in, "we've actually got a quiet moment. How about you two sit and eat, I'll make us some coffee, and then the boss here can tell us what we're doing for our party."

"Deal." Emily nodded. "Now you—" she nodded at Kate, "—go sit."

"Done." Kate turned and headed for the nearest table and sank down into the chair with a sigh of relief.

A few minutes later, Emily carried over two plates bearing lunch and set them down before taking a seat. "Thanks." Kate gave a grateful smile and then picked one up and took a bite. "God, these are good."

Emily took a bite of her own and stared at the display cabinet while she chewed thoughtfully. Stocks were holding well, and she took a moment to admire the latest offerings. Kate had been expanding her repertoire on an exponential basis, and Emily gave a quiet sigh as she looked at the blueberry and pear tarts that had been artfully dusted with powdered sugar and slivered almonds; one day she'd be able to bake things like that.

Wren made the coffees and served another customer before making her way over to the table and taking a seat herself, although she sat facing the door so that she could see any new customers.

"You're not eating?" Kate looked up from her plate with surprise.

"I'll grab a protein shake later." Wren shrugged. "Or a bagel if there's one going."

"Any reason for the lack of appetite?" Emily raised an eyebrow and laughed when Wren gave her an indignant look.

"Yeah," Wren said after giving them both a very pointed look. "It's because David insisted on cooking an enormous breakfast, so don't go getting any ideas." She sipped at her coffee and then set it down and looking at Kate. "So, c'mon, boss, spill."

"Okay." Kate finished her mouthful and sipped at her coffee before beginning to speak. "I've booked some *great* catering. Seriously, guys, you're going to love it, and Michael said that he and David are going to arrange the drinks. Paul's coming, and I think Thomas is going to stop by, so if there's anyone else you want to invite just let me know." Kate paused with a gleam in her eye. "Actually, Bear's being a little bit secretive lately; I think he could be seeing someone."

"Do you think he'll bring her?" Emily looked interested.

"Hope so." Kate smiled. "I'm as curious as all hell, so he'd better."

"Music?" Wren asked after a ruminative pause.

"Whatever you want." Kate shrugged. "Just remember we're going for an intimate kinda gathering."

"Right." Wren nodded, her mind ticking over with ideas. "What did you think of the window idea?"

"The sheers?" Kate squinted over at the windows. "I think it could work but…" She gave Wren a hesitant look. "I really want to avoid you guys going to any trouble. The party is my thank-you to you both, so how about we come up with something else?"

"Stars," Emily said suddenly, blinking as Kate and Wren turned to look at her. "Sorry."

"Care to elaborate?" Wren smiled over the rim of her cup.

"We've got to get the Christmas decorations finished," Emily went on. "I was thinking we could just get some metallic paper and cut out all different size stars and hang them on different lengths of ribbon." Emily took a sip of her coffee. "It's simple enough."

"And a nice classic look," Wren mused. "I like it."

"You do?" Emily was surprised and flattered at their resident style guru's acceptance of her simple suggestion.

"Sure." Wren nodded. "We can do that this week. It'll be fun."

"Do you always get excited over the prospect of extra work?" Kate grinned at her.

"When it's creative stuff, it never feels like work so…" Wren broke off as she remembered David's comments from a few weeks ago. "Anyway," she went on, "I'll take care of it." She finished off her coffee and stood up to get back to work.

"Interesting," Emily mused as they both watched Wren put away her cup and turn toward a new customer with a bright smile.

"Very," Kate commented before taking another bite of her lunch.

In the end, the three women only managed to grab twenty minutes apiece for lunch, and even that was disrupted by the occasional order. Kate was thinking about this as she locked up and began to head toward home. Ten minutes later, she realized with a start that she was heading in the direction of her old apartment and changed direction at the next intersection with an inward sigh. She was going to be late. Shoving her hands deeper into her pockets, she walked on.

Michael flicked the catch on the front door and walked back into the kitchen to give dinner another stir. A few moments later, he heard the door close and walked into the living room to see Kate standing in the hallway shedding her overcoat.

"Hey," he greeted her as he gave her a soft kiss. "You okay?"

"I'm fine," Kate grumbled before relaxing against his chest with a sigh. "I took the wrong way home, and then forgot my key."

"So that's why I had to buzz you in. I thought you were going all formal on me," Michael said with a teasing smile.

Kate gave a tired laugh against his chest, and then lifted her head as she gave an appreciative sniff. "Do I smell dinner?"

"Porcini mushroom risotto," Michael said with a pleased smile at her look of delight. "You go unwind, I'll finish up and then I've got a surprise for you."

"Which is?" Kate gave him a hopeful look.

"Not telling until you've shed your day," Michael said as he turned her in the direction of the bedroom and gave her a gentle push. "Go."

❧

Kate put down her fork with a sigh of satisfaction and smiled at Michael across the kitchen island. By the time she had showered off her day and changed into some old sweats and a T-shirt, Michael was dishing up dinner. It had all smelled so good that she had relaxed her usual rule and enjoyed a glass of red wine with the meal. Now she sat back in her seat and watched as Michael gathered up the plates and put them in the dishwasher.

"That was fantastic," she said as she swirled the wine in her glass, admiring the color of the liquid in the light.

"Let's see if you're saying that in a few days' time. I made enough of it to feed an army," Michael commented. "Mom gave me the recipe this morning, but she didn't think to scale back the quantities." He turned and saw Kate gazing thoughtfully into her glass. "Ready for your surprise?"

Kate perked up at that. "I'd forgotten," she admitted with a smile, "but hell, yeah."

"C'mon." Michael held out a hand and pulled Kate to her feet. "You can bring your drink," he offered as he began to lead her back out into the living room. "It's nothing much, but it's something I know we're going to get a lot of use out of." He gestured to the walls of the room, and Kate gave him a puzzled look before looking at where he was pointing.

"Is that ... picture rails?" She took a step toward the wall as she peered up at the ceiling. She gave him a look of delight before turning and following the tracks that Michael had installed on every wall. "It just keeps going. How much did you put up?"

"I've done the whole living room, a wall in the kitchen and the whole bedroom." Michael grinned at her. "C'mon, I know how many pictures you've got and you know we're going to keep getting more."

"You don't mind?" Kate stepped toward him, and then remembered she was still holding her wine glass. She turned and set it down on his desk before wrapping her arms around his waist. "I was worried that you'd feel a bit overwhelmed."

"Is that why you didn't hang anything up over the weekend?" Michael pulled her closer.

"Maybe," she admitted to his shirtfront. "I mean, your apartment is gorgeous and I didn't want to cramp your style too much."

"Kate, I'm a guy," Michael said, sighing. "Style isn't something I chart my life by, but I want you to feel like this is your home now."

"Okay." Kate offered him a shy smile that became wider as she glanced around at the wide expanse of living room walls. Oh, she was going to have *fun*.

❧

The days went by in a blur of activity and baking. Since the review, business had been building at a steady rate which had led Kate to wondering if she needed to find another new employee.

"I don't know if lightning can strike a third time," she said to Michael over breakfast on the day of the party. "I mean, first Wren and then Emily. What do you think the chances are finding someone else that will fit in?"

"All you can do is try." Michael shrugged as he spread some butter on his raspberry muffin and bit into it with a satisfied groan.

Michael could appreciate Kate's concern, but at the same time, he couldn't help but reflect on how good life was being to them. He got up and began to make himself another latte; Kate had been a very patient teacher, and although it was going to be a long time before he could consider himself a barista to Wren's exacting standards, he could make a decent coffee for himself. Carrying his cup back to his seat at the kitchen island, he sipped at it as he studied the long expanse of the apartment.

Kate had taken his advice to heart and set about making the apartment homey. Michael's framed vintage movie posters were now interspersed with Kate's collection of prints and found objects that made for a riot of color on the walls. Kate's latest interest was butterflies, and she had somehow acquired some framed specimens that floated on the wall beside some Indian shadow puppets and Michael's 1960s Modesty Blaise poster. It was a collection that logically made no sense at all, and yet somehow it all seemed to work.

"So what time do you want me there today?" Michael asked before biting into his muffin again.

"Has David called you about the wine?" Kate looked up from the notebook in front of her where she was ticking items off a list.

"Sure. He and I made a list of wines we're getting, so we'll deliver that to the store before you guys close for the afternoon. Anything else?"

"I don't think so." Kate tapped her pen against the pages as she thought. "The decorations are all up, Emily's bringing the candles, and Wren is bringing our dresses to work this morning." Kate paused and gave a short laugh. "I still can't believe she won't let us see them until tonight. Do you know anything?"

"Nope, only that she told me what I was allowed to buy," Michael said as he gave her a satisfied smirk.

"Fine," Kate sighed. "Be like that, then."

"Okay." Michael grinned at her as he licked some residual crumbs off his fingers and followed it with his coffee.

Kate stood up with some reluctance and rounded the island to stand between Michael's knees with her arms around his neck.

"Guess this is the part where I leave for the day," Kate murmured as she gave him a soft kiss.

Michael ran his hands up her sides and around her waist so that he could pull her closer. "Something like that," he agreed as he kissed her again. Kate smiled against his lips, and he took the opportunity to dip his tongue into her sweetness. It was so nice that he went back for more. By the time Kate managed to lean back, her eyes were heavy and dilated.

"Wow," she managed. "What was I doing?"

"I have no idea," Michael said as he pulled her back, "but I can think of a few things." He slid his hand up and under her shirt to feel her smooth warm skin beneath his fingertips. Kate moved closer still, and he felt his stomach clench as she tangled her fingers in his hair to hold his face to hers as they kissed. He'd been thinking about getting another haircut soon, but the feel of her fingers in his hair had him re-thinking his options.

"So those things you were thinking about," Kate ventured when they broke apart, "I don't suppose you could give me a general idea?"

"I believe I could," Michael said as he tried to look thoughtful before giving up and cupping her bottom with his hands and squeezing gently. "But it might take some time. I know you've got a busy day ahead and—" He stopped when Kate kissed him again.

"I'm ahead of schedule," she said in between kisses as Michael got up from his seat and began to walk her toward the bedroom. "And Emily has a key."

After making love, Kate had to shower and get ready for work all over again, which was probably a good thing as Michael had left her with a spectacular case of sex hair. She was late enough that Michael insisted on calling her a cab and joining her for the ride, kissing her all the way so that she entered the store pink and flustered but with a smile that would last the whole morning.

"Don't tell me," Wren deadpanned as Kate swept past them with a sheepish grin to hang up her coat in the kitchen. "Something came up?"

"I'm not even going to dignify that with a response," Kate called back after a snuffle of laughter.

"Just means I'm right," Wren retaliated as she got a cup to make Kate a coffee.

Kate was tying on her apron when she saw two zipped up garment bags hanging on one of the coat hooks in the kitchen. "Are these in here what I think they are?"

"No peeking," Wren hollered back before fixing Emily with a beady stare. "And that means you too."

"Gotcha." Emily nodded with a smile. Emily was feeling quite pleased with herself this morning. Although she hadn't beaten Wren to work—and suspected that she never would—she had arrived at the store earlier than usual to get the day going. It was Saturday, two days before Christmas, and they were all looking forward to the party that night. Emily had quickly set about making more cranberry muffins while Wren had made up some of their lunch bagels and wraps. The two of them had agreed a few days ago to get a head start on the day, and so far it seemed to be working well.

Kate stood at the counter, sipping her coffee and gazing around the store with approval. True to her word, Wren had cut out dozens of gold and silver stars in different colors and suspended them from the ceiling and windows with red metallic ribbon. The stars swirled and danced in the air and added a distinctive festive touch to the store. There were boxes of beeswax pillar candles waiting to be arranged throughout the store that evening for the party, and Kate could already tell that it was going to be a very enjoyable evening, especially if the morning had been anything to go by. She sipped at her coffee to hide her blush and satisfied smile.

"So, Wren," Kate said as she finished her coffee, "last quote before Christmas. Bring it on, baby.'"

"Oh, you're going *down*," Wren said with an evil grin as she grabbed the chalkboard and began writing. And kept writing. After a long moment, Kate and Emily exchanged a look of concern.

"Uh, you're not writing your life story there, are you?" Emily ventured.

"Hush," Wren scolded as she kept writing. Finally she held up the board, and the two women gaped at the board in unison.

The Four Phases of Life:
You believe in Santa;
You don't believe in Santa;
You are Santa;
You look like Santa.

Kate stared at the board for a long time, and then walked into the kitchen. Wren hung up the board and walked back inside to get herself another coffee. Ten minutes later, the kitchen was still silent. Wren and Emily glanced at each other, and then peered around the doorway to see something that they never thought they'd see: Kate flicking furiously through her recipe notebook, looking frustrated. Aware of their scrutiny, Kate looked up at them and offered Wren a wry smile.

"Damn, woman, I think you've got me."

"Are you shitting me?" Wren gaped at her and then looked at Emily in wonderment. "Do you have any idea how long I've been working toward this moment?"

"Yeah," Kate sighed and shook her head. "I guess it had to happen sometime."

"Wow." Wren was still stunned. "I mean—" She stopped as Kate pushed herself away from the counter and walked toward one of the smaller cupboards, and then dropped to her knees to forage toward the back of the lowest shelf. "Boss, what *are* you doing?"

"Getting your trophy," Kate's reply was muffled, but she emerged triumphant and got to her feet to walk toward Wren and hand over what she had been looking for.

"Ohhh." Wren's eyes were like saucers as Kate handed her a bottle of Bollinger champagne. "For me?"

"You've totally earned it." Kate grinned and then gave her a huge hug. "I'm so proud of you." She was startled, therefore, when Wren handed the bottle back to her.

"Put this in to chill," Wren advised. "We're having it tonight."

"What? No, that's yours, you earned it," Kate protested.

"C'mon, boss, I couldn't have done it without you providing the competition. Besides, it'll get the party off to a great start, don't you think?"

"If you say so," Kate said as she accepted the bottle. "But while we're in such a giving mood, I'd like to give you two your Christmas presents."

"What?" Emily squeaked. "You can't. I've got yours at home."

"That's fine, but I want my gifts to you to be opened when it's just the three of us," Kate explained. She went to her bag and pulled out the two embossed envelopes that she had arranged while she was out dropping off the day's takings at the bank. She walked back to Wren and Emily with a broad smile and handed them each an envelope.

Wren and Emily paused to glance at each other for a moment before Wren shrugged. "The hell with waiting," she said. "I'm going in."

Emily turned the heavy envelope over in her hands and noted the gold seal before she carefully opened it and removed the gold embossed card inside. As she read it carefully, she felt her mouth drop open with surprise.

"Holy sh—" she began just as Wren stepped forward and threw her arms around Kate.

"I love it, but it's too much," Wren protested.

Emily glanced at the card and had to agree. Kate had purchased them each "The Ultimate" treatment at the Tribeca Beauty Spa: a day of pampering and indulgence that didn't come cheap.

"Guys…" Kate disentangled herself from Wren and submitted to an equally fervent hug from Emily. "You totally deserve it. You two work so hard here, and my appreciation wasn't something that could be wrapped up in some sorta ornament." She gave them both a fond look. "I wanted to give you something really special, so I figured the gift of time that's just for *you* would be perfect."

"And it is," Emily gasped as she re-read the card. "I've never had anything like this."

"Which is why I did it," Kate went on. "Over the years, a lot of gifts just become *stuff*, so I wanted to get you an experience." She looked down and picked at an imaginary thread on her apron as she kept talking. "I couldn't do any of this—" she waved a hand to indicate the store, "—without the kind of help I get from you guys, so this is just…" She looked up and gave them a watery smile.

Emily and Wren stepped forward as one, and the three women wrapped each other up in a group hug that ended up with sniffles and laughter. The coffee machine gave a loud beep to indicate it was ready for work, and Kate set to making their coffees before disappearing into the kitchen to make some Christmas themed *Jack's Favorite* cupcakes.

It was going to be a good day, and an even better party. She just knew it.

ↄ

"You're sure there's nothing else you need?" Michael called over his shoulder as he walked into the living room tucking his dress shirt into his trousers.

"I'm as sure as I can be," Kate answered from the bathroom as she finished her makeup. "David delivered the wine, you dropped off the extras, Paul is bringing some music, the girls just have to bring themselves, and we're getting there early to meet the caterers and set up. Have I missed anything?"

Michael ran through a mental checklist: food, drink, music, friends. He slipped on his jacket and patted the pocket to make sure it was still there. Wren had given him instructions on what he was allowed to buy to match whatever it was Kate was going to be wearing, and he had taken her advice to heart.

"I think we're good," he called back.

"Okay then," Kate replied, and he heard the sound of a long zipper being opened. Kate had arrived home toting a garment bag that Wren wouldn't let her look at while she was still at the store. "Wow," Kate said at last.

"What? Can I see?"

"Not yet, let me get it on," Kate answered.

"Whatever it is, I bet it'll look great on the floor later tonight," Michael called back with a huge grin.

There was an amused pause. "And you're a *writer?*" Kate retorted, making him laugh.

Moments later when she appeared in the doorway, he was definitely at a loss for words.

The dress was simplicity itself: a wrap dress in a gray wool/jersey blend, offset by a black cherry blossom print and jet bead detailing. It hugged Kate's curves before falling in soft waves to mid-calf. Kate had teamed it with knee-high black leather boots, and she stood there a little uncertainly before Michael's silent scrutiny.

"You like?" she asked with a shy smile.

Michael licked his lips before replying. "Parts of me are already applauding."

Kate gave a delighted smile and walked toward him for a kiss, which he was only too happy to oblige. Michael ran his hands up her sides, and then held her out at arm's length, cocking his head this way and that as he studied her. "It needs something, though," he said at last.

"Ah." Kate nodded. This would be the accessorizing part that Wren had told her about.

Michael reached into his jacket pocket and produced a small box that he handed over with a smile. Kate looked into his eyes before lifting the lid, her lips forming an "O" of surprise. It was a vintage marcasite necklace, the polished jet and pyrite detail glinting as she removed it from the box to admire it.

"Allow me." Michael took it gently from her hands and moved to stand behind her so that he could fasten it around her neck where it swung to rest between her breasts. Michael's breath was warm against her neck as he nuzzled her for a kiss. "You like?"

"I love it." Kate turned to smile at him and was surprised at the nervous look on his face.

"There's something else that would look good on you too," Michael ventured. He dipped into his pocket again, and this time the box was smaller.

❧

Wren looked excitedly out the window of the cab as it pulled up outside the store.

"I don't think I've ever seen you so excited to get to work," David commented with a soft laugh as she scrambled out.

"I want to see how the girls look," Wren said as she stood and waited for David to settle the fare and follow her to the door.

The store looked warm and festive against the winter chill that was howling down the street. Kate had arrived early as promised, and the candles were all lit and glowing on various surfaces around the store, glinting off the dozens of stars the casting festive shadows on the walls as Michael Bublé's latest album crooned out of the speakers. Some of the tables and chairs had been moved to give them room to mingle, and the caterers were ensconced in the kitchen with all manner of enticing smells wafting out into the store.

"I knew you'd be the first one here," Kate called with a smile as she looked up from where she and Michael had been having a quiet conversation at one of the tables.

"Stand up, let me look" Wren commanded as Michael and David exchanged greetings. Kate dutifully got to her feet and did a slow twirl for her inspection. Wren felt very pleased with herself. "What did Michael get you?" Kate tipped her chin back to set off the necklace, and Wren stepped forward to look at it. "Oh, it's gorgeous. I love it." She grinned her approval at Michael, who inclined his head in a gracious nod. He was sporting a beaming smile, one that seemed out of proportion to her compliment, and she squinted at him in puzzlement before turning back to Kate and giving her the same look. Kate contrived to look innocent but a matching smile kept breaking through.

"What else did he—" Wren began, and then her eyes widened as she grabbed at Kate's hand. "Oh, my God," she squealed as she wrapped her arms around Kate for the second time that day.

"How did it go?" David asked Michael in a quiet voice as the women exchanged hugs and kisses of delight.

"Just like I hoped," Michael said with a smile. "You?"

"Soon," David commented, "but not yet."

"You'll know when," Michael assured him, and they both turned their attention back to the women they loved.

Emily and Brad soon followed Wren and David's arrival at the store. Like Kate, Emily had to offer herself up for inspection and approval, which was, of course, duly forthcoming by the designer. Emily was wearing a periwinkle blue tunic over black leggings, teamed with what looked to be a vintage cardigan, and of course like Kate, she had followed Wren's footwear suggestion. Emily had been eager to open her garment bag when she got home and had spent a long time pouring over the hidden details that Wren had included. The cardigan buttons had been replaced with black and white crystal creations that resembled snowflakes, and Emily had been delighted to discover the same buttons on the tunic's pockets and in a row down the back where Brad had to fasten her into the dress instead of zipping her up.

"You like?" Wren said after inspecting her with a proprietary air.

"Love it," Emily confirmed. She glanced at Brad and, seeing he was exchanging slightly star-struck greetings with Michael, stepped closer. "It's comfortable and sexy, and it does wonders for my confidence," she added with a grin. "I've never seen anything like it," she added in a slightly louder voice.

"You will soon." David had turned at Emily's pronouncement and draped an arm around Wren's shoulders with a smile.

"Really?" Kate hadn't missed that comment and her face lit up. "Wonderful!"

Anything else she had been about to say was drowned out by Paul's booming welcome as he entered the store with a date in tow, his gaze seeking out Michael's almost immediately. When he saw Michael's triumphant smile, he let out a war whoop of delight and lunged for his sister in a way that *really* got the party started.

"Kate, I'd like you to meet Christine." Paul wore a beaming smile as he put his arm around his date's shoulders to draw her closer.

"It's a pleasure." Kate smiled as the two women shook hands. "I'm really glad you could make it."

"Thanks." Christine smiled as she glanced up at Paul who winked at Kate. "It feels a bit like I'm crashing the party, but Paul insisted it would be fine."

"And rightly so," Kate assured her. "It's great to have you here." Kate considered her for a moment, cocking her head to one side. "Actually, this is going to sound really cheesy, but I think I might have seen you somewhere before."

Christine laughed at this.

"Oh, you sound like me. I say that to people all the time, but it's because I meet so many people. I've got a stall at the—" Christine broke off as she glanced over Kate's shoulder and a pleased smile appeared on her face.

"You were saying?" Paul asked with amusement.

"Um, I think we *have* met," Christine went on. "You've got my fox on your wall over there." She pointed, and Kate obediently turned to look at the wall before glancing back at Christine with a beaming smile.

"That was you? But this is wonderful." Kate was delighted. The night just kept getting better.

Wren darted into the kitchen and a few minutes later reappeared holding the Bollinger aloft and a waitress with a tray of champagne glasses in tow.

"Celebrations all round!" she crowed to Kate as she handed the bottle to David for him to open.

"You knew?" Kate asked, jumping when the cork was removed with a loud "pop."

"About that?" Wren gestured to Kate's hand. "Not at all, but I just knew this party was going to be one to remember."

"Big occasion?" the waitress asked as David began to pour the champagne into the waiting glasses.

"Pretty big." He nodded with a grin. "The owner there—" he indicated Kate with a nod, "—and my best friend—" another nod, "—just got engaged, plus it's the store's Christmas party."

"Oh, that's wonderful," she enthused as she watched the wine bubble into the delicate glasses. "This looks like a great place. They must have a lot of fun," she observed in a wistful tone.

"They sure do." David smiled.

The glasses were dispensed and held high for a toast of congratulations and wishes for the holiday season. Kate gave a gracious speech conceding victory to Wren, who in return offered her heartfelt congratulations to Kate and Michael as David stood by her side stroking her back. The store was warm against the chill outside, and the joy everyone felt just made everything seem warmer. Food began to circulate into the store from the kitchen, the music got turned up, and the party began in earnest.

A couple of hours later, Kate looked up as Michael leaned down to kiss her neck and whisper in her ear. The door was opening, and Thomas stepped inside with a smile. Kate blinked at him, trying to work out what was different and then realized what it was. He was fashionably dressed as always, but this time his smile of greeting seemed more authentic. There was no showman style greeting, no flamboyant expressions, just Thomas looking at her with a warm smile that reached his eyes, and he walked toward her holding someone's hand.

"Kate," Thomas greeted her, "hey, girl." He released his partner's hand to wrap his arms around her for a hug. Stepping back, he reached out and pulled his date to his side. "I'd like you to met Stephan."

"It's a pleasure." Kate smiled as she shook Stephan's warm and calloused hand. "Tom, I'm so happy you could make it. Things wouldn't have seemed the same without you here." Kate looked around to see that Michael was already arranging drinks for the new arrivals, and she beamed at Michael as he appeared at her elbow with two more glasses.

"Tom, it's been a while. How the hell are you?" Michael smiled as he handed over the glasses.

Kate watched as both men fell into an easy conversation. She sometimes doubted that Michael and Tom would ever enjoy a true friendship; Thomas still got territorial from time to time in an "I was here first" kind of way, which Michael matched with an unspoken "finders keepers." Fortunately, they were both able to recognize that their common bond was love and protectiveness for the woman that connected their lives.

"He was nervous, you know," Stephan mentioned in an undertone to Kate as Paul greeted Tom with the kind of cheer that indicated a major headache would be forthcoming the following day.

"Really? Why?" Kate looked at Stephan in surprise. They hadn't been talking for long, but Kate had taken to him immediately. Stephan was a furniture restorer, whose quiet, deliberate manner seemed to soften Tom's edges and bring a measure of peace to her friend. Watching the two of them together, she could see that Tom was genuinely happy in a way that made him relax at long last. It seemed that everyone had found a measure of completion to his or her life that had already seemed happy and full.

"It still bothers him," Stephan went on. "You know, the history with you and the way he came out."

"I don't see why. Things are fine now," Kate said as she sipped at her drink and accepted another canapé from the circulating tray.

"They are," Stephan agreed, "but now that he's happy." He gave a self-effacing laugh. "Sorry, I'm not trying to talk myself up here," he explained.

"S'okay, go on." Kate waved for him to continue as she chewed.

"Being happy now makes him realize how long he wasn't. Happy, I mean. I think he worries that he took it out on you or held you back some."

"I think it's safe to say that things have moved on," Kate answered, and at Stephan's questioning look, held up her hand so that he could see the ring.

"Is that what I think it is?" Tom appeared at her side. "Paul just told me." He wrapped his arms around Kate for another squeeze. "Sweet girl, I'm so happy for you," he murmured into her ear.

"Thanks, babe," Kate whispered as Stephan silently relieved her of her glass so that she could wrap her arms around Tom. She looked over his shoulder to see Stephan approach Michael and shake his hand as he offered his congratulations. "Looks like we all got our happy this year." They released each other, and Tom stepped back and looked at his feet as he cleared his throat, and then called for another drink. "I've just got one problem," Thomas announced as he accepted a glass.

"What's that?" Kate looked at him with concern.

"The music," Thomas sighed. "Let me guess. Bear?"

"Some of it," Kate agreed. "Not up to your standards?"

Thomas gave her a pitying look. "Oh, honey, we can do so much better, which is why I came prepared." He threw back his drink and went over to the small pile of discs Stephan had set down on one of the tables beside their keys and made for the stereo. The music was changed, the volume turned up, and then the evening just kept getting better.

Sometime later, Kate made her way over to where Brad and Emily were laughing and chatting with Bear. Christine had zeroed in on Wren as soon as she had discovered who had been behind the outfits Kate and Emily were wearing. Soon they were talking about the markets and their creative outlets.

"So, Brad," Kate began, smiling when she felt Michael's arm snake around her waist. They had been in constant contact with each other all night as their delight in each other seemed to grow. "Emily tells me that you knew about Michael here long before the rest of us."

"Sure." Brad nodded with a grin. He had been a little intimidated when first introduced to Michael, but the two men had talked about mutual authors of interest and Brad's work in the store. When he had heard that Michael's book was entering the production phase soon, he had scored a minor coup for his workplace with Michael agreeing to appear for a book signing and literary luncheon event.

"Brad, I think we might need to do something about this. Do you think she needs to know what she's marrying?" Michael teased as he kissed Kate simply because he could.

"Maybe some reading material?" Brad guessed.

"Sounds good," Kate replied as she grinned at Michael. "I guess I've got some catching up to do."

"I'd better get in on that given he's about to become family." Paul appeared between them and put his arms around their shoulders. He gave a theatrical sigh. "It's not often a new family member comes with study obligations."

"Sorry to cause all the extra paperwork." Michael laughed.

"I'll live," Paul sighed, and then he grinned at Kate as he released them both and reached for her hand. "Nice." He gave a low whistle as he looked at the ring. "You know you're giving Christine all sorts of ideas, right?"

"Christine?" Kate challenged him.

"Okay, me," he conceded. "I was hoping he'd ask you soon. The suspense has been killing me."

"You knew?" Kate looked in surprise at Michael, who nodded and took her glass to go get a refill. "Don't tell me he asked you for my hand in marriage."

"Oh, hell, no." Paul shook his head. "And besides, you're not mine to give away. It's your choice entirely. Michael just wanted to make sure I'd be okay with it."

"Really?" Kate was looking puzzled now. David had been standing nearby and, hearing their conversation, stepped forward after seeing Michael had been collared by Wren and Christine.

"Think about it. He's an only child of two academics. He didn't want for love, but his whole social interactions were very different. He grew up on college campuses, surrounded by adults, and then fell into an introspective career," David went on. "He's never been one to go around with his heart on his sleeve, but you've loosened him up more than anyone has before." David looked at his oldest friend and smiled. "I think you'll find he surprises you with how he goes about some things, but never doubt his sincerity."

"I don't," Kate vowed, her words brushing past David and flowing toward Michael who took a breath as he turned to her and smiled.

Michael looked at Kate enjoying herself, surrounded by people she loved. The walls of the bakery shimmered in the golden candlelight as laughter lilted around the room. Another bottle of champagne popped and was cheered by those nearby before it was poured into the waiting glasses. Words bubbled in the air, flowing from one person to the next, the argon tying them all irrevocably together for eternity. Words began whispering in the back of Michael's mind, and he returned to Kate's side to give her another kiss. The words were gathering momentum now, growing louder in his head, but they were tied to such a happy moment in his life that he knew he would be able to recall them with ease when the time came to begin writing again. He'd never felt more content.

Beginnings, Endings, and the Eternal Breath

Kate darted out of the kitchen to peer up at the wall clock in the store, and then returned to the kitchen with a sigh where she picked up her piping bag and got back to work.

"You okay, boss?" Kristyn paused in the doorway and looked at Kate with concern.

"I'm fine," Kate assured her. "Just waiting for something."

"Oh." Kristyn half-turned back to the storefront before stopping and looking at Kate. "So long as you're okay."

"Sure." Kate nodded at her again and poised the piping bag over the waiting cupcake. It was true; she felt perfectly okay although she wasn't sure she could say the same about Michael.

The store phone rang, and Kate re-appeared from the kitchen to snatch up the receiver before Kristyn or Emily could react. They could tell from Kate's smile that it was Michael on the line. The conversation was brief and ended with "I love you" before Kate hung up and turned to face them with a grimace.

"Tomorrow," she sighed. "There's been a hold up, and Michael will get his advance copy tomorrow."

"What's this?" Kristyn looked up from drying cups from the dishwasher and stacking them on top of the coffee machine.

"Michael's book," Emily explained.

"It's out?" Kristyn looked excited at the news. "Fantastic. I'll get a copy on the way home." She beamed at Kate. "I love his books. I can't believe you guys are married." She shook her head at the memory, amazed that she had been there the night one of her favorite authors had announced his engagement at a private party she happened to be working at.

"Sorry, Kristyn, you'll have to wait a few more days, but Michael gets a copy ahead of the stores."

"Figures." Kristyn shrugged. "He wrote it, after all. What do you think of his others?"

"Can you believe Kate hasn't read any of his books yet?" Emily nodded toward Kate who glanced at the wall clock and then took down three cups to make them a mid-morning coffee. Kate's reading habits—or lack thereof when it came to Michael's body of work—had been a recurring joke over the last few months, but Kate had stuck to her guns.

"You haven't?" Kristyn was amazed. "But what about the one with—"

"Nope." Kate shook her head. "I figured I'd start with the latest one when it's out, and then work my way backwards from there."

"Oh, I see," Kristyn replied, although she wasn't sure she understood at all. Kate seemed easygoing about it all, but she was bound to have her reasons. "Well, I'm sure you'll love it when it arrives."

"It just better arrive soon, that's all I'm sayin'," Kate muttered as she got back to work.

❧

The next day, Michael stood in the apartment doorway, signing for the special delivery package with a hand that was remarkably steady. Closing the door, he carried the parcel to the sofa and sat down to unwrap it. Discarding the wrapping paper, he sat turning the book over and over in his hands, and then after huffing out a long sigh, leaned back onto the cushions and began to read. Two chapters later, he remembered himself and snatched up his cell phone to send Kate a message.

It's here. Reading now xM

He picked up the book again and looked back at his phone when it chirped a few minutes later.

Cant wait. See you 2nite. xK

❧

Kate let herself into the apartment with a sigh of relief. After getting Michael's message, the hours had crawled by. Emily had finally snapped during the late afternoon and told her to go home. Kicking off her shoes and leaving them by the door, she walked into the living room.

"Hey," she greeted Michael who was sprawled on the couch with a book on his chest. "Is that it?"

"Sure is." Michael gave her a tired smile.

"Have you been reading it?" Kate crossed the room toward him and gave him an inquiring smile.

"All day," Michael admitted. "I finished it about half an hour ago."

"But I thought you already knew what it was all about," Kate commented as she nudged his legs on the sofa so that he could make room for her to sit down. She sat and picked up the book, running her fingertips over the embossed jacket.

"It wasn't a book when it left me." Michael shrugged as he sat up and scissored his legs around her waist to anchor her against him as he nuzzled at her neck, making her squirm as his stubble rasped against her skin.

"So what's your verdict of the finished product?" Kate asked as she gently set the book down on the coffee table in front of them and wriggled around so that she was curled up in his lap.

"I think I like it," Michael admitted, "but I'll feel better after you've read it."

"I'll start it tonight," she promised. "Can't have you suffering any longer."

"I'm relieved and terrified all at once," Michael admitted, and then gave a short bark of laughter. "And all these years I thought hearing back from Alistair was the hardest part."

"I'll be gentle," Kate assured him.

"You always are." He smiled back and ran his hands up her neck and into her hair. "Hey, wife."

"Hey, husband." Kate smiled before dipping in for a kiss.

True to her word, Kate read late into the night.

❧

Michael rolled over onto his side and buried his head in the pillow, blinking against the light that was flooding into the bedroom. He lifted his head and peered over Kate's shoulder toward the bedside clock, blinking until the displayed time could register.

"Baby." He gave Kate's shoulder a gentle shake. "Kate," he said a little louder this time. "You're going to be late."

"Not gonna," Kate mumbled as she rolled over and buried her head against his chest, frowning as she tried not to wake up.

"Yeah, you will." Michael swallowed a laugh as Kate shook her head again and curled herself tightly around him.

"Day off," Kate mumbled. She was waking up now, and rubbed her cheek against his bare chest as she began to rub her instep up and down his calf.

"Really?" Michael glanced at the clock and then down at his wife. Well, that just changed everything. "What for?"

"Emily told me that I had some reading to do, but I can think of a few things we could do first," Kate replied as she began to dust kisses across Michael's chest, swirling her tongue on his skin and nipping in a way that made him give an involuntary squirm. She offered him an impish smile as she began to wriggle around in the bed, working her way downward with her hands and lips and smiling at Michael as his face lit up with a delighted smile of understanding.

"If that's the way you feel," Michael murmured, his words ending in a soft gasp as Kate's hands and tongue swirled lower still.

"Oh, I'm feeling quite a few things," Kate said with a muffled laugh as her head disappeared beneath the sheets. Soon she was quite incapable of speech, but then again so was Michael, so it all worked out rather well.

An hour later, Kate was freshly showered and dressed. She walked out into the living room in time to see Michael padding toward her with a cup in his hand.

"What's this?" she asked as Michael handed her the cup and gave her a kiss.

"The start of breakfast," Michael said as he turned to go back to the kitchen. "Where do you want it?"

"Uh, I'll have it in the kitchen." Kate blinked at his departing back, and then sipped at the coffee. She followed him slowly and arrived to see him scooping the last pancake onto the short stack he'd made before spooning mixed berries and powdered sugar over the lot.

"Wow." Kate was impressed. "What brought this on?"

Michael looked up with a slight smile. "Can't a guy make breakfast for his wife?"

"Every morning as far as I'm concerned," Kate agreed and then waved a hand at the small feast he had created. "But this looks pretty special."

"I figured you need your strength for all the reading you've got ahead of you today." Michael rounded the island and guided Kate to her seat. Kate sank into the chair and picked up the small jug of maple syrup Michael had set beside the plate. A moment later, she looked up at Michael with round eyes as she chewed, giving him an enthusiastic thumbs up.

"Good?" Michael smiled and leaned down. It was meant to be a short kiss, but the sweetness of her answering smile and the maple syrup on her lips rapidly turned it into something more. "Whoa," he replied and stepped back licking his lips.

"Oh, I don't know about that, c'mere." Kate reached toward him with a gleam, but Michael stepped back, neatly evading her grab at his shirt.

"Breakfast, then reading," he admonished.

"Spoilsport," Kate grumbled, but she was smiling again as she returned her attention to her pancakes. She looked up in surprise minutes later when Michael reappeared wearing his running gear. "You're going out?"

"I need to run off some steam," he explained. He had been full of nervous energy ever since the book had arrived. The manuscript had been a ghost in their lives throughout their relationship. Now that it was published, its potential impact on their lives had become all the more real. He couldn't wait for Kate to read it, but that didn't mean he wanted to be there when she did.

"Okay." Kate sipped her coffee and nodded. "You go have fun; I'll see you when you get back."

"See you soon." Michael walked up behind her to kiss her neck before snatching up his keys and walking toward the door.

Kate watched him go with resigned amusement and then returned her attention to breakfast.

❧

Michael paused in the foyer downstairs to do some quick stretches, and then broke into a light jog as soon as he hit the pavement. He started by counting his steps, the number of pedestrians he had to jog around as he steadily increased his pace, and then settled for counting his breaths. By the time he got to Washington Square Park and saw David pacing in a slow circle, he was warmed up and ready to go.

"Hey," Michael greeted him as he caught up and they set off.

"Dude." David nodded. "So she has a copy?"

"Yup, got it yesterday." Michael nodded.

They jogged on in a companionable silence for a while.

"You okay?" David ventured.

Michael shot him a sidelong look. "Fine. She was just about to start reading again when I left."

"Ah." David gave a sage nod. "So that's why you wanted to get out this morning."

"I figured it'd be better for her if I wasn't pacing the apartment all day, watching her turn the pages."

"Good call." David nodded. He studied Michael as they jogged, noting with amusement that he hadn't seen Michael this nervous since his and Kate's wedding day. The day had been kept as low-key as humanly possible, and still, Michael had been a roiling mass of nerves until he had seen Kate enter the room laughing with Susan. Over the past six months, David had watched his friend reach a level of peace and contentment in his life that he had never known before. David hoped it would be the same for him, which was something he looked forward to discovering in the very near future.

"What time do you have to get to work?" Michael grunted as they rounded another curve of the trail.

"Late," David replied. "Juggled my schedule with one of the faculty so I could keep you company for a while."

"Yeah?" Michael looked surprised.

"Yeah, and get over it, Forrester." David jogged closer so that he could nudge Michael hard enough to send him staggering off the path. "We all know what you're like at times like this. I'm just doing my bit for misery control."

They jogged on in silence while Michael processed David's words.

"Thanks, man," he said at last.

"No charge," David replied with a placid smile.

❧

"…and there's your change." Kristyn smiled at her customer as she handed over some coins and a takeout coffee cup before turning to Emily. "Do you think Kate will come in today?"

"Doubt it," Wren commented on her way past. "Michael's books are *huge,* so if she can read his latest in a day, I'll be surprised."

Emily had called an emergency summit meeting of the troops when she had discovered the publication date of Michael's book. She, Wren, and Kristyn had banded together to tell Kate her services would not be required on the coming Wednesday—a decision Kate received with mild shock.

"But what about the store?"

"Hello?" Wren chimed in. "Have we burned it down on any other day that you haven't been here?"

"Well, no, but things are so busy lately," Kate began, stopping when Emily waved her down. The store had been reviewed again, this time by the *New York Times,* and trade continued to increase as a result.

"Enough," Emily said. "The three of us will be fine, and I have a cunning plan."

"How cunning?" Kate regarded her with a slight smile, touched at the girls' concern for her.

"So cunning you could put a tail on it and call it a weasel," Emily deadpanned before continuing. "The lovely Kristyn here has a barista friend who can come help out at short notice." She indicated Kristyn, who bobbed a quick curtsey. Kristyn and Wren had the same slight build and, it seemed, the same humming-bird energy level. "We'll be fine, which is why you need to stay at home and read."

Emily leaned against the workbench and surveyed the store. Business was going well, and she was delighted to see that her cupcakes for the day had been well received by the customers.

"Hey, Kristyn," Emily said, "how about you call your friend and ask if she can work here for a few days. I think Kate's going to be busy for longer than she thinks."

"Will do." Kristyn nodded and went into the kitchen to get her cell phone out of her bag.

❧

Michael fished his cell phone out of his pocket and checked the screen again. No calls. He sighed and put it away as he kept walking aimlessly. It was now Friday afternoon, and Kate had nearly finished the book. By unspoken agreement there had been no discussion about what Kate had read so far; they both wanted to wait until she had completed it so that they could discuss the story in full, but the nervous anticipation was killing him. Hours later, he was reaching a breaking point, walking out of yet another store after realizing he was doing little but staring sightlessly at the merchandise. He snatched at his pocket as he felt his phone begin to vibrate.

All done. Come home xK

Michael put the phone away, and then looked at the traffic around him. There were no cabs in sight, and so he broke into a run. Arriving home, Michael fumbled with the keys, cursing under his breath when he dropped them in his haste. As soon as he was inside, he was looking for Kate.

"I'm in here," he heard her call, and he headed for the bedroom, stopping dead in his tracks when he saw her.

Kate was curled up against the pillows, a pile of crumpled tissues beside the now completed book.

"Hey." She gave him a tremulous smile.

"Kate…" Michael paused and swallowed hard as he walked toward her and stopped at the foot of the bed.

"You're too far away." Kate held up her arms. "I need you here."

Michael shrugged off his jacket and kicked off his shoes before crawling across the bed to take her in his arms. Kate turned into his embrace with a sigh, and he only realized she was crying when he felt the damp warmth on his chest.

"Hey." He kissed the top of her head. "Hey, now." He reached down and gently tipped her face up so that he could look at her. Her eyes were pink and puffy from crying, and her bottom lip trembled as she looked at him. "Is it really that bad?"

"Michael." Kate reached for him, and he was surprised at the intensity of her kiss.

"I guess you liked it." He offered her a lopsided smile as she hiccuped.

"I love it." Kate nodded. "Really, Michael. I love it."

"Then I'm glad," he answered as he pushed her hair off her face with gentle fingers. He felt his whole body relax as Kate smiled and settled herself against him, wrapping her arms around his waist.

"He lived," Kate said after a moment of peaceful quiet. Michael's hand stilled on her hair, and she propped her chin on Michael's chest to look up at him. "Jack lived, in your book."

Michael resumed stroking her hair. "Is that okay?"

"Better than," she confirmed, and then snuggled into his chest again. "It was perfect." She thought back over the story and gave a sad smile. Michael had been truthful; there was enough characterizations and anecdotes in the book for Kate to recognize herself, but done in such a way that her privacy remained intact. Jack was in there too, alive and well on the printed page along with Paul and Gwen. There were even shadows of Emily, Wren, and David that she had smiled over. They weren't lifelike portraits, but after knowing the real thing, she had recognized each of them when they had ghosted across the pages. Michael pulled Kate closer and kissed her again, feeling more relief than he had imagined possible.

"I sent Paul a copy," Kate offered after a contemplative silence had descended over the room again.

"You did? I thought you'd been here all day," Michael said, surprised.

"I called Alistair and got him to send Bear a copy. He's reading it now," Kate explained. She patted his chest with a reassuring hand. "He'll love it too."

"You called Alistair?" Michael's surprise was growing. "I'm surprised he agreed to do that."

"Well, it came at a cost," Kate admitted.

"Ah." Michael nodded. "Which was…" He raised an eyebrow and smiled as Kate's shoulders shook with silent laughter.

"Oreo cupcakes," she replied. "He wants some this week."

"He's a pushy bastard." Michael sighed.

"Yeah, he told me that too." Kate pushed herself up into a sitting position and looked at Michael after knuckling her tired eyes. "I figured I'd make some over the weekend, and we can take them into his office on Monday."

"Sounds like a plan." Michael nodded. "It's probably about time you two met each other."

"That's what I thought." Kate looked at him for a moment, and then shifted herself so that she was straddling Michael, rocking herself gently against him. Michael reached up and grabbed her hips out of sheer reflex.

"Anything else you're thinking?" he asked as Kate settled herself comfortably against his core, and then reached up to pull off her shirt in one fluid gesture.

"One or two ideas come to mind," she offered with a smile. "Shall I tell you about them?"

"Words can be overrated." Michael gave an elaborately casual shrug. "How about you show me instead."

"If you insist," Kate murmured, and then bent her head to kiss him.

☙

"Morning, boss," Emily greeted her as Kate breezed into the store the next morning.

"Emily, don't call me boss."

"Sorry, boss." Emily gave a delighted laugh. "I can't tell you how weird it is to be a part of that routine."

"What routine's that?" Kate asked as she rounded the counter to go and collect her apron from the kitchen.

"The Wren routine you guys always had going," Emily explained. "First the cupcakes and quotes, and now the morning greeting. It felt strange at first, but on the days Wren isn't here, it still feels like she is, you know?"

"I do." Kate stopped and gave a fond smile.

Wren was following her dream, and the promise her talent had always foreshadowed at the store was at last coming to fruition. She had worked with Christine on getting a stand at the market, and within weeks had established herself. Christine had reported back to Kate that Wren's fashions were generating a lot of buzz, and she was acquiring herself a small-but-devoted following. She was still working at the store and thoroughly enjoying herself, but everyone involved knew that it was only a matter of time before Wren's fashions would be able to keep her financially self-sufficient.

Yielding to the inevitable, Wren had moved in with David before Easter, and although the stress of sharing her life with someone on such a permanent basis had created some memorable fireworks, Kate had never seen her happier. Michael and Paul had helped with the move, and Michael had watched as David had lugged boxes upstairs with the tired but happy smile of a man who held a winning ticket.

Emily and Brad's relationship remained as steady as ever, and it had been bolstered further after Brad had at last met Michael at the Christmas party. Brad had been quick to secure Michael's presence for a special literary event at the bookstore, which had been well publicized in the weeks leading up to the book's release. In literary circles, the opportunity to meet the somewhat reclusive Michael Forrester had made it one of the hottest tickets in town. Kate had avoided the event, as she hadn't wanted it to spoil any surprises before she read the book for herself, but Emily had made sure she was there at Brad's side. Listening to Michael's voice as he read an excerpt from the book, Emily had reached out to find Brad's hand already seeking out her own. They had stood there hand in hand, spellbound at the words Michael wove around them.

"Kate," Emily had told her the next day, "when that book comes out, you are going to drop everything. You are going to do *nothing* until you have read it. Have I made myself clear?"

"Crystal." Kate had nodded and then after a pause. "So, it's good?"

"I'm not saying another word about it." Emily had pointed an admonishing finger at Kate. "Now you make the coffee, and I'll get the chalk."

"So ..." Emily began as she got down some cups and slid them over to Kate, "now that you've had a chance to read it, what did you think?"

"Oh." Kate blinked at the coffee machine in front of her, and then gathered herself to start making coffee. "Well, it was ... unexpected."

"Unexpected how?"

Kate moved as if to speak and settled for frothing the milk instead. When the coffees were made, the conversation resumed.

"Unexpected in a sad and beautiful way," Kate said after a long pause. "It made me laugh, cry." She paused and sipped at her coffee again. "It made me think." Another pause as she gave the book some more thought and then offered a short laugh. "I don't know that I'll ever look at fluorescent lighting in the same way again."

"Huh?" Emily looked blank.

"The argon," Kate clarified.

"Oh, right." Emily gave a knowing nod. "Michael read that part out at the store."

"What did *you* think?" Kate was the curious one this time.

"Beautiful," Emily sighed. "That part really ..." She waved a hand. "I mean I've always admired writers and artists and all their creations over the centuries. Now I realize that I'm connected to them. Even if it's only on a cellular level, it's all connected. What did Michael call it?"

"The eternal breath," Kate said quietly as her throat tightened.

"Yeah," Emily sighed. "That's it."

"Beautiful," Kate added, and both women nodded in thoughtful silence.

"Oh, my God." Alistair's eyes all but rolled up in his head as he took another bite. "Beautiful, incredible." He licked crumbs off his lips, and then called out for his assistant. "Molly, could you take some of these to Fiona with my compliments."

True to her word, Kate had baked a batch of cupcakes for Michael's editor over the weekend, and he had escorted her to the office for the delivery and introductions.

"Will do." Molly nodded as she scooped the proffered cupcakes onto a small plate and disappeared.

"Fiona?" Michael raised an eyebrow.

"Food Editor," Alistair clarified as he licked some frosting off his fingers. "Seriously, Kate, if you weren't already a married woman—" he began, breaking off when Michael gave a low growl and reached out to interlace his fingers with Kate's.

"She's taken," Michael stated.

"Quite taken," Kate affirmed as she gave her husband a fond smile. They had been married for five months now, and the novelty still hadn't worn off. They were still exchanging small talk when a smartly dressed woman appeared in the doorway.

"Alistair, where did—" She stopped when she saw that he had company. "I'm sorry, I didn't realize you were with someone."

"Fiona." Alistair leaned back in his chair and waved her in with a proprietary grin. "I'd like you to meet Michael Forrester and his wife, Kate."

"It's a pleasure." Fiona nodded and shook their hands. "I'm sorry to interrupt, but, Alistair, where did you get those cupcakes?"

"Kate here brought some in for me as a thank you." Alistair smiled. "She has a bakery in the Village that you might be interested in."

"I am." She nodded. "Especially if there are more where these came from."

"Plenty," Michael confirmed with a pleased nod. "Kate's becoming famous for them."

"Really." Fiona looked thoughtful now. "Ever thought of publishing?"

"Huh?" Kate blinked at Fiona, and then looked over at Michael. This was an unexpected development. "Well, uh ..." she floundered, and then looked at Michael again. "Help," she peeped.

"Maybe it's best if you pay the store a visit sometime," Michael suggested, "see where these creations come from. I can tell you now," he went on with a proud grin, "they just keep getting better."

"Good to hear." Fiona nodded. "Let me get you my card, and we'll arrange a time."

"Okay." Kate nodded. "Sounds good."

The three of them watched Fiona depart, and then Michael caught Alistair looking very pleased with himself.

"You knew what you were doing," he accused.

"What?" Alistair tried to look surprised.

"Getting Kate in here with cupcakes, sending some to Fiona. What's going on in that head of yours?"

"Just the next phase of something that could be very exciting," Alistair said, and then looked disappointed. "Of course, it'd be even more exciting if you told me you have another story in the works."

"Oh, give me a break." Michael leaned back in his seat with a tone of exasperation that made Kate laugh. "Can't this book keep you occupied for at least a few more days before you start hounding me again?"

"Don't worry." Alistair waved him off. "Once that book hits the stores, my phone is going to be running hot. I'll be kept busy for a while. Just don't get too relaxed."

☙

"Kat," Paul was saying as Kate paced around the apartment with the phone, "I read it before I went to work and on my breaks; I wanna get off the phone to read it now." There was a pause as he replayed his words in his head. "Not that I don't wanna talk to my baby sister," he added hastily.

"It's okay, Bear," Kate assured him as she tried not to laugh. "I was the same way."

"They're in there, Kat," Paul went on in a quiet voice. "Mom and Dad, they're there. They're alive and they're together."

"I know." Kate swallowed hard.

"Hey, you remember the time Mom decided she wanted the family to go camping?"

Kate gave a whoop of laughter at the memory. "Oh, my God, and you ate so many s'mores you nearly threw up. What about the time when you ..." The conversation between brother and sister went on late into the night, punctuated with tears and laughter on both sides. Michael appeared at her side from time to time with a fresh drink or a quick kiss, but he left the siblings alone with their memories, grateful that he had in some small part been the medium to encourage it.

It was late when Kate finally got off the phone, and her expression was peaceful when she strolled out of the bathroom to see Michael turning down the bed for the night.

"All good?" he asked as he got into bed and watched Kate finish her bedtime ritual. She plumped her pillows and brushed her hair before getting into bed and nodding at him to lift up his arm so that she curl up beside him.

"Better than good," she assured him with a smile. "Paul and Christine are getting *real* serious."

"How serious?" Michael looked down at her, curious.

"He's-got-a-ring type of serious," Kate confirmed. "Now that he's finished reading, he's going over there to propose tonight."

"Now?" Michael was astonished. "But it's ten o'clock at night."

"He said there was no time like the present, and now he's got the ring, he wants to start spending the rest of his life with her as soon as possible."

"Good man." Michael nodded. "I know the feeling."

"Now that you mention it, is there something else that you know?" Kate peered up at him.

"I don't know." Michael yawned. "Name your subject, and we'll take it from there."

"Alistair and Fiona," Kate stated. "Anything going on there that you want to tell me about?"

"I have my suspicions," Michael admitted, "but how about we hold off until Fiona pays you a visit?"

"Guess I won't have long to wait," Kate said as she settled down again. "She's coming into the store tomorrow."

"She works fast. I can see why Alistair speaks so highly of her."

❧

The next day, Kate was serving a customer when she looked up and saw Fiona pausing in the doorway, her eyes darting everywhere to try to take in everything at once.

"Honey," she called out. Michael looked up from his laptop and nodded when he saw Fiona. To Kate's surprise and delight, Michael had offered to visit the store and keep her company when Fiona arrived.

"Not for any negotiating," Michael had said. "I know you can look after yourself, and the store is your baby, but can I just be there to watch it happen?"

"Watch what happen?" Kate had given him a suspicious look. What did he know?

"I dunno." He had shrugged. "But I think it's going to be something good."

"Sure, why not?" Kate had nodded. "It'd be kinda fun to have you there."

"Done."

"Is this the part where we spit on our palms and shake hands?" Kate had asked as she wrinkled up her nose.

"If that's how you want to play it," Michael had said, looking dubious at the prospect. "How about we kiss instead?"

"So long as that isn't how you close all your deals," Kate had said with a smile as she submitted.

Now Kate stood waiting by the coffee machine as Fiona approached. The woman strolled through the store looking entirely unhurried: stopping to look at the artwork, smiling at the children's books stacked on a low shelf, and then stopping dead in her tracks when she saw the display cabinet.

"God." Fiona's jaw dropped as she gazed at the sugary temptations in wonderment. "Tell me you made these."

"Sure did." Kate nodded.

"And the quote outside?" Fiona waved a hand to indicate the chalkboard by the door.

"Ah, that's the work of Wren today, sometimes Emily, sometimes Kristyn."

"I see." Fiona was looking thoughtful now. She stood and turned in a slow circle as she looked at the store again. "Okay," she said as she reached a decision. "You got a moment?"

Kate glanced over at Wren, who gave her an encouraging nod. "Sure, coffee?"

"Please." Fiona nodded and walked the table where Michael was sitting. "Michael." She nodded as she sat down. "Working on something?"

"Just a few notes." He smiled.

"Anything for me to tell Alistair about?" she said with an inquiring gleam in her eye.

"Not yet," he answered, "but when there is, I'd like to be the one to tell him, if you don't mind."

"Point taken." She gave a gracious nod, and then beamed at Wren as a coffee was set down in front of her. "Smells good," she said as she picked up her cup, and then her eyes widened as Kate set down a plate for her with the cupcake of the day. "And *that* looks even better."

"So, Fiona, to what do I owe the pleasure?" Kate handed Michael a fresh coffee and took a seat with a cup of her own.

"Well, going by what I tasted yesterday, you clearly know what you're doing," Fiona began, "and the style I see here in the shop tells me a lot more."

"More about what?" Kate asked as she sipped at her coffee.

"Enough to know that if you agree to publish a book with us, it'll be the kind of cupcake book that no one has ever seen before," Fiona said as she leaned forward in her chair. She hesitated and then, unable to resist any longer, picked up the cupcake and took a bite.

Kate and Michael sat and watched as Fiona chewed and swallowed, before setting the cake back down on its plate and giving Kate a particularly intense stare. As they talked, Fiona revealed that she had done her research last night and had read both newspaper reviews. She said the store had delivered on its promise: the coffee was the best she'd tasted in a long time and the cupcake had exceeded her every expectation. Even better, the display cabinet held an array of tarts and almond petit fours that showed Kate was more than a one-trick pony.

"Kate, just say yes, and I promise you it will be a book that changes your life," Fiona said as she sipped at her coffee with an inward sigh of pleasure.

"Oh, I don't know about that," Kate said as she gave Michael a loving smile. "The books I've come across lately have all been pretty life-changing."

"Well, then," Michael replied and, heedless of Fiona's presence, leaned forward to give her a kiss. "I guess we'll just have to see if we can make the next one even better."

"You've got yourself a deal." Kate smiled.

"Is that to me, or Michael?" Fiona inquired as she leaned forward again.

Kate looked from her soon-to-be editor and then back at her husband.

"Both," she replied. "Let's get to work."

THE END

ACKNOWLEDGMENTS

The quotes and cupcakes have come from a combination of my own imagination and the many café chalkboards I've encountered, which are too numerous to mention.

Credit is also given to Dr. David Suzuki, whose 2008 Commonwealth Lecture provided the inspiration for the argon discussions found in this story.

Freshly baked cupcake thanks to: Autumn Barowski, Nicole Dean, Lisa Allen, Leisa Voysey, Shannon Helton, Adeline Remy, Siobhan Melia, Kari Hansbarger, Kathryn Robertson and the mini U.N.

Grammatically correct thanks to my editor, Meredith MacLeod, and all at Omnific.

Sandra was born in Gnowangerup, and lives in Perth at the end of the earth—get a map and look it up. She shares her windswept and interesting existence with good friends and the biggest, laziest cat in the known universe. Having had a number of different occupations, Sandra aspires to be rich and famous so she can travel aimlessly around the world, drinking good wine and writing novels. She smiles often, cries sometimes and generally loves life.

www.sandrawright.com.au